THE GOLDEN AGE OF MURDER

The Detection Club library bookplate, designed by Edward Ardizzone.

The Golden Age
of Murder

*The Mystery of the Writers Who
Invented the Modern Detective Story*

MARTIN EDWARDS

HarperCollins*Publishers*

HarperCollins*Publishers*
1 London Bridge Street
London SE1 9GF
www.harpercollins.co.uk

Published by HarperCollins*Publishers* 2015

1

ISBN 978-0-00-810596-9

Printed and bound in the United States of America

To the members of the Detection Club,
past and present.

Acknowledgments

The Golden Age of Murder is a very different book from any other study of this fascinating yet neglected subject. I could not have written it, however, without a great deal of help, or without building on foundations laid by others, above all Julian Symons, a former President of the Detection Club and author of *Bloody Murder*, a study which broke fresh ground. I am deeply grateful to the countless people who have given me assistance, directly and indirectly, during long years of reading and research, and while it is impossible to mention everyone by name, I'd like to express my thanks to all of them.

I am especially appreciative of my family, who have spent years surrounded by mountains of old books and magazines, and patiently (well, fairly patiently!) accompanied me to second hand bookshops up and down the country in search of elusive titles. This book would not exist in its present form if my agent, James Wills, and my publisher, David Brawn, had not believed in it, and I owe a great deal to them, to my copy-editor, John Garth, as well as to Simon Brett and my colleagues in the Detection Club. Among the latter, those distinguished writers Peter Lovesey, Ruth Dudley Edwards, Jessica Mann and Ann Cleeves read early drafts, and offered generous insight and guidance. So did Tony Medawar, one of Britain's Golden Age experts, as well as John Curran, who decoded Agatha Christie's secret note-books, and two American authorities on traditional detection,

Douglas Greene and Tom Schantz. Their input was invaluable, and saved me from many errors, yet there is still much more to be discovered about Golden Age detective fiction and the people who wrote it. This book is not the last word, but I hope it may form a landmark, and encourage further research and discovery. I bear in mind the wisdom of Julian Symons, who made clear that he was always receptive to 'reasoned contradiction' and lived up to that promise, responding generously and with a willingness to revisit his opinions when, as a young man, I wrote to him about the first two Francis Iles books.

In the course of my investigations, I met, spoke to or corresponded with members of the families of several early members of the Detection Club. Understandably, memories of events dating back more than half a century were often hazy, but their reminiscences gave me a fuller understanding of the past. Once or twice, I felt there was a danger of intruding on private unhappiness; the legitimate public interest in such things has its limits, and I have striven to reflect that in writing this book. I will not, therefore, mention individual family members by name, but I am indebted to various members of the families of Anthony Berkeley, Anthony Gilbert, Helen Simpson, Christopher Bush, Josephine Bell and Margot Bennett, and deceased members of the Detection Club Robert Barnard, Harry Keating and Margaret Yorke, for their assistance and consideration.

Many lovers of Golden Age detective fiction in a number of different countries have given me useful information, as well as taking part in lively but good-natured debate about the respective merits of some writers, and the right way to assess Golden Age stories. Some supplied illustrations, some loaned me rare first editions. Space permits only a selective list of specific thank-yous, but the British contingent include Geoff Bradley and many contributors to *CADS*, including Liz Gilbey and Philip L. Scowcroft; the late Christopher Dean; Seona Ford and their colleagues in the Dorothy L. Sayers Society; the Sayers estate; Barry Pike and Julia Jones of the Margery Allingham Society: the late Bob Adey, Celia Down, David M. Chapman, Nigel Moss, Mark Sutcliffe, Jamie Sturgeon, Ralph Spurrier, James M. Pickard, Lyndsey

Greenslade, Chris Garrod, Christine Simpson, Ann Granger, P. D. James, Sheila Mitchell, Catherine Aird, Charles Gordon Clark, Mike Ashley, Christine Poulson, Jennifer Palmer, Alan Hamilton, Emma Wilson, the late Chris Peers, and the late R. F. Stewart. I benefited from help from American friends and correspondents, notably Laura Schmidt and her colleagues at Wheaton, home of the Dorothy L. Sayers archive, Steve Steinbock, Arthur Robinson, B.J. Rahn, Arthur Vidro, Curtis Evans, Howard Lakin, George Easter, and Marvin Lachman. Italy's Mauro Boncompagni, Germany's Almuth Heuner, France's Xavier Lechard, and Australia's Malcolm J. Turnbull were a mine of information. So were contacts I made via social media, and in particular members of the GA Detection forum and Facebook group. To all of them, my sincere thanks.

Martin Edwards

Contents

Introduction

The origins of my quest to solve the mysteries of the Detection Club date back to when I was eight years old. A rich American called John L. Snyder II, who retired to the picturesque Cheshire village of Great Budworth after making a fortune in Hollywood, hosted the annual summer fete at his country house, Sandicroft. He decided to show a film in a marquee in Sandicroft's extensive grounds – and set about pulling strings with Metro-Goldwyn-Mayer. A remarkably persuasive man, Snyder secured permission to present the world premiere of MGM's brand new movie, *Murder Most Foul*.

This stranger-than-fiction initiative guaranteed publicity in the local and national Press. Snyder's ambition was demonstrated by his search for a celebrity to open the fete. He began by approaching Brigitte Bardot, but when Brigitte declared herself unavailable (did this surprise him? I wonder), he changed tack and recruited the star of the film – Margaret Rutherford. My family lived near Great Budworth, and my parents took me to the fete as a birthday treat. So many people wanted to go that it was impossible to drive there. A fleet of coaches bussed everyone to Sandicroft.

I can still picture that afternoon among the crowds under the July sun. And I remember the excitement as a noisy helicopter circled overhead, coming in to land on a cleared patch of lawn before disgorging Margaret Rutherford, alias Miss Jane

Marple. After much queuing, we squeezed into a showing of the film. Already I loved reading and writing stories, but this was my first exposure to Agatha Christie, and I was thrilled by the confection of clues and red herrings, suspects and surprises. I went home in a daze, dreaming that one day I would concoct a story that fascinated others as this light-hearted murder puzzle had fascinated me. I soon discovered the film bore little resemblance to the novel on which it was based, but that didn't matter. I was hooked.

How fitting that my love of traditional detective fiction was inspired by a country house party in a village reminiscent of St Mary Mead. That evening, I took from a bookshelf a paperback copy of *The Murder at the Vicarage,* and my fate was sealed. I devoured every book Christie wrote, and tried to learn anything I could about the woman whose story-telling entranced me. In the mid-Sixties, with no internet, no social media, and not much of a celebrity culture (apart from Bardot and Margaret Rutherford, of course), finding out more about Christie proved surprisingly difficult. Eventually I moved on to other crime writers, ranging from past masters like Dorothy L. Sayers and Anthony Berkeley to Julian Symons, then at the cutting edge of the present. From Symons' masterly study of the genre, *Bloody Murder*, I learned about the Detection Club, an elite but mysterious group of crime writers over which Sayers, Christie and Symons presided for nearly forty years.

Years later, I became a published detective novelist, writing books set in the here and now. A delightful moment came when a letter arrived out of the blue from Simon Brett, President of the Detection Club, explaining that the members had elected me by secret ballot to join their number. Subsequently, I was invited to become the Detection Club's first Archivist.

The only snag was that there were no archives. Although the Detection Club once possessed a Minute Book, it has not been seen since the Blitz. Even the extensive Club library, packed with rare treasures, had been sold off.

At the time of writing, there seems little hope of ever recovering all the missing papers, in the absence of one of those lucky breaks from which fictional detectives so often benefit. But inevitably the loss of the Club's records of its early days sharpened my curiosity. To a lover of detective stories, what more teasing challenge than to solve the mysteries of the people who formed the original Detection Club? I quickly discovered far more puzzles, especially about Christie and other early members of the Club, than I expected. I began to question my own assumptions, as well as those of critics whose judgements were often based on guesswork and prejudice.

My investigation sent me travelling around Britain, as I tracked down and interviewed relatives of former Detection Club members and other witnesses to the curious case of the Golden Age of murder. Some of the people I talked to joined in with the detective work, and the more I discovered, the more I came to believe that the story of the Club and its members demanded to be told. I explored remote libraries and dusty second bookshops, and badgered people in Australia, the United States, Japan and elsewhere in the hunt for answers. Sometimes memories proved maddeningly vague or erroneously definite. Biographies of Club members were packed with as many inconsistencies as the testimony of witnesses with something to hide.

I met with much kindness and generosity, often from those I shall never meet in person. One or two who knew secrets about the Detection Club did not want to be traced, or to recall past traumas, and this I understood. A couple of times, I reined in my curiosity when the quest risked becoming intrusive or hurtful – as Poirot recognises at the end of *Murder on the Orient Express*, sometimes the truth is not the only thing that matters. Exciting breakthroughs spurred me on, as when two clues, one in the form of an email address, and another discovered on my own bookshelves, led me to identify someone with personal knowledge of the dark side of one of my prime suspects.

Luck often played a part, as when I stumbled across Dorothy L. Sayers' personal copy of the transcript of the murder trial described in *The Suspicions of Mr Whicher*, with pages of detailed notes in her neat hand recording her own interpretation of the evidence. Authors' inscriptions in rare novels supplied fresh leads, and even an apparent confession by Agatha Christie to 'crimes unsuspected, not detected'. The chance acquisition of a signed book led to my learning of a secret diary written in a unique code.

Clues to extraordinary personal secrets were hidden in the writers' work. I sifted through the evidence with an open mind, and as real-life detectives often find, I needed to use my imagination from time to time, to fill in the inevitable gaps. Studying the work of two writers over the course of a decade and a half of their lives helped to build a convincing picture of their doomed love affair, and to understand a strange relationship that changed their lives, but has eluded all previous literary critics and their biographers. Many of the finest Golden Age sleuths sometimes relied on intuition, and what was good enough for Father Brown and Miss Marple was good enough for me. In the end, I uncovered enough of the truth to round up the prime suspects for a suitable *denouement* in the final chapter.

How can one discuss detective stories without giving away the endings? Some reference books contain 'spoiler alerts', but these can result in a fragmented read. I've tried not to give too much away, although in the case of a few books, readers will be able to put the pieces together.

My respect for the earliest members of the Detection Club did not diminish as I spotted flaws in their detectives' reasoning, or chanced upon curious and sometimes embarrassing incidents in their own lives. On the contrary, I came to respect their prowess in skating over thin ice, in fiction and in everyday life. They were writing during a dangerous period in our history, years when recovery from the shocking experience of one war became overshadowed by dread of another. At this distance of time, we can see that Detection Club members had much more to say about the world in which they lived than either they acknowledged or critics have appreciated. They entertained their readers royally, but there was more to their work than that.

Even the most gifted Golden Age detectives did not work in isolation, and my own investigation benefited enormously from the help and hard work of others. My profoundest thanks go to Christie, Sayers, Berkeley and all their colleagues, who have given me so much pleasure – not only in their writing, but in the puzzles they posed as I followed their trail. That trail reaches back to the long ago July afternoon when I was lucky enough to see Miss Marple make her improbable descent from the skies, and discover a new world which, from that day to this, I have found utterly spellbinding.

Notes

Even in a book of this length, it is impossible to explore in detail every issue touched on in the text. The notes provided at the end of each chapter, inevitably selective, seek to amplify some facets of the story of the Golden Age and its exponents, and to encourage further reading, research – and enjoyment.

Members of the Detection Club elected 1930–49

1930

G. K. Chesterton 1874–1936
H. C. Bailey 1878–1961
E. C. Bentley 1875–1956
Anthony Berkeley 1893–1971
Agatha Christie 1890–1976
G. D. H. Cole 1889–1959
M. Cole 1893–1980
J. J. Connington 1880–1947
Freeman Wills Crofts
    1879–1957
Clemence Dane 1887–1965
Robert Eustace 1871–1943
R. Austin Freeman 1862–1943
Lord Gorell 1884–1963
Edgar Jepson 1863–1938
Ianthe Jerrold 1898–1977
Milward Kennedy 1894–1968
Ronald A. Knox 1888–1957
A. E. W. Mason 1865–1948
A. A. Milne 1882–1956
Arthur Morrison 1863–1945
Baroness Orczy 1865–1947

Mrs Victor Rickard 1876–1963
John Rhode 1884–1965
Dorothy L. Sayers 1893–1957
Henry Wade 1887–1969
Victor L. Whitechurch
    1868–1933
Helen Simpson (Associate
    Member) 1897–1940
Hugh Walpole (Associate
    Member) 1884–1941

1933

Anthony Gilbert 1899–1971
E. R. Punshon 1872–1956
Gladys Mitchell 1901–1983

1934

Margery Allingham 1904–66

1935

Norman Kendal 1880–1966
R. C. Woodthorpe 1886–1971

1936
John Dickson Carr 1906–77

1937
Nicholas Blake 1904–72
Newton Gayle (Muna Lee
    1895–1965 and Maurice
    Guinness 1897–1991)
E. C. R. Lorac 1894–1958
Christopher Bush 1888–1973

1946
Cyril Hare 1900–58
Christianna Brand 1907–88
Richard Hull 1896–1973
Alice Campbell 1887–1976

1947
Val Gielgud 1900–81
Edmund Crispin 1921–78

1948
Dorothy Bowers 1902–48

1949
Michael Innes 1906–94
Michael Gilbert 1912–2006
Douglas G. Browne 1884–1963

Author Gallery

G. K. Chesterton   H. C. Bailey   E. C. Bentley

Anthony Berkeley   Agatha Christie   G. D. H. Cole

M. Cole   J. J. Connington   Freeman Wills Crofts

Clemence Dane   R. Austin Freeman   Lord Gorell

Edgar Jepson   Ianthe Jerrold   Milward Kennedy

Ronald A. Knox   A. E. W. Mason   A. A. Milne

Arthur Morrison   Baroness Orczy   John Rhode

Dorothy L. Sayers

Henry Wade

Victor L. Whitechurch

Helen Simpson

Hugh Walpole

Anthony Gilbert

Gladys Mitchell

Margery Allingham

R. C. Woodthorpe

John Dickson Carr

Nicholas Blake

Muna Lee

Christopher Bush

Cyril Hare

Christianna Brand

Richard Hull

Val Gielgud

Edmund Crispin

Michael Innes

Michael Gilbert

Part One

The Unusual Suspects

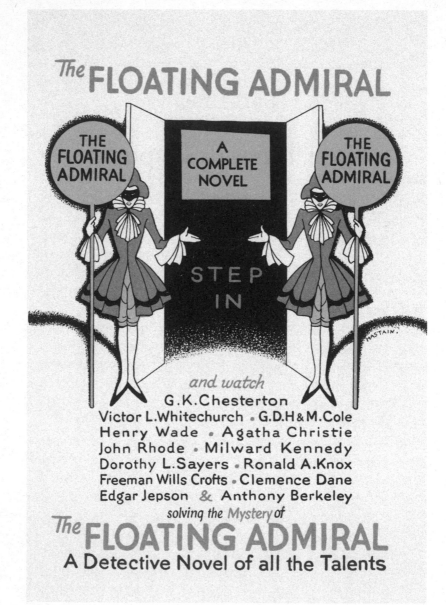

The first of the Detection Club novels, published by Hodder & Stoughton in 1931.

1

The Ritual in the Dark

On a summer evening in 1937, a group of men and women gathered in darkness to perform a macabre ritual. They had invited a special guest to witness their ceremony. She was visiting London from New Zealand and a thrill of excitement ran through her as the appointed time drew near. She loved drama, and at home she worked in the theatre. Now she felt as tense as when the curtain was about to rise. To be a guest at this dinner was a special honour. What would happen next she could not imagine.

Striking to look at, the New Zealander was almost six feet tall, with dark, close-set eyes. Elegant yet enigmatic, she exuded a quiet, natural charm that contrasted with her flamboyant dress sense and artistic taste for the exotic. Fond of wearing men's clothes, smart slacks, a tie and a beret, this evening she had opted for feminine finery, her favourite fur wrap and extravagant costume jewellery. In common with her hosts, she had a passion for writing detective stories. Like them, she guarded her private life jealously.

Until tonight, she had only known these people from reading about them – and from reading their books. Many were household names, distinguished in politics, education, journalism, religion, and science, as well as literature. Most were British, a handful came from overseas. A young American was here, and so were the Australian granddaughter of a French marquis, and an elderly Hungarian countess who each year made a special journey for the occasion, travelling to England from her home in Monte Carlo.

The ritual was preceded by a lavish banquet in an opulent dining room. As the wine flowed, the visitor fought to conquer her nerves. Her escort, a discreet young Englishman, attentive and admiring, did his best to put her at ease. The food was superb, and the company convivial, but she preferred to let others talk rather than chatter herself. Sipping at her coffee, she half-listened to the speeches. At last came the moment she was waiting for. Everyone rose, and the party retired to another room. At the far end stood a large chair, almost like a throne. On the right side was a little table, and on the left, a lectern and a flagon of wine, its mouth covered with cloth.

All of a sudden, the lights went out, plunging the room into darkness. As if at a given signal, everyone else swept out through the door, leaving the woman from New Zealand and her companion alone. She became conscious of a faint chill in the air. Both of them were afraid to break the silence. As the moments ticked away, they dared to exchange a few words, speaking in whispers, as if in church.

Without warning, a door swung open. The Orator had arrived.

Resplendent in scarlet and black robes, and wearing pince-nez, a statuesque woman entered the room. She marched towards the lectern, holding a single taper to light the way. As she mounted the rostrum, the New Zealander saw that, in the folds of her gown, the Orator had secreted a side-arm. The visitor caught her breath. In the gloom, she could not identify the weapon. Was it a pistol, or a six-shooter?

Stern and purposeful, the Orator lit a candle. She gave no hint that she knew anyone was watching. At her command, a sombre procession of men and women in evening dress filed into the room. In the flickering candle-light, the visitor glimpsed unsmiling faces. Four members of the group carried flaming torches. Others clutched lethal weapons: a rope, a blunt instrument, a sword, and a phial of poison. A giant of a man brought up the rear. On the cushion that he carried, beneath a black cloth, squatted a grinning human skull.

The New Zealander was spellbound. The Orator cleared her throat and began to speak. She administered a lengthy oath to a burly man in his sixties. This secretive and elitist gathering had elected him to preside over their affairs, and he pledged to honour the rules of the game they played:

'To do and detect all crimes by fair and reasonable means; to conceal no vital clues from the reader; to honour the King's English . . . and to observe the oath of secrecy in all matters communicated to me within the brotherhood of the Club.'

As the ritual approached its end, the Orator lifted her revolver. Giving a faint smile, she fired a single shot. In the enclosed space, the noise was deafening. Her colleagues let out blood-curdling cries and waved their weapons in the air.

The eyes of the skull lit up the blackness, shining with a fierce red glow.

Stunned, the New Zealander found herself unable to speak. Her companion, familiar with the eccentric humour of crime writers, laughed like a hyena.

The visitor from New Zealand was Ngaio Marsh, who became one of her country's most admired detective novelists, as well as a legendary theatre director. Her escort, Edmund Cork, was her literary agent, and he also represented Agatha Christie. The Orator who led the procession was Dorothy L. Sayers, and the bearer of the skull was another popular detective novelist, John Rhode. The satiric ritual followed a script so elaborate that Sayers, its author, thoughtfully supplied an explanatory diagram. The occasion was the installation of Edmund Clerihew Bentley as second President of the Detection Club.

Ngaio Marsh remembered that night for the rest of her life. Long after she returned home, she dined out on stories about what she had seen, embellishing details as time passed, and memory played tricks. In one account, she identified the setting for the ritual as Grosvenor House; in her biography, written in old age, she said it was the Dorchester. She also made conflicting

LEFT AND RIGHT: Dorothy
L. Sayers and John Rhode
with Eric the Skull,
photographed by Clarice
Carr (by permission of
Douglas G. Greene).

BELOW: The Detection
Club annual dinner,
presided over by G.K.
Chesterton.

claims about whether or not she met Agatha Christie that night. Detective novelists, like their characters, often make suspect witnesses and unreliable narrators.

The Detection Club was an elite social network of writers whose work earned a reputation for literary excellence, and exerted a profound long-term influence on storytelling in fiction, film and television. Their impact continues to be felt, not only in Britain but throughout the world, in the twenty-first century. Yet a mere thirty-nine members were elected between the Club's inception in 1930 and the end of the Second World War. The process of selecting suitable candidates for membership was rigorous, sometimes bizarrely so. The founders wanted to ensure that members had produced work of 'admitted merit' – a code for excluding the likes of 'Sapper' and Sydney Horler, whose thrillers starring Bulldog Drummond and Tiger Standish earned a huge readership, but were crude and jingoistic.

Those thirty-nine men and women were as extraordinary an assortment of characters as the cast of *Murder on the Orient Express*. They included some of the country's most famous authors of popular fiction: not only the creators of Hercule Poirot and Lord Peter Wimsey, but also authors better known for writing about the Scarlet Pimpernel or Winnie-the-Pooh. Detection Club members came from all walks of life. Several had fought in the First World War and suffered life-changing harm, some played a prominent part in British political life. Members ranged from right-wing Tory to red-blooded Marxist, and everything in between. The aristocracy was represented, along with the middle and working classes, and the Anglican and Catholic clergy.

The Club's first President, G. K. Chesterton, is currently regarded as a potential candidate for canonisation by the Pope – even though today he is remembered less for his spiritual-ity than his detective fiction. The lives of his colleagues, for all their surface respectability, were much less saintly. Several were promiscuous, two had unacknowledged children. Long before homosexual acts between men were decriminalized, there were gay and lesbian members, as well as a husband and wife literary duo – one of whom nursed a passion for a young man who eventually became leader of the Labour Party. And one cherished a secret fantasy about murdering a man who stood between him and the woman he adored.

The movers and shakers in the Detection Club were young writers who at first pretended to write according to a set of light-hearted 'rules'. This symptomized the 'play fever' that swept through Britain after the First World War, when games as different as contract bridge and mah-jongg captured the popular imagination, and crossword puzzles were all the rage. After the loss of millions of lives in combat, and then during the Spanish flu epidemic, games offered escape from the horrors of wartime – as well as from the bleak realities of peace. Economic misery seemed never-ending. The national debt ballooned, and politicians imposed an age of austerity. Industrial output fell, and so did consumer spending. The cost of living soared, and so did unemployment. The threat of slashed wages for miners led to Britain's one and only General Strike, and the ruling classes had to cling to wealth and power by their fingertips. The sun had not quite set on the British Empire, but this was the twilight of the imperial era. While Bright Young Things partied the night away, millions of ordinary people couldn't sleep for worrying about how to pay their bills.

Detective stories offered readers pleasure at a time when they feared for the future. As the Wall Street Crash brought the Roaring Twenties to a shuddering end, writers prided themselves on coming up with fresh ways of disguising whodunit or howdunit, but the most gifted novelists itched to do more, to explore human relationships and the complications of psychology. The work of Sigmund Freud, himself a detective fiction fan, became influential. The social mores of the Thirties prevented novelists from writing graphic sex scenes, but strong sexual undercurrents are evident in many of the best detective stories of the Thirties, above all in the extraordinary final novels of Anthony Berkeley and Hugh Walpole. Increasingly, Detection Club members relished breaking the so-called 'rules' of their game. They experimented with the form of the novel, deploying untrustworthy narrators as well as unexpected culprits. Their books reflected social attitudes and political change, more than they intended, and more than critics have realized.

Three remarkable people became the Club's leading lights. In the vanguard was Sayers, brilliant and idiosyncratic as any maverick detective. By her side stood Berkeley, crime fiction's Jekyll and Hyde – suave and scintillating one minute, sardonic and sinister the next. And then there was Agatha Christie, a quiet, pleasant woman who was easy to read unless you wanted to know what was going on in her mind.

Christie's legendary ingenuity with plot was matched by Berkeley's biting cynicism about conventional justice and his obsession with criminal psychology. Sayers, a woman as forceful as she was erudite, believed the detective story could become something more than mere light entertainment. 'If there is any serious aim behind the avowedly frivolous organisation of the Detection Club,' she said shortly after its formation, 'it is to keep the detective story up to the highest standard that its nature permits, and to free it from the bad legacy of sensationalism, clap-trap and jargon with which it was unhappily burdened in the past.'

Appearances are deceptive. When we look at pictures of Christie and Sayers today, we usually see the women in their later years: respectable, well-upholstered, grandmotherly. The few published photographs of the publicity-hating Berkeley show a dapper fellow, wearing a trim moustache in his younger days, bald and pipe-smoking in later life. How tempting to fall into the trap of dismissing them as strait-laced middle-class English people. Yet in private, they led extraordinary lives and endured disastrous marriages. All three took secrets to the grave.

Their novels are often sneered at as 'cosy', and the claim that their characters were made from cardboard has become a lazy critical cliché. The very idea that detective fiction between the wars represented a 'Golden Age' seems like the misty-eyed nostalgia of an aged romantic hankering after a past that never existed. Many argue that the quality of crime fiction written today matches, or surpasses, that of any other period. But today's writers often owe something to their predecessors, and the term 'the Golden Age of detective fiction' was popularized, not by some genteel old lady or retired brigadier, but by John Strachey, a young Marxist who later became Minister of War in the post-war Labour government.

Strachey recognised that the *best* detective novels of the Thirties were exhilarating, innovative and unforgettable. They explored miscarriages of justice, forensic pathology and serial killings long before these topics became fashionable (and before the term 'serial killer' was invented). Many of the finest books defied stereotypes. The received wisdom is that Golden Age fiction set out to reassure readers by showing order restored to society, and plenty of orthodox novels did just that. But many of the finest bucked the trend, and ended on a note of uncertainty or paradox. In some, people were executed for crimes they did not commit; in others, murderers escaped unpunished. The climax of one of Berkeley's novels was so shocking that when Alfred Hitchcock came to film it, even the legendary master of suspense, the man who would direct *Psycho*, lost his nerve. He substituted a final scene that was a feeble cop-out in comparison to Berkeley's dark and horrific vision.

Sayers, Berkeley and Christie came to detective fiction young – in their late twenties and early thirties. All three were full of energy and imagination, fizzing with fresh ideas. Each was an obsessive risk-taker. The First World War changed them, as it changed Britain. After the bloodshed of the trenches, writers craved escapism just as much as their readers. Though their stories often seem as artificial as they are ingenious, Sayers, Christie and Berkeley were intent on transforming the genre. Along the way, they fought against personal catastrophes, and suffered spells of deep despair. The lonely nature of their work – no publicity tours, no fan conventions, no glitzy awards ceremonies – contributed to their torments. Thanks to Detection Club meetings, writers found new friends who shared their literary enthusiasms. Not only did members eat, drink and talk together – they wrote and broadcast together, raising money by collaborating on crime stories in unique cross-media initiatives. For Sayers and Christie in particular, the Detection Club became a lifeline.

Christie's controversial eleven-day disappearance in 1926 is by far the most high profile of the numerous disasters that befell Club members, affecting their writing as well their lives. Much as they wanted to promote their books, they were determined to keep their personal lives out of the public gaze. Many hid their private agonies in a way impossible in the age of paparazzi and Press intrusion, and of blogs, Facebook and Twitter. Beneath the façade of middle class respectability lay human stories as complex and enthralling as any fiction.

Christie, Sayers and Berkeley were fascinated by murder in real life. True crime stories influenced and inspired them. And they did much more than borrow plot elements from actual cases. There is a long tradition of mystery writers undertaking detective work for themselves – from Edgar Allan Poe and Arthur Conan Doyle, to P. D. James's re-evaluation of the murder of Julia Wallace, and Patricia Cornwell's investment of two million dollars in her efforts to establish that Walter Sickert really was Jack the Ripper. Other than Conan Doyle, however, none have investigated real-life mysteries with the zeal of the Detection Club in the Thirties.

Anyone researching the Club must navigate a labyrinth of blind alleys and wrong turnings. The challenge is to unravel three sets of mysteries – about the books, the real-life murder puzzles, and the dark secrets of the writers' personal lives. All are woven together in a tangled web.

The simpler riddles are literary. Who wrote the first serial killer mysteries? What game did Club members play with a superintendent from Scotland Yard? Who pioneered the novel of psychological suspense? How did Anthony Berkeley anticipate *Lord of the Flies*?

Trickier questions arise about real-life crimes. Did a young woman's horrific death trigger Berkeley's infatuation with a married magistrate? Why was Christie haunted by the drowning of the man who adapted her work for the stage? What convinced Sayers of the innocence of a man convicted of battering his wife to death with a poker? And what did she make of the blood-stained garment that supplied a vital clue in the murder investigated by the legendary Inspector Whicher?

Detection Club members seldom confessed to writing about themselves, or the increasingly fragile social order to which they belonged. Yet they scattered hints throughout their writing, just as their fictional culprits made mistakes that gave away their clever schemes. We can deduce more from reading between the lines of the books than the authors realized.

Which novelist wrote a secret diary in an unbreakable code? How did two famous writers conduct a forbidden love affair through hidden messages in their stories? Why did Sayers and Berkeley suddenly abandon detective fiction at the height of their fame? Clues, outlandish as any ever picked up by Poirot, lurk in the unlikeliest settings – an inscribed first edition, a unique form of shorthand, a murderous fantasy transformed into fiction, even the abdication of a king.

Christie once hinted she was guilty of 'crimes unsuspected, not detected.' Sayers found herself confronting a blackmailer. And Berkeley fantasized about murdering the man who stood between him and happiness. Searching for the truth about this gifted trio is as enthralling as any hunt for fictional culprits.

After a series of economic earthquakes on a scale not seen for generations, uncanny parallels exist between our time and the years between the wars. This is the perfect moment for a cold case review of the Detection Club: to unmask the Golden Age writers and their work, against the backdrop of the extraordinary times in which they lived.

Notes to Chapter 1

In one account, she identified the setting for the ritual as Grosvenor House; in her biography, written in old age, she said it was the Dorchester.
The former version of events, referred to by Joanne Drayton, in *Ngaio Marsh: Her Life in Crime*, seems more reliable than Marsh's later recollection in *Black Beech and Honeydew*. The ritual has been held at a variety of prestigious venues in central London over the years. By coincidence, it currently takes place at the Dorchester.

Sigmund Freud, himself a detective fiction fan
Freud 'relished in particular Agatha Christie's *Murder on the Orient Express*': Paul Roazen, 'Orwell, Freud and 1984', *Virginia Quarterly Review*, Autumn 1978.

'If there is any serious aim behind the avowedly frivolous organisation of the Detection Club,' she said
In Christianna Brand's Introduction to the 1979 edition of Sayers' *The Floating Admiral*.

the term 'the Golden Age of detective fiction' was popularised . . . by John Strachey
The first use of the term seems to be in Strachey's 'The Golden Age of Detective Fiction', *The Saturday Review*, 7 January 1939. Another Marxist critic, Ernest Mandel, echoed Strachey forty-five years later in *Delightful Murder*: 'The inter-war period was the golden age of the detective story.' Over the years, there has been extensive debate about the distinction between 'detective stories', 'crime novels', and 'mysteries', but precise and satisfactory definitions of the differences between them have remained elusive. For the sake of simplicity, the terms are treated broadly as synonyms in this book.

2

A Bitter Sin

One dark November day in 1923, Dorothy Leigh Sayers sat in her London office, rehearsing a lie until it sounded like the unvarnished truth. She excelled at playing with words, and making things up, whether in advertising copy or detective fiction. Now her imagination faced its sternest challenge. The daughter of a vicar and a devout Christian, she possessed fierce moral principles and an acute sense of sin, but she felt afraid and alone, and saw no alternative to deceiving the people she worked with. She hated what she was doing, but desperation drove her to bury her scruples.

She had invented a mysterious illness to justify taking eight weeks off work, hoping none of the men she reported to would enquire too closely into the medical problems of a valued female member of staff. This was the first step in an elaborate charade, designed with the same attention to detail she lavished on her fictional mysteries. Family and friends must be fooled as well.

Sayers worked for S. H. Benson Ltd, an advertising agency based in Kingsway Hall, close to the newspapers of Fleet Street, and ten minutes from her flat in Great James Street. Her room sat at the top of a steep and slippery spiral staircase made of iron which looked stylish, but was a death-trap for anyone unlucky enough to lose her footing. One day, she would turn that staircase into a fictional murder scene. Benson's boasted an eclectic roster of clients, and had been quick to adopt fashionable American methods of 'psychological' and 'scientific' advertising. In her first published piece of copy, which she admitted was 'a tissue of exaggeration', Sayers extolled the virtues of 'Sailor Savouries'. Soon she was rhapsodizing about 'Lytup' handbags and Colman's Starch.

Innovative and industrious, Sayers was perfectly suited to her job. She liked the way the copywriters were collectively known as the 'Literary Department', and the buzz and gossip of office life reminded her of student days in the common rooms of Oxford. Philip Benson and his management team regarded her highly, and some thought Dorothy's talents might one day take her all the way to the boardroom. Her colleagues regarded her as eccentric but gifted, an outspoken bluestocking with a startlingly earthy sense of humour. None of them knew she was nursing a secret which she dared not allow to leak out.

Disaster had struck at a time when life brimmed with exciting possibilities. Publishing her first detective novel fulfilled a long-held ambition, and although sales were modest, Benson's had raised her salary to six pounds ten shillings a week, and promised a bonus. Even her troubled love life had taken a turn for the better. Although a man she adored had deserted her, a new lover turned up to offer the sexual satisfaction she craved. She nicknamed him 'the Beast'.

But then the worst happened. With 'the Beast', she overcame her loathing of contraceptives, but despite her precautions, something went wrong, and she fell pregnant. When she broke the news to 'the Beast', he flounced out in a temper, pausing only to blurt out that he already had a wife and daughter. Sayers had slept with him on the rebound, and she dared not tell her friends about her humiliation. Confiding in her elderly, respectable parents, who were the embodiment of Victorian values, was equally unthinkable. Her father, an elderly vicar, would be horrified, while her mother had no time for babies. She had no confidence that Philip Benson would sympathize. Probably he would sack her. Money was tight, and she dared not risk being thrown out of work.

Overwhelmed by shame and misery, she thought about parting with the child to an orphanage or a charity for waifs and
strays. Adoption was impossible; it would not become legal for
another three years. In despair, she contemplated abortion, but
quite apart from the fact that it was a crime, and highly dangerous, her religious faith made such a 'solution' unthinkable.

She had first encountered 'the Beast', alias Bill White, when
he rented a small flat above hers. Seeking work in the motor
trade, he had left his wife Beatrice and young daughter Valerie
in an attic flat in Southbourne, near Bournemouth. He stained
the wooden floor of Sayers' sitting-room for her, and took her for
trips on his motor-cycle. After teaching her fashionable dance-
steps – the bunny-hug, the shimmy and the black bottom – he
accompanied her to a dance at Benson's, wearing a borrowed
dinner jacket. Two lonely people, with not much in common,
each craving a little fun. She lent him cash, and even introduced
him to her parents. The fun stopped the moment she told him
about the baby.

With a chilling mixture of cheek and selfishness, Bill asked
his wife to help him wriggle out of this calamity. Shocked as she
was, Beatrice White agreed, and met up with Sayers. It was an
excruciating encounter. They were both tormented by distress
and embarrassment, but they were also sensible and decent
women whose only mistake had been to fall for an unworthy
man. A problem needed to be solved – so what should they do?

They talked things over constructively, without wasting time
on recriminations. The outcome was a pragmatic deal. Sayers
promised not to see Bill again, and to have the child fostered. Beatrice arranged for Sayers to stay in a guest house at
Southbourne, and for her brother, a doctor, to attend the birth
at a nearby nursing home. Meanwhile, Beatrice moved into
Sayers' flat in Great James Street, and forwarded her post, so
that Sayers could correspond from her London address. This
meant she could keep everyone in the dark about the truth of
her absence. She cobbled together an excuse to explain to her
mother why she would not be home for Christmas. The baby
was due to be born at around the turn of the year.

She was a good liar. Once she summoned the courage to ask for time off, the hierarchy at Benson's accepted what she said at face value. So did her parents. Resting in bed at Southbourne, Sayers scribbled away at *Clouds of Witness*, her second book about the aristocratic detective, Lord Peter Wimsey, and mapped out the future in her mind. On New Year's Day, she wrote to her much-loved cousin Ivy Shrimpton, asking if Ivy and her mother, both experienced and trustworthy foster careers, would look after another infant. She didn't mention she was the mother. Two days later her son, John Anthony, was born.

When Ivy agreed to look after him, Sayers told her the truth. Her parents must not be told, she insisted. The news would mortify them. Giving birth to an illegitimate child was not, she told Ivy, the kind of 'ill-doing' which her mother would tolerate. The Sayers were proud of their clever, lively daughter, and she could not bear to let them down. Perhaps she underestimated their love for her, but Ivy proved utterly reliable. The Sayers went to their graves without ever learning that they had a grandchild. Bill White had no further contact with his son John Anthony. Within four years, he had met someone else, and divorced Beatrice. After that, he never saw his daughter Valerie again either.

To the end of Sayers' life, the existence of her child was known only to Ivy and a handful of trusted confidants. Beatrice kept quiet too. Not until Sayers died did she tell Valerie that she had a half-brother. Valerie and John Anthony never met, because by the time she plucked up the nerve to contact him, he was dead.

Did anyone else guess the truth? At first, Sayers congratulated herself on managing her absence from Benson's with the utmost discretion, although on returning to work, people noticed she had put on weight. One colleague at least, it seems, saw though the mysterious 'illness'. Suspecting what had happened, he tried to make mischief, terrifying Sayers with the threat of exposure.

Courage was a quality Dorothy Sayers never lacked. Her tormentor had no hard evidence to support his guesswork, and she faced him down. Somehow she found the strength to say, 'Publish and be damned', and made sure he kept his mouth shut. Her secret was secure. Later, she would take her revenge on him, but not until it became safer to do so.

Before and after Benson's, Oxford played a pivotal role in Sayers' life. She was born in the city on 13 June 1893. Her father, an ordained priest, had been a contemporary of Oscar Wilde at Magdalen College, but his life followed a much less exotic course than Oscar's. When his daughter was four, he was offered the living at Bluntisham, in East Anglia's fen country. Oxford and Fenland provided the settings for two of Sayers' most admired novels, *Gaudy Night* and *The Nine Tailors*. After the Godolphin School in Salisbury, she won a scholarship to Somerville College, where she studied modern languages and medieval literature.

The feminist and pacifist Vera Brittain, an Oxford contemporary, described Sayers as 'a bouncing and exuberant young female'. That bounce and exuberance never deserted Sayers, despite the blows that rained down on her over the years. Tall, thin, and with a neck that earned her the nickname 'Swanny', she stood out from the crowd, and made up for her lack of natural beauty with a flamboyant taste in clothes. She liked to wear a three-inch-wide scarlet riband round her head, and earrings in the form of miniature cages containing brightly-coloured parrots. Often she strode down the High, smoking a cigar while a cloak billowed around her.

Her busy social life included attending a lecture by G. K. Chesterton, whom she admired as a man, as well as for his detective stories. She also developed crushes on Dr Hugh Allen, director of the Bach Choir, and Roy Ridley, a handsome Balliol student who later became the college's chaplain. Ridley was the physical original of a fictional Balliol man, Lord Peter Wimsey.

In August 1914, oblivious of the tense political climate in Europe, she set off for a long holiday in France, which was duly interrupted by the outbreak of war: for all her intellectual gifts, she could be hopelessly naïve. The following year Douglas Cole (like Chesterton, a future Detection Club colleague), a co-editor of *Oxford Poetry*, accepted one of her poems for publication. Before long, she produced a slim volume of verse. Having

achieved a First in French, she applied for a job in the French
Red Cross, but was turned down because she was too young.
After a spell as a teacher, she worked for Blackwell's, the
publishers, in Oxford, where she fell in love with Eric Whelpton,
a handsome soldier who have been invalided out of the Army.

After the war ended, Whelpton started teaching in France.
Sayers chased him across the Channel, and took a job as his
assistant. When he teased her about her enthusiasm for crime
fiction, she told him some friends from Oxford were planning to
make a fortune by writing detective stories. The group included
Douglas Cole, his wife Margaret, and Michael Sadleir, later a
successful publisher. They thought they could create a market,
and had it in mind to set up a writing syndicate together. Sayers
urged Whelpton to join them, but he was not interested. Worse,
he did not reciprocate her devotion.

Whelpton became involved with a married woman, and a
chastened Sayers returned to London to lick her wounds. Her
morale received a much-needed boost when – in the same post-
war mood that saw women given the vote (provided they were
thirty years old), the first female MP returned to office, and
the first woman called to the Bar – Oxford University allowed
women to graduate formally. Sayers was among the first group
of female students from Oxford to be invested with both a B.A.
and, because five years had passed since she had taken her
finals, an M.A.

Equal rights for women remained, however, a distant dream.
Working men worried about women taking their jobs, and trade
union pressure pushed women towards the career cul-de-sac
of domestic service. Even highly educated women found their
horizons narrowing. Their choice was often between a career
coupled with a life of celibacy, or redundancy and marriage.

With so many young men killed in combat, marriage was
often not an option. The problem of the 'surplus woman' was
widely debated by the chattering classes. One successful Golden
Age suspense novel (written by a single woman) even saw a
deranged serial killer decide to solve that problem by ridding
the world of unmarried females. For Sayers, the answer lay in

building an independent and fulfilling career, preferably as a writer. After being turned down for a series of jobs, she returned to teaching as a stopgap. Meanwhile, she tried her hand at a detective story.

She began with the mystery of 'a fat lady found dead in her bath with nothing on but her pince-nez'. After the victim – a sympathetically presented Jew – underwent a sex change, this became the opening of *Whose Body?* In Sayers' original version, Lord Peter Wimsey deduces that a body in a bath is not that of Sir Reuben Levy, a financier, because it is not circumcised. The publishers thought this too coarse for the delicate sensibilities of readers, and required her to change the physical evidence so as to suggest that the corpse belonged to a manual worker, rather than a rich man.

Originally, Wimsey featured as a minor character in an unpublished story. This was probably intended for the Sexton Blake series, produced by a writing syndicate. Sayers also toyed with the idea of introducing Wimsey in a play ('a detective fantasia' called *The Mousehole*) that she did not finish. When she embarked on a novel, she decided this son of a duke would be her detective.

Her intentions were satiric rather than snobbish. A detective who was not a professional police officer, she reasoned, needed to be rich and to have plenty of leisure time to devote to solving mysteries. She conceived Wimsey as a caricature of the gifted amateur sleuth, and found it amusing to soak herself in the lifestyle of someone for whom money was no object. When Wimsey first comes into the story, 'his long amiable face looked as if it had generated spontaneously from his top hat, as white maggots breed from Gorgonzola.'

Sayers endowed Wimsey with criminology, bibliophily, music and cricket as favourite recreations. He is a Balliol man, equipped with a magnifying glass disguised as a monocle, a habit of literary quotation and an engaging, if often frivolous, demeanour. His valet and former batman, the imperturbable Mervyn Bunter, became devoted to him when they fought together during the war. Conveniently, his sister, Lady Mary, is to marry Detective

Chief Inspector Charles Parker of Scotland Yard. Like many amateur sleuths, Wimsey benefits from keeping close to the police. The dialogue is flippant, but Wimsey's worldview is darkened by his wartime experiences. He suffered shell-shock and had a nervous breakdown. When Parker is bothered by the idea of a corpse being shaved and manicured, Wimsey retorts, 'Worse things happen in war.'

A distinctive amateur sleuth, a lively style and unorthodox storyline compensated for the fact that it is easy to guess whodunit. Sayers was always more interested in describing the culprit's methods of carrying out and concealing the crime. In a nod to E. C. Bentley's ground-breaking whodunit *Trent's Last Case*, she had the killer refer to 'that well-thought-out work of Mr. Bentley's'. Later, it became a regular in-joke for Detection Club members to reference each other in their books.

Having fun with Wimsey offered relief from the depressing reality of life on a tight budget. The rent for her flat was seventy pounds a year, and she struggled to make ends meet. As she told her parents, in one of her innumerable frank and entertaining letters, writing about Wimsey 'prevents me from wanting too badly the kind of life I *do* want, and see no chance of getting. . . .' If the novel did not sell, she intended to abandon her literary ambitions, and take up a permanent job as a teacher. But it was not what she wanted. When an American publisher offered to take *Whose Body?* she was overjoyed. Soon a British publisher accepted it as well.

While Sayers was working on her first novel, she began a relationship with someone very different from Whelpton, the writer John Cournos. Russian-born, Cournos came from a Jewish background, and his first language was Yiddish. His family emigrated to the United States when he was ten, but he moved to England and established a reputation as a novelist, poet and journalist. Cournos was disdainful about Sayers' aristocratic detective, but she cheered up when Philip Guedella, a Jewish historian, asserted in the *Daily News* that 'the detective story is the normal recreation of noble minds'.

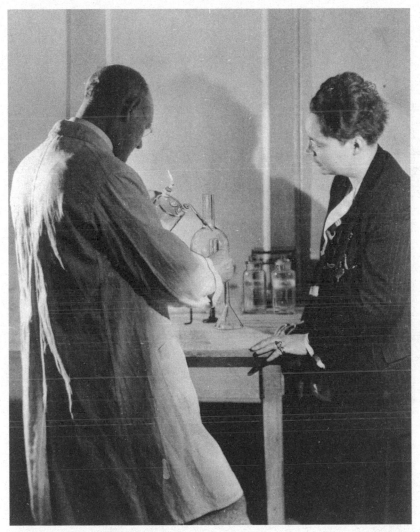

Dorothy L. Sayers and the mysterious Robert Eustace – photographed to publicise *The Documents in the Case* (by permission of the Marion E. Wade Center, Wheaton College, Wheaton, IL).

Dorothy L. Sayers (by permission of the Dorothy L. Sayers Society).

Cournos believed in free love, but Sayers, a High Anglican, was wary about sex outside marriage. Times were changing, and Marie Stopes, author of *Married Love*, had recently set up the country's first clinic dispensing contraceptive products and advice – a crucial step towards making birth control socially acceptable. Sayers, however, had not yet overcome her objection to contraception as she did later with the Beast, Bill White. She did not want her relationship with Cournos to have the 'taint of the rubber shop'.

This mismatch of expectations killed off their affair. She presented a fictionalized version of her emotional battle with Cournos eight years later, when she published *Strong Poison*. Harriet Vane, a detective novelist and Oxford graduate, is accused of murdering her selfish former lover Philip Boyes. She tells Wimsey that Boyes demanded her devotion, but 'I didn't like having matrimony offered as a bad-conduct prize'.

Cournos retaliated with a more intimate and brutal account of their relationship in *The Devil is an English Gentleman*. Stella, based on Sayers, resists Richard's overtures, thinking: 'If I give myself to him, he'll forsake me.' Meanwhile Richard 'waited for the generous gesture, for a token of abandonment on her part; it did not come'. Cournos, who eventually emigrated to the USA, continued to publish books until the early Sixties. His destiny was to be remembered for his doomed romance with Sayers rather than for his own literary efforts.

Sayers started working for Benson's shortly before *Whose Body?* was accepted. The job taught her how to use publicity to promote her writing, and the value of branding (before it was known as branding). Not from cussedness, but because she knew the value of a distinctive brand, she insisted on being known as Dorothy L. Sayers, not simply Dorothy Sayers. When her publisher, Ernest Benn, missed out her middle initial on the spine of one book a few years later, she was incandescent. After all, she said, people did not talk about E. Bentley, or G. Chesterton or G. Shaw.

Bill White was earthier than Cournos, and part of his appeal was that he did not share his predecessor's lofty disdain for crossword puzzles and vulgar limericks. Thanks to him, Sayers experienced at last the sexual pleasure she craved. But once again, a man let her down. It was becoming a pattern in her life.

Sayers had never intended her affair with Bill White to be more than 'an episode'. On returning to Benson's, she worked furiously during the day, and then on her new book in the evenings. But the pretence of business as usual took a toll on her health. Her hair fell out, a visible symptom of severe emotional strain, and when it grew again, she decided her 'little rat's-tail plaits' were hideous, and had her hair cut short and started wearing a silver wig.

She kept in touch with Cournos, but was deeply wounded when, having said he was not the marrying kind, he married Helen Kestner Satterthwaite, an American who wrote detective stories under the pen name of Sybil Norton. Biting back despair, Sayers wrote him a letter of congratulation, confiding that she had 'gone over the rocks', and that the result was John Anthony. Cournos's reaction was anger that she had given herself to someone else, after refusing him. 'Why not me?' he demanded.

Sayers' reply amounted to a scream of pain. 'I have been so bitterly punished by God already, need you really dance on the body?' The correspondence continued, as she agonized over what had gone wrong between them. One line explains a great deal about the way she led the rest of her life: 'I am so terrified of emotion, now.'

That terror of emotion never left her. Sayers was devoted to her child, but in her own mind, she had committed 'a bitter sin'. These were dark days, and she told Cournos, 'It frightens me to be so unhappy.' Although she had hoped things would improve, each day seemed worse than the last, and her work was suffering. She dared not even resort to suicide, 'because what would poor Anthony do then?' In Cournos's novel, Stella threatens to kill herself, and Sayers did more than talk about self-harm in her correspondence: suicide forms a significant plot element in each of the first five Wimsey novels.

Yet there were lighter interludes. Cournos sent her an article by Chesterton about writing detective fiction, and she responded with a four-page critique. Game-playing mattered more to detective novelists at this point than the study of psychology, and she argued that characters in the detective story did not need to be drawn in depth. *Clouds of Witness* was most notable for a trial scene in the House of Lords where Peter Wimsey's elder brother is accused of murder, a plot element she hoped would attract American readers.

Her next novel, *Unnatural Death*, displayed more interest in character, although the lesbianism of the heiress Mary Whittaker is implied rather than explicit. Thrifty as good novelists are, Sayers used a snippet of information from Bill White about an air-lock in a motorcycle feed pipe to provide a clue to the mystery. In a far from cosy passage, she describes how the arms of a corpse had been nibbled by rats. Years later, she explained to George Orwell (who had spoken of Wimsey's 'morbid interest' in corpses) that in a detective novel, 'where the writer has exerted himself to be extra gruesome, *look out for the clue*'. The *frisson* induced by the image of hungry rats was a ruse to distract readers from the possibility that the arm had been pricked by a hypodermic.

Wimsey is assisted by Miss Climpson and her undercover employment agency for single women. Climpson's irrepressible verve was Sayers' riposte to the likes of Charlotte Haldane, wife of the Marxist geneticist J. B. S. Haldane, who argued in *Motherhood and its Enemies* that a woman's personal fulfilment depends on her inborn maternal instinct. Haldane is remembered as a feminist, but Sayers' fiction was more sympathetic to single women, and her attitude towards them more progressive. *Unnatural Death* focused, as Sayers' stories often did, more on the means by which death was caused than on whodunit; the culprit is obvious. The murder method involved injecting an air bubble into a vein. An ingenious idea, even if its feasibility was open to question.

She earned money by writing short stories, drawing on her own know-how for material. 'The Problem of Uncle Meleager's Will' included a crossword puzzle clue, a nod to the fashionable craze which was also one of her own favourite pastimes. Motorcycling was an unlikely passion. She bought a 'Ner-a-Car' motorcycle, complete with sidecar, and rode it 'in light skirmishing trim . . . with two packed saddle-bags and a coat tied on with string.' 'The Fantastic Horror of the Cat in the Bag' features a race with a motorbike rejoicing in the improbable but factually accurate name of the Scott Flying-Squirrel.

The weirder realms of advertising presented her with the germ of 'The Abominable History of the Man with Copper Fingers', which is perhaps the best Wimsey short story. Sayers' inspiration came from an American firm of morticians whose advertisements demanded: *Why lay your loved ones in the cold earth? Let us electroplate them for you in gold and silver.*

In April 1926, Sayers summoned up the nerve to drop a bombshell on her parents. She wrote a letter telling them, after a lengthy preamble including thanks for the present of an Easter egg, that she was 'getting married on Tuesday (weather permitting) to a man named Fleming, who is at the moment Motoring Correspondent to the *News of the World*'. Hoping to soften the shock, she added, 'I think you will rather like him.' To her relief, they did.

The new man in her life, Oswald Arthur Fleming, was a divorced journalist twelve years her senior. She had only known him for a few months. A Scot hailing from the Orkneys, he liked to be known as 'Mac', though he wrote under the name Atherton Fleming. John Anthony, who knew Sayers as 'Cousin Dorothy', remained in Ivy Shrimpton's care after the death of Ivy's mother, and did not join the couple in their London flat.

Mac Fleming was a hard-living, hard-drinking newspaper-man, keen on motor racing, and chronically hard up. He had two children by his first wife, but provided them with no financial support. He had written a book called *How to See the Battlefields*, based on his time as a war correspondent for the *Daily Chronicle*. For a time, he worked in advertising, which may explain how he and Sayers met.

She took to married life with gusto. She accompanied him to race meetings at Brooklands, and bought a motorcycle to ride herself, clad in goggles, gauntlets, and leather helmet. Motor racing was the latest craze, and leading drivers like Malcolm Campbell, Henry Segrave and J. G. Parry-Thomas – all of whom held the world land speed record in quick succession – were household names.

Racing offered thrills in abundance, but danger was ever present. The long, flat beach at Pendine Sands in Carmarthenshire was vaunted as 'the finest natural speedway imaginable', but while trying to regain the record, Parry-Thomas crashed his car. He was severely burned, and his head was ripped away from his neck by the drive chain. Mac, a friend of the dead man, was given the wretched task of reporting the horrific crash.

A less personally distressing project saw the *News of the World* pay for both Mac and Sayers to travel to France. Their task was to solve the murder of the English-born nurse May Daniels. Nurse Daniels had disappeared from a quayside waiting room when about to return to England after crossing the Channel with a friend for a day trip. Months later, her decomposed body, bearing signs of strangulation, was found by the roadside near Boulogne, and her gold wristwatch was missing. Clues (or red herrings) found near the body included a discarded hypodermic syringe, and an umbrella, while Nurse Daniels' friend said she had spoken about a meeting with 'Egyptian princes'.

Rumours spread that the dead woman was pregnant by a prominent member of the British establishment, and that the real purpose of her trip was to have an abortion performed by a mysterious Egyptian called Suliman. Questions were asked in Parliament about a baffling lack of cooperation between the British and French authorities, and the Press scented a cover-up. Mac and Sayers faced competition from other journalists, including former Chief Inspector Gough, hired as a 'special investigator' by the *Daily Mail*, and Netley Lucas, a conman turned crime correspondent for the *Sunday News*. None matched the brilliance of Lord Peter Wimsey, although Netley Lucas' lifestyle was equally colourful: he later applied his talents to twin careers as a literary agent and a publisher before being sentenced to eighteen months with hard labour for fraud and plagiarism.

The Daniels puzzle remained unsolved. Despite this setback to her embryonic career as an amateur detective, Sayers became entranced by real-life mysteries, and introduced aspects of the Nurse Daniels case into *Unnatural Death*. After the excitement of the trip to France, Sayers fantasized about moving abroad, but this would have meant an even greater separation from John Anthony, and was out of the question. She hated the way that the Defence of the Realm Act – unaffectionately known as 'Dora' – curtailed individual liberties. In her eyes, the curbs on alcohol consumption, and restricted licensing hours, coupled with high levels of income tax, meant England was 'no country for free men'.

She threw herself into work at Benson's with renewed vigour. Colman's of Norwich was a key client, and Sayers wrote *The Recipe Book of the Mustard Club* to promote Colman's Mustard. Typically, she littered the text with quotations, and devised a frivolously elaborate history of the club, claiming it was founded by Aesculapius, god of medicine, and that Nebuchadnezzar was an early member. At first, the club was purely imaginary, featuring characters such as Lord Bacon of Cookham, and the club secretary Miss Di Gester, but the campaign was such a huge success that a real club was created. At its height, it boasted half a million members.

Sayers' creative flair was ideally suited to marketing. She is credited with coining the phrase 'it pays to advertise', and collaborated on the most memorable advertisement of the time, part of a long campaign on behalf of Guinness stout. An artist called John Gilroy joined Benson's in 1925, and he and Sayers became friends as well as colleagues. After a visit to the circus, Gilroy dreamed up the idea of using birds and animals to advertise Guinness. He sketched a pelican with a glass of Guinness on his beak, and Sayers suggested replacing that bird with a toucan. She wrote the lines:

> *If he can say as you can*
> *Guinness is good for you,*
> *How good to be a Toucan:*
> *Just think what Toucan do.*

To this day, there is a healthy market for Guinness toucan collectibles. Gilroy, a young man from Whitley Bay who had started out as a cartoonist, combined his advertising work with portrait painting, and Sayers was one of the first people to sit for him, sporting her silver wig. Gilroy was alive to her earthy physicality, and unexpected sex appeal, and rhapsodized about her: 'terrific size – lovely fat fingers – lovely snub nose – lovely curly lips – a baby's face in a way'.

Sayers was ready to spread her creative wings. She began to translate the *Chanson de Roland* into rhymed couplets, as well as a medieval poem, *Tristan in Brittany*. In addition, she dipped in and out of a projected book about Wilkie Collins. She never finished it, but her study of Collins' methods influenced her own literary style. Her main focus remained on writing detective fiction. Spurred by the desire to support herself and her family, she became intensely productive. In 1928 alone she published three books, including a Wimsey novel, *The Unpleasantness at the Bellona Club*. The novel was reviewed by Dashiell Hammett, shortly before the former Pinkerton's gumshoe established himself as a writer of hard-boiled private eye novels. Hammett's writing, tastes, politics, and life experiences were a world away from Sayers', but he felt her novel only missed being 'a pretty good detective story' because of a lack of pace: 'Its developments come just a little too late to knock the reader off his chair.'

She had written enough short stories to publish a collection, *Lord Peter Views the Body*, under the new imprint of Victor Gollancz. A left-wing firebrand, Gollancz had rejected his orthodox Jewish upbringing and become a highly successful businessman with an unrivalled flair for marketing. As managing director of Sayers' publishers, he revolutionized the advertising of fiction, with two-column splashes in the broadsheets which made his books seem important and exciting.

When he left Ernest Benn to set up on his own, Gollancz built a list of talented detective novelists, promoting newcomers like Milward Kennedy and Gladys Mitchell. But Sayers was much more bankable, and he begged her to join him. She admired Gollancz's intelligence and drive, and trusted his judgement – it was Gollancz who recommended her to a new literary agent, David Higham. Author and publisher had starkly contrasting political and religious views, but they enjoyed each other's company, and their mutual respect and loyalty was lifelong.

Since her next novel was under contract to Benn, Gollancz started with the short stories, and came up with a simple but striking yellow and black dust jacket. Gollancz, who was as desperate as his authors for his titles to be noticed (oddly, this is not a trait which all writers associate with their publishers), honed this technique to perfection in the next few years. The bold, yellow jackets, with typography in varying sizes and typefaces, were as recognizable as advertising posters – and Gollancz duly hired Edward McKnight Kauffer, an American modernist whose posters for the London Underground were much admired, to produce eye-catching abstract artwork for works of detective fiction.

Gollancz claimed to have invented the term 'omnibus volume'; long before the era of the fat airport thriller, he was convinced that readers liked bulky books, which yielded good profits. He had an idea for a huge anthology of mystery stories, and persuaded Sayers to edit it. With his encouragement, she researched the history of the detective story in the course of compiling a weighty gathering of genre fiction. She was probably influenced by Wright and Wrong – that is, by comparable projects undertaken in the United States by Willard Huntington Wright (better known as detective novelist S. S. Van Dine) and in Britain by E. M. Wrong. Her lengthy essay introducing the first series of *Great Short Stories of Detection, Mystery and Horror* showed the breadth of her reading and her critical insight.

As Sayers' reputation blossomed, the intense happiness of the early days of marriage faded. Pressure of work, and personal circumstances, took their toll. During the war, Mac had been gassed, two of his brothers had died and another was badly injured. His previous wife reckoned that this sequence of personal disasters transformed his personality, and not in a good way. Now Mac was afflicted by a series of health problems, and owed money to the taxman. When he had to give up his job and go freelance, his morale – and temper – suffered. Once again Sayers found herself let down by a man. Her reaction was to feast on comfort food and to drink more than was good for her.

Despairing of her 'rapidly fattening frame', she had her hair cut in an Eton crop, a severe, boyish style that had recently supplanted the 'bob'. Her choice of clothes became even more outlandish, and on one occasion she turned up to a public function in a man's rugby shirt. Her plain appearance and fondness for masculine dress led some people to assume she was a lesbian. But with detective novelists, as with detective novels, it is a mistake to judge a book by its cover.

After her father died in September 1928, Sayers and Mac bought a house in Witham, Essex. Today, her statue stands across the road from her home in Newland Street. Sayers' mother died ten months after her father, and the double bereavement was a crushing blow. A contract with an American publisher enabled her to resign from Benson's, but she took on responsibility for caring for an elderly aunt, as well as supporting John Anthony. Money remained tight. Mac Fleming's health worsened, and as her increasing fame provoked his jealousy, he became depressive and difficult. He had promised to adopt John Anthony, but kept putting off any action. So the boy stayed with Ivy, and when Ivy suggested moving nearer to Witham, Sayers discouraged her. She had her hands full with Mac.

When Anthony Berkeley invited her to dine with fellow detective novelists, he offered her much more than simply the opportunity to socialize with people who played the same literary game. For Sayers, the Detection Club came to mean an opportunity to escape for a few hours, just as the stories the Club members wrote were enjoyed by people in search of escapism.

Sayers was becoming interested in real-life murders, absorbing herself in the fears and passions of victims, suspects and culprits alike. She and her colleagues in the Detection Club understood that these cases posed puzzles of their own – and itched to solve them. These puzzles differed from the contrived complexities of the typical detective story. They concerned guilt and innocence, the mysteries of human motivation, and the frighteningly unpredictable workings of justice. And the crime that made the greatest impression on the Detection Club was the brutal stabbing that led to the equally shocking execution of Edith Thompson.

Notes to Chapter 2

My account of Sayers' life and work owes much to information supplied by the Dorothy L. Sayers Society, Sayers' reviews of detective fiction, and the biographies and collections of letters mentioned in the Select Bibliography, in particular Barbara Reynolds' *Dorothy L. Sayers: Her Life and Soul*, together with material held in the Sayers Archive at the Marion E. Wade Center, Wheaton College, Illinois.

One successful Golden Age suspense novel (written by a single woman) even saw a deranged serial killer decide to solve that problem by ridding the world of unmarried females.
To identify the book in question would be too much of a spoiler, but the author was Ethel Lina White (1876–1944), a specialist in 'women in jeopardy' novels, and best known for *The Wheel Spins* (1936), filmed by Hitchcock as *The Lady Vanishes*. Raymond Chandler co-wrote the screenplay for *The Unseen*, also based on a White novel, *Midnight House* (1942).

the Sexton Blake series
Blake was another private eye with rooms in Baker Street; he was originally created by Harry Blyth in 1893. The many later, often pseudonymous, writers of Blake stories (Margery Allingham may have been among them) included the science fiction and fantasy novelist Michael Moorcock (born 1939) whose first Blake story, *Caribbean Crisis* (1962), a locked room mystery with a corpse in a bathysphere, is now a sought-after rarity. Blake was brought to the television screen in the Sixties, with Laurence Payne (1919–2009) in the title role; Payne later wrote crime novels, starting with *The Nose on My Face* (1961), a whodunit filmed as *Girl in the Headlines*.

Philip Guedella, a Jewish historian
Guedella (1889–1954) was a barrister and popular writer who stood five times as a Liberal candidate for Parliament without success. His epigrams include 'Even reviewers read a Preface', while his remark about detective stories is quoted in Antony Shaffer's play *Sleuth*.

The Daniels puzzle remained unsolved.
Three years later, a workman called Prudhomme was interrogated
by police after his wife accused him of stealing a gold watch, which
was discovered at his home. But the watch proved not to be May
Daniels', and justice went no further than seeing the French police
charge Prudhomme with the theft of a bicycle, and his wife with
stealing vegetables.

a projected book about Wilkie Collins
The surviving fragment was published posthumously: E. R. Gregory,
ed., *Wilkie Collins. A Critical and Bibliographical Study* (Toledo:
Friends of the University of Toledo Libraries, 1977).

Clouds of Witness *was most notable for a trial scene in the House
of Lords*
Charles Parker mentions to Wimsey the real-life precedent of Earl
Ferrers, the last peer to be hanged, in 1760 (for the murder of his
land steward). The novel achieved a strange form of notoriety in
1962, as one of the library books mischievously vandalised by the
playwright Joe Orton and his lover and eventual murderer, Kenneth
Halliwell; the pair were sent to prison for malicious damage to the
property of Islington Public Library.

*George Orwell (who had spoken of Wimsey's 'morbid interest' in
corpses)*
In 'Raffles and Miss Blandish', *Horizon*, October 1944. Drawing a
contrast with the stories about Holmes, Ernest Bramah's blind detective Max Carrados, and Dr John Thorndyke, Orwell argues that: 'Since
1918 . . . a detective story not containing a murder has been a great
rarity, and the most disgusting details of dismemberment and exhumation are commonly exploited.' A modern perspective is supplied
in Jake Kerridge, 'Does Crime Writing Have a Misogynistic Heart?',
Daily Telegraph, 17 July 2014. Thanks to the success of the Carrados
stories, Ernest Brammah Smith (1864–1942), who wrote as Ernest
Bramah, was an obvious candidate for membership of the Detection
Club, but although he corresponded amiably with Sayers, probably
his natural reclusiveness led him to decline the chance to join.

under the new imprint of Victor Gollancz
Details about Gollancz's life and career are drawn from Ruth Dudley
Edwards' *Victor Gollancz: a Biography* (London: Gollancz, 1987).

influenced by Wright and Wrong
The seminal essays were Willard Huntington Wright's 'Detective Story' in *Scribners*, November 1926, and E. M. Wrong's 'Introduction' to *Crime and Detection* (London: Oxford University Press, 1926).

3

Conversations about
a Hanged Woman

On a cold, damp January morning in 1923, a terrified woman was dragged to the gallows at Holloway Prison. Even after a judge put on the black cap at the end of a calamitous trial and sentenced her to death, Edith Thompson never believed she would really hang. Her morale only collapsed when the date was fixed for her execution. On that final morning, when no last-minute reprieve arrived, she started to sob and scream. She was injected with a cocktail of drugs to calm her, and given a large measure of brandy and a cigarette. The hangman strapped her wrists, and his assistant tied her skirt and ankles, but it took four men to manhandle her outside into the drizzle, and then into the shelter of a brick shed. The scaffold stood waiting for her.

Edith was put in a wooden bosun's chair, so the noose could be tied around her neck. She was barely conscious as a white hood was placed over her head. After the trapdoor opened and she fell, her underclothes were drenched with blood. Lurid rumours claimed that her 'insides' fell out. The bleeding was so severe that the authorities insisted that any woman to be hanged subsequently must wear canvas pants. One possibility is that Edith suffered a haemorrhage, another that she was pregnant.

Edith Thompson's name was on everyone's lips. She had become notorious as the 'Messalina of Ilford', a scandalous modern successor to the predatory and sexually insatiable wife of the Emperor Claudius. Yet Edith's beginnings could not have been more ordinary, and the events leading to her death were more like a blend of *crime passionnel* and black farce than a story of calculated and cold-blooded cruelty.

Born on Christmas Day, six months after Sayers, Edith Graydon was a pretty, vivacious Londoner. Her father was a clerk with a profitable sideline as a dancing teacher. One of his pupils, a neighbour in Leytonstone, was Alfred Hitchcock. Despite his physical bulk, the young Hitchcock was surprisingly nimble. He knew the Graydon family, and formed a lasting friendship with Edith's younger sister Avis.

Dancing and acting were Edith's favourite pastimes. Her imagination was fired by a touch of drama and romance, but she wasn't afraid of hard work, and became head buyer for a milliner's. Edith met Percy Thompson, a shipping clerk, when she was fifteen. After a six-year courtship they married and settled down in Ilford. Their life was comfortable, but lacked glamour and excitement, and Edith craved both. There was nothing dowdy or old-before-her-time about her. She bobbed her hair, wore calf-length sleeveless dresses and spoke French.

When she was twenty-six, she took a fancy to Frederick Bywaters, an eighteen-year-old ship's laundry steward who had previously courted Avis. Handsome and widely travelled, Bywaters was not staid and set in his ways, like Percy. The three of them, and Avis, went on holiday to the Isle of Wight, and Percy suggested that Bywaters stay with them in Ilford in between voyages. Before long Edith was skipping work for breakfast in bed with the lodger, but Percy discovered that they were having an affair. He refused Bywaters' demand to allow Edith a divorce, and threw the lad out of the house.

Undeterred, Edith and Bywaters kept seeing each other. When he went back to sea, she sent him dozens of intimate letters. She claimed that she had tried to poison Percy, grinding up broken glass from light bulbs and feeding the shards to him, mixed up with mashed potato. Begging Bywaters to 'do something desperate', she sent him press cuttings with accounts of poisonings, and said she had become pregnant by him, but had carried out an abortion herself. All this was probably fantasy rather than fact. Unfortunately for Edith, Bywaters could not bring himself to throw away the letters, and became obsessed by the idea of having her for himself.

Late at night on 4 October 1922, he waited in the darkness for Edith and Percy as they came home from a trip to the Criterion Theatre, and pounced on Percy, stabbing him repeatedly. Panic-stricken, Edith called out, 'Oh don't! Oh don't!', but her cries made no difference. Bywaters had done something desperate, just as her letters had asked. He fled, and Percy died at the scene. When the police questioned Edith, she became hysterical and insisted that a stranger had attacked her husband. But she was a poor liar. Her affair was soon uncovered, and so were the incriminating letters.

Edith Thompson and Frederick Bywaters were both charged with murder. At the trial, Bywaters said he had only meant to injure Percy, and that Edith was not involved. Against her lawyers' advice, she gave evidence in her own defence, and her naïve answers when questioned destroyed her credibility. The judge's summing-up oozed stern Victorian moralism, and the couple were sentenced to death. Their appeals failed, but public opinion, perverse as ever, swung from hatred for Edith to horror at her fate. A woman had not been hanged in Britain for sixteen years, and Bywaters never faltered in his insistence that she was innocent. A petition signed by a million people failed to persuade the Home Secretary to grant a reprieve. Edith and Bywaters were executed in separate prisons, Holloway and Pentonville, on the stroke of nine on 9 January.

Edith Thompson's final moments tormented her hangman, John Ellis, a former hairdresser and newsagent from Rochdale. Britain's chief executioner, Ellis hanged Doctor Crippen and Herbert Rowse Armstrong before descending into misery and alcoholism. Eight years after snapping Edith's neck, he cut his own throat.

The Thompson–Bywaters case marked, in George Orwell's phrase, the end of an 'Elizabethan Age' of English murder. The more talented detective novelists realized that, whilst their fictional mysteries were bound to be very different from real-life cases, they could and should learn from what had happened to people who did kill others in the real world.

Anthony Berkeley was appalled by Edith Thompson's fate. So was Alfred Hitchcock, who toyed with the idea of filming her life story. Unlike Berkeley, he decided to steer clear, perhaps because of his continuing friendship with Edith's sister, although some aspects of *Stage Fright* echo the case.

For Berkeley, the outcome of the trial showed that the British legal system was more fallible than the general public fondly believed. He devoted several of his novels to subversive attacks on conventional justice, yet he was no-one's idea of a bleeding heart. His sympathy for Edith was driven at least in part by his scorn for the prevailing sexual mores. He had no time for people who condemned adultery.

In Berkeley, wit, charm and flair warred with demons. He loved to confound people's expectations. The contradictions of his personality infuriated many of his contemporaries. He was the most vociferous advocate of the need for the detective novel to focus on the motivation for murder rather than mere puzzles. Yet the complexities of his own psychological make-up would baffle the most expert profiler.

Unlike almost everyone else, he never felt overawed by Sayers' intellect and strength of character. He was cheeky enough to put her into one of his most celebrated novels, and tease her about Lord Peter Wimsey. In the long run, his temper tantrums drove Sayers to despair. Yet Agatha Christie wrote about him – not just for publication, but in her private notebook – with unqualified admiration.

Berkeley loved hiding behind the masks he presented to the outside world. One of his literary disguises was so successful that it prompted lengthy – and often wild – speculation in the national press, as well as in two novels by other writers. In later years, the concealment took physical form. Ailing and asthmatic, he would 'disconcert anybody carrying on a conversation with him by suddenly placing a mask over his face, pumping away at little rubber ball and then taking deep breaths'. Julian Symons, a post-war President of the Detection Club, was one of the disconcerted, believing that Berkeley's 'ruddy-faced geniality' concealed a disturbingly shy and secretive character. He was an obsessive by nature, whose eccentricities (which included a fruitless campaign against King Edward VIII's marriage to Wallis Simpson) persisted to the end of his life. His will instructed his trustees to make sure that he really was dead. He was terrified of being buried alive.

For all his strange behaviour, Berkeley's contribution to detective fiction was dazzling. 'Detection and crime at its wittiest', Agatha Christie said. 'All his stories are amusing, intriguing, and he is a master of the final twist.' His influence can also be detected in the plotting of Christie novels such as *Murder on the Orient Express*.

His real name was Anthony Berkeley Cox. Born in the same year as Sayers and Edith Thompson, he was the son of a doctor who invented a form of X-ray machine enabling the detection of shrapnel in wounded patients. Sybil Iles, his mother, claimed descent from the seventeenth-century Earl of Monmouth, and from a smuggler called Francis Iles. The family inheritance included two properties in Watford: Monmouth House and The Platts. Sybil was a strong-minded intellectual who studied at Oxford before women's colleges were formally admitted to the university. A head teacher prior to her marriage, she had published a novel called *The School of Life*. Berkeley found her powerful and intimidating, and the complexities of their relationship probably explain his schizophrenic attitude towards women – adoring and hurtful by turns.

Berkeley had a younger sister, Cynthia, and a brother, Stephen. An Edwardian photograph shows all three of them posed together in the style of the period. Berkeley seems pensive, with a hint of a suppressed smile, as if enjoying a private joke. He attended Sherborne School before reading Classics at University College, Oxford, and was a contemporary of Sayers, although their paths seem not to have crossed. Yet in a family of high achievers, Berkeley felt overshadowed by his gifted siblings. He took a miserable third-class degree, whereas Stephen won a scholarship to King's College, Cambridge, and Cynthia achieved a doctorate in music. Stephen became a prominent mathematician, while Cynthia enjoyed success as a musician as well as notoriety because she lived with a man to whom she wasn't married.

Unlike Sayers, whose letters are now held in hundreds of folders at an American university archive, and Christie, who wrote an (admittedly selective) autobiography, Berkeley cultivated an air of mystery. It appealed to his sense of humour to fob off anyone who sought biographical information, whilst hiding clues to his personal life in plain sight by putting them into his detective stories. His darkest secret was concealed in a book with a title borrowed from the judge's remarks in Thompson–Bywaters case, but its catastrophic failure marked the end of his career as a novelist.

It is naïve to assume that crime stories routinely reveal secrets about their creators' personalities. Detective novelists specialize in misdirection. But Berkeley's mother had fictionalized aspects of her own life in her novel, and he took the same approach to astonishing extremes. For Berkeley, fiction gave a licence to say the unsayable. His skill was such that none of his contemporaries had a clue about how much his novels owed to his private passions.

Alan Littlewood, the hapless protagonist of *As for the Woman*, is a self-portrait, and Alan's family bears a close resemblance to Berkeley's. Alan is an Oxford graduate, the oldest of three children, and feels inadequate in comparison to his sister, a musician, and his brother, a Cambridge scholar. Like Berkeley, he has literary ambitions; and as a teenager he publishes a romantic sonnet. Alan inadvertently overhears Mrs Littlewood, probably echoing Berkeley's own mother, dismiss his poetry as 'empty, pretentious nonsense'. Like Berkeley, he suffers from poor health, and an inferiority complex which is exacerbated by a sense that his powerful and intelligent mother finds him a disappointment. And like Berkeley, he finds women both fascinating and frightening. Alan lusts after a married woman, who encourages his devotion, but proves unworthy of it. Was this strange and disastrous relationship based on an early episode in Berkeley's love life – or is there another interpretation?

Berkeley's sense of humour was acute but idiosyncratic. Julian Symons recalled that when, inexplicably, a rusty nail appeared in Berkeley's soup at a literary luncheon, he could not tell whether it had been put there by a careless cook, by a fellow guest Berkeley had insulted, or by Berkeley himself: 'With Anthony Berkeley Cox, such a joke was possible.' Even when relatively young, Berkeley relished playing the grumpy old man, and liked to give the impression that he was a misanthrope. Perhaps he used this as a cover to hide his compulsive womanizing. The glamorous Christianna Brand, who joined the Detection Club after the Second World War, and certainly caught Berkeley's eye, said he once confided that there was 'not one soul in the world he did not cordially dislike'. Thin-skinned and quick to take offence, he was a rich man who earned a reputation for stinginess. Legend has it that the reason why books signed by Berkeley are rare is because he charged for giving his autograph.

Yet he showed kindness and generosity to little-known writers, inspired loyalty in those who worked for him, and was renowned as a genial host. Christianna Brand judged him 'an excellent companion, clever, erudite and very well read', and Symons said he was 'particularly sympathetic to the young'. When he published a fiercely opinionated book about England's social and political ills, some of his arguments were not merely perceptive and enlightened, but decades ahead of their time. He argued in favour of equal pay for women, a minimum wage, fairer rents and worker participation on company boards. He also forecast the creation of a League of European Nations.

When the First World War broke out, Berkeley joined up, reaching the rank of lieutenant. He was gassed while serving in France, and also wounded by shrapnel before being invalided out of the army. Bouts of ill-health contributed to the uncertainty of his temperament throughout the rest of his life. In the reckless whirl of wartime, he married Margaret Farrar while on leave in 1917. He was twenty-one, she was just nineteen. They were too young, but what was the point of thinking long-term? Soldiers did not know whether they would ever come back from their next tour of duty. Nor did their lovers.

In peacetime, the marriage ran into difficulties, and eventually they divorced. Margaret (known as Peggy to those close to her) remarried, but Berkeley stayed on surprisingly good terms with her. When he died, decades after their divorce, she received a legacy under his will. The image he liked to cultivate of a tight-fisted misanthrope was not the whole story.

Not long after Berkeley and Margaret split up, he put his own views into the mouth of his (unmarried) detective, Roger Sheringham: 'I never think a first marriage ought to count, do you? One's so busy learning how to be married at all that one can hardly help acquiring a kind of resentment against one's partner in error. And once resentment has crept in, the thing's finished.' This is the best evidence we have about why the marriage collapsed.

Like so many other men returning to Britain after serving on the Front, Berkeley found it hard to adjust. He dabbled in activities ranging from farming, property management, and what he described as 'social work' (although he was scarcely a conventional do-gooder), to 'work in a Government office' (given his contempt for bureaucrats, that job was presumably short-lived). Keen on shooting, he became a good enough marksman to compete at Bisley, but amateur theatricals appealed to him even more, because they afforded a chance to assume a different personality. When his two-act comic opera, *The Family Witch* was performed in Watford, he played the Major-Domo, and Margaret designed the women's costumes.

Berkeley contributed scores of humorous sketches to *Punch* and other periodicals. These included a Conan Doyle spoof written in the style of Wodehouse. He also wrote a series of sketches featuring a small girl, some of which were collected as

Brenda Entertains, and a comic fantasy with elements of 'biological science fiction', *The Professor on Paws*, in which part of a dead scientist's brain is transplanted into a kitten. He had a facility for catching on to what was currently popular, and detective fiction caught his fancy at a time when, as M. R. James said (drawing a contrast with the ghost story), 'The detective story cannot be too much up-to-date: the motor, the telephone, the aeroplane, the newest slang, are all in place there.'

His first detective novel, *The Layton Court Mystery*, was published anonymously. The cover said the book was written by '?'. Berkeley wrote it 'for pure amusement, just to see if I could,' but it sold twenty times better than his earlier books. A country house mystery, it introduced the breezy nosy parker Roger Sheringham and his sidekick Alec Grierson. Berkeley made Sheringham rude and vain, 'an offensive person, founded on an offensive person I once knew, because in my original innocence I thought it would be amusing to have an offensive detective'. This may explain why Sheringham is portrayed as anti-Semitic. Berkeley developed a taste for taking revenge through fiction that became an addiction.

Yet Sheringham bears an uncanny resemblance to his creator. The son of a doctor, from whom he has inherited a love of puzzles, he is educated at public school and Oxford before military service. He writes successful novels and also for the newspapers. Berkeley was talking about himself and people he knew when he said in a biographical note about Roger: 'Privately, he had quite a poor opinion of his own books, combined with a horror of ever becoming like some of the people with whom his new work brought him into contact: authors who take their own work with such deadly seriousness, talk about it all the time and consider themselves geniuses.'

Roger comes up with a plausible explanation of who shot the blackmailer Victor Stanworth – only to find that he is wrong. This becomes a familiar pattern for Sheringham, the most fallible of 'great' detectives. When he does discover the truth, he helps the culprit to escape punishment, and this thwarting of conventional justice became his trademark. As Berkeley said,

Sheringham's self-confidence was limitless and he was 'never afraid of taking grave decisions, and often quite illegal ones, when he thinks that pure justice can be served better in this way than by twelve possibly stupid jurymen'. The striking twist in this novel concerns the murderer's identity. Months later, Agatha Christie used a similar ploy in *The Murder of Roger Ackroyd*, but took it a stage further.

An odd connection arose between Berkeley and Christie when, in March 1926, he serialized *The Wintringham Mystery* in the *Daily Mirror*. The newspaper offered a total of £500 in prizes to readers who provided the best answers to questions about the story: how did Stella disappear, and who caused her disappearance and why? When the prize winners were announced, one of the runners-up was Colonel Archie Christie, who was awarded five pounds. Presumably Agatha either helped her husband to solve the puzzle or entered the competition under his name. She had already won prize money for solving a previous newspaper mystery competition, but given her growing celebrity, may have been reluctant to enter as herself. Even better, the incident gave her the idea for a novel she wrote a few years later. The plot depends upon one character winning a competition prize under someone else's name.

Sheringham's second outing came in *The Wychford Poisoning Case*. At first, it was again published anonymously. Long after writing the book, Berkeley urged a correspondent to throw his copy into the incinerator, saying, 'I blush hotly whenever I look now at its intolerably facetious pages.' Yet the story offers clues to his own bizarre psychological make-up.

Spanking and sado-masochistic scenes crop up several times in Berkeley's work. When the mother of Alec Grierson's girl-friend Sheila Purefoy says that Sheila and most of her friends deserve a good spanking, Roger heartily agrees that a public spanker ought to be appointed. In a chapter accurately titled 'Mostly Irrelevant', Alec spanks Sheila in the presence of her father, who genially remarks, 'Don't mind me.' A few chapters later, it is Roger's turn to inflict discipline on Sheila, with a rolled-up magazine. Berkeley's interest in spanking was matched by his loathing of bureaucrats, and a few years later he argued in *O England!* that 'The President of the Metropolitan Water Board ought to be spanked publicly on Tower Green' because of the Board's failure to deal with water shortages.

Roger Sheringham is at his worst when he rants about women: 'Most women are potential devils. . . . They live entirely by their emotions . . . they are fundamentally incapable of reason and their one idea in life is to appear attractive to men.' Yet Sheringham adds, 'A man without his woman is only half an entity and . . . a woman . . . can . . . turn his life, however drab, into something really rather staggeringly wonderful.' When Alec Grierson asks why Roger remains a bachelor, the answer is that 'the right woman in my case . . . happens unfortunately to be married to someone else.'

Sheringham has few qualms about adultery. Attitudes were changing rapidly in the post-war era, and novels were becoming franker in their treatment of sex. Berkeley took advantage of this, and Sheringham was almost certainly expressing his creator's opinions. The central mystery of Berkeley's life is which particular married woman he thought, at that time, was the right woman for him.

Berkeley subtitled the novel 'An Essay in Criminology', and he based the plot on a classic Victorian poisoning puzzle. At the age of nineteen, Florence Chandler, a southern belle from Alabama with gold ringlets and large violet eyes, had a shipboard romance with an Englishman called James Maybrick. He was twenty-three years older, a portly man with a fondness for eating arsenic as an aphrodisiac. More appealingly, Maybrick had made a small fortune as a cotton broker, and Florence agreed to marry him. After settling into Battlecrease House, Maybrick's home in the suburbs of Liverpool, she gave birth to a son and a daughter, but discovered that her husband had several mistresses, including one who had borne him five children. He also had a vile temper and an unshakeable belief that adultery was acceptable for husbands but not wives. When she had the temerity to take a lover of her own, he was so infuriated that he ripped her dress and blacked her eye.

Gloomy, gothic Battlecrease House made a suitably sinister setting for a macabre domestic mystery populated by a cast of inquisitive servants and members of a family hostile to the young American interloper. Florence bought flypapers from a chemist, and soaked them in bowls to extract arsenic from them – to use as a facial cream, she said. Her husband succumbed to a severe gastric illness, and when the children's nanny intercepted compromising letters between Florence and her lover, she alerted Maybrick's brother. The next day, a nurse saw Florence tampering with a bottle of meat juice in her husband's bedroom; within twenty-four hours, he was dead. Florence was convicted of his murder, even thought there was doubt about whether arsenic poisoning was the cause of death. She fell victim to a fit of popular moral outrage fuelled by the Press, and a hostile summing-up from a judge, who was committed to an asylum two years later, after his sanity finally gave way.

Locked in the condemned cell in Walton Gaol, Florence had the excruciating experience of listening to workmen hammering in the prison yard as they assembled the gallows on which she was to hang. In a bizarre twist of fortune, the death sentence was belatedly replaced with life imprisonment for 'administering and attempting to administer arsenic to her husband with intent to murder'. Since this was a crime for which she never stood trial, she suffered from the most outrageous compromise in British legal history, serving fifteen years before her release. She fled back to the United States under an assumed name, where she lived to a ripe old age in a squalid cabin in Connecticut. She only had her cats for company, but no doubt she felt safer with them than in the sinister household at Battlecrease House. Decades after her death, a diary was published purporting to amount to a confession by her late husband that he was Jack the Ripper.

The Maybrick mystery, and its multiple interpretations, fascinated Berkeley and also a new friend of his. This was Elizabeth Delafield, a stylish and often poignant novelist widely regarded as a twentieth-century Jane Austen. He dedicated the novel to her, saying it grew out of 'those long criminological discussions of ours'. He hoped that Delafield would 'recognise the attempt I have made to substitute for the materialism of the usual crime-puzzle of fiction those psychological values which are . . . the basis of the universal interest in the far more absorbing criminological dramas of real life. In other words, I have tried to write what might be described as a psychological detective story.'

The psychological puzzle of the relationship between Berkeley and E. M. Delafield is the great untold story of the Golden Age. Born Edmée Elizabeth Monica de la Pasture (her pen name was a jokey version of de la Pasture), Delafield was the daughter of a count whose family fled to England to escape the French revolution and of a novelist. At nineteen, she made a beautiful debutante, but was too tall for most of her dancing partners. She joined a French religious order based in Belgium, but a life of chastity as a Bride of Heaven was not for her. After leaving the convent, she worked in the Voluntary Aid Detachment during the war, published her first novel, and married Major Paul Dashwood, an engineer and third son of a baronet.

The couple had two children, and after three years in Malaya, they moved to Kentisbeare in Devon, where Dashwood acted as land agent for a large estate. Delafield became a pillar of the community, and a doyenne of the Women's Institute. She was appointed as Cullompton's first female Justice of the Peace, causing one elderly magistrate to resign from the bench in protest at this invasion of male territory. Like Berkeley, she wrote under a pseudonym, but they had much more in common than that. Each hid deep-rooted feelings of inferiority beneath a veneer of sophistication. They shared a taste for irony, an acute sense of humour, and a risky delight in turning their private lives into fiction.

Delafield and Berkeley talked long into the night about the hanging of Edith Thompson, and Florence Maybrick's narrow escape from the rope. They regarded both women as victims of a hypocritical morality that punished them for having sex outside marriage. Delafield empathized with their craving for excitement, although unlike Edith and Florence she did not make the mistake of writing letters revealing her intimate secrets. Today, she is never considered as a crime writer, but she was the first author to base a novel on the Thompson–Bywaters case, years before Sayers, Berkeley and the rest. *Messalina of the Suburbs* appeared just a year after the double execution.

Berkeley's interest in married women was not confined to Delafield. He nursed a hopeless passion for a budding actress called Hilary Reynolds, but unfortunately she was the wife of his brother, Stephen Cox. She had starred in the West End under the name Hilary Brough, but she and Stephen emigrated briefly to Canada, returning when she became pregnant. By the time their daughter was born, the marriage was on the rocks, and Hilary decided to return to the stage. A brief reunion with Stephen resulted in another pregnancy, and Hilary abandoned her career in the theatre. She and Stephen stayed together until the end of the Thirties for the sake of their son and daughter.

Brenda's elder sister in *Brenda Entertains* is a fictional counterpart of Hilary, an early example of Berkeley's penchant for populating his books with women who appealed to him. Stephen discovered Berkeley's interest in his wife, and for years he and Hilary broke off contact with Berkeley. Berkeley's interest in Hilary did not go unnoticed by Delafield, whose *No One Now Will Know* features the seduction of a sister-in-law.

Berkeley was undaunted. He began to dream of another dangerous liaison, this time with Helen Peters, a gentle and attractive woman. Once again, there was a stumbling block which would have deterred any other writer, no matter how lustful. Not only was Helen married, her husband was Berkeley's literary agent.

The storyline of *The Wintringham Mystery* resurfaced in revised form as a novel entitled *Cicely Disappears*. Berkeley borrowed the names of his Watford properties for a new pseudonym, A. Monmouth Platts, and gave repeated nods and winks to Delafield. One character is named Cúllompton, another Kentisbeare, while the heroine marries someone who takes a job as a land agent, like Paul Dashwood. The changes to the story and author's name may have been designed to evade an agreement that he should not publish the original without the newspaper's consent. The novel is flimsy, but for Berkeley, its publication represented a shrewd bit of business.

A scene in *Mr Priestley's Problem* takes place at a cocktail party where two people discover a shared fascination in criminology, as Berkeley and Delafield had done. The story is a Wodehousian romp in which a group of pranksters trick a naïve man into thinking that he has shot and killed a supposed blackmailer. Berkeley was a member of the Gnats, an amateur dramatic group based in Watford, and wrote the libretto and music for several musicals, including two which reached the London stage – a comic opera, and a stage version of *Mr Priestley's Problem*.

Priestley is handcuffed to an attractive woman during the story. Did Alfred Hitchcock read the book or see the play? The situation bears an uncanny resemblance to the scene in Hitchcock's version of *The 39 Steps* in which Robert Donat is handcuffed to Madeleine Carroll. There was a touch of sado-masochism in Hitchcock, as there was in Berkeley. For both men, the scenario was a sexual turn-on.

The Vane Mystery saw Berkeley playing with the conventions of the genre. Sherlock Holmes' superiority over Inspector Lestrade led to innumerable stories contrasting incompetent professional policemen with gifted amateurs, but in this book, Sheringham is humiliated by Inspector Moresby of Scotland Yard, who prefers evidence to psychology, believing that 'No good detective ought to have too much imagination.' As if unable to help himself, Berkeley not only gave his own name to Sheringham's amiable cousin, but audaciously named two key characters with guilty secrets after the two people who stood in the way of a relationship with Helen Peters. They were his wife Margaret, and Helen's husband. Given such effrontery, to dedicate the book to his parents-in-law was hardly an olive branch.

Unabashed by his humiliation, Sheringham triumphs over Moresby, now promoted to Chief Inspector, in *The Silk Stocking Murders*. The title illustrates Berkeley's knack of gaining attention for his detective novels. The first two had been published anonymously, to create a *frisson* of mystery, and now he calculated that silk stockings, suggestive of sex and suspense, would capture people's attention. As so often in his literary career, he was ahead of his time, creating a serial killer before the term 'serial killer' was invented. Again, he borrowed from a real life crime – the strangling six years earlier of Lilian Othen, a prostitute who worked in the West End under the name Lily Ray. One evening, she picked up a young petty crook called Anthony Castor in Regent Street. He had been drinking heavily, and after going for a late-night walk on the Embankment, they took a tram ride back to her flat in Brixton. During a quarrel, he seized her by the throat, and squeezed until she was dead. He then took off one of her silk stockings and tied it around her neck to make it seem that she had killed herself. But in the early hours of the morning, a policeman saw him trying to break into a shop, and he admitted at once that he had killed a girl. 'I didn't think it was so easy to kill anyone,' he said. He was found guilty of manslaughter and sentenced to eight years' penal servitude.

Berkeley's killer adopts Castor's *modus operandi.* An aspiring actress, a chorus girl, and a diplomat's daughter are found dead in quick succession, hanged with silk stockings. Roger deduces that they have been murdered by a sex maniac who seeks out victims whose deaths he can twist into apparent suicides. Berkeley dedicated the book to 'A. B. Cox, who kindly wrote it for me in his spare time.' He even inscribed a copy 'To A. B. Cox from the Author' and kept it himself. A sign of a split personality, perhaps, or one more example of his weird sense of humour.

In July 1928, he wrote a letter – in French, for some reason – to his agent, A. D. Peters about a play he was writing, and sent 'Mes salutations à la belle Hélène.' This is the first known record of his interest in Helen Peters (who was not French but Scottish, the daughter of MacGregor of Glengyle, a distant descendant of Rob Roy). Perhaps Helen was flattered. For all his faults, women found Berkeley attractive. He was rather like those handsome cads who so often crop up in Golden Age novels, and cannot be trusted with other men's wives. Years later, Clarice Dickson Carr, wife of American detective author John, recalled that Berkeley was 'very good looking in an English film star way'. And he did not lack stamina. As the Twenties drew to a close, in addition to writing prolifically and pursuing his amorous adventures, he was busily laying the foundations of the Detection Club.

Notes to Chapter 3

Edith Thompson never believed she would really hang
Among the many accounts of the Thompson–Bywaters case (which, as is invariably the way with discussion of past cases, contain much conflicting information) I have found René Weis's *Criminal Justice* especially useful.

in George Orwell's phrase, the end of an 'Elizabethan Age' of English murder
See Orwell, 'Decline of the English Murder', *Tribune*, 15 February 1946.

Anthony Berkeley was appalled by Edith Thompson's fate.
For convenience, I refer to authors such as Berkeley, Henry Wade, John Rhode, Milward Kennedy, J. J. Connington, and Anthony Gillbert by their principal pseudonyms; they were for the most part known to their fellow Detection Club members by their pen names rather than by their real names. Sometimes their novels appeared under alternative titles, typically when an American publisher made a change. Titles mentioned in this book are generally those first used in the UK, although there are exceptions, notably Christie's *And Then There Were None*.

In Berkeley, wit, charm and flair warred with demons.
Information about Berkeley's life is notoriously hard to come by, and I am indebted to Malcolm J. Turnbull (author of *Elusion Aforethought*), George Locke (author, under the name Ayresome Johns, of a slim but informative volume about Berkeley's writings), Arthur Robinson, Tony Medawar, and members of Berkeley's family for supplying material that has proved invaluable in writing this book. Medawar and Robinson (jointly) and Locke have written informative introductions to two collections of Berkeley's shorter work, *The Avenging Chance and other Mysteries from Roger Sheringham's Casebook*, and the privately published *The Roger Sheringham Stories* respectively. William F. Stickland's chapter 'Anthony Berkeley Cox' in Earl F. Bargainnier's *Twelve Englishmen of Mystery*, and the sources he quotes, also offer useful insight.

Julian Symons . . . believing that Berkeley's 'ruddy-faced geniality'
concealed a disturbingly shy and secretive character.
Symons' posthumous memories of Berkeley, quoted in *Elusion*
Aforethought, appeared in an obituary for *The Sunday Times* on 14
March 1971, and in the *Times Literary Supplement* of 10 March 1978.

'Detection and crime at its wittiest', Agatha Christie said.
In 'Detective Writers in England'; see *CADS* 58, December 2008,
and below.

The glamorous Christianna Brand . . . said he once confided that
there was 'not one soul in the world he did not cordially dislike'.
Christianna Brand (1907–1988), a distinguished post-war practi-
tioner of books in the Golden Age tradition, had mixed feelings about
Berkeley, which she expressed in private correspondence with a
younger Detection Club colleague, Robert Barnard (1936–2013), and
in several versions of an essay which appeared as the Introduction
to *The Floating Admiral*, on the book's republication in the US in
1979; see also Tony Medawar, ed., 'Detection Club Memories:
Christianna Brand', *CADS* 52, August 2007.

as M. R. James said . . .'The detective story cannot be too much
up-to-date . . .'
In an Introduction he wrote in 1924 to *Ghosts and Marvels*, edited
by V. H. Collins.

An odd connection arose between Berkeley and Christie
See Tony Medawar, 'On This Day: 9 April 1926', *CADS* 64, November
2012.

The newspaper offered a total of £500 in prizes to readers who
provided the best answers to questions about the story
During the Golden Age, prize competitions linked to detective stories
were highly popular. They can be cost-effective marketing devices – if
carefully handled. In 1905, Edgar Wallace offered £1,000 in prize
money for readers who solved the puzzle in his debut thriller, *The*
Four Just Men, and found himself courting bankruptcy as a result.
Almost sixty years later, Len Deighton's second spy novel, *Horse Under*
Water, included a crossword with clues which could be solved through
reading the novel. The clues were printed on the endpapers of first
editions, and readers were given ten days to complete the puzzle;
the first ten to send in correct solutions were awarded book tokens.

4

The Mystery of the Silent Pool

On the morning of Saturday 4 December 1926, a gypsy boy called George Best came across a Morris Cowley motor car at Newlands Corner, near Guildford in Surrey. The lights were on, but nobody was inside, although a fur coat and small suitcase had been left. The police soon traced the car to Agatha Christie, who lived with her husband in the stockbroker belt at Sunningdale in Berkshire. At the age of thirty-six, Christie had already established a reputation as a detective novelist, and the couple had named their house Styles, after the scene of the crime in her debut novel, *The Mysterious Affair at Styles*.

When the police called at Styles, they spoke to Charlotte ('Carlo') Fisher, who acted as Christie's secretary and helped to look after her daughter Rosalind. Carlo said the author had left home, driving off without telling anyone where she was going. According to Carlo, Christie had been unwell recently, and her family were worried about her. Christie's husband Archie was staying with friends, along with his secretary Nancy Neele. He'd recently confessed to Agatha that he'd fallen in love with Nancy.

The police took Archie and Carlo to the spot where the car had been found. The news had already leaked out, and the car was surrounded by a crowd. The area rapidly became a magnet for sensation-seekers, and the Press salivated over the puzzle, indulging in feverish guesswork about the mysterious affair of the beautiful young writer, and her dashing war hero husband.

Words of wisdom from Superintendent Kenward, the Deputy Chief Constable of Surrey Police, featured prominently in their reports.

'The most baffling mystery ever set me for solution' was Kenward's quotable description of the case. An early theory was that Agatha had crashed her car and wandered into nearby woodland in a disorientated state and become lost. The area was searched, with help from members of the public, but there was no sign of Agatha. When questioned by the police and newspapers, Archie was defensive. He dreaded the truth about his relationship with Nancy coming to light. The police guarded his house, and monitored his phone calls.

'They suspect me of doing away with Agatha,' he told a business colleague. To deflect suspicion, he revealed to the *Daily News* that his wife had been thinking of 'engineering her disappearance'. The newspaper offered a £100 reward for information leading to her discovery, helpfully printing a set of photographs showing how she might have altered her appearance with a disguise.

Close to Newlands Corner, in a hollow shaded by box trees, lay the Silent Pool. Fed by underground springs, the water was clear and still. A woodcutter's daughter had been surprised there by wicked King John, so legend said, while she was bathing naked. She drowned while trying to flee from him. Her ghost was seen by local people from time to time, floating on the surface of the pool.

Had Christie chosen this serene yet spooky place to end her life? There was only one way to find out. The Silent Pool was dredged with the aid of a pump and large grappling irons to slash the weeds. Tractors and a light aircraft scoured the countryside, and dogs searched the land. They found no sign of a corpse.

With each passing day, the theories became wilder. A clairvoyant called in by the *Daily Sketch* suggested that Agatha's body might be found in a log-house. Cynics suggested that the 'disappearance' was a stunt to publicize her latest novel, *The Murder of Roger Ackroyd*. Or had she disguised herself in male clothing and gone into hiding, like Dr Crippen's mistress Ethel Le Neve sixteen years earlier? The *Daily Express* consulted a former Chief Inspector of the CID, Walter Dew, renowned as 'the man who caught Crippen', who reinvented himself as an occasional media pundit on matters criminal and mysterious after retiring from Scotland Yard. Dew doubted whether Christie was the victim of foul play, or had vanished for publicity or financial reasons. 'All women are subject to hysteria at times,' he pronounced, opining that perhaps the fact that she 'thought about crooks and murder all day' had affected her. Reporters thirsting for sensation found leading crime writers equally keen to share their wisdom.

On Friday 10 December, Dorothy L. Sayers (whose father had jumped to 'a scandalous explanation' of the puzzle) wrote about the case for the *Daily News*. She assessed the possible scenarios: loss of memory, foul play, suicide, and voluntary disappearance, but her article was apparently written without personal knowledge of Christie's character. Her speculations highlighted the questions about the case, but yielded no answers.

Was Agatha conducting a form of 'mental reprisal' against someone who had hurt her? Edgar Wallace advanced this theory in the *Daily Mail*, guessing that she was taking revenge on Archie for his adultery. A year or so later, Wallace wrote a story inspired by the case, 'The Sunningdale Murder'. The *Daily Mail* also featured Max Pemberton, author of several bestselling Victorian thrillers, fearing the worst. He thought Agatha was dead.

Sherlock Holmes' creator, Sir Arthur Conan Doyle, was a former Deputy Lieutenant of Surrey, although he had resigned after developing a passionate belief in spiritualism. He had investigated real-life crimes, such as the Edalji and Oscar Slater cases, with much success. The Surrey police supplied him with one of Agatha's gloves, which he took to a medium and psychometrist named Horace Leaf. Leaf's considered opinion was that 'trouble' was connected to the glove. If this insight was of limited value, Leaf did say that Agatha was still alive. Conan Doyle informed Archie of this breakthrough, and announced that the case was 'an excellent example of the uses of psycho-metry as an aid to the detective'.

The police appealed for public help in searching the Surrey Downs, and 'the Great Sunday Hunt' took place on 12 December. About two thousand civilians took part, wrapped up warm against the cold. It was like a massive outdoor pre-Christmas party. Ice creams and hot drinks were sold from vans to refresh the spectators. Sayers could not resist joining in the excitement, and persuaded John Gilroy, her artist friend from Benson's, to drive her to the Silent Pool. The outcome for her was even more of an anticlimax than her foray to France to investigate the Nurse Daniels mystery. During a brief look around, Sayers failed to spot any tell-tale clues that the police had missed, and was left to pronounce, with all the authority she could muster, 'No, she isn't here.' Yet if she failed to contribute to the detective effort, at least her day out amounted to useful research. Aspects of her visit featured in *Unnatural Death*, in which two women go missing from a car left abandoned on the south coast.

As darkness fell, the hunt was called off. A flare was lit to help searchers who had lost their bearings find their way home. Weary and deflated, Kenward told journalists that he did not believe Agatha Christie's disappearance was a gimmick designed to sell her books.

What he did not know was that the answer lay more than two hundred miles north. A banjo player and a fellow bandsman performing at the Hydropathic Hotel in Harrogate, the North Yorkshire spa town, were keeping a close eye on a woman guest. They concluded she was the missing novelist, and their detective work proved superior to anyone else's. Within forty-eight hours, the whole world learned that Agatha Christie had been discovered, safe and well.

After travelling by train to Harrogate, Christie had taken a first-floor room at five guineas a week and bought herself some new clothes, including a glamorous pink georgette evening dress. She followed the reports about her disappearance in the Press, and played bridge – and billiards – in the public rooms. At night she danced in the Winter Garden Ballroom to the music of the Happy Hydro Boys. Otherwise she relaxed by having massages, solving crossword puzzles and borrowing books from the W.H. Smith's lending library. Her favourite reading comprised thrillers rejoicing in titles such as *The Double Thumb* and *The Phantom Train*. She had assumed the identity of a Mrs Teresa Neele, recently returned to Britain from Cape Town. Her chosen surname was that of her husband's mistress.

Today Agatha Christie remains, almost half a century after her death, a household name. More than that, she has become a global brand. Big business. Two billion (or is it four billion? – estimates vary, and at such a stratospheric level, it scarcely seems to matter) copies of her books have been sold, and she has been translated more often than any other author. About two hundred film and television versions of her work have been screened, and the stories have been adapted into video games, graphic novels and Japanese *anime*. She was the most performed female British playwright of the twentieth century, and *The Mousetrap* is the longest-running stage play of all time, with more than 25,000 performances in London alone. The sixtieth anniversary of its first performance was celebrated by sixty specially licensed performances worldwide. Her home overlooking the River Dart is in the care of the National Trust and a popular tourist destination, while her native Torquay boasts an Agatha Christie Mile, along which visitors can retrace her steps.

A statue featuring a bust of Christie stands in Covent Garden, the Pera Palace Hotel in Istanbul has an Agatha Christie room, and her face smiles from a billboard welcoming tourists to Gran Canaria. On the 120th anniversary of her birth, cooks around the world baked a Delicious Death cake from a recipe by Jane Asher. The book with the thickest spine in the world has been created from the complete Miss Marple stories. In Harrogate, a plaque in the Old Swan Hotel (formerly the Hydropathic Hydro) commemorates her disappearance, the reason for which continues to provoke debate. Agatha Christie is, in short, an icon whose name is synonymous with detective fiction and mystery.

The enduring nature and astonishing scale of her fame would

have amazed, and possibly appalled her. Not only was she genuinely modest, she was fanatical about preserving her privacy.
She had always been shy, but the media frenzy that surrounded
her disappearance left her with a lifelong detestation of the
Press.

At first sight, Christie seems as genteel as her books are
supposed to be. With Christie, however, nothing was quite as
it seemed. In person, she combined a straightforward outlook
on life with hidden depths, just as her simple and accessible
writing style contrasted with her devious plots. Her father was
American, and from childhood she spent long periods abroad,
gaining a breadth of understanding and experience of the world
that helps to explain why her work has enjoyed unceasing popularity when so much more sophisticated fiction has vanished
from sight.

Agatha Mary Clarissa Miller was born on 15 September 1890,
the third child of Frederick and Clara Miller. Frederick had
inherited enough money from the family business not to need to
work, and not long after Agatha's elder sister Margaret (known
as Madge) was born, the family settled in Torquay. Frederick
was good-natured but lazy, and his failure to keep a close eye
on the family fortune proved financially calamitous. To econo-
mize, he let the Torquay house, and took his family to France
for over six months. Agatha enjoyed such an idyllic summer in
Pau that she never went back there, unwilling to diminish the
magical memories of that first foreign adventure. Her novels are
stereotypically associated with settings in country houses and
seemingly Home Counties villages for which detective novelist
Colin Watson coined the generic term 'Mayhem Parva'. In fact, a
high proportion of her stories are set overseas. This reflects her
love of travel, but above all her core belief that, in its fundamentals, human nature is much the same everywhere.

Madge was regarded as 'the clever one' in the family, and
attended boarding school, but one of Clara's unorthodox ideas
was to school Agatha at home. Frederick Miller's health deterio-
rated along with the family finances, and he died in 1901. Money
was short, but Madge had married James Watt, who came from

a wealthy Mancunian family, and Agatha often stayed with them at Abney Hall in Cheshire. She loved Abney, and fictitious versions of it appeared in *After the Funeral* and 'The Adventure of the Christmas Pudding'. After a brief and unsatisfactory spell at a Torquay school, attending two days a week, she completed her education at three *pensions* in France.

She lived in her imagination, and loved writing stories and poems. Her instinct was to watch and listen to others rather than take centre stage herself. A keen eavesdropper, she gathered plot ideas from stray phrases in overheard conversations between strangers. She was as curious about other people as she was reluctant to reveal her own thoughts. Her innate modesty meant she felt under no compulsion to talk too much, and so she never gave herself away.

She wrote a novel set in Cairo, where she and her mother had taken a three-month holiday, but a literary agent, Hughes Massie, turned *Snow upon the Desert* down. Undaunted, she continued to write, as well as taking singing lessons, while receiving plenty of overtures from young men attracted by her serene manner and quiet good looks. Tall, slim and pale-haired, she rejected several marriage proposals before becoming engaged to Reggie Lucy, a major in the Gunners. Yet she broke with Reggie after meeting a dashing young airman.

Lieutenant Archie Christie was the son of a judge in the Indian Civil Service, and Christie later said she fell for him because she found him unpredictable and fascinating. When war broke out, she realized he was likely to be killed. Three days before Christmas, he suddenly obtained leave from duty and they decided to marry. The wedding took place on Christmas Eve 1914, and Archie returned to France on Boxing Day. Life at this time was heady, exhilarating, and impulsive. It was also frighteningly insecure. Agatha's brother Monty, a feckless charmer, was badly wounded while serving with the King's African Rifles, and although he survived, he suffered psychological damage. To Clara's distress, he liked to take up his revolver and shoot at people passing the family home in Torquay – a hobby Christie gave to a character, decades later, in her play *The Unexpected Guest*.

Archie was decorated for bravery and promoted to the rank of colonel before being invalided out of the Royal Flying Corps. At one point the couple did not see each other for almost two years. Agatha became a V.A.D. (Volunteer Aid Detachment) nurse, later transferring to the dispensary. A rather sinister pharmacist who told her he enjoyed the power afforded by dealing with poisons stuck in her mind, and nearly fifty years later, provided her with a key character in *The Pale Horse*. She blew up a Cona coffee maker whilst attempting the Marsh test to detect the presence of arsenic, but acquired an extensive knowledge of poisons, which she soon put to use – in fiction.

Madge shared Agatha's enthusiasm for detectives such as Sherlock Holmes and his French rivals Arsène Lupin and Joseph Rouletabille, and challenged her to write a whodunit. Having encountered a few Belgian war refugees, Christie decided that her detective would be Belgian too. She created someone who was vain but brilliant: Hercule Poirot. His foreign nationality was a clever stroke, and so was his conceit: British people were often suspicious of foreigners, and distrustful of cleverness. Christie poked fun at her fellow countrymen's insularity, while making it plausible that suspects who concocted ingenious murder schemes made the catastrophic mistake of underestimating this seemingly ridiculous figure, with his broken English, extravagant moustache and insistence on using 'the little grey cells' of the brain. Christie's prime literary influence was Conan Doyle, and she equipped Poirot with an amiable if rather obtuse Watson in Captain Arthur Hastings.

Christie finished *The Mysterious Affair at Styles* in 1918, and the following year she gave birth to Rosalind. After a series of rejections from publishers, John Lane offered a less-than-generous contract which gave him an option over her next five books. She made the revisions he asked for, and her ingenious country house mystery finally appeared in the US in 1920 and in Britain the following year. Next came *The Secret Adversary*, a light and breezy thriller which introduced a young couple who went on to marry and to feature in four subsequent books, the last published more than half a century after the first. Tommy and Tuppence Beresford represent wish fulfilment on Christie's part. She imagined herself as the lovely, sharp-witted Tuppence, while the courageous and eternally reliable Tommy was an idealized portrait of the man she thought she had married.

In January 1922, Christie and Archie took the extraordinary step of leaving their young daughter for almost a year so that they could take part in a 'Mission to the Dominions'. This was an international publicity exercise meant to pave the way for the forthcoming British Empire Exhibition. The grand tour was the brainchild of Major Belcher, a friend of Archie's with a genius for self-promotion, the highlight of whose war service was a spell as Controller of the Supplies of Potatoes. Belcher offered Archie, who had worked in the City since the war, the job of financial adviser to the mission, and Agatha's travel expenses were covered, with a month's holiday in Honolulu thrown in. Archie's employers were unwilling to keep his job open for him, but he was bored with civilian life, and Agatha loved to travel. She said in her autobiography: 'We had never been people who played safe.'

Although Madge and her mother agreed to look after Rosalind, Madge felt Agatha should have stayed in England, but Clara Miller was supportive, arguing that a wife's priority was to be with her husband. Agatha fell in love with South Africa, and the experience provided material not only for her next book, but also for creating the make-believe life of Mrs Teresa Neele. On board ship, she often played bridge, and sometimes quoits, once defeating the captain. In Waikiki, the couple were among the first British people to master the art of stand-up surfing. An added pleasure for Agatha was the chance to show off her figure in an emerald green wool bathing dress.

The tour was long and often gruelling, but although Belcher proved a cantankerous and selfish companion, who sent Agatha out to buy socks or on other errands, and then forget to reimburse her, she had no regrets. On their return, however, Rosalind treated them as strangers. Perhaps her mother's long absence during her childhood accounted for some of the complexities in the relationship between mother and daughter that persisted for the rest of Christie's life.

Christie's naïveté is illustrated by the fact that she did not realize that the money she earned from writing was subject to income tax, and this was the start of a long and unhappy relationship with the Revenue. She needed a literary agent, and although Hughes Massie had died, she was taken on by his youthful successor whose trustworthiness made him someone she relied on for the rest of her life. This was Edmund Cork, who later escorted Ngaio Marsh to Bentley's installation as President of the Detection Club.

Poirot had returned in *The Murder on the Links*, whose plot was influenced by a recent murder in France, and she tried to supplement her finances by entering newspaper competitions. The *Daily Sketch* serialized *The Mystery of Norman's Court*, by John Chancellor, a crime writer who enjoyed a brief vogue but is now forgotten. The first prize for the solution to Chancellor's puzzle was an eye-watering £1,300, illustrating the lengths newspapers were willing to go to in order to attract readers. Christie did not win, but was one of twelve people who shared in the runners-up prize of £800.

At this time, she did not have the loathing of publicity stunts that developed later. She even took part in a mock trial to promote a mystery play, *In the Next Room*, a dramatization of a locked room mystery by Burton E. Stevenson. Christie was one of four writers on a jury presided over by G. K. Chesterton. The accused was found not guilty, and Chesterton announced that in any case he would have 'refused to convict a Frenchman for the humane and understandable act of murdering an American millionaire'.

Poirot's popularity prompted her to feature him in a string of sub-Sherlockian short stories, but *The Man in the Brown Suit* broke fresh ground. It is almost unique among early Golden Age novels in being narrated (mostly) by a woman. Anne Bedingfeld, the heroine, was an idealized self-portrait of an independently minded young woman with a taste for adventure. After arriving in South Africa, Anne goes surfing at Muizenberg, as Christie had done, and finds the sport equally exhilarating. By the end of the book, she has also found love, and is happily married, with a child.

At Belcher's request, a character based upon him played a prominent part. Much of the story is presented through extracts from two diaries, and the surprise solution paved the way for an even more daring and skilful means of confounding the reader's expectations in *The Murder of Roger Ackroyd*. Christie took care to ensure that this breakthrough novel did not appear until after she had completed her contractual obligation to John Lane with a collection of the Poirot tales and a third light-hearted thriller, *The Secret of Chimneys*.

The events of 1926 changed everything. The year began pleasantly, with a holiday in Corsica, and winning the prize (under husband Archie's name) for solving Berkeley's serial, *The Wintringham Mystery*. In June, the publication of *The Murder of Roger Ackroyd* catapulted her into the front rank of crime novelists. The book remains a landmark title of classic detective fiction. The story is told not by Captain Hastings but by Dr Sheppard, who lives with his busybody sister Caroline in the sleepy village of King's Abbot, and their new neighbour is Poirot, who has retired to grow vegetable marrows.

The arrival of a fictional detective in a tranquil location invariably presages an outbreak of homicide, and when the little Belgian starts to investigate, Dr Sheppard acts as a surrogate Hastings. Christie enjoyed writing about the doctor's sister, Caroline Sheppard, someone who is intensely inquisitive, 'knowing everything, hearing everything: the complete detective service in the home'. More fully developed than most of Christie's puppets, Caroline was the prototype for Jane Marple. The village setting and dazzling plot combine to make this the definitive Christie novel.

Christie's masterstroke was to give an ingenious extra twist to Berkeley's central idea in *The Layton Court Mystery*. Her spin on the 'least likely person' theme resembled the trick in a book written more than forty years earlier. *The Shooting Party* was a remarkable early novel by that least likely of crime writers, Anton Chekhov. The Swedish writer Major Samuel August Duse (it is not true that Swedish crime fiction began with Henning Mankell and Stieg Larsson) had previously used a comparable device in *Dr*

Smirno's Diary and *The Dagmar Case*. However, since Chekhov's book was not translated into English until 1926, and Duse's books not at all, it is unlikely that Christie was aware of them.

A minority moaned that Christie had failed to 'play fair'. One reader wrote a letter of complaint to *The Times*, and the *News Chronicle* harrumphed that the book was a 'tasteless and unfortunate letdown by a writer we had grown to admire.' This was an absurdly harsh judgment, even though Christie's telling of the story was economical with the truth. T. S. Eliot reckoned it was a 'brilliant Maskelyne trick', while Sayers insisted, 'It's the reader's business to suspect everybody.'

Before the year was out, Christie's comfortable existence was ripped apart. Clara died, and as Christie struggled to cope with grief and the task of sorting out her mother's affairs in Torquay, she felt increasingly run down and lonely. She was acutely conscious that she was no longer the svelte young woman who made admirers swoon. Her delicate beauty was fading, and since Rosalind's birth, she had put on weight. Archie stayed in London, and when he rejoined her, he broke the news that he had fallen in love with Belcher's former secretary, Nancy Neele. At that moment, Agatha's 'happy, successful, confident life' ended.

She tried to persuade Archie to stay, but he became increasingly unkind, perhaps a sign of a guilty conscience. He walked out on his family on the morning of 3 December to be with Nancy. That same evening, Agatha drove away from home, leaving Rosalind asleep in the house.

After Agatha was tracked down to Harrogate, Archie maintained in public that she had been suffering from amnesia, a claim supported by two doctors. In a forerunner of a tabloid witch-hunt, hostile journalists accused her of simply seeking publicity. She also found herself caught up in a row between two formidable bruisers from opposite ends of the political spectrum.

When the Home Office announced that the cost to Scotland Yard of the search for Christie was twelve pounds, 10 shillings, the MP and former miner William Lunn ranted about the expense of a 'cruel hoax'. The Home Secretary, William

Joynson-Hicks, promptly revised the cost to nil, on the basis that it was absorbed by the general police budget. The real argument was not about Christie, but the bitter aftermath of the failed General Strike. Lunn was angry about expenditure on the moneyed classes when the poor were suffering. Joynson-Hicks was a right-wing hawk, unwilling to give his opponents an inch, and quite prepared to juggle the figures to suit his purpose.

Lunn's condemnation was as brutal as the Press coverage. Christie was a victim, though she was too strong to wallow in victimhood, and too proud to seek help before she cracked. Her experiences left a mark on her future writing, in which the idea of the 'ordeal by innocence' undergone by ordinary people whose lives are disrupted by murder crops up as often as the 'wronged man' in the films of Alfred Hitchcock.

The trauma left her barely able to work. Drained of energy and enthusiasm for writing, she recuperated at Abney Hall and then took a holiday in the Canary Islands; her visit features in their tourist literature to this day. But the process of recovery was slow and tortuous. She had lost her trust in people, and had developed a loathing for crowds and for the Press. She admitted in her autobiography that she could hardly bear to go on living. Yet she, like Sayers, had a young child to whom she felt not only devotion but a sense of duty. Suicide was not an option.

With her marriage in ruins, and her confidence shattered, she struggled to earn money to look after herself and Rosalind. Inspiration had deserted her. As a stop-gap measure, she was helped by Archie's brother, Campbell Christie, to cobble some previously published short stories together to form *The Big Four*. The resulting thriller was lively but ludicrous, featuring not only an evil Chinese mastermind and an exotic *femme fatale*, but also, in a nod to Mycroft Holmes, Poirot's smarter brother, Achille.

When Christie did force herself to produce a fresh novel, it was simply an expanded version of an earlier short story. By her standards, it was dismally dull. Even Christie admitted she hated *The Mystery of the Blue Train*. The book is dedicated to Carlo Fisher, one of the few people whom Christie felt she could trust. In April 1928, she was granted a divorce, and Archie promptly married Nancy Neele. Hoping to rid herself of her former husband's name, she tried to persuade her publishers to allow her to adopt a male pseudonym, but they refused. The Agatha Christie brand was already too valuable to be sacrificed.

She tried her hand at various types of story in an attempt to recapture her joy in writing, but struggled to recapture her zest and originality. *The Seven Dials Mystery*, another thriller, resurrected characters from *The Secret of Chimneys*, while Tommy and Tuppence Beresford returned in *Partners in Crime*, a collection of short stories which had mostly appeared five years earlier.

The worst was not yet over, as Agatha's brother died. She and Madge had paid for Monty to live in a house on Dartmoor; his poor health was exacerbated by a drug habit, although his personal magnetism attracted women willing to look after him. He emigrated to the south of France, and his final companion was a nurse. A stroke killed him while he was having a drink in a seafront café in Marseilles. Christie had been fond of him, but acutely aware of his failings. Attractive but weak-willed men like Monty often figure in her novels.

As *Partners in Crime* was published, there was at last a hint of better times to come. Anthony Berkeley introduced Christie to a new social circle, which gave her the chance to meet people with whom she had a great deal in common. Crucially, they were people whom she could trust. Her determination to stay out of the public gaze was shared by many of her new friends. They believed their books should speak for themselves. The camaraderie of their dinners helped her to patch up her self-confidence as she embarked on the long journey towards a new life.

Notes to Chapter 4

Christie had already established a reputation as a detective novelist
The principal sources for my account of Christie's life and work,
including her disappearance, are listed in the Select Bibliography.
The tireless research work undertaken by both Tony Medawar and
John Curran has proved especially valuable.

his French rivals Arsene Lupin and Joseph Rouletabille
Created respectively by Maurice Leblanc (1864–1941) and Gaston
Leroux (1868–1927). Rouletabille first appeared in the classic 'locked
room' novel, *The Mystery of the Yellow Room*, but thanks to Andrew
Lloyd Webber's musical, Leroux is now better remembered as author
of *The Phantom of the Opera*.

*she tried to supplement her finances by entering newspaper
competitions*
See Tony Medawar, 'On this Day', *CADS* 64, November 2012, for
accounts of Christie's prize competition entry, and the mock trials
mentioned here and in chapter 6.

*The Swedish writer Major Samuel August Duse . . . had previously
used a comparable device*
Duse's work is discussed by Bo Lundin in *The Swedish Crime Story*
(1981).

T. S. Eliot reckoned it was a 'brilliant Maskelyne trick'
Jasper Maskelyne (1902–73) was a British stage magician, and a
member of a family of stage magicians, the son of Nevil Maskelyne
and a grandson of John Nevil Maskelyne. The Maskelynes' claims
to fame include not only the creation of countless tricks that fascinated Carr, but also the invention of the coin-in-the-slot toilet door,
which has yet to be deployed in a locked cubicle whodunit. John
Nevil invented a character dressed in a Chinese-style silk tunic,
capable of playing hands of the card games whist and nap, and
named Psycho. Psycho appeared to move of its own accord, but was
in fact operated by concealed bellows.

5

A Bolshevik Soul in a
Fabian Muzzle

A tediously repetitive complaint about Sayers and other Golden Age novelists is that their books were dominated by 'snobbery with violence'. This is a neat phrase, but a lazy criticism. In reality, Golden Age writers suffered under snobbish attitudes (and still do) at least as often as they were guilty of them. Douglas Cole, a leading socialist intellectual, liked to tell a story from his time as an Oxford don. He remarked to a reactionary acquaintance, Colonel Farquharson, that the BBC had broadcast one of his detective stories the previous week. The Colonel replied: 'What a pity. Had I known earlier, I could have asked the servants to listen to it.'

Christie, Sayers and Berkeley were conservative in outlook, and their success has caused a peculiar amnesia to afflict critical discussion of the Golden Age. Detective novelists with radical views have become the men – and women – who never were. Even the distinguished historian of the genre Julian Symons, who should have known better, thought it 'safe to say that almost all of the British writers of the Twenties and Thirties . . . were unquestionably right-wing.' In fact, the Liberal Party and centre-left were well represented among Golden Age authors, while others joined the Communist Party or flirted with it. One led the Jarrow Crusade, another married one of Stalin's senior lieutenants, yet another was killed fighting for the Republican cause in Spain. Some mocked Nazis and Fascists in their detective novels long before it was fashionable to do so. Others wrote mysteries which debated the merits of assassinating dictators.

Douglas and Margaret Cole were the leading lights of the Left among Golden Age detective novelists. Their personal lives seem, at first glance, more straightforward than the emotionally turbulent experiences of Sayers, Berkeley and Christie. Yet the Coles' apparently happy marriage was more complicated than it seemed.

Douglas Cole was already a pillar of the Labour Research Department, when Margaret Postgate joined after a spell teaching classics at Hammersmith's prestigious St Paul's Girls' School. Margaret was a dynamic young woman, with 'a mop of short thick black wavy hair in which is set swarthy complexion, sharp nose and chin and most brilliantly defiant eyes'. Instantly smitten by Douglas, she wrote the name 'Mrs G. D. H. Cole' on a piece of paper to see how it looked before hastily crumpling it up.

Her brother Raymond described Douglas as 'slender, fairly tall and quite handsome; his eyes were set in a curiously straight line and he could look at you in an oddly hypnotic manner.' This expression reminded Raymond of a snake, while Raymond's son Oliver gave Douglas a curious immortality by taking him as the model for the character of Professor Yaffle in the children's television series *Bagpuss*. Yaffle was a woodpecker carved from wood, a brilliant academic with a grumpy demeanour, who at times of inactivity served as a bookend.

Margaret debated political theory with Douglas, and secretly wrote 'a bad poem or two about him', but was dismayed to find the Department 'as nearly as possible sexless – it did not fornicate – hardly even"neck".' One wet winter night, she spent the evening in Douglas' flat in Battersea, discussing a propaganda pamphlet. When he offered her the loan of an umbrella for her walk back to Fulham, rather than a bed for the night, she felt aggrieved. Although he did not seem to reciprocate the physical desire she felt for him, she put this down to the all-consuming nature of his dedication to socialism.

After a year or so, it dawned on him that Margaret's interest in his company was not solely due to her love of politics, and he took her out to the theatre and a concert. When he invited her for a country walk, it turned into 'a pretty fast march' along the Thames towpath. He brought along dates and biscuits for them to eat, but forgot about anything to drink. The walk passed mostly in silence. Margaret's throat was dry with thirst, and she could not think of anything to say. Douglas did not help her out.

Undeterred, a couple of months later, she accepted another invitation for a walk. They went down to Hampden Woods on a fine day in May. 'Some kind of tension seemed to develop,' she recalled, and they sat down on a log in the midst of the young beech trees. No-one else was around, apart from an 'indignant pigeon' which flew out of the log. With something less than the panache of a born Casanova, Douglas stretched an arm around her and said, 'I suppose this has got to happen.'

On returning to the Labour Research Department, the couple announced their engagement. The wedding took place at a registry office adorned by a sign warning: '*No Confetti: Defence of the Realm Act.*' Margaret wrote a poem, 'Beechwood', about that close encounter on the log: the pigeon was mentioned, but not the fact that Douglas fell asleep on the train home. People were startled by their marriage, since Douglas was widely assumed to be more interested in men than women. His idea of a stab at humour was to claim he had been forced into matrimony, but Margaret did not care.

'Physically,' she said, 'he was always under-sexed – low-powered. If he had not married, I doubt very much whether he would have had any sex life at all in the ordinary sense. . . . Up to this time, his physical affections, his desire to caress, had been generally directed towards his own sex; he had fallen in love with various young men . . . and had written poems to them. But it was all very mild, and needed no sort of legal sanction . . . his sympathy with homosexuals was intellectual chiefly. For women generally, except his wife, he never seemed to have any sexual use at all . . . he thought that the mass of women were not good Socialist material.'

In 1926, Christie lost a husband, Sayers found one, and Berkeley was contemplating a change of wife. That year was equally momentous for Douglas and Margaret Cole, but for different reasons. Having abandoned the plans they had discussed with Sayers for forming a crime-writing syndicate, they were now writing detective stories together to supplement their academic income. Fiction, however, was put on hold as they rallied to the cause of the workers during the General Strike.

The Coles and their allies on the British Left were convinced that a determined and united industrial movement 'could make its will prevail'. That confidence was mirrored by the apprehension of people who supported the status quo, such as Christie. Her anxieties were reflected in *The Secret Adversary*. The spy-master Mr Carter warns Tommy and Tuppence Beresford about the threat to trade posed by a Labour government. 'Bolshevist gold' is pouring into the country, in an attempt to foment unrest among the workers. Thanks to the plucky Beresfords, the 'strike menace' and the 'inauguration of a reign of terror' feared by the newspapers are averted.

While Christie dreaded the prospect of seismic political change, the Coles devoted their lives to trying to achieve it. The General Strike offered the prospect of worker solidarity toppling the established order. After Ramsay MacDonald, the first Labour Prime Minister, lost office in 1924, Churchill's 'Silk Stocking Budget' reintroduced the Gold Standard, creating pressure to cut wages, and when the mine owners threatened to slash pay, the miners threatened to strike. The government bought off the employers with a temporary subsidy, unable to risk a confrontation because stocks of coal were low. Trade unionists rejoiced over their victory, but their celebrations proved premature.

Margaret concluded afterwards that the General Strike was provoked by the government, once it had bought time to prepare for a fight. Coal was stockpiled, and Churchill set up a strike-breaking force, the Organisation for the Maintenance of

Supplies. Once the subsidy ended, the mine owners again proposed lower pay and longer hours. 'Not a penny, not a minute' was the trade union side's response, but concessions were not forthcoming. Compositors at the *Daily Mail* refused to set a leader article attacking the miners, and Baldwin retaliated by calling off negotiations. The next day, the 'front-line troops' were called out on strike.

At a rowdy protest meeting, members of Oxford University's Labour Club argued about how to fight back if the Vice-Chancellor conscripted students into the O.M.S. to keep essential services moving. They were interrupted by the arrival of Douglas and Sandie Lindsay, the Master of Balliol, who came to announce a triumph. They had persuaded the authorities to reject compulsory conscription. Douglas, the ascetic intellectual, became an instant hero. A University Strike Committee was set up, based at the Coles' house in Holywell, to produce propaganda with an 'inky duplicator', and organise speakers to address meetings and rally public support.

It was an exciting time. The team of activists borrowed cars to run a courier service between Oxford and London. The plan was to collect messages and instructions from the Trades Union Congress, along with copies of the union newsletter, the *British Worker*. Margaret was appointed chief courier, and Hugh Gaitskell, one of Douglas's most gifted students, did most of the driving. Another undergraduate volunteer was Cecil Day-Lewis. He worked on a bulletin arguing that the Archbishop of Canterbury should mediate in the strike., and ruined his only good suit by spilling violet ink over it. Eleven years later, having assumed the identity of crime writer Nicholas Blake, he joined the Coles in the Detection Club.

Margaret was thrilled by the solidarity shown by long-serving employees of the Clarendon Press, who showed the courage of their convictions by walking out of work, even though it meant risking their pensions. For all their brilliance, however, the Coles failed to spot the obvious. The trade union leaders had blundered by calling the print workers out, as this made it harder to get their message across to a fearful public. The government, conversely, was able to influence debate on the radio. After eight days, the engineers and ship workers were called out, but although the miners opposed any compromise, the battle proved unwinnable, and the TUC told its members to go back to work.

Douglas struggled to come to terms with the scale of this defeat, but Margaret concluded that the government's victory marked the 'final throw' of mass industrial action. Yet the Coles' spirit was unquenchable. Before long they turned their minds back to detective fiction, as well as what to do next in the name of socialism. For all their deeply-felt dismay, they were lucky. The General Strike did not hurt their pockets, as it did those who lost pay they could ill afford. For Margaret, the strike was an enthralling experience, and she had enjoyed Hugh Gaitskell's company, although it was Douglas who fell in love with him.

Sayers and the Coles bonded on an intellectual level, even though their opinions about life and society were poles apart. Sayers' priority was to earn a living, and she threw herself into the advertising business with gusto. The Coles believed capitalism was in crisis, and opted for seclusion among the dreaming spires, although Douglas did become honorary research officer to the Amalgamated Society of Engineers.

He was always known as G. D. H. Cole; this was as much a brand name as Sayers' insistence on her middle initial, although he would have been horrified by anything as redolent of capitalism as the idea of a 'brand'. Although born in Cambridge, Margaret said later that he 'developed a violent dislike of Cambridge, partly because it was not Oxford'. At St Paul's School, he worked on a magazine which G. K. Chesterton praised, and became a devotee of William Morris. By the time he went to study Classics at Balliol, he had embraced socialism.

Douglas fantasized about Britain developing into a society based on 'Guild Socialism', with production run and organized by self-governing democratic organisations of workers. He became prominent in the Fabian Society. Chesterton's novel *The Napoleon of Notting Hill*, set in London in 1984 (perhaps a date that stuck in George Orwell's mind) struck a chord with the Guild Socialists, and Chesterton's often radical views had much more in common with Douglas's than those of Berkeley, Sayers or Christie. His friend and fellow Guild Socialist Maurice Reckitt found him kindly, but impatient and hot-tempered: 'He was always resigning . . . from bodies which failed to do what he required of them.' His 'haughty ruthlessness' prompted Reckitt to write a short poem:

> 'Mr G. D. H. Cole
> Is a bit of a puzzle.
> A curious role
> That of G. D. H. Cole,
> With a Bolshevik soul
> In a Fabian muzzle.'

Margaret's brother, Raymond Postgate, also admired Douglas's intellect, but thought him rude. Postgate later wrote *Verdict of Twelve*, a superb study of jurors in a murder case, biting enough to confound any lawyer with a sentimental attachment to the notion of trial by jury. The book's ironic and innovative style owed much more to Anthony Berkeley than to Douglas, but Raymond became better known for founding *The Good Food Guide*, and as the father of Oliver.

Margaret was born a few weeks before Sayers. Because the Postgates' father was a classical professor and grammarian who invented a 'new' pronunciation of Latin, at the age of six Margaret was required to ask for Sunday dinner in Latin. After leaving Roedean, she combined the study of Classics at Girton College, Cambridge, with helping to educate five younger brothers and sisters. Rebelling against her father's right-wing views, she embraced socialism, atheism, feminism and pipe-smoking. Like her future husband, she wrote poetry, and 'The Falling Leaves', a poignant perspective on the consequences of war, has featured on the GCSE syllabus for English Literature students. Her father was so outraged when she chose to share her life with a socialist that he disinherited her.

In the aftermath of the war, arguments about the Russian Revolution led to divisions on the left. Raymond Postgate joined the newly formed British Communist Party, but although Douglas Cole was sympathetic to the party's aims, he did not follow suit, and neither did Margaret. The dream of Guild Socialism turned to dust, and the Coles moved to Hampstead, where Douglas threw himself into writing and what Margaret described as 'the pleasures of bourgeois family life'. They socialized with the likes of Leonard and Virginia Woolf, and relaxed by watching Sussex play cricket. Margaret gave birth to two daughters in quick succession, and Douglas, while recovering from a bout of pneumonia, started work on a detective novel. Margaret bet he would not finish it, which provoked him to carry on to the end.

His approach was influenced by the success of Freeman Wills Crofts' novels about policemen who got results by sheer hard work. Douglas was in good company in admiring Crofts; T. S. Eliot rated him as the finest detective story writer to have emerged during the Twenties. Crofts was born in Dublin, but moved to Ulster in his youth, ultimately becoming Chief Assistant Engineer of the Belfast and Northern Counties Railway. During a long illness, he wrote *The Cask*, which became a bestseller. A cask unloaded at St Katharine's Dock breaks open and is found to contain sawdust, gold coins – and a dismembered female corpse; but the cask and its contents vanish before the police arrive at the scene. Inspector Burnley of Scotland Yard travels to Paris in order to crack an ingenious alibi, working with the unflagging attention to detail that became the hallmark of Crofts' detectives. The book sold so well that eventually Crofts moved to England to write full-time. In his fifth book he introduced the painstaking and utterly relentless Inspector Joseph French, whose arrival on the scene invariably spelled disaster for murderers whose chances of escaping the gallows depended on intricate alibis.

Crofts was published by Collins, and Douglas submitted his first novel to them, but at first they turned it down, saying it contained too many murders. He cut out one 'gory death', although what counted as 'gory' then seems cosy today. This was the only time, his wife said, that he agreed to make a significant change to any of his books. The touch of arrogance in Douglas's unwillingness to accept that his work could be improved, coupled with furious productivity, contributed to the sterility of much of his later writing.

The Brooklyn Murders introduced Superintendent Henry Wilson, sleuthing alongside a young couple in the same mould as Tommy and Tuppence Beresford. The Coles decided to play the detective game together, and co-write a follow-up. *Death of a Millionaire* appeared under the joint by-line of 'G. D. H. and M. Cole', the brand name for all the subsequent novels, whoever wrote most of the text. The book was unusual in its day for its sympathetic portrayal of trade union leaders and refusal to demonize Bolsheviks. Unfortunately, Superintendent Wilson's lack of charisma made Inspector French seem like a quirky maverick. Even when he resigned briefly from Scotland Yard to operate as a private eye, Wilson was no Sam Spade. The most exciting thing that happens to him during the series is that he grows six inches taller – a simple mistake, Margaret confessed. Even so, his career lasted for two decades. Having settled a plot in outline, one spouse wrote a first draft which the couple then discussed and worked on together.

The Murder at Crome House features a self-portrait of Douglas in the form of James Flint, a lecturer and tutor in history and economics. Flint turns amateur detective after discovering a bizarre photograph showing an apparent murder. It has been concealed inside a library book on the subject of psychoanalysis and autosuggestion. After the astonishingly careless owner of the photograph turns up on his doorstep, hoping to retrieve it, Flint tries to establish the truth about the crime. An elaborate alibi is unravelled with tedious persistence, and at the end of the book Flint contemplates marriage to the deceased's widow – but the Coles amuse themselves by describing his relief when he is talked out of it. The don is not the marrying kind. The same is true of Dr Preedy in the locked room mystery novella *Disgrace to the College* – he is 'fastidious to the point of confirmed celibacy in his relations with women' but enjoys the intimacy of private conversations with his male students. Unlike Berkeley, Douglas was reluctant to fictionalize his private sexual predilections, and this is as close as the Coles came to including a homoerotic subtext in their stories. Raymond Postgate featured a gay academic in *Verdict of Twelve*, differentiating the character from Douglas simply by making clear that he was neither handsome nor an economist.

In a fit of optimism during a short-lived economic recovery, Douglas wrote a massive tome, *The Next Ten Years in British Social and Economic Policy*, suggesting that a Labour government with a majority in Parliament might 'socialize' all the land in Britain within a decade. Margaret later described his proposals as a testament to the 'irresistible buoyancy' of his spirit. Soon he had plenty to be buoyant about. After five years of Conservative rule, the general election of 1929 returned a minority Labour government led by Ramsay MacDonald.

Douglas sent MacDonald a copy of his book, and the Coles were invited to spend a day at Chequers. The new Prime Minister held court over a meal of 'most superior' salmon fishcakes washed down with wine, and invited Douglas, along with John Maynard Keynes, to join a new Economic Council. Margaret admitted that this produced 'very little positive result'.

These were hectic years for radical activists, and on returning to live in London the Coles kept in touch with the working classes by engaging three servants. The children were looked after by a nurse, and an unemployed Yorkshire miner and his wife were hired to do the housework. Before long the family moved to a house in Hendon with grounds large enough for both badminton and tennis courts.

Hugh Gaitskell accompanied Douglas on a series of walking tours, and Douglas eventually declared his love for his former pupil. Gaitskell was flattered but embarrassed. Resolutely heterosexual, he was probably more attracted to Margaret, and his subsequent conquests included Ann Fleming, wife of the creator of James Bond. Douglas accepted defeat, as he had to do so often in his life, and climbed back into the closet. Gaitskell became leader of the Labour Party in the Fifties, and after his death he was succeeded by another of Cole's brilliant Oxford pupils, Harold Wilson, who made it all the way to 10 Downing Street.

Margaret's startlingly candid posthumous biography of Douglas included an appendix written by the family doctor. A classic example of 'too much information', this contained exhaustive detail about her husband's ailments, including a refractory bowel and a degenerative narrowing of the arteries. Margaret suggested that Douglas's lack of interest in sex may have been due to the lack of a robust constitution; 'bleeding piles . . . were a constant drain on his energy. . . . One feels that he would scarcely have had energy for vigorous love-making; and the idea of 'love-play' would have shocked him. . . . His sex-life diminished gradually to zero for the last twenty years of his life. . . . He came to feel that it was all revolting.'

Margaret's frankness did not extend to describing how she felt about all this, but she confided in her friend, the Scottish writer Naomi Mitchison, that she 'was made monogamous but not faithful'. She and Berkeley got on remarkably well, but even if he had designs on her, their political views were irreconcilable. Instead, she fell for Naomi's husband Dick, an affable lawyer and future Labour MP, whose oysters-and-champagne lifestyle and baronial Scottish castle appealed to her almost as much as his personality and socialism. She described him slyly in her autobiography as 'deceptive . . . because he looks so large and so respectable. He did, when I first knew him, all the things that a gentleman should, except play cricket.' Their relationship did not jeopardize either marriage, and Margaret remained steadfast in her commitment to Douglas and their shared political values. When she wanted a break from politics, she took refuge in the Detection Club.

Notes to Chapter 5

'snobbery with violence'
This phrase, often attributed to Alan Bennett, seems to have been coined as the title of a pamphlet published in 1932 by Count Geoffrey Potocki de Montalk (1903–1997). Colin Watson, himself a member of the Detection Club, borrowed it for his critique of pre-war thrillers and detective novels.

He remarked to a reactionary acquaintance, Colonel Farquharson
For this anecdote, I am indebted to crime novelist Keith Miles, also known as Edward Marston, who found it in L. G. Mitchell's article *'Murder, Univ and G. D. H. Cole'*, in the *University College Record*, vol. xiv, no. 1 (2005).

the Liberal Party and centre-left were well represented among Golden Age authors
To take a few examples, A. E. W. Mason served briefly as Liberal MP for Coventry, and Helen Simpson campaigned as a Liberal candidate prior to her early death. Lord Gorell served in David Lloyd George's government before defecting to the Labour Party.

One led the Jarrow Crusade, another married one of Stalin's senior lieutenants, yet another was killed fighting for the Republican cause in Spain.
The writers concerned were Ellen Wilkinson, Ivy Low (also known as Ivy Litvinov) and Christopher St John Sprigg.

Douglas and Margaret Cole were the leading lights of the Left among Golden Age detective novelists.
The Coles' lives have been extensively documented, with the predominant focus on their political activities. I have found Margaret's autobiography, her biography of Douglas, and Betty Vernon's biography of her especially valuable.

Margaret's brother, Raymond Postgate
Postgate (1896–1971) published three crime novels in all, but neither *Somebody at the Door* (1943) nor *The Ledger is Kept* (1953) matched the success of *Verdict of Twelve*. His father-in-law, George Lansbury, leader of the Labour Party from 1932–35, was grandfather to Angela

Lansbury, who played Jessica Fletcher in the television series *Murder, She Wrote* and Miss Marple in the film *The Mirror Crack'd*.

Freeman Wills Crofts' novels about policemen who got results by sheer hard work
Authors whose early work shows the influence of Crofts include not only Douglas Cole and Henry Wade but also John Bude, the name under which Ernest Carpenter Elmore (1901–57) wrote a long series of detective novels.

Crofts explained his painstaking method of story construction in 'The Writing of a Detective Novel', reprinted in *CADS* 54, July 2008 with an introduction by Tony Medawar. Extensive discussion of his life and work is to be found in Curtis Evans' Masters of the 'Humdrum' Mystery. 'Humdrum' is a term that Julian Symons applied in *Bloody Murder* to Crofts, Rhode and certain other novelists who 'had some skill in constructing puzzles, nothing more'. An entertaining overview of their work is supplied in H. R. F. Keating's *Murder Must Appetize*. Symons' assessment was challenged by B. A. Pike and Stephen Leadbeatter in 'Give a Dog a Bad Name . . .', *CADS* 21, August 1993. Pike and Leadbeatter are champions of the 'humdrums', as is Evans.

T. S. Eliot rated him as the finest detective story writer to have emerged during the Twenties
See Curtis Evans, 'Murder in the *Criterion*: T. S. Eliot on Detective Fiction', in *Mysteries Unlocked*. Eliot's other favourite was Richard Austin Freeman, who started writing detective stories much earlier.

Having settled a plot in outline, one spouse wrote a first draft which the couple then discussed and worked on together.
See 'Meet Superintendent Wilson' in *Meet the Detectives*. However, the extent to which the Coles' books were joint endeavours is open to debate; see Curtis Evans, 'By G. D. H. *AND* Margaret Cole?', *CADS* 63, July 2012, which strives to identify the books written solely or predominantly by one or other of the Coles.

the Coles kept in touch with the working classes by engaging three servants
The Coles' novels sometimes offered gentle satire, but penetrating social critiques tended to be in short supply. In *Dead Man's Watch* (1931), for instance, the cast includes an eccentric and unpleasant

husband and wife called Mr and Mrs Cole, who are members of a Pentecostal sect. Mention is made of a young unmarried woman who becomes pregnant, faints at work, and is sacked when her condition is revealed by the doctor called to attend her, but there is no hint that anyone would or should be surprised by this. Unusually, in *Knife in the Dark* (1941) a motive for murder is rooted in a xenophobe's hostility towards foreign refugees; the well-evoked atmosphere of a university town in wartime compensates for a thin plot.

6

Wearing their Criminological Spurs

The first person who set out to solve 'the riddle of the Detection Club' was Clair Price, the London correspondent of *The New York Times*. Her quest led to a top-floor flat 'in a remote suburb of London'. By this, she meant Watford. There, 'a cloud of cigarette smoke, rising from the depths of an easy chair' revealed the debonair presence of Anthony Berkeley. Having conducted the first press interview about the recently formed Club with its debonair but daunting founder, Price was left in no doubt whatsoever that its members were 'neither meek nor humble'.

It was typical of Berkeley that, despite his occasional professions of misanthropy, he not only decided to create the first social network of crime writers, but also possessed the charisma and drive to transform his idea into reality. It was equally characteristic that he embarked on this initiative a mere three years after publishing his first detective novel.

Mystery has shrouded the origins of the Detection Club. Julian Symons, a historian as well as a crime writer of distinction and former Club President, mistakenly wrote that the Club started in 1932. The Club itself continues to circulate a private list of members' details giving the same date. The misunderstanding arose because a formal constitution and rules were not adopted until 11 March 1932, but the Club effectively came into existence two years earlier, and its origins date back to 1928.

Anthony Berkeley (by permission of Celia Down).

The Cox siblings: Stephen, Anthony Berkeley, and Cynthia.

Berkeley approached several writers of detective fiction with, as John Rhode put it, 'the suggestion that they should dine together at stated intervals for the purpose of discussing matters concerned with their craft'. He was taking a lead from the Crimes Club, a dining society focused on legal and criminological topics, with members including Sir Arthur Conan Doyle, P. G. Wodehouse, and A. E. W. Mason, a former spy and MP whose books featuring Inspector Hanaud also earned him membership of the Detection Club.

The first dinners were hosted by Berkeley and his wife Peggy, and held at their home. These were convivial occasions, and although no known records identify those who attended, it is safe to assume they included Sayers, Christie, Douglas and Margaret Cole, Ronald Knox, Henry Wade, H. C. Bailey, and John Rhode. All of them lived either in London or within easy reach, and were members of the generation of detective novelists whose careers began after the end of the war.

In the era of globalized media, when social networking by authors is encouraged by publishers to the extent that it feels almost compulsory, it is easy to forget that, in the Twenties, writers' lives were often unconnected. Beyond small cliques whose members first met at public school or Oxbridge, writers had few opportunities to meet and talk together. Most of them prized their privacy, and not only loathed personal publicity, but kept direct contact with readers to a minimum.

'I never supply biographical notes or photographs: a form of publicity which I deplore,' Berkeley said, when refusing to allow his likeness to appear on Penguin paperback editions of his novels. 'But seeing how often I myself am put off by a photograph of the author on the back of a book, I cannot but feel that some reason at any rate is on my side.'

Christie would never be so rude. She replied to fan letters by saying that she never sent out photographs of herself to anyone but personal friends, though she was willing to send autographed cards instead. Sayers took a similar line, happy to advertise her books but determined at all costs to keep her personal life under wraps. Berkeley may have been poking fun at a post-war Detection Club member, Mary Fitt (in real life, the classicist Kathleen Freeman), who did permit Penguin to publish a photograph of her, resembling a grim Borstal boy, complete with a short back and sides. In other respects Fitt, who lived with another woman, was as reticent as Berkeley: 'It is, I think, the writer of fiction who is of interest to the public, not the person of whom the writer is part. Therefore I do not propose to give details of where I was born, where educated and so forth. . . .' As late as the mid-Fifties, it was perfectly credible for Christianna Brand (who was far from diffident) to conjure up a detective novel with a plot depending upon a successful writer's hatred of personal publicity.

Keeping a distance from inquisitive strangers was one thing. A chance to meet fellow detective novelists was something special. It is no surprise that so many of those Berkeley approached leapt at the chance, just as Ngaio Marsh was thrilled to attend E. C. Bentley's installation as President. Younger writers loved playing the game of whodunit, but that was not quite enough. Could the detective novel metamorphose into something more than a mere puzzle? Conversations over dinner at the Detection Club promoted fresh thinking, above all about collaborative writing projects.

For Sayers, as for Christie and Berkeley, the dinners offered a break from the acute stresses of their personal lives. Christie had been deserted by Archie, Berkeley wanted to be free of Margaret, and Sayers was finding Mac a trial. They were working long hours. Financial pressures meant the two women felt under pressure to write without let-up, while Berkeley was driven by the urge to show that he was as gifted as the rest of his family.

Margaret Cole was much more sociable than Douglas, and enjoyed crossing swords with intellectual equals, such as Sayers, Berkeley, and Ronald Knox, whose attitudes differed sharply from hers. They talked about real-life murder cases, crime writing, and (a constant refrain of writers the world over) the shortcomings of publishers. The dinners proved so popular that, within a year or so, about twenty writers had attended. Excited by the success of his initiative, Berkeley decided the time had come for them to organize themselves into a permanent club.

Berkeley reimagined his get-togethers as the Crimes Circle, whose activities are at the heart of *The Poisoned Chocolates Case*, published in 1929. The novel was an expansion of 'The Avenging Chance', a story often cited as an all-time classic, in which Roger Sheringham solves an ingenious murder committed by means of chocolates injected with nitrobenzene. The crime is broadly replicated in the novel, but this time Chief Inspector Moresby recounts the story to the Crimes Circle, a group of criminologists founded by Sheringham. Scotland Yard has given up hope of solving the mystery – can the amateurs do better?

Sheringham, like Berkeley, rejoiced in assembling a talented array of colleagues, and his elitist group prefigures the Detection Club: 'Entry into the charmed Crimes Circle's dinners was not to be gained by all and hungry.' Membership was by election 'and a single adverse vote meant rejection'. The intention was to have thirteen members, though only six had so far been admitted, and it is easy to imagine that plans for the Detection Club were at a similar stage of development. In addition to Sheringham, the Circle included a distinguished KC, a famous woman dramatist, 'the most famous (if not the most amiable) living detective-story writer', a meek little man called Ambrose Chitterwick, and 'a brilliant novelist who ought to have been more famous than she was'.

Each of the six armchair detectives is tasked with looking into the murder of Joan Bendix and finding a culprit, and this enables Berkeley to poke fun at the methods of detective story writers. 'Just tell the reader very loudly what he's to think, and he'll think it all right,' proclaims Morton Harrogate Bradley, a crime novelist and former car salesman (like Berkeley). He makes his point by seeming to prove that he was the culprit, emphasizing: 'Artistic proof is . . . simply a matter of selection. If you know what to put in and what to leave out, you can prove anything you like, quite conclusively.'

One by one, the members propound their solutions – and each identifies a different murderer. Sheringham takes fourth turn and comes up with the explanation from 'The Avenging Chance'. He is followed by Alicia Dammers, who puts forward an even more convincing solution, which wins over all her colleagues except the diffident Chitterwick. He draws up a chart analysing the deductions of the other five members before explaining how they all went wrong. His is a classic 'least likely culprit' solution, delightfully revealed. Berkeley's belief in the infinite possibilities of solutions to mysteries was confirmed half a century after the book's publication when Christianna Brand devised yet another surprise ending to the book for an American publisher.

The Poisoned Chocolates Case is a *tour de force*. Julian Symons, a demanding critic, called it 'one of the most stunning trick stories in the history of detective fiction'. Agatha Christie and P. G. Wodehouse admired each other's work, but – regrettably – never collaborated with each other. Had they done so, they might have produced such a novel, blending wit with dazzling ingenuity. And as if to underline his cleverness while indulging in his new-found fascination with true crime, Berkeley drew a parallel between each of the solutions to the puzzle put forward by his characters and a real-life murder mystery. These included the story of Constance Kent, Carlyle Harris's killing of his wife by morphine in New York, and the startling case of Christiana Edmunds, 'the Chocolate Cream Poisoner'.

'This correspondence must cease,' declared Dr William Beard during the summer of 1870, in a frantic attempt to break off contact with a woman he had treated for nervous trouble. Christiana Edmunds had begun to frighten him. She lived quietly with her widowed mother in Brighton, but Beard failed to diagnose her long-standing mental illness, and Christiana started deluging him with letters proclaiming her devotion. Beard's suspicions were not aroused when she turned up at his house with a box of chocolates as a present for his wife, but when his wife became sick after eating them, belatedly he put two and two together. However, Emily Beard recovered, and Beard said nothing to the police.

Christiana blamed Mrs Beard's illness on a confectioner called Maynard, and set about acquiring supplies of strychnine from a local dentist, telling him that she meant to poison stray cats. She paid a number of boys to buy chocolate creams from Maynard's shop, and duly laced them with strychnine, before leaving them around the town. One set of poisoned creams was returned to Maynard's, and subsequently eaten by Sidney Barker, the four-year-old nephew of the man who bought them. Sidney died, and at his inquest, Christiana testified that she too had fallen ill after eating chocolates bought from Maynard's. A verdict of accidental death was recorded, prompting Christiana to step up her campaign against the luckless scapegoat. She sent Sidney's parents a series of anonymous letters blaming Maynard for the boy's death, and gave arsenic-laced fruit and cake to a handful of local people, including the dentist who supplied the strychnine and Emily Beard. At last Dr Beard contacted the police, and showed them Christiana's letters, although he always denied having had a sexual relationship with her. Christiana was tried at the Old Bailey for Sidney's murder.

The Press loves nothing better than a sensational murder, and the journalists deduced homicidal tendencies from Christiana's appearance in the dock: 'Short of stature, attired in sombre velvet, bareheaded, with a certain self-possessed demureness in her bearing . . . a rather careworn, hard-featured woman. . . . The character of the face lies in the lower features. The profile is irregular, but not unpleasing; the upper lip is long and convex; . . . chin straight, long, and cruel; the lower jaw heavy, massive, and animal in its development.'

Christiana was found guilty and sentenced to death. She tried to avoid the gallows by claiming that she was pregnant, a lie easily disproved, but the Home Secretary granted a reprieve on the ground of her insanity. She was sent to Broadmoor, where she made a memorable entrance, complete with rouged cheeks and an enormous wig. Thriving on her celebrity and self-image as a *femme fatale*, she remained incarcerated until her death, thirty-five years later.

Even before *The Poisoned Chocolates Case* appeared, Ronald Knox's *The Footsteps at the Lock* hinted that Berkeley's dinner parties might develop into a formal club. Knox's story opens wittily with an account of two cousins who detest each other and are rival heirs to a fortune. They take a canoe trip together, and when one of them disappears, the other is the obvious suspect. The Indescribable Insurance Company calls in the amiable Miles Bredon to investigate. In the course of his enquiries, Bredon encounters an American called Erasmus Quirk, who says he is 'a member of the Detective Club of America; and it was his duty to write up a detective mystery of some kind before the fall, as a condition of his membership'. Quirk, however, is not what he seems.

The pleasure of Berkeley's dinners prompted Agatha Christie to add to her series of short stories parodying celebrated fictional detectives. 'The Unbreakable Alibi' sees the Beresfords tackling a puzzle in the manner of Freeman Wills Crofts' Inspector French. She amalgamated the stories into *Partners in Crime*, which poked gentle fun at the detectives of twelve other writers, including eight founder members of the Detection Club, as well as Poirot. By an odd coincidence, given Conan Doyle's interest in her disappearance, the Sherlock Holmes spoof story, written two years before she was discovered in Harrogate, was 'The Case of the Missing Lady'. The lady in question had disappeared simply to indulge in a slimming cure.

On 27 December 1929, Berkeley wrote to G. K. Chesterton describing plans for the Club. The tone of the letter blended charm, dynamism, and impatience: 'I do hope you will join. A club of the kind I have in mind would be quite incomplete without the creator of "Father Brown", and one who has evolved such a very original turn to the detective story as you have. . . . I want if possible to get things going for a first meeting in about the middle of January.'

He kept up the momentum. By 4 January 1930, a list of twelve 'members to date' was typed, along with a list of twenty-one writers invited to be the original members. Eight proposed Rules of the Club were sent to Chesterton, and the number of Rules grew to a dozen within days. Gathering members took time, and the Rules kept evolving. By the time the final version of the Rules and Constitution came into force, twenty-eight people had been elected to membership, although two were described as Associate Members.

With Sayers' enthusiastic support, Berkeley asked Sir Arthur Conan Doyle to become Honorary President. Conan Doyle was the obvious choice, having created the most famous of all fictional characters, although like Douglas Cole he regarded his work in the genre as less 'important' than some of his other writing. The best Holmes stories belong to the nineteenth century, but Conan Doyle was still writing detective stories in the Golden Age. By now, though, his health was poor, and he could not accept Berkeley's invitation.

Chesterton ranked second only to Conan Doyle in the pantheon of detective story writers, and he duly agreed to become President of the Detection Club. A committee was formed, and Berkeley became Honorary Secretary. He also awarded himself the title of 'First Freeman'. This was a jokey way of distinguishing himself from R. Austin Freeman and Freeman Wills Crofts, although eventually the title's supposed significance became a source of friction when Berkeley claimed it allowed him special privileges.

That lay far in the future. In the meantime, half a dozen members responded to an invitation from the BBC's Talks Department to collaborate on a detective story for radio. Already, the Detection Club had earned a mention in the *Daily Mirror*'s gossip column – alongside snippets about horse racing and Gracie Fields' holiday in Italy – as a dining club for writers whose stories 'rely more upon genuine detective merit than upon melodramatic thrills'. Sayers probably fed the snippet to the newspaper. She was determined to make the public aware of the Club, and its meritocratic ethos.

The first episode of *Behind the Screen* aired on 14 June 1930, trumpeted in *The Listener* as a 'co-operative effort on the part of six members of the well-known Detection Club', a phrase that showed how effective Sayers' promotional efforts had been in a short space of time. Ronald Knox brought the story to what the BBC called 'a nerve-shattering and brain-racking conclusion' on 19 July. Four days later, as a postscript to the serial, the BBC broadcast a conversation between Sayers and Berkeley on the subject of 'Plotting a Detective Story'. As The *Radio Times* explained: 'Miss Sayers will come to the microphone with a theme for a mystery story, Mr Berkeley with a new method of murder. They will endeavour to combine the two to form a plot for a story.'

Detection Club membership meant writers were no longer isolated when publishers annoyed them, and Sayers organized a rebuke to Collins, which launched a 'Crime Club' imprint for its detective fiction list, with a hooded gunman logo. Collins announced that 'the sole and only object of the Crime Club is to help its members by suggesting the best and most entertaining detective novels of the day'. The books were supposedly chosen by a 'panel of experts'. This was a shrewd public relations ploy, but the Crime Club was not a club in any meaningful sense. Fans' addresses simply constituted a database for the despatch of quarterly newsletters about forthcoming titles. Detection Club members who were *not* published by Collins fumed at the implication that their books did not rank with the best. Sayers and Berkeley flexed their muscles with a letter to the *Times Literary Supplement*, signed by eight Club members. With icy understatement, they said: 'We wish . . . to raise our eyebrows at a method of advertisement which is likely to mislead the public.' Collective pressure made more impact than a moan from a single author, and although the Collins Crime Club flourished for more than half a century, its publicity became less provocative.

Arthur Conan Doyle died on 7 July 1930, and Sayers spotted an opportunity to promote the new Club. Shamelessly, she told Berkeley: 'Old Conan Doyle chose this moment to pop off the books. I just put on a card 'To the creator of 'Sherlock Holmes' from the members of the Detective [*sic*] Club with reveration [*sic*] and deep regret.' I thought it would look well and be a bit of publicity.'

In January 1931, Berkeley suggested that Club members might put together a 'Detection Annual', modelled on the popular, though sporadically published, *Printer's Pie*. Baroness Orczy was among those willing to contribute, but before long, this proposal was superseded by the concept of a full-length Detection Club novel, and the result was *The Floating Admiral*.

At the same time, Christie contemplated writing a novel set around a 'Detective Story Club' involving '13 at Dinner'. In one of her private notebooks, she listed the cast of characters. Sayers and her husband are included, alongside a mention of 'Poisons', as are Freeman Wills Crofts and his wife ('Alibis'), Christie herself, John Rhode, Edmund Bentley, Douglas and Margaret Cole, and Clemence Dane. Anthony Berkeley (and his wife, which suggests the couple contrived to keep their matrimonial difficulties to themselves) also appeared on the list.

Christie adds the note 'fantastic writer' next to Berkeley's name. The admiration they had for each other's skill and originality with mystery plots was genuine and deeply felt. Perhaps because she feared she could not out-do *The Poisoned Chocolates Case*, Christie never pursued the story idea. The sinister implications of an unlucky number of dinner guests were, however, soon realized in *Lord Edgware Dies*, the American title of which was *Thirteen at Dinner*. The other writer named on the list in her journal was the American S. S. Van Dine. This was odd, since Van Dine was never a member of the Detection Club. He had, however, visited England not long before, and may have been invited to one of Berkeley's dinners as a guest. In later years, Christie jotted down an idea about her character Ariadne Oliver, a scatty detective novelist, attending a Detection Club dinner with guests. Murder was to take place when the Club's initiation ritual began. It is a shame that she never developed this appealing idea.

On 1 May 1931, Berkeley wrote to tell Chesterton that a new member, Helen Simpson, was to be initiated in a 'ceremonious

Book II.

She 13. at dinner.

Detective Story Club (?).

Miss Sayers - Shibkart.
Mr Van Dine. +
Mr Wills Croft - +mfr
Mrs Christie
Mr Rhode.
Mr & Mrs Cole.

Mr Bentley.
Miss Clemence Dane.
Mr Berkeley. + wife.

Agatha Christie's notebook 41: extract featuring a story idea based on the Detection Club (by permission of the Christie Archive Trust).

Berkeley — fantastic uncle.
& wife.
Miss S.   Poisons.
& husband.
F.W.C. —   Alibi.
    — wife.

ritual' devised by Sayers. He thought the idea of giving solemn pledges to honour the values of fine detective writing would be amusing. This is the first recorded mention of the Detection Club's initiation ritual.

Club members took a strikingly modern approach to combining self-promotion with supporting a good cause, and four members collaborated in a fundraising event for a hospital charity on 31 May 1932. Berkeley (described in the publicity as the Club Secretary), Bentley, Crofts and Margaret Cole were subjected to a 'mock trial' at the London School of Economics, charged with 'faking the evidence' by a prosecuting barrister, with a King's Counsel sitting in judgment.

Less than three months earlier, on 11 March, the Rules and Constitution of the Club had been adopted. They stated that the Club was instituted 'for the association of writers of detective novels and for promoting and continuing a mutual fellowship between them.' To promote the Club's aims, the suitability of every candidate for membership was to be 'fully and carefully examined' to ensure that he or she had written 'at least two detective novels of admitted merit or (in exceptional cases) one such novel; it being understood that the term 'detective novel' does not include adventure stories or "thrillers" or stories in which the detection is not the main interest, and that it is a demerit in a detective novel if the author does not "play fair" with the reader.'

Why exclude thriller writers? Christie and many other members wrote thrillers from time to time, and even Sayers had contemplated adding to the mountain of stories about Sexton Blake. The answer was that Sayers and her friends had no time for crude blood-and-thunder merchants. However, the rule did mean that Bentley's old friend John Buchan, a pillar of the establishment and by a distance the most distinguished British thriller writer, was ineligible for membership, since none of his books could be classed as a detective novel.

In total there were twenty-three rules. They provided that a member who was guilty of a deliberate breach of the rules or damaged the Club's interests was liable to expulsion. Nobody

THE CRIME CLUB NEWS

AUTUMN 1939

CRIME CLUB

SIGN OF A GOOD DETECTIVE NOVEL

The cover of Collins' Crime Club newsletter for autumn 1939.

WHEN first we introduced Rex Stout to Crime Club readers, we made no attempt to hide our conviction that he would henceforth always be one of the big names on any Crime Club programme. As their July Selection, the Crime Club panel chose his new book SOME BURIED CÆSAR, and immediately saw it acclaimed as one of the year's most distinguished detective novels. "One of the most entertaining murder mysteries I have ever had the luck to encounter. I recommend it to all searchers after exciting entertainment," wrote one reviewer. "An excellently contrived story, and (what is is almost better) it is well and wittily told," wrote another. "An unusually entertaining story, well worked out and amusingly told," was the *Times Literary Supplement's* confirmation of the Crime Club panel's judgment. The murder of a prize bull may be said to be something of an innovation in detective fiction, but it provides the incomparable Nero Wolfe with a problem of fitting proportions. *Stout work*, Mr. Stout!

We featured this month another detective novel with a transatlantic setting, Leslie Ford's MR. CROMWELL IS DEAD. Here, beside a problem that was baffling and fast-moving, there was the novelty of a description of Reno, city of divorce, more devastating than has yet been achieved by any straight novelist.

The best qualities of English detective fiction were this month represented by Miss Alice Campbell (A DOOR CLOSED SOFTLY) and Mr. Miles Burton

THESE AUTHORS GAVE YOU
YOUR SUMMER
CRIME CLUB BOOKS

G.D.H. & M.COLE

ALICE CAMPBELL

M.G.EBERHART

HERBERT ADAMS

REX STOUT

Have you read them yet?

(MR. BABBACOMBE DIES). Miss Campbell's story was in the suspense category, giving the reader a real Ethel-Lina-White chill down the spine. Mr. Burton's was another of his brilliantly ingenious poison mysteries.

OUR August selection, DOUBLE BLACKMAIL, is probably one of the cleverest detective stories that even that great combination, the Coles, have ever achieved. Amelia Selvidge had established herself as a Public Figure, well-known for her devotion to good causes, not so well-known as the wife of an exile in Australia. But everything was going well—until the blackmail started. Even the sudden death of the blackmailer does not put an end to her troubles, for the blackmail still continued. "Double Blackmail" indeed only in part describes the doubleness of this detective mystery.

Herbert Adams has made a great hit with his golfing mysteries. He has added murder to the hazards of several of the eighteen holes, but in his latest he gives us MURDER AT THE 19TH HOLE!

R. Philmore in DEATH IN ARMS tells an up-to-the minute story of the death of a man in the Intelligence Department of the Ministry of Defence.

M. G. Eberhart has an unusually tense opening to her new novel of atmosphere and suspense. Three women are sitting in the semi-darkness of evening, happy and at peace, when a man whom they had believed to be dead steps from the shadows and shatters their security.

July Selection
SOME BURIED CAESAR
by Rex Stout

Recommendations
MR. CROMWELL IS DEAD
by Leslie Ford

A DOOR CLOSED SOFTLY
by Alice Campbell

MR. BABBACOMBE DIES
by Miles Burton

August Selection
DOUBLE BLACKMAIL
by G. D. H. & M. Cole

Recommendations
THE 19TH HOLE MYSTERY
by Herbert Adams

DEATH IN ARMS
by R. Philmore

BRIEF RETURN
by M. G. Eberhart

Two sample pages from Collins' Crime Club newsletter.

THE COLES AT HOME

A delightful photograph of G. D. H. & Margaret Cole taken at their Hendon home. They have contrived again to provide us with our special Christmas Choice. *(Photo by Howard Coster)*

The Crime Club News' back page advertisement for Milward Kennedy's reviews in the *Sunday Times*.

has ever been expelled, which shows the value of a rigorous approach to recruitment. By the time the Rules and Constitution came into force, there were twenty-eight members. The rules make no provision for 'Associate Members', yet Hugh Walpole and Helen Simpson have been described as such in the Club's list of members. In the list for 1939–40, Walpole is described as an 'Honorary Member', as is Sir Norman Kendal, who was not a writer at all, and there is no suggestion that Simpson was not a full member. Presumably this untidiness is due to doubt as to whether Walpole's psychological thrillers qualified as 'detective novels', despite his participation in the *Behind the Screen* project. Simpson was eminently qualified for full membership, whereas Kendal's election was a goodwill gesture. One mystery is why the name of R. C. Woodthorpe, elected in 1935, has not appeared in the list of members for the last half-century. Was he thrown out, and his name expunged from the records, for some unspeakable transgression? The likeliest solution is that the omission of his name was a simple mistake.

Despite the veneer of formality, nobody cared about inconsistencies of detail, as long as the Club's core values were preserved. When creative people get together, sparks often fly, and that happened from time to time in the Detection Club. It was rare, though, for members to risk damage to their relationships through backbiting. They were excited by the prospect of exploiting the potential of the detective story. The mix of strong personalities and varied talents was a source of strength. Berkeley had the vision, Chesterton supplied gravitas, and Sayers led by energetic example. Her study of the history of detective fiction broke new ground, paying tribute to the contribution to the genre made by older members of the Club, and signalling how the modern writers could take it to fresh heights. Like any good detective, she knew that to understand the present, and what the future may hold, one needs to understand the past.

Notes to Chapter 6

The first person who set out to solve 'the riddle of the Detection Club' was Clair Price
See Clair Price, 'A New Code for Crime between Covers', *New York Times*, 24 July 1932.

Julian Symons, a historian as well as a crime writer of distinction and former Club President, mistakenly wrote that the Club started in 1932.
Symons said this in his introduction to *Verdict of 13: A Detection Club Anthology* (London, Faber, 1979), where he also expressed the belief that John Dickson Carr was 'the only member ever elected who was not British'. A more reliable account of the Club's early days was supplied by John Rhode's Foreword to an earlier Club anthology, *Detection Medley*.

In other respects, Mary Fitt . . . was as reticent as Berkeley
Even so, she was persuaded by *Picture Post* to be photographed on her hands and knees, peering through a magnifying glass at a Greek vase.

The novel was an expansion of 'The Avenging Chance'
Curiously, the story appears to have been published *after* the novel. A latter-day Berkeley might come up with multiple explanations for this little mystery. Perhaps he realized the strength of his short story's plot, and delayed its publication until he had exploited it more fully, and more lucratively, through the novel.

On 27 December 1929, Berkeley wrote to G. K. Chesterton
No original correspondence relating to the early days of the Detection Club remains in the Club's possession; while the Minute Book has apparently not been seen since the Second World War. The Club's archive is, at the time of writing, in the process of development. I have gleaned information about the correspondence mentioned in this book from a wide variety of sources, in particular the Marion E. Wade Center at Wheaton, from Arthur Robinson, Tony Medawar, George Locke, Douglas G. Greene and Curtis Evans, as well as from occasional sales of material on www.abebooks.com.

'Plotting a Detective Story'
See Tony Medawar, 'Plotting a Detective Story – Dorothy L. Sayers and Anthony Berkeley', *CADS* 51, April 2007.

four members collaborated in a fundraising event for a hospital charity on 31 May 1932
A fifth collaborator was Captain Alan Thomas (1896–1969). His *The Death of Laurence Vining* (1928) was a well-regarded 'impossible crime' novel, and he later became editor of *The Listener*. *Death of the Home Secretary* (1932) is one of a host of Golden Age mysteries in which politicians meet an untimely end.

7

The Art of Self-Tormenting

'The art of self-tormenting is an ancient one,' Sayers proclaimed in her essay introducing the first volume of *Great Short Stories of Detection, Mystery and Horror*. She knew more than most people about self-torment. Keeping her son's existence secret was a constant strain, and on one occasion before she married Mac her self-discipline snapped. She confided in a total stranger, a woman with a boy of ten who had just divorced her husband, and who envied Sayers because nobody else was laying claim to her son. Sayers told John Cournos that contemplating someone else's misfortune made her feel better, but she still wanted to find a man 'to help me to handle the kid later on'. Mac never offered such help.

The self-torment she was talking about was the way that people love to be teased by a mystery. To trace the roots of detective fiction, she delved into ancient texts like a gumshoe determined to leave no stone unturned. Her hunt for early fore-runners of the detective story yielded some unlikely suspects. Analysis of evidence featured in the Apocrypha, the fabrication of false clues appeared in Herodotus, and psychological detection underpinned the story of Rhampsinitus. Sayers was stretching to prove her point, but not as far as it might seem. Nine years after her anthology appeared, the murderer in John Dickson Carr's *To Wake the Dead* relied on an intricate scheme echoing the story of Rhampsinitus.

Why had detective fiction not developed sooner? The Jews, 'with their strongly moral preoccupation' were, Sayers felt, well suited to create detective stories. So were the Romans, with their taste for logic and law-making. She identified elements of detection in one of the Grimms' tales, and in an Indian folk-tale. Yet although stories about crime had flourished for centuries, the *detective* story could not thrive until the wider public sympathized more with the forces of law and order than the law-breakers.

Sayers argued that the ground rules for the genre were set forever in the United States, in the 1840s, when Edgar Allan Poe wrote five seminal tales of mystery and imagination. First came 'The Murders in the Rue Morgue', a 'locked room' story. A woman and her daughter are found savagely murdered inside a locked room. The central puzzle, borrowed by hundreds of Poe's successors was – how could the murderer have got in and out?

Poe created a gifted and eccentric amateur sleuth, Chevalier C. Auguste Dupin, the first of fiction's Great Detectives. Dupin's cases were told by an unnamed chronicler, setting the template for Holmes and Watson, Poirot and Hastings, and dozens of less celebrated pairings, in which admiring sidekicks ranging from the obtuse to the sophisticated recount the exploits of amateur sleuths who almost always outsmart the professional police. The neat twist in 'The Purloined Letter' was that the solution was so obvious that everyone overlooked it. Chesterton's 'The Invisible Man' was the most famous of many later stories using this trick of a clue hidden in plain sight. Even more influential was 'The Mystery of Marie Roget', in which Dupin plays the 'armchair detective'. This was the very first detective story based on a criminal puzzle from real life.

Marie Roget was the fictional counterpart of Mary Rogers. She worked in a New York tobacconist's, and her 'raven tresses', womanly figure and tantalising smile inspired young male customers to poetry and earned her the sobriquet 'the beautiful cigar girl'. Among Mary's admirers was a young lawyer called

Alfred Crommelin. She rejected his advances, and became engaged to Daniel Payne, a cork cutter. Subsequently, she left a note at Crommelin's apartment, hinting at a reconciliation. When he did not reply, she sent him a series of letters, and asked for money. Shortly afterwards, on 23 July 1841, she disappeared. This was not the first time she had vanished without explanation; the same thing had happened three years earlier.

A few days after she went missing, a group of young men decided to escape the steamy heat of the city by walking out to Sybil's Cave at Hoboken. They noticed clothes floating in the shallow waters of the North River, and thought someone had fallen in. Finding a wooden scull nearby, they rowed over to the bobbing objects, to discover the body of a young woman, whose long black hair rippled in the water like seaweed. A slip of cloth was knotted around her neck. One report said, 'Her forehead and face appeared to have been battered and butchered, to a mummy.'

The remains were identified as Mary's. A popular theory was that she had been killed by a gang, although Payne and Crommelin also came under the microscope. The plot thickened when some of her garments were found close to a tavern run by a Mrs Frederica Loss. Daniel Payne committed suicide, and Frederica Loss was shot by one of her sons, but the precise details of Mary Rogers' death were never established. Mrs Loss supplemented her income with work as an abortionist, and Mary's death probably followed a termination that went wrong.

Poe hinted at the truth in his story (transplanted to Dupin's home turf in Paris) as well as offering a more imaginative alternative theory. Sayers was impressed by his efforts at solving a real-life mystery, and by Arthur Conan Doyle's 'splendid efforts' on behalf of George Edalji and Oscar Slater, wrongly accused men who benefited from his work as an amateur detective. Detection Club members were keen to follow the lead given by Poe and Conan Doyle – none more so than Sayers herself.

Poe showed how to transform a real-life case into detective fiction, and a generation later Wilkie Collins followed his example in *The Moonstone*. He borrowed details from the Constance Kent case, and based Inspector Cuff on the real-life Inspector Whicher. For Sayers, *The Moonstone* came closer to perfection than any other detective story, even though Arthur Conan Doyle's Sherlock Holmes was incontestably the greatest detective. Collins was the most gifted author of Victorian 'sensation novels', but the short story remained the dominant form in detective fiction until the Golden Age.

Sayers loved the Holmes tales, and admired the way Conan Doyle enriched English literature with countless memorable lines. There is a striking resemblance between lines from 'The Musgrave Ritual' and a passage in Eliot's *Murder in the Cathedral*, while the success of Mark Haddon's novel *The Curious Incident of the Dog in the Night-Time* and the television show *Sherlock* demonstrate that Holmes-speak still appeals in the twenty-first century.

Sherlock Holmes' leading rivals were created by three contrasting writers – a socially mobile Cockney, a rural dean, and a Hungarian baroness – who would become Detection Club members. Arthur Morrison, son of an engine fitter, exploited his literary gifts to escape London's slums. A journalist, he hit his stride with *Tales of the Mean Streets*, but could scarcely have guessed that 'mean streets' would become a phrase associated with American private eyes. Morrison depicted the East End with an insider's expertise, but became embarrassed by his humble origins. He even falsified data on the national census to conceal his date and place of birth. It is a pity he was so sensitive, since the strength of his writing lies in an understanding of working class life that Berkeley, Sayers and Christie could never match.

Morrison's Martin Hewitt, a lawyer turned private investigator, was meant to fill the gap left by Holmes' plunge into the Reichenbach Falls. Portly and good-natured, Hewitt was too ordinary to outshine the sage of 221b Baker Street, dead or alive. More distinctive was Horace Dorrington, a suave villain who plans a murder at the start of *The Dorrington Deed-Box*. His scheme fails, and although he escapes justice, his intended victim discovers the records of several cases in which Dorrington combines work as a private inquiry agent with shameless criminality. Morrison abandoned Dorrington after one book, but had created the literary ancestor of the murderous charmer Tom Ripley, created by Patricia Highsmith, herself a member of the Detection Club, and of Jeff Lindsay's serial killer Dexter Morgan.

Thorpe Hazell was another eccentric Great Detective. Hazell is a specialist railway detective, a vegetarian and health fanatic. After solving the puzzle of 'Sir Gilbert Murrell's Picture', he declines Sir Gilbert's offer of a cooked lunch. He has already ordered lentils and salad to eat at a railway station, and starts to perform his 'physical training ante-luncheon exercises'. As the bewildered baronet watches him 'whirling his arms like a windmill', Hazell explains, 'Digestion should be considered *before* a meal.' He was created by Victor Lorenzo Whitechurch, rural dean of Aylesbury and an honorary canon of Christ Church. Whitechurch was supposedly the first detective story writer to devote such care to his description of police procedure that he checked the authenticity of his manuscripts with Scotland Yard.

Sayers believed detective fiction should never become predictable. She felt Baroness Orczy's stories became formulaic, and perhaps Orczy came to the same conclusion. After making a fortune from her historical melodramas featuring the Scarlet Pimpernel, she moved away from writing detective fiction, although she was a loyal member of the Detection Club. Orczy was born Emma Magdolna Rozália Mária Jozefa Borbála Orczy de Orczi, in Hungary. Her father, Baron Felix Orczy, was a composer and a friend of Liszt, but disgruntled workers set his crops and farm buildings on fire when he introduced farm machinery, and the family fled when she was three. They lived in Budapest, Brussels and Paris, before moving to London, where she learned English and studied painting. She married an English illustrator, and the couple translated children's stories together. Orczy published detective short stories before concentrating on the Pimpernel, alias Sir Percy Blakeney, who helped French aristocrats to escape from the Revolution.

Orczy created two detectives as different from Sherlock as could be. Bill Owen, the enigmatic Old Man in the Corner, sits in the ABC Teashop on the corner of Norfolk Street and the Strand, fiddling with a piece of string as he unravels criminal puzzles on the basis of what he has read in newspaper reports and from occasional visits to court. He enjoys a contentious relationship with his 'Watson', Polly Burton, a young journalist. In the final story, it appears that the Old Man himself is the culprit.

Lady Molly of Scotland Yard is a collection starring Molly Robertson-Kirk, whose unique selling point as a detective is her ability is to use her domestic experience to spot clues that would elude a man. Yet the stories would make any feminist despair. Lady Molly has risen to the top of the 'female department' at Scotland Yard motivated solely by the urge to save her falsely convicted fiancé from prison. Having achieved her aim, she duly marries him, and retires from the force to spend more time in the kitchen and bedroom.

Sayers had no time for Lady Molly, and lamented the way fictional female detectives relied on intuition rather than their experience of the world. A brilliant female detective, Sayers reluctantly concluded, had yet to be created. There was a huge gap in the market, waiting for Agatha Christie to fill it with Miss Jane Marple. In the meantime, Sherlock Holmes' most memorable rival was the unlikeliest – a diminutive Roman Catholic priest called Father Brown.

On a blustery March morning in 1904, Gilbert Keith Chesterton, who had given a lecture in Keighley the night before, tramped across the Yorkshire moors to the house where his wife was staying. By his side was a recent acquaintance, a priest called Father John O'Connor. They made an odd couple – Chesterton, six feet four and twenty-one stone, dwarfed the priest – but they enjoyed each other's company, and their conversation ranged far and wide. Lunacy, the problem of vagrancy, and the burning of heretics, as they headed towards Ilkley Moor. The shortcomings of Zola and anti-clericalism as they climbed the slope of Morton Bank. To keep out the cold, they recited ballads, and on the high moorland, they burst into song. When they reached Ilkley, they met two Cambridge students, who patronized the humble priest. But Chesterton realized that Father O'Connor had fought 'solid Satanism' all his life, and in comparison, the undergraduates were 'two babies in the same perambulator'. From that unforgettable day sprang the idea for Father Brown, whose deep understanding of evil makes him a detective of extraordinary insight, and who is all the more formidable because he is so easy to underestimate, with his umbrella, brown parcels and inoffensive manner.

G. K. Chesterton never stopped coming up with ideas, and Father Brown was the best of them. He and E. C. Bentley met at St Paul's School in London at the age of twelve, and formed a lifelong friendship. Bentley said Chesterton 'was by nature the happiest boy and man I have ever known'. A larger-than-life character, fond of wearing a cape and crumpled hat, and carrying a swordstick, Chesterton wrote dozens of books and contributed to many more, besides producing hundreds of poems, a couple of hundred short stories, five plays, and more than four thousand articles for newspapers and magazines. Some of his views have stood the test of time, others now seem eccentric and questionable. Yet the strength of his spiritual values has caused Pope Francis to regard him as a potential candidate for sainthood.

In 1922, Chesterton published *Eugenics and Other Evils* (the title speaks for itself) in the face of a tide of contrary opinion. As the reality of Nazism became clear, 'progressive' backers of eugenics melted away, and Chesterton was vindicated. His natural sympathy for the underdog meant that during the Boer War, he was pro-Boer, while he detested imperialism. In partnership with the essayist and former Liberal MP Hilaire Belloc, he advocated 'distributism', an airy-fairy concept based on the notion that accumulation of capital should become the occupation of the many rather than the few. This was in keeping with Douglas and Margaret Cole's enthusiasm for Guild Socialism, but the distributists saw 'Jewish bankers' as part of the problem facing society, and this led to accusations of anti-Semitism. The danger of pouring opinions endlessly into print is that not all of them stand up to scrutiny, especially after the passage of time.

Chesterton was on safer ground when he wrote his essay 'A Defence of Detective Stories', arguing that the detective story 'is the earliest and only form of popular literature in which is expressed some sense of the poetry of modern life'. That reference to poetry is significant. From Poe onwards, a strikingly high proportion of detective novelists have also been poets. They are drawn to each form by its structural challenges.

As for the work of the detective, Chesterton wrote: 'The whole noiseless and unnoticeable police management by which we are ruled and protected is only a successful knight-errantry.' This is not so far away from Raymond Chandler's honourable private eye prowling the mean streets, neither tarnished nor afraid.

The Innocence of Father Brown, a collection of twelve stories, appeared in 1911. Whereas Sherlock Holmes specialized in deductive reasoning and used scientific aids – fingerprinting, microscope and magnifying glass – to investigate crime, Father Brown is intuitive. He relies on philosophy and his knowledge of sin to solve mysteries. Holmes had his Watson, but the little priest had God on his side. The starting point of a story is often a clever puzzle – in 'The Hammer of God', for instance, the question is how a man's skull could be smashed to bits by a tiny hammer – but the real force of the tales lies in a pungent moral or social precept. In 'The Blue Cross', Father Brown recognises that the disguised criminal, Flambeau, is not a priest because he attacks reason, which is 'bad theology'.

In 'The Queer Feet', Father Brown makes a witty and telling point about social class: 'It must be very hard work to be a gentleman, but, do you know, I have sometimes thought was it may be almost as laborious to be a waiter.' Similarly, in 'The Invisible Man', a story of an apparently impossible murder, Father Brown realises that the culprit is *mentally* invisible: 'Nobody ever notices a postman, somehow, yet they have passions like other men.' In 'The Mistake of the Machine', Father Brown shows contempt for the newly fashionable lie-detector, which he thought as valuable as 'that interesting idea in the Dark Ages that blood would flow from a corpse if the murderer touched it'.

Chesterton was not a Catholic when he started writing about Father Brown, but was received into the Catholic Church in 1922. The cost of launching *G.K.'s Weekly*, a personal soapbox, prompted him to resurrect Father Brown, just as Conan Doyle's desire to fund work in the field of spiritualism caused him to write further Sherlock Holmes stories. Chesterton had prudently avoided hurling his detective into a waterfall, and attributed the priest's long absence to years spent working in South America.

The Incredulity of Father Brown appeared in the same year as *The Murder of Roger Ackroyd*, but although Chesterton and Christie both displayed a flair for misdirection, they were very different writers. Poirot's Catholicism is incidental, and Christie never allowed theological argument to interrupt the careful unravelling of her puzzles, even when her subject was murder at the vicarage. Father Brown has more in common with Jane Marple than with Poirot. Like the priest, the spinster from St Mary Mead relies on a deep understanding of human nature, coupled with an unassuming personality which keeps criminals off their guard. Just as the quality of the Sherlock Holmes stories sank after his disappearance at the Reichenbach Falls, so the later Father Brown stories made less impact than their predecessors. Chesterton could not help preaching, but detective fiction and didacticism seldom mix well.

Like Chesterton, E. C. Bentley came up with his best story while walking – although on his own, and over a period of six to eight weeks. He lived in Hampstead, and it took him an hour to stride to Fleet Street, where he worked as a political journalist. Commuting each day on foot, he worked out the storyline of *Trent's Last Case*. He wrote the book at a standing-up desk, because he disliked the idea of a sedentary occupation, and the only place where he could stand up to write was in his own house. The novel achieved a success Bentley never repeated. Yet it is no mean feat to have changed the course of detective fiction history. And that is what *Trent's Last Case* did.

As a schoolboy, Edmund Clerihew Bentley devised a simple verse form, to which he gave his middle name. In 1905, he published a selection of 'clerihews', with illustrations by Chesterton, under the name 'E. Clerihew'. Typically, a clerihew is biographical and whimsical, comprising four lines of irregular length and the rhyme structure AABB. For all their inherent limitations, clerihews have never gone completely out of fashion, with examples composed by writers as diverse as W. H. Auden and Spike Milligan. Bentley even wrote a clerihew about Sayers:

> *Miss Dorothy Sayers*
> *Never cared about the Himalayas*
> *The height that gave her a thrill*
> *Was Primrose Hill.*

Bentley's son Nicolas, an illustrator and occasional crime writer, accompanied the verse with a caricature of her, but privately Sayers expressed her dissatisfaction: 'It makes me all chin and no forehead, whereas in fact I am all head and no features, like a tadpole.'

In 1910, Bentley decided 'to write a detective story of a new sort'. He intended a swipe against a lack of realism in the portrayal of fictional Great Detectives like Holmes: 'It should be possible, I thought, to write a detective story in which the detective was recognizable as a human being.' His aim was to make 'the hero's hard-won and obviously correct solution of the mystery turn out to be completely wrong. Why not show up the infallibility of the Holmesian method?' Readers took *Trent's Last Case* at face value, not caring that it was meant to be 'not so much a detective story as an exposure of detective stories'. The book became an immediate and an enduring success, and has been filmed three times.

Bentley did more than mock literary convention. He stumbled across a format for the twisting mystery, a blend of game-playing and mental gymnastics that still fascinates readers in the twenty-first century. His ground-breaking experiment inspired a new generation of writers who turned to detective fiction once 'the war to end wars' was over. They found that the length of a novel offered much greater scope for elaborately plotted whodunits. Sherlock Holmes and Father Brown (as well as Martin Hewitt, Thorpe Hazell, and Lady Molly) enjoyed their finest hours in short stories. The plots were too slender to sustain full-length novels. In the hands of Detection Club members during the Golden Age, the novel at last became the natural form for the detective story. It has remained so ever since.

The phrase 'Golden Age of detective fiction', coined in 1939, has stuck. Yet opinions vary about how long the Golden Age lasted, as well as whether it really was as golden as admirers claim. Julian Symons thought it logical to define the Golden Age as the period between the two world wars, and it is difficult to argue. Of course, Christie and her disciples continued to produce new books, and enjoy much success, long after that time, but most of the classic detective fiction appeared between the wars. To begin with, many Detection Club members treated their novels like a game, and consciously tried to 'play fair' with their readers. Before long, subversives like Berkeley found it was more exciting to break the rules.

Notes to Chapter 7

her essay introducing the first volume of Great Short Stories of Detection, Mystery and Horror
Sayers' essay remains among the most insightful examinations of the genre's development. Other influential studies are listed in the Select Bibliography.

his essay 'A Defence of Detective Stories'
The essay first appeared in 'The Speaker' in October 1901, and was included in Chesterton, *The Defendant* (London: Johnson, 1902).

Bentley decided 'to write a detective story of a new sort'
He described planning and writing the book in *Those Days*.

Part Two

The Rules of the Game

Ask A Policeman, the second book from the Detection Club, published by Arthur Barker in 1933.

8

Setting a Good Example to the Mafia

The Golden Age detective novel was not dreamed up on the playing fields of Eton, yet readers might be forgiven for thinking otherwise. In *Trent's Last Case*, Philip Trent refers to 'detective sportsmanship', and the notion of playing by the rules of the game in detective fiction was not new even then. The prominent Jewish writer Israel Zangwill, author of a Victorian locked room classic, *The Big Bow Mystery* (which features a Scotland Yard detective with the marvellous name of Wimp) argued that everything in the solution must derive logically from clues already given to the reader.

One of the earliest detective novelists to focus on 'fair play' was the old Etonian Lord Gorell, who had a spell as Under-Secretary of State for Air in David Lloyd George's government before defecting to the Labour Party. He gave a clue to his strengths and limitations in the title of his autobiography, *One Man, Many Parts*. A jack of all trades, yes, but it would be harsh to dismiss Gorell as a master of none.

Ronald Gorell Barnes was the second son of a High Court judge who received a peerage. During the war, his bravery earned him the Military Cross, but his career as an infantry officer ended when a German machine gunner shot him in the leg. His elder brother, who inherited the title, was killed not long after winning a DSO on the Somme, and Ronald became the third Baron Gorell in 1917. In the same year, he published his first crime novel, *In the Night*.

Gorell (like Arthur Conan Doyle before him) was a good enough cricketer to play at first-class level. For people of his station in society, whatever their political views, the sport was idealized as exemplifying high moral standards in action. Cheating simply 'was not cricket'. During the Golden Age, cricket mattered, and so did the idea that one should play by the rules – and abide by their spirit. In the early Thirties, when an England team touring Australia intimidated and injured opposing batsmen with fast bowling that was regarded as unsporting, it sparked an international diplomatic incident. The English euphemism for these tactics was 'leg theory'; the Australians called the bowling 'bodyline'. The West Indian cricket writer and Marxist C. L. R. James went so far as to argue that the 'Bodyline Affair' signalled 'the decline of the West'.

Gorell's aim was 'to deal fairly with its readers. . . . Every essential fact is related as it is discovered and readers are, as far as possible, given the eyes of the investigators and equal opportunities with them of arriving at the truth.' He supplied a floor plan of the crime scene, the kind of garnish that became a familiar ingredient of Golden Age novels. An unpleasant elderly businessman is bludgeoned to death in his own country house, and the apparent solution is that 'the butler did it', but Gorell offers a neat final twist and an unexpected culprit. He wrote occasional crime novels until the Fifties, but never surpassed *In the Night*.

Alan Alexander Milne, another cricket lover, wrote only one detective novel, *The Red House Mystery*, but it enjoyed enormous popularity. Again the setting was an English country house. A family black sheep recently returned from Australia is found shot dead in a locked library and two guests, Antony Gillingham and his friend Bill Beverley, decide it would be fun to ape Holmes and Watson. Even at this early point, the tropes of the detective story are gently guyed, and Antony says, 'I oughtn't to explain 'til the last chapter, but I always think that's so unfair.' One chapter is called 'Mr Gillingham Talks Nonsense', which captures the spirit of the enterprise. A. A. Milne was, like Berkeley, a regular contributor to *Punch*, and became assistant editor. He was an early screenwriter for the British film industry, as well as a prolific playwright, and two years after *The Red House Mystery* appeared, he immortalized his son Christopher Robin in *Winnie-the-Pooh*.

For all its associations with sportsmanship, cricket is governed by complicated laws, and Milne reckoned that if the detective novel was a game, readers and writers needed to know the rules. When *The Red House Mystery* was reprinted, he set out half a dozen key points:

1. The story should be written in good English.
2. Love interest is undesirable.
3. Both detective and villain should be amateurs.
4. Scientific detection is 'too easy'.
5. The reader should know as much as the detective.
6. There should be a Watson: it is better for the detective 'to watsonize' than soliloquize.

Even T. S. Eliot took a stab at devising rules for detective stories. Thus, 'disguises must only be occasional and incidental,' 'elaborate and bizarre machinery is an irrelevance,' and 'the detective should be highly intelligent but not superhuman.' Eliot was a stickler for fair play: 'We should feel that we have a sporting chance to solve the mystery ourselves.'

This idea of rules of the game was taken to extremes on the other side of the Atlantic. Using the pen name S. S. Van Dine, the American aesthete Willard Huntington Wright wrote ornately plotted detective novels starring the smug gentleman sleuth Philo Vance. Like Crofts and Douglas Cole, Van Dine turned to crime fiction during a period of illness, although in his case the cause was a secret cocaine habit. His literary addiction was to overdoing things, and he came up with no fewer than twenty rules for writers.

Van Dine's rules, like Milne's, banned 'love interest', and he also decreed that the detective should never be the culprit. Depressingly, he argued that: 'A detective novel should contain . . . no subtly worked-out character analyses, no 'atmospheric' preoccupations. . . . They hold up the action and introduce issues irrelevant to the main purpose, which is to state a problem, analyse it, and bring it to a successful conclusion.' Sayers proved more far-sighted, but both writers shared a fascination with unsolved murders, and Van Dine's debut, *The Benson Murder Case*, was inspired by a killing that came closer than any other to supplying a real-life locked room mystery.

Shortly after half past eight on a warm June morning in 1920, a housekeeper called Marie Larsen arrived at the Manhattan home of her employer, Joseph Bowne Elwell. The front double doors were locked, but she had a key and let herself in. An inner door was also locked, and again she opened it. Making her way into the reception room, she found Elwell sitting in an upright armchair, wearing only red silk pyjamas. His eyes were shut, but his mouth was open, as he fought noisily for breath. Although a vain man, he was wearing neither his toupee nor his dentures. She saw a cone-shaped bullet hole in his forehead, with blood trickling from it. He died without giving a clue to his killer's identity.

Elwell was a well-known man-about-town in Jazz Age New York. Nicknamed 'the Wizard of Whist', he was the most famous bridge-player of his day, and a leading teacher of the game to pupils including King Edward VII. A gambler, racehorse owner, unofficial 'spy-catcher', and dealer in bootleg liquor, he was also an energetic 'chicken chaser' (that is, philanderer). This multi-faceted life supplied so many possible motives for murder that the police were spoiled for choice. Was the culprit an abandoned mistress, a cuckolded husband, someone Elwell had cheated at cards, a fellow bootlegger, or the agent of a foreign power?

Nobody was ever convicted of the crime, and there was probably a disappointingly mundane explanation for the 'locked room' aspect of the case. Some police officers suspected the killer slipped inside the house when the doors were opened to admit the postman. The likeliest murderer was Walter Lewisohn, a disturbed man jealous of Elwell's interest in a beautiful dancer called Leonora Hughes, described in her publicity as 'the dimpled wisp of grace from Flatbush'. Four years after the murder, Lewisohn was diagnosed with chronic delusional insanity and confined to a sanatorium for the rest of his life. Leonora enjoyed better luck, marrying an Argentinian known as 'the Cattle Croesus' because of his fabulous wealth, and living in luxury until her death in Buenos Aires in 1978.

As for Elwell, his lifestyle is said to have influenced F. Scott Fitzgerald's characterisation of Jay Gatsby, while the colossal success of *The Benson Murder Case* led to a string of best-sellers featuring Philo Vance. For *The Canary Murder Case*, Van Dine fictionalised another unsolved murder – the killing by chloroform of Dot King, hostess of a New York speakeasy. The Vance stories were filmed, and inspired a host of lucrative spin-offs, including a Philo Vance cocktail and a Canary ice-cream sundae.

Van Dine's fellow American writers of detective stories in the Golden Age style included Rufus King, Milton Propper, Todd Downing, and the psychologist and creator of super-elaborate whodunits, C. Daly King (whom Sayers called 'a highbrow of highbrows', her idea of the ultimate compliment.) The names of Q. Patrick, Jonathan Stagge and Patrick Quentin were used over the years by four writers in all – two men, two women – who between them produced a long run of high-calibre mysteries. *The Grindle Nightmare*, co-written by Richard Wilson Webb and Mary Louise Aswell, is a stunning example of Golden Age *noir*, complete with the killing and maiming of a child and animals. Sayers found the book disturbing, and no wonder.

American fans of classic detective fiction who tried their hand at the genre included such unlikely figures as Georges Antheil, the avant-garde composer and author of an 'impossible crime' mystery, *Death in the Dark* (edited in the UK by T. S. Eliot for Faber) and Gertrude Stein, whose output included both

Blood on the Dining Room Floor and an essay called 'Why I Like Detective Stories'.

The towering figure among American Golden Age writers was Ellery Queen, a pseudonym used by Frederic Dannay and Manfred Lee, two cousins whom *The Benson Murder Case* inspired to write mysteries themselves. They heightened the interactive nature of 'fair play' novels by including 'formal challenges to the reader' to guess whodunit once all the clues had been supplied. Dannay and Lee were, like Sayers, shrewd and imaginative when it came to marketing. They also wrote as Barnaby Ross, and they publicized their books through a series of debates in which Lee pretended to be Queen while Dannay posed as Ross. Both wore black domino masks with ruffles underneath, so their faces could not be seen. Rumour-mongers claimed that Queen was really Van Dine, while Ross was said to be the critic and raconteur Alexander Woollcott, who later became Anthony Berkeley's *bête noire*.

A myth has grown up that Golden Age detective fiction was an essentially British form of escapism in response to the First World War, an effete counterpart to the tough and realistic crime fiction produced in the United States. Pulp magazine stories grew rapidly in popularity during the Twenties, as gifted writers such as Dashiell Hammett, James M. Cain and Chandler emerged. Hammett's first two crime novels appeared in 1929, and *The Maltese Falcon* followed as the Detection Club was becoming established. Yet the distinction often drawn between the two countries is simplistic. In the US, tough guys and traditionalists co-existed until the Second World War.

The key difference between the two countries, according to the American critic Howard Haycraft, was 'the existence of the highly honourable company of the Detection Club . . . a virtual Academy of the genre . . . and constituting a goal and reward for ambitious newcomers'. Haycraft believed the Club gave British writers 'one inestimable advantage denied to their American brethren' – and to their colleagues in continental Europe, he might have added if crime fiction in translation had been as popular then as it is today.

Is this why British Golden Age writers enjoyed greater success and had a more lasting influence than authors writing in a similar style in the US and elsewhere? The Detection Club fostered a collegiate spirit which buttressed members' determination to try out fresh ideas – and to keep going in the face of the disappointments which are part and parcel of a writer's life. Members did more than simply respect tradition – they were constantly challenging each other to take the genre to a higher level. As a result, they developed detective fiction in ways that lasted much longer than anyone expected.

Britain's leading standard-bearer for the principle of fair play in detective fiction was Ronald Knox. Monsignor Knox, as he was known, famously promoted the idea of 'rules of the game'. Unlike Van Dine, Knox never took himself, or the idea of rules for detective novelists, too seriously. Born in 1888, he was one of the Bishop of Manchester's six children, and the family was astonishingly talented. His eldest brother, E. V. Knox, became editor of *Punch* and wrote one of the wittiest parodies of Golden Age detection, 'The Murder at the Towers'. Another brother, Dillwyn, became an eminent cryptographer, cracking German codes in both world wars. Their sister Winifred – later, Lady Winifred Peck – produced several mainstream novels along with a couple of mysteries of her own. Ronald's niece, Penelope Fitzgerald, another novelist, won the Booker Prize.

Ronald was educated at Eton and Balliol, and became President of the Oxford Union. Having taken a vow of celibacy at the age of seventeen, he converted to Catholicism, taking up the Catholic chaplaincy in Oxford, before encountering the young and lovely Daphne, Lady Acton. She had married a Catholic and sought tuition from Knox. Later, she confided in Evelyn Waugh that she had fallen in love with her priest, though he was twice her age. Knox either did not realize or pretended not to notice. Sayers, however, thought Knox unreliable, and he found her overbearing.

During the First World War, Knox worked with Dillwyn, code-breaking for naval intelligence, and became addicted to word games. He published *A Book of Acrostics*, and his 'Studies in the Literature of Sherlock Holmes', an early example of Sherlockian scholarship, earned the appreciation of Conan Doyle. His second detective novel, *The Three Taps*, introduced Miles Bredon, the investigator from the Indescribable Insurance Company. Bredon's wife Angela assists him, while dutiful nannies take care of the children. One of Knox's biographers speculated that Dashiell Hammett modelled one of his most famous characters, Nora Charles, on Angela Bredon.

Knox's introduction to *Best Detective Stories of the Year (1928)* included what he called a 'Decalogue': ten command-ments for the detective story writer. Many of these 'rules' were conceived tongue-in-cheek. He would have been amazed, as well as amused, to find so many commentators in later years taking his jokes at face value. According to Knox, 'The criminal must be someone mentioned in the early part of the story, but must not be anyone whose thoughts the reader has been allowed to follow. . . . All supernatural or preternatural agencies are ruled out as a matter of course. . . . Not more than one secret room or passage is allowable. . . . No hitherto undiscovered poisons should be used, nor any appliance which need a long scientific explanation at the end.'

'No Chinaman must figure in the story,' Knox also insisted, poking fun at thriller writers whose reliance on sinister Oriental villains had already become a racist cliché. The most famous culprit was Sax Rohmer (the exotic pseudonym of Birmingham-born Arthur Ward), creator of the villainous Fu Manchu, embod-iment of 'the Yellow Peril'.

Knox knew perfectly well that most of his 'rules' were ludicrously strict: 'No accident must ever help the detective, nor must he ever have an unaccountable intuition which proves to be right. . . . The detective must not himself commit the crime. . . . The detective must not light on any clues are not instantly produced for the inspection of the reader.' Some rules did make sense in terms of constructing an artistically satisfactory narrative: 'The stupid friend of the detective, the Watson, must not conceal any thoughts which pass through his mind. . . . Twin brothers, and doubles generally, must not appear unless we have been duly prepared for them.'

Tellingly, Knox added: 'Rules so numerous and so stringent cannot fail to cramp the style of the author. . . . The game is getting played out; before long, it is to be feared, all the possible combinations will have been used up.' Many books written during the Golden Age were certainly formulaic and dull. In the hands of writers of real ability, though, the detective story proved highly flexible and capable of almost infinite development. Almost half a century after Knox devised his Decalogue, the distinguished Czech writer Josef Skvorecky published *Sins of Father Knox*, a collection paying homage to the classic form. Skvorecky challenges the reader in each story not only to identify the criminal but to spot which of Knox's commandments has been broken.

When Sayers hit upon the idea of an initiation ritual for new members of the Detection Club, she cannibalized Knox's Decalogue. The ritual is often described as cloaked in secrecy, which is odd, given that Chesterton set it out in full in an article for *The Strand*. He said he did this 'in the age of publicity and public opinion' to set a good example to 'the Mafia, the Ku Klux Klan, the Freemasons, the Illuminati . . . and all the other secret societies which now govern the greater part of public life'.

Since the Thirties, the ritual has been revised regularly as each generation of members tries to combine the essence of what binds them together with a touch of humour, although the concept of an oath taken by the initiate endures. The original version quoted by Chesterton included a catechism conducted by the President (or 'Ruler'):

Ruler: Do you promise that your detectives shall well and truly detect the crimes presented to them, using those wits which it may please you to bestow upon them and not placing reliance on, nor making use of Divine Revelation, Feminine Intuition, Mumbo-Jumbo, Jiggery-Pokery, Coincidence or the Act of God?

Candidate: I do.

Ruler: Do you solemnly swear never to conceal a vital clue from the reader?

Candidate: I do.

Ruler: Do you promise to observe a seemly moderation in the use of Gangs, Conspiracies, Death-Rays, Ghosts, Hypnotism, Trap-Doors, Chinamen, Super-Criminals and Lunatics; and utterly and forever to forswear Mysterious Poisons unknown to Science?

Candidate: I do.

Ruler: Will you honour the King's English?

Candidate: I will.'

But the ritual had a sting in the tail, with the Ruler's final remarks having a touch of menace: 'You are duly elected a Member of the Detection Club, and if you fail to keep your promises, may other writers anticipate your plots, may your publishers do you down in your contracts, may total strangers sue you for libel, may your pages swarm with misprints and may your sales continually diminish. Amen.'

Was this finale contributed by Anthony Berkeley? It smacks of the waspish humour that was his trademark. Yet while he and Sayers adored the fun of the ritual, their detective stories were becoming increasingly realistic and ambitious.

Notes to Chapter 8

a floor plan of the crime scene, the kind of garnish that became a familiar ingredient of Golden Age novels
See R. F. Stewart, 'Die-agrams', *CADS* 18, February 1992, one of the most amusing articles ever written about Golden Age detective fiction.

Even T. S. Eliot took a stab at devising rules for detective stories.
See Curtis Evans, 'T. S. Eliot, Detective Fiction Critic', *CADS* 62, February 2012.

he came up with no fewer than twenty rules for writers
See S. S. Van Dine, 'Twenty Rules for Writing Detective Stories', *American Magazine*, September 1928.

Van Dine's fellow American writers of detective stories in the Golden Age style
My understanding of American Golden Age fiction derives in particular from the work of Howard Haycraft, Ellery Queen and the novelist and critic Anthony Boucher. Charles Daly King (1895–1963) was an American writer whose elaborate and idiosyncratic whodunits appealed even more to British readers than his fellow countrymen. Daly King, a psychologist whose other published work includes texts on psychology, coined the word 'obelist', and used it in three book titles. It is typical of his eccentricity that, having defined the word in *Obelists at Sea* (1932) as 'a person of little or no value', he then re-defined it in *Obelists en Route* (1934) as 'one who harbours suspicion'. The latter novel includes no fewer than seven diagrams, a 'cluefinder', and a 'bibliography of references'.

The towering figure among American Golden Age writers was Ellery Queen, a pseudonym used by Frederic Dannay and Manfred Lee
The influence of Daniel Nathan, alias Dannay (1905–82) and to a lesser extent Manford Emanuel Lepovsky, alias Lee, (1905–71) on the genre's development was long-lasting, especially in the United States. That influence was not confined to novels, and was enhanced by the success of Ellery Queen's Mystery Magazine, which flourishes to this day, as well as criticism and commentary relating to the genre.

Chesterton set it out in full in an article for The Strand.
See G. K. Chesterton, 'The Detection Club', *The Strand* (May 1933).

Since the Thirties, the ritual has been revised regularly
An account of changes to the ritual appears in Gavin Lyall, 'A Brief Historical Monograph on the Detection Club Initiation Ceremony' (unpublished; Detection Club archive).

9

The Fungus-Story
and the Meaning of Life

'Our worthy friend Harrison passed away this evening in excruciating agony,' Sayers announced gleefully on 11 January 1930.
She was breaking the news to an enigmatic collaborator about
a novel they were writing together, just as the Detection Club
came into existence. Their book became a landmark in detective fiction – but the pair never worked together again.

They became writing partners as a result of Sayers' work
on *Great Short Stories of Detection, Mystery and Horror*. To
highlight scientific and medical detection, she chose two stories
co-authored by Robert Eustace. 'The Face in the Dark' was an
innovative scientific detective story from the late 1890s; Eustace
had supplied technical expertise, with the writing undertaken
by the prolific Victorian, L. T. Meade (the pseudonym of an early
feminist, Elizabeth Thomasina Meade Smith). 'The Tea Leaf', a
Golden Age classic that Eustace co-wrote with Edgar Jepson,
was a locked room mystery. A man is stabbed in a Turkish bath,
but the weapon vanishes inexplicably.

Despite a career in crime fiction spanning more than forty
years, Robert Eustace was the most mysterious member of the
Detection Club. For decades after his death, students of the genre
speculated about his identity, his date of birth, and even his
sexual orientation. One wild theory suggested he was married

to Sayers. In fact, he was born in 1871, his real name was Robert Eustace Barton, and he was a doctor working at a mental hospital in Northampton. Sayers invited him to lunch, and they got along famously. Within a matter of weeks, he had inspired her to contemplate a detective novel more ambitious than, anything she had attempted so far. Given her long-standing interest in 'howdunit', she liked the idea of utilizing Eustace's scientific imagination to produce a novel of a new sort. She wanted to give Wimsey a rest, and create a detective with scientific expertise.

Eustace suggested a murder committed by adding poisonous muscarine to a meal containing otherwise harmless mushrooms. The difference between natural and artificially produced muscarine, he explained, was that the latter is optically inactive. They can be differentiated by using a polariscope, so if the presence of synthetically created muscarine can be shown, murder may be proved. This seized Sayers' imagination, especially when Eustace proposed that the story might explore 'the most fundamental problems of the phenomena of life itself'.

Sayers realized she must abandon her hostility to 'love interest', and that the story demanded a 'modern and powerful' relationship between the key characters. She quizzed Eustace about the medical aspects of the plots of Wilkie Collins' novels, and raised a question about arsenic as she mulled over the idea for the next Wimsey novel, *Strong Poison*. Although she had several projects in mind, she announced, 'This fungus-story must be the next thing I tackle.'

Soon she was ready to begin: 'I will . . . make suitable arrangements for the Villain to poison the mushrooms without

a) Poisoning himself

b) Being obviously unwilling to share the poisoned dish

c) *Being suspected of popping a genuine 'death cap' into the dish*

If possible the trap should poop off while the villain is away in Town, or something. By the way, I shall want to know:

1. What muscarine (artificial) looks like (whether clear or coloured, cloudy or transparent)
2. What is the fatal dose
3. *What it smells and tastes like. . . .*'

Their excitement grew rapidly. Eustace thought this 'the best idea of my life' and Sayers' mood was ecstatic: 'The sodium slaying scene sounds absolutely great!' She was afraid that, as in the initiation ritual, somebody else might anticipate the plot: 'I'm not breathing a word about it to anybody – hardly, even, to my husband – but these things seem to get "into the air", and it would be dreadful to be forestalled.'

Eustace researched the scientific means for solving the crime, while Sayers focused on character and story development. Eustace suggested the book might be called *The Death Cap*, but eventually they opted for *The Documents in the Case*. The pair signed a collaboration agreement, and their correspondence remained upbeat throughout 1929. In April, Sayers told Eustace that their American publisher was 'tremendously thrilled' by the idea of a detective story embodying 'the very latest scientific ideas'.

She pushed round to the press a news item about their joint project, to remind people of his track record as a writer of detective fiction. Her next brainwave was to propose 'publicity photographs of Miss Dorothy Sayers and her mysterious collaborator in the laboratory – you know, showing just the back of your head and your hands, with really fine melodramatic lighting effects'. Just such a picture was taken of the co-authors by a firm of theatrical photographers in Soho. The striking image typifies Sayers' flair for coming up with fresh angles to promote her books. She made sure that nobody outside her closest circle knew of her young son's existence, but when it came to developing a public profile, she was the most modern of the Detection Club's members.

Edith Thompson's doomed affair with Frederick Bywaters supplied the storyline, along with 'all the usual claptrap about their having been made and destined by heaven for one another'. Accustomed to hiding her own emotions, Sayers was scornful of people who lacked the same discipline. Anthony Berkeley had much more sympathy for Edith's love of fantasy and adulterous sex.

The murder method and its detection were Sayers' priorities. Her approach to story structure was influenced by the multiple viewpoints Wilkie Collins employed in *The Moonstone*. She composed fifty-three 'documents' in all, most of them letters. Pleased with what they had done, Eustace suggested further collaboration, but Sayers, still grieving for her parents, and worrying about how to make a good living after leaving Benson's, was becoming anxious: 'The story is turning out rather grim and sordid.'

The book was finished on 8 February, but Sayers usually found, as many authors do, that once she had finished a book, she went through a phase of self-doubt, because the execution had not lived up to her original concept. When she sent the manuscript to Eustace, she said that she felt she had failed: 'I wish I could have done better with the brilliant plot.'

The Documents in the Case was daring and original, and Sayers was too harsh on herself. Yet it is a flawed novel. By focusing on the ingenuity required to detect the murder method, she sacrificed verve, and the characterization did not live up to the potential of the storyline. She lacked sympathy for her version of Edith Thompson, the bored and frustrated Margaret Harrison, who yearns to sweep away 'the useless people' who 'get in the way of love and youth'.

The Book Guild named the book as detective story of the year. 'I'm famous!' Sayers whooped, and the prize money paid for her and Mac to take a trip on the *Mauretania*. But disaster struck when she heard from one of those knowledgeable readers whose correspondence writers dread. He claimed that the scientific solution did not work, and in a broadcast talk for the BBC, Sayers admitted to 'a first-class howler'. Her confession proved premature. Eustace's further researches led him to reassure her that the criticism was unfounded: 'very comforting after all the agonies and the criticisms we had'. Eustace was now a member of the Detection Club, but their proposed scientific detective character never materialized, and they never wrote together again.

Eustace was left to resume his infrequent collaboration with Edgar Jepson, who owed his place among the founder members of the Detection Club more to his clubbability than to his detective fiction, of which only 'The Tea Leaf' has stood the test of time. Jepson wrote thrillers and supernatural stories as well as mysteries, and was briefly an editor of *Vanity Fair*. His son Selwyn also became a crime writer, while his daughter Margaret, also a novelist, was mother of the writer Fay Weldon.

Sayers enjoyed editing anthologies for Victor Gollancz, and corresponded with dozens of authors, agents and publishers in her quest for stories of distinction. Milward Kennedy offered two stories which had won prizes in a *Manchester Guardian* competition when submitted under the improbable pseudonyms of E. Grubb and Gasko. Another unlikely pen name, Loel Yeo, concealed the identity of P. G. Wodehouse's stepdaughter Leonora. She wrote 'Inquest', a story so witty and original that it is sad she never published a crime novel prior to her tragic early death following a 'routine' operation.

To keep her readers happy, Sayers brought back Wimsey, but she decided his priorities needed to change, and in *Strong Poison*, he fell for Harriet Vane (whose surname might just have been a nod to Berkeley's *The Vane Mystery*). Their relationship suffered various setbacks, but developed over the next few years, setting a pattern for detective series that broke decisively with the past. Previously, detectives had not 'grown' in the course of a series, however long-running. Sherlock Holmes and Father Brown are much the same in their final appearance as in their first, because the stories shy away from their emotional lives. The same is true of Hercule Poirot, whose exaggerated characteristics scarcely varied over half a century. Sayers' decision to give new depth to Wimsey, and to set up a relationship with Harriet that was psychologically credible, paved the way for her successors to create series detectives who were much more than ciphers.

After an unhappy affair with the unworthy Philip Boyes, Harriet buys arsenic from a chemist's while researching for a book. Boyes duly dies of arsenic poisoning, and she is tried for murder. The outcome is a hung jury, and while she awaits a retrial, Wimsey rides to the rescue. The detective interest lies in working out howdunit rather than whodunit, but the real focus is on the relationship between Wimsey and Harriet. Sayers' technique for achieving realism was to draw on the experience of her own doomed affair with John Cournos – a cathartic but risky strategy which provoked Cournos to retaliate with his own barbed fictional version of their relationship. She was rapidly transforming the detective story into something more than a game between writer and reader. So, in a very different way, was Anthony Berkeley.

Notes to Chapter 9

'Our worthy friend Harrison passed away this evening in excruciating agony . . .'
This account of the collaboration between Sayers and Eustace is based on Sayers' letters, the chapter in Barbara Reynolds' biography about the writing of *The Documents in the Case*, and 'Proceedings of the 1983 Seminar' (Witham, Dorothy L. Sayers Society, 1983).

and even his sexual orientation
Trevor Hall's 'Dorothy L. Sayers and Robert Eustace' in *Dorothy L. Sayers: Nine Literary Studies* offers imaginative but questionable speculation about Eustace's sexual proclivities that is reminiscent of Roger Sheringham's less successful detective work. Professor Lars L. Bottiger's paper in the 'Proceedings of the 1983 Seminar' portrays Eustace as an 'open, charming and easy-going' man with a taste for gambling, drink and women, whose happiest days were spent in the army, but who found it difficult to adjust to peacetime. Eustace supplemented his income from medicine by writing, and was an eccentric whose dislikes ranged from seagulls to women wearing trousers. At the start of the Second World War, when age and drink were taking their toll, Eustace found 'a temporary job in the mental hospital in Cornwall, fitting the lunatics with gas masks'.

the improbable pseudonyms of E. Grubb and Gasko
Kennedy was so taken with the name E. Grubb that he gave it to a character in *Angel in the Case*, published under the pen name Evelyn Elder.

P. G. Wodehouse's stepdaughter Leonora
See Sophie Ratcliffe, 'P.G. Wodehouse: a Life in Letters', *The Guardian*, 4 November 2011. In marrying the twice-widowed actress and dancer Ethel Wayman, 'Wodehouse not only gained a wife. He also "inherited" her 11-year-old daughter Leonora. Wodehouse adored being a stepfather. . . . Leonora – or "Snorky" as she soon became – was far more precious to Wodehouse than any of his biological relations.' Her sudden death in 1944 was a crushing blow: 'I really feel that nothing matters much now.' Her widowed husband, Peter Cazalet, went on to train Devon Loch, the Queen Mother's

racehorse that mysteriously collapsed fifty yards short of winning the 1956 Grand National while being ridden by Dick Francis (later, like his son Felix, a member of the Detection Club).

10

Wistful Plans for Killing off Wives

Berkeley bought his very own country house, Linton Hills, in a remote part of north Devon, and promptly set a murder there. His detective stories were now as convoluted as his love life, but more successful. The acclaim which greeted *The Poisoned Chocolates Case* prompted him to bring Ambrose Chitterwick back in *The Piccadilly Murder*. At the Piccadilly Palace Hotel, Chitterwick witnesses a murder, and as a result of his evidence a Major Sinclair is arrested and charged with poisoning his wealthy aunt. But a group of people, including Major Sinclair's wife, try to persuade Chitterwick that all is not as it seems.

Chitterwick and Sheringham reflected exaggerated aspects of Berkeley's complex personality. Where Sheringham was outspoken and offensive, Chitterwick was meek and mild, yet surprisingly tenacious when the need arose. Like Berkeley, he was fascinated by criminology – and had issues with women. When, in *The Piccadilly Murder*, Judith Sinclair offers him her body in return for help in saving her husband from the gallows, he is terrified. Sigmund Freud enjoyed the mysteries of Christie and Sayers, but he seems not to have read Berkeley – a pity, since understanding Berkeley's psychology would have been a challenge even for him.

The Linton Hills house, renamed 'Minton Deeps', featured in *The Second Shot*, another Berkeley novel which expanded a short story, this time 'Perfect Alibi'. In finest Golden Age

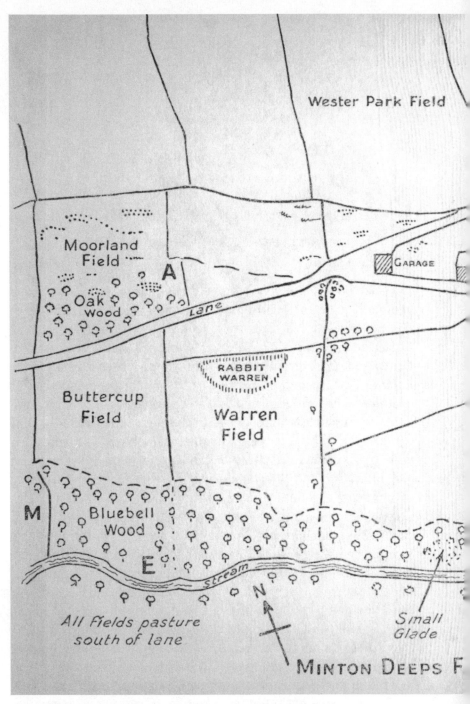

The endpapers for Anthony Berkeley's *The Second Shot*, showing
Minton Deeps, and 'supposed positions' of the prime suspects.

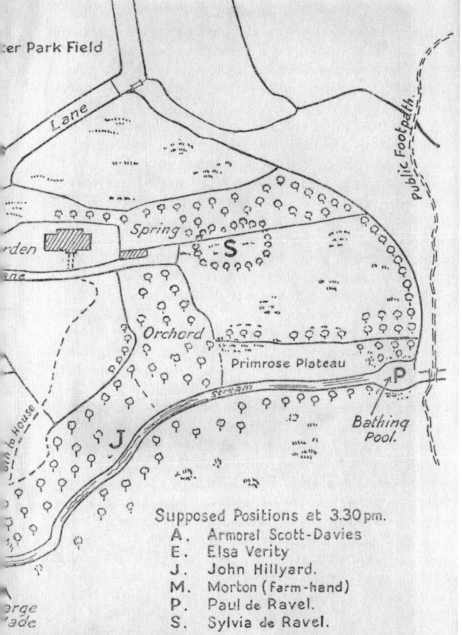

er Park Field

Lane

Spring

S

rden

ne

Orchard

Primrose Plateau

P

Stream

Bathing Pool.

J

to House

rge
ade

Supposed Positions at 3.30 pm.
A. Armorel Scott-Davies
E. Elsa Verity
J. John Hillyard.
M. Morton (farm-hand)
P. Paul de Ravel.
S. Sylvia de Ravel.

: 8ᵀᴴ June, 1930.

tradition, the book included an elaborate map of the estate on the endpapers, showing the positions of the main suspects at a critical time on the afternoon of the murder. But Berkeley recognized that the conventional country house murder story was becoming played out.

His fresh twist was an idea which Christie later adapted for *Towards Zero*, namely that, although detective stories typically begin with the discovery of a murder, events preceding the crime are key to the process of detection. Roger Sheringham – fallible as ever – distracts the police into believing that the victim suffered an accidental death, when really the case involves a 'justifiable homicide'. Murder motivated by good intentions became a recurrent theme in detective fiction in the Thirties. But the real significance of *The Second Shot* is that it shows Berkeley beginning to focus on the point of view of the criminal, rather than the detective.

In November 1930, he and Sayers exchanged their latest novels, and he inscribed her copy of *The Second Shot*: 'Take ye in one another's washing.' He shared her ambitions for the genre. In a prefatory note to *The Second Shot* he argued: 'The days of the old crime puzzle pure and simple, relying entirely upon plot, and without any added attractions of character, style, or even humour, are, if not numbered, at any rate in the hands of the auditors. . . . The detective story is already in process of developing into the novel with a detective or a crime interest, holding its readers less by mathematical than by psychological ties. . . . It will become a puzzle of character rather than the puzzle of time, place, motive and opportunity. . . . There is a complication of emotion, drama, psychology and adventure behind the most ordinary murder in real life, the possibilities of which for fictional purposes the conventional detective story misses completely.'

These far-sighted remarks hint at an astonishingly personal puzzle of character. He addressed his remarks to the dedicatee of *The Second Shot*, his agent A. D. Peters. He had included a Doctor Peters in a story about wife-seduction, 'Unsound Mind', and, still unable to drive the name out of his head, gave it to a detective in 'The Mystery of Horne's Corpse', a 'vanishing body' puzzle about a corpse that keeps disappearing from the apparent scene of the crime. These clues suggest his fascination with Peters' wife, Helen. And the mishaps of marriage coupled with dangerous desires prompted him to write his masterpiece.

With *Malice Aforethought*, Berkeley slipped into a fresh identity as smoothly as a fictional villain adopting a disguise. He amused himself by borrowing the name of that old family black sheep, his smuggler ancestor Francis Iles, and keeping his authorship a secret. *Malice Aforethought* was a stunning breakthrough. The novel focuses throughout on the perspective of the criminal, not the detective. The tone is set in the famous opening paragraph: 'It was not until several weeks after he had decided to murder his wife that Dr Bickleigh took active steps in the matter. Murder is a serious business. The slightest step may be disastrous. Dr Bickleigh had no intention of risking disaster.'

Meek, seemingly insignificant men who reveal unexpected personal qualities – good and bad – under pressure are staples of Berkeley's fiction. Dr Bickleigh is a striking example. Henpecked by his unlovely older wife Julia, Bickleigh suffers from an inferiority complex, which he fails to cure through a combination of an active and entertainingly described fantasy life and a series of affairs. The Devon village where gossip is a way of life is described with satiric glee. Berkeley charts the doctor's self-deceptions with ironic precision: 'From what he had seen of marriage he did not doubt that most married men spend no small part of their lives devising wistful plans for killing off their wives – if only they had the courage to do it.'

Bickleigh reads Thomas de Quincey, and concludes, 'Murder could be a fine art: but it was not for everyone. Murder was a fine art for the superman. It was a pity that Nietzsche could not have developed de Quincey's propositions. Dr Bickleigh had no doubt whatever that in murder he had qualified, not only as a fine artist, but as a superman.' When the doctor becomes infatuated with an attractive but neurotic and unreliable heiress, he resolves to do away with Julia. Bickleigh's perspective on his changing fortunes during his trial for murder is as naïve as ever, and paves the way for a bitterly ironic ending.

Reflecting Berkeley's jaundiced world view, *Malice Afore-thought* was crammed with unsympathetic characters. As a result Bickleigh, for all his failings, is someone the reader roots for – while fearing for him. The finale sees a miscarriage of justice perpetrated by a legal system whose crude and clumsy workings Berkeley despised. But he could not resist playing jokey games. During Bickleigh's trial, an expert named Clerihew makes a fleeting appearance. The character was named in honour of E. C. Bentley, and soon Detection Club members were including references to each other, or their detectives, in their novels as a matter of course.

All three novels written under the Francis Iles name draw heavily on Berkeley's personal life. So Bickleigh not only has a name sounding much the same as Berkeley, but is the same age as his creator, suffers from an inferiority complex, and is an incurable womanizer and fantasist. Berkeley dedicated the book to Margaret, and since it tells the story of a man who is planning to kill his wife, the compliment could hardly have been more barbed. Although the reader is invited to identify with Bickleigh, there is a shocking side to his nature quite apart from his willingness to commit murder. When a whiny former lover, Ivy Ridgeway, makes a nuisance of herself, he hits her in the face, and reacts to what he has done 'with mixed emotion; half of it was disgust, and half of it a queer, shouting exultation'.

Berkeley seems aware here, as in his other books, that his attitudes towards women were deeply unhealthy. Was he using detective fiction as a substitute for a psychiatrist's couch? Wrestling with his own confused feelings, he wrote: 'The normal man's attitude towards women is far, far more compli-cated than those women ever suppose, or than theirs towards him – interlaced with totally conflicting likes and dislikes, self-contradictory, altogether much more illogical and irrational than anything of the kind he has ever deplored in the women themselves.'

Berkeley did not let any of this slow down the story, and

'Francis Iles' became an overnight sensation. Critics marvelled at the cleverness and wit of *Malice Aforethought*, with *The English Review* raving that the book was 'possibly the best shocker ever written. It is psychologically extraordinarily good; it is the work of a born novelist; it is humorous and witty as well as tragic.' But not everyone was ready for such daring crime stories. Berkeley believed firmly in distinguishing between detective fiction, thrillers and novels of psychological interest, and deplored the general term 'mystery'. Almost twenty-five years after the second Iles book, *Before the Fact*, he lamented that it had been 'killed stone dead' in the US because it was marketed as a 'detective story', and so disappointed those who simply wanted a well-clued whodunit.

Young, good-looking and sexually adventurous women like the supposed murderers Florence Maybrick and Edith Thompson exerted an irresistible attraction for Berkeley. He also displayed a disturbing empathy with apparently respectable middle-class Englishmen who commit murder. The inspiration for Dr Bickleigh's crimes in *Malice Aforethought* came from the misadventures of Major Herbert Rowse Armstrong, a solicitor, church warden and freemason best known as the Hay-on-Wye Poisoner.

'Excuse fingers,' Armstrong said, handing a buttered scone laced with arsenic to a fellow solicitor called Oswald Martin. He had invited Martin for afternoon tea at Mayfield, his home in Hay. This legendary occasion captures perfectly the genteel nature of the kind of murder for which the Golden Age is famous.

Martin became violently sick after the tea party. His father-in-law, a local chemist, already had suspicions of Armstrong, because he bought arsenic in such large quantities. When tests on Martin's urine revealed the presence of arsenic, the police were called in. While they carried out their investigations, Armstrong made repeated, and increasingly frantic, attempts to invite Martin and his wife back for another tea party. Like actors in a black comedy, the Martins found themselves resorting to ever more desperate reasons for their refusal.

Armstrong was arrested in his office on New Year's Eve 1921. In his pocket was a pack of arsenic. After more arsenic was discovered at Mayfield, the body of his wife Katharine was exhumed. She had died the previous year, apparently of gastritis, but Bernard Spilsbury, the pathologist in the Crippen case, was called in to conduct a post-mortem. Her remains were in a relatively good state of preservation – due to the mummifying effects of arsenic. Armstrong was duly charged with her murder. He had been irritated by her nagging and domineering personality, and wanted the freedom to pursue his interest in other women, but at the time of her death nobody suspected foul play. Soon after that, he had found himself on the opposite side from Martin in a legal dispute. The Martins had received a box of chocolates from an anonymous well-wisher, which were later found to contain arsenic.

At his trial, Armstrong said he kept arsenic to kill off dandelions growing in the garden of Mayfield. His counsel suggested that Katharine was a hypochondriac who had dosed herself with arsenic either by mistake or intending suicide. But the prosecution called Spilsbury, whose implacably definite way with evidence in court spelled disaster for the accused. Spilsbury testified that the amount of arsenic found in Mrs Armstrong's remains could only have resulted from poisoning. The judge's summing-up extolled Spilsbury's impartiality, and Armstrong was found guilty. He remains the only English solicitor to have died on the scaffold. True to type, he was wearing his best tweed suit.

The mystery of the identity of Francis Iles kept everyone guessing. Berkeley may have hated self-promotion, but his insistence upon anonymity proved a masterstroke, cleverly exploited by his new publisher. Victor Gollancz sparked a long-running debate by indicating that the pseudonym masked the identity of a well-known writer. So successfully was the secret kept that Berkeley's authorship was still unknown when *Before the Fact* was published a year later. Gollancz seized his chance with gusto. '*Who is Iles?*' demanded the dust jacket, which listed twenty candidates put forward in 'the public prints'.

Literary detectives proposed solutions to the riddle ranging from the plausible to the crazy. Names put forward included such diverse writers as Hugh Walpole, E. M. Forster, Aldous Huxley, Edgar Wallace, and H. G. Wells. Some suspected that the author was a woman, suggesting Marie Belloc Lowndes, F. Tennyson Jesse, Stella Benson, Rose Macaulay – and E. M. Delafield. Trying her hand at a literary form of psychological profiling, Naomi Royde-Smith argued that the author could not be a woman, in view of the relentlessly cynical portrayal of the female characters. A clue in the text was the author's familiarity with rural Devon. Berkeley had bought a country house there, Linton Hills, the previous year. None of the sleuths, however, discovered the biggest giveaway of Francis Iles' identity: similarities between an obscure story signed by A. B. Cox, 'Over the Telephone' and *Malice Aforethought* made it obvious both were written by the same man.

Berkeley revelled in the speculation. In his cuttings book, he kept a record of all the mistaken guesses. However, he cringed at a suggestion by New York critic Alexander Woollcott that his rough drafts had been polished up by his friend Delafield. The jibe prompted Berkeley to take a pot shot at Woollcott in *Panic Party*. Even after that the hurt lingered, and Berkeley made a wounded reference to Woollcott when dedicating *As for the Woman* to Delafield.

Reflecting the level of interest in the puzzle of Francis Iles' identity, two contemporary novels joked about it. In *X v Rex*, a thriller about a serial murderer of policemen, written under the pen name of Martin Porlock, Philip MacDonald amused himself by having Gollancz deny that Francis Iles was in reality Porlock. In *The Provincial Lady Goes Further*, Delafield included a scene in which she is assured by a fellow party guest 'that Mr Francis Iles is really Mr Aldous Huxley. She happens to know. Am much impressed . . . but am disconcerted by unknown gentleman who tells me . . . he happens to know that Francis Iles is really Miss Edith Sitwell.'

There was a hidden edge to this joke. Given their closeness, Berkeley must have confided the truth to Delafield, and she was teasing him with the crack about Sitwell, an odd and famously unattractive woman whose poetry Berkeley no doubt detested. Hardly anyone else was in on the secret, not even his colleagues in the Detection Club. The success of the Iles puzzle prompted Gollancz's old firm, Ernest Benn, to offer a prize of ten pounds for the first person to guess the identity of the successful novelist who published *Murder at School* under the pseudonym Glen Trevor. Keeping a secret was easier then than it is today. When J. K. Rowling, a long-time fan of Sayers and Margery Allingham, published a pseudonymous detective novel in 2013, elaborate precautions failed to prevent the truth about her identity leaking out within weeks. But two years passed before the public learned that Anthony Berkeley and Francis Iles were one and the same.

The next two Anthony Berkeley books, *Top Storey Murder* and *Murder in the Basement*, saw the return of Roger Sheringham and Chief Inspector Moresby. In the former, Sheringham is again too clever for his own good, coming up with an ingenious explanation when the truth proves simple and anti-climactic. One of the suspects is an Australian novelist, Evadne Delamere, a blend of Helen Simpson and Delafield.

Murder in the Basement begins and ends with a police procedural story, but includes an incomplete novel written by Roger. A woman's body is later found in the cellar of a suburban house, and she is traced to a prep school, but her identity is not revealed. Roger's manuscript, set in the recent past, describes mounting tensions in the school where, improbably, he had provided cover for a sick teacher friend, and where several female characters are potential murderees. Back in the present, Moresby tells him which of the women has been killed.

'Whowasdunin?' was a new question for puzzle addicts. An unidentified corpse is often found in crime novels, but here the challenge was to deduce which person, out of a number of possible candidates, was the victim. For good measure, Berkeley came up with a traditional 'whodunit' twist, and a murder motive, sexual repression, that was daring for the early Thirties.

In a further refusal to conform to genre conventions, Roger is persuaded not to tell the police what he has discovered, and once again justice goes begging.

The idea of putting a mystery about the identity of a murder victim at the heart of a novel was borrowed by Raymond Postgate for *Verdict of Twelve*, and by the Americans Anita Boutell and Patricia McGerr on either side of the Second World War. Whowasdunins remain uncommon, but in 2013 Mark Lawson's *The Deaths* adopted the form for a novel satirising a 'closed circle' of four rich couples in the aftermath of the near-collapse of the banking system in the twenty-first century. Once again, Berkeley's influence was long-lasting.

As well as writing at a furious pace, Berkeley seized the moment with Helen Peters. Helen's husband had built an agency with a glittering list of clients including the actor and writer Frank Vosper, Henry Wade and E. M. Delafield. A tough nego-tiator, Peters had several run-ins with Victor Gollancz, whose attitude towards authors was rather like Hitchcock's attitude towards actors.

Peters' eye roved as much as Berkeley's. Having met a woman who became the second of his three wives, he left Helen in the spring of 1932. Helen had two young children on her hands, but she and Berkeley became romantically involved, and he sought a divorce from Margaret. Although it took time for the Peters' divorce to be made final, Berkeley set up home with Helen at Linton Hills. He liked to spend his summers in the countryside, returning to London for the winter.

Berkeley may be the only crime novelist in history to have married his literary agent's former wife. With anyone else, this would spell career suicide, but Peters felt relieved that Helen had found someone else. Outwardly, at least, the two men's relations remained civilised. Berkeley's career remained on an upward curve. His effrontery was as breathtaking in life as in fiction. He was the sort of man who could get away with murder.

After the success of *Malice Aforethought*, Berkeley was itching to resume his work as Francis Iles. When he did so, he based his novel on an astonishingly bold premise, and amused himself (if not the new woman in his life) by dedicating this latest novel of wife-murder to Helen.

Before the Fact recounts the fate of a born victim. As with *Malice Aforethought*, the book dazzles from the opening paragraph: 'Some women give birth to murderers, some go to bed with them, and some marry them. Lina Aysgarth had lived with her husband nearly eight years before she realized that she was married to a murderer.'

Lina Aysgarth ought to be far more appealing than Dr Bickleigh. She suffers, whereas he inflicts suffering. The snag is that her reluctance to face up to unpalatable facts, and then to save herself, is maddening. She is swept off her feet by the amiable but selfish Johnnie Aysgarth, and, although appalled by each fresh example of his ruthless self-indulgence, she turns a blind eye to forgery, infidelity and ultimately murder. At one point, he conducts a rehearsal of a proposed murder. Agatha Christie soon took the same idea a step further in a clever whodunit of her own, in which an apparently inexplicable crime turns out to have been committed by an actor – who else? – as a rehearsal for another killing.

For all her intelligence, Lina is breathtakingly naïve, with an inferiority complex to rival those of Chitterwick and Bickleigh. Beneath a quiet exterior runs a streak of masochism, evident not only in her devotion to Johnnie but also during her brief separation from her husband. She flees to her sister, who lives (as Berkeley did, when in town) in Hamilton Terrace in St John's Wood, and is introduced to Ronald Kirby, with whom she has an unconsummated fling. Berkeley indulges a favourite interest when he has Lina provoke Kirby into spanking her, an experience which causes her to exult: 'That's the *stuff*!'

The Aysgarths live in a house called Dellfield – yet another nod to Delafield. Did elements of Lina's personality reflect Berkeley's frustration about Delafield's commitment to an unsatisfactory marriage with an unworthy man? As in *Malice Aforethought*, there are tennis parties and dismal social gatherings of people who do not like each other much, mirroring Berkeley's view of

Devon life: 'For one who takes pleasure in despising his neighbour more than himself, the English countryside of this decade offers exceptional opportunities.'

Sayers makes a delightful guest appearance in the book. She is thinly disguised as Isobel Sedbusk, whom Lina's sister Joyce describes as 'not nearly so formidable as she looks. In fact, she's a very good sort. No nonsense. And intelligent; but keep off religion.' Berkeley had learned from experience to keep off religion when talking with Sayers over dinner at the Detection Club. But he enjoyed her company, and was amused by her assertiveness, as well as her dress sense: Sedbusk 'boasted of weighing fifteen stone, and boomed in proportion. . . . She was inclined to talk a little too much about her own line of work, and liked showing her familiarity with the tools of her trade, such as blood and *rigor mortis*: but she was amusing and had plenty of other interests as well. In spite of the fact that she wore black sombreros and had a masculine cut about her clothes, she was an ardent feminist.'

Sedbusk shares Sayers' interest in unusual methods of committing murder. She chats cheerfully about 'live electric wires inside the springs of an easy chair', and Lina learns from her that Johnnie adapted a murder method used in real life by a Victorian doctor called William Palmer. Sedbusk also unwittingly reveals to Johnnie an undetectable means by which he can kill Lina. This never-revealed method was an invention, calculated to irritate traditionalists, but Berkeley did not care about scientific accuracy. He was focusing on the psychological make-up of a sociopath and his victim.

Upper-middle-class characters at leisure in rural England might dominate the story, but there is nothing cosy about *Before the Fact*. The final scene is daring and unique. Berkeley contrives one of the most shocking climaxes to any British crime novel of any era. What is even more extraordinary is that it had its origins in real life.

'When will it all end?' asked Annie Palmer, after a series of mysterious deaths in the small Staffordshire town of Rugeley, where her husband William practised medicine. The answer was that Dr Palmer would be executed on 14 June 1856 in front of a crowd of thirty thousand people. Unfortunately, Annie too was dead by then, and so were four of their children.

The first member of Palmer's circle to die was a man called Abley, whose wife was rumoured to be having an affair with the doctor. Abley met his end in 1846, after sharing a drink of brandy with Palmer at the local infirmary. The doctor then married Annie Palmer, and her mother was next to go. The former mistress of a wealthy colonel, she had inherited his fortune when he committed suicide, but died while visiting the Palmers. An obliging local doctor called Bamford certified the cause of death as 'apoplexy'. A bookmaker to whom Palmer owed a handsome sum also died after coming to stay with the Palmers, and the cash he was carrying and his betting book, which recorded Palmers' losses, went missing.

Four of Palmer's five children by Annie (he was also said to have fourteen illegitimate children from his days as a medical student) died in infancy from 'convulsions', although a story later circulated that they had licked honey from their father's fingers. They were followed to the grave by one of his creditors, and an uncle whom he challenged to a brandy-drinking contest. Annie surely feared the worst when her husband took out an insurance policy worth £13,000 on her life. Yet she seemed incapable of doing anything to save herself in the face of over-whelming circumstantial evidence that she was married to a man who, for all his amiability and regular church-going, was extremely dangerous to know. She died not long after he paid the first premium.

'My poorest dear Annie expired at ten minutes past one,' Palmer recorded in his diary, adding, 'She was called by God to the house of bliss she so well deserves.' Any distress he felt did not prevent him from proceeding to have sex with their housemaid, who soon became pregnant. According to the ever-helpful Dr Bamford, Annie died from 'English cholera'. Palmer's alcoholic brother Walter, whom he plied relentlessly with gin and brandy, was no more fortunate. This time, the insurance company carried out an investigation, and a boot boy told them that he had seen Palmer pouring something into Walter's glass. A further setback was that Walter's wife made a claim on the insurance policy.

After a race meeting at Shrewsbury, Palmer went for a celebratory drink with a horse-owner called John Parsons Cook, who had just won more than two thousand pounds. On downing a brandy, Cook cried, 'Good God, there's something in that which burns my throat!' Palmer ministered to him, naturally to no avail, and Cook died eight days later. By that time Palmer had already forged a cheque to draw on Cook's account, as well as a document purporting to show that Cook owed him £3,500. He had also secured another death certificate from Dr Bamford, now eighty years old, stating the cause of death as 'apoplexy'. Palmer attended the post-mortem, and tried to take away the jar containing the stomach, saying, 'I thought it more convenient.'

He did not stop there, intercepting the post-mortem report, and attempting to win the local coroner's goodwill with gifts of a twenty-pound turkey, a brace of pheasants, a barrel of oysters and a cod. But Professor Alfred Swaine Taylor, the leading toxicologist of the day, found traces of antimony in Cook's remains. Annie's body was exhumed, and once again antimony was found. Palmer was charged with murder, but because local feeling against him was running high, special legislation was passed to enable him to be tried at the Old Bailey. The evidence against him was circumstantial, and his denial of guilt sufficiently plausible to persuade his barrister to express a personal, if unprofessional, belief in his client's innocence. None of this made any difference to the verdict, but Palmer's composure did not falter. Legend has it that, standing on the scaffold, he looked at the trapdoor, and said, 'Are you sure it's safe?'

Annie Palmer's refusal to face reality made a superb subject for a novelist obsessed with the psychology of killers and victims. Lina Aysgarth represents Berkeley's attempt to get inside Annie's mind, but his portrayal is flawed. When Lina becomes pregnant, she concludes that 'at all costs Johnnie must not be allowed to reproduce himself'. Yet Berkeley, whose wives never bore him children, fails to answer a crucial question that would surely preoccupy a woman writer, or a man more instinctively empathetic with women – why Lina does not do more to protect her unborn baby.

Before the Fact repeated the success of *Malice Aforethought,* although Berkeley was acutely self-critical. Six years after publication, he wrote that there were several real-life cases in which a wife must have known that her husband was poisoning or intended to poison her, and yet did nothing to save herself: 'My aim was to explore this curious twist of female psychology and try to make it clear how such a thing can happen.' He felt he had underplayed the way Lina's bossy manner concealed an 'instinctive submissiveness'. He thought her exasperating because she was always on the lookout for slights, never answering a question actually asked but rather responding to some implied criticism which she thought lay behind it. He concluded his mistake had been to tone down Lina's awfulness in order to keep the reader's sympathy for her. In later books, he took the opposite approach. Increasingly, his female protagonists came to resemble monsters.

In 1941, Hitchcock filmed *Before the Fact* as *Suspicion,* with Cary Grant miscast as Johnnie. Not even the Master of Suspense could match Berkeley's sheer nerve, and the ending of the film reversed that of the book, a change which Hitchcock later sought to blame on the studio. Berkeley told a correspondent that Hitchcock had never shared with him an idea of casting Alec Guinness as Dr Bickleigh in *Malice Aforethought* – 'but then he wouldn't. Authors do not exist for Mr Hitchcock, except as some low form of insect life to spin plots and characters like silkworms, for him to muck about.'

So infuriated was Berkeley with the mess that Hitchcock made of *Suspicion* that for the first Iles book he 'stepped up the price high enough to discourage him'. He was rich enough, and pig-headed enough, to refuse to allow the director to have his way. Yet if Berkeley and Hitchcock had made the effort to get to know each other, they would have found they had more in common than they realized. Two complicated and often unhappy men, they risked allowing their fascination with women to be soured by sadistic fantasies.

Notes to Chapter 10

Malice Aforethought *was a stunning breakthrough.*
For all its originality, some aspects of the plot are reminiscent of C.
S. Forester's *Payment Deferred* (1926). This bleak and brilliant novel
tells the story of William Marble, who murders a rich nephew for
gain, only to receive his just deserts at the end in a savage twist
similar to Berkeley's. *Plain Murder* (1930) repeated the formula, with
the background of an advertising agency, a setting Sayers used three
years later. Forester was the pen name of Cecil Louis Troughton Smith
(1899–1966). The manuscript of his third crime novel, *The Pursued*,
was lost, and the book did not achieve publication until 2011; some
events in the story are reminiscent of the Crippen case. Forester
turned away from crime fiction, and became celebrated for his adventure stories, including the naval series featuring Horatio Hornblower.

A handful of ambitious 'studies in murder' were produced by
authors outside the Detection Club, such as Joanna Cannan's *No
Walls of Jasper* (1930) and Lynn Brock's untypical yet oddly compelling *Nightmare* (1932). Brock was a pseudonym for the Irish novelist
and playwright Alister McAllister (1877–1943), whose convoluted
whodunits featuring Colonel Warwick Gore were admired by T. S.
Eliot. Cannan (1898–1961) wrote several detective novels, but is
remembered mainly for writing pony stories for children. An even
earlier example, often overlooked, is *The House by the River* (1921)
by A.P. Herbert, which was filmed by Fritz Lang in 1950. Herbert
(1890–1971) did not pursue his early interest in crime writing, but
earned fame (and a knighthood) as a playwright, novelist, and advocate of law reform; he was also one of the more talented humorists
to spend time as a Member of Parliament.

the successful novelist who published Murder at School *under the
pseudonym Glen Trevor*
This was James Hilton (1900–1954), who achieved fame and fortune
with novels such as *Lost Horizon*, *We Are Not Alone*, *Random
Harvest*, and *Goodbye, Mr Chips*, all of which were filmed. The
quality of his solitary detective novel and his few crime short stories
make it regrettable that he abandoned the genre.

*When J. K. Rowling . . . published a pseudonymous detective novel
The Cuckoo's Calling* (2013), published as by Robert Galbraith.

Two years passed before the public learned that Anthony Berkeley and Francis Iles were one and the same
The identities lurking behind less celebrated pseudonyms sometimes remained unknown for decades. The fact that Miles Burton was a pen-name of Cecil John Street did not become widely known for forty years, while Cecil Waye was only revealed as another of his aliases in the twenty-first century.

'Whowasdunin?' was a new question for puzzle addicts
See Martin Edwards, 'Whowasdunin?' in *The Oxford Companion to Crime and Mystery Writing*.

She chats cheerfully about 'live electric wires inside the springs of an easy chair'
See Tony Medawar, 'Plotting a Detective Story – Dorothy L. Sayers and Anthony Berkeley', *CADS* 51, April 2007.

Critics marvelled at the cleverness and wit of Malice Aforethought, *with The English Review raving that the book was 'possibly the best shocker ever written . . .'*
Berkeley deplored Gollancz's description of one of the Iles novels as a 'shocker', which he felt halved his sales. See Francis Iles, 'When is a Thriller not a Thriller?', *The Crime Writer*, vol. i, no. 2, Summer 1954. This publication was the newsletter of the Crime Writers' Association, founded by John Creasey on 5 November 1953. Unlike the Detection Club, the CWA has never elected members by secret ballot. Berkeley said that Gollancz 'was handsome enough to admit later that he had been wrong, but the damage had been done'. Evidently the hurt lingered.

11

The Least Likely Person

For Agatha Christie, the urge to explore real-life crimes was a natural outgrowth of dinner table discussions *chez* Berkeley. In 1929, she was prompted to write an article for the *Sunday Chronicle* about a recent series of mysterious poisonings in Croydon which became one of her favourite cases, a lifelong source of fascination. The Croydon mystery was also crawled over by such diverse investigators as Edgar Wallace, R. Austin Freeman, and former Inspector Walter Dew, 'the man who caught Crippen', but to this day it remains officially unsolved.

'Something has gone wrong with my throat. I can't speak. I can't breathe.' These were the last words of Edmund Duff to his wife Grace at their suburban villa in Croydon, on 27 April 1928. Edmund, a retired colonial civil servant, was fifty-nine years old and Grace seventeen years his junior. Edmund had been taken ill following a fishing trip, and after eating supper he complained of leg cramps and nausea. Grace called in the family doctor, Dr Elwell, who thought there was no cause for alarm, but twenty-four hours later Edmund was dead. At the inquest, a pathologist said, 'One can quite exclude the possibility of poisoning,' and a verdict of death by natural causes was recorded. The coroner sympathized with the tearful widow, who portrayed her married life as idyllic.

Ten months later, Grace's unmarried sister Vera Sidney said she felt 'seedy' after lunch. Her mother Violet, and the cook, and

the family cat also became unwell, but Vera's condition deterio-
rated, and she died a couple of days later. The doctor attributed
her death to 'gastric influenza'. Less than three weeks later,
Violet Sidney also fell ill after eating her lunch, and blamed the
'gritty tonic' prescribed by her doctor as a pick-me-up following
her bereavement. She died within hours.

This disastrous series of events provoked suspicion, and
the police decided to look into what had happened. When the
bodies of Violet and Vera were exhumed, analysis revealed traces
of arsenic. Subsequently, despite Grace's protests, Edmund's
remains were also exhumed, and again arsenic was found. Three
separate inquests were held over a period of five months, com-
plicating the search for the truth. Verdicts of murder by person
or persons unknown were reached in relation to Edmund and
Vera, but there was insufficient evidence to prove that Violet had
been murdered.

The Sidney and Duff family circle supplied several potential
culprits, but nobody was charged with the crimes, and Christie
took care not to invite a libel claim by making any allegations.
She wondered if the murderer was driven simply by a lust for
killing, but thought it likelier that a personal and domestic
motive lurked beneath the contented façade of suburban life.
The Croydon mystery had many possible interpretations, and
she borrowed elements from the case for three of her novels.
Above all, she sympathized with the innocent, whose lives were
ruined by the sins of someone else. Remembering her own
trauma, she spoke with feeling about the nightmarish existence
of people who come into the public eye through no fault of their
own, and who find their friends look at them wonderingly, and
who become targets for autograph hunters and 'curious idle
crowds'.

At one point, Grace's brother Tom was the prime suspect,
because he possessed a quantity of arsenical weed-killer. He
emigrated to the United States, and never saw his sister again.
Much later, he said he thought her dangerous. The likelihood is
that Grace was the secret poisoner. One theory is that she murdered her husband because she had fallen for Dr Elwell, and

killed her sister and mother for money. She left Croydon after
the deaths, supposedly to make a new life in Australia. In fact,
she ran a boarding house on the English south coast for many
years, her guests suffering no known ill-effects, and she lived
until her eighty-seventh year.

Late in her life, the noted criminologist Richard Whittington-
Egan turned up on Grace's doorstep. He accused her of having
committed the murders, but promised not to publish his theory
until she was dead. With the menacing confidence of a born
survivor, she retorted by pointing out that he might die before
her, but he lived to tell the tale.

Christie was as intrigued by real life murders as Berkeley,
but her private fantasies were very different from his. While
he tortured himself with dreams of an unattainable woman,
Christie's idea of heaven was a trip on board the legendary
Simplon-Orient Express. The steam train represented the last
word in luxury. Even the list of stops *en route* sounded irresistibly romantic: London–Paris–Lausanne–Milan–Venice–Trieste–
Zagreb–Venice–Sofia–Stamboul. And then on, by the Taurus
Express, to Aleppo and Beirut. For Christie, a ticket for the train
was a passport to freedom.

Train travel offered surprise, excitement, and mystery.
Impossible to predict who one's companions might be, those
people with whom one would be thrown together for a few
short days and then never meet again. The Orient Express
brought together people from widely diverging backgrounds.
The compartments of one of its coaches might become a closed-
off world, where anything might happen. Even murder.

Christie loved to discover new places, and new people. For
all her shyness, she appreciated good company. This was why
the Detection Club meant so much to her. What she hated was
occupying centre stage. Archie's betrayal and the disaster of her
disappearance made her wary of strangers, and in the immediate aftermath of divorce, she felt lonely.

Meeting fellow detective novelists lifted her spirits, and she
rediscovered her zest for writing, and for life. Travel offered

escape from harrowing memories. Two years after her disappearance, with Rosalind away at school, she decided to take a
break abroad. She bought tickets for a trip to the West Indies,
but a conversation over dinner led to a last-minute change of
plan. A couple she met had just returned from Baghdad, and
their vivid holiday memories captivated her. They rhapsodized about the joy of travelling there by train rather than sea.
Entranced by the prospect of taking the Orient Express to visit
the cradle of civilization, Christie rushed off to Thomas Cook's
office to change her tickets. She wanted to see for herself the
archaeological excavations at Ur.

The prospect of discovering the secrets of the Middle East at
first hand was irresistible. As a form of detective work, archaeology was in vogue. Five years earlier, Lord Carnarvon's long-
running excavations in Egypt's Valley of the Kings had resulted
in Howard Carter opening a sealed door leading to a burial
chamber. Venturing inside, he set eyes on the sarcophagus of
the Boy King, Tutankhamun. The discovery caused a sensation,
and Ancient Egypt became the height of fashion. Hieroglyphic
embroideries taken from the walls of the tomb featured in dress
designs, while garish scarabs were sought-after accessories
which played a part in novels as diverse as Sayers' *Murder Must
Advertise* and Walpole's *The Killer and the Slain*. Carnarvon's
sudden death, soon after the tomb was opened, fuelled talk of
'the Mummy's Curse'.

Christie had been quick to jump on the bandwagon with a
Poirot story, 'The Adventure of the Egyptian Tomb', and she later
mined her knowledge of Ancient Egypt for a ground-breaking
historical detective novel, *Death Comes as the End*. Now her
priority was to visit Mesopotamia, as Leonard Woolley's claim
to have identified the site of the Biblical Flood was all over the
news. She intended to travel on her own, believing she had
become too dependent on other people – Archie, her secretary
Carlo Fisher, her agent Edmund Cork. Her aim was to find out
what sort of person she really was.

The Orient Express took her from Calais to Istanbul. She
crossed the Bosphorus and, after a short stay in Damascus,

reached Baghdad and found herself in what she called 'Memsahib Land'. She was no colonialist, not a woman who wanted to spend her time in idle gossip, treating the British-governed city as an outpost of London. Taking a letter of introduction, she headed off for the excavations at Ur.

Before the First World War, Leonard Woolley had worked with T. E. Lawrence in Syria and Egypt. His work made it possible for scholars to trace the history of Ur from its beginnings in 4000 BC. Woolley's wife Katharine had recently enjoyed *The Murder of Roger Ackroyd*, and the couple went out of their way to make Christie welcome. For her part, she relished being treated as a writer of note and honoured guest, rather than merely Archie's wife.

Katharine Woolley was beautiful, controlling, and volatile. Her first husband had shot himself at the foot of the Great Pyramid shortly after their honeymoon – possibly a reaction to being told that she did not intend to consummate their marriage. She preferred the company of men to women, but the men were required to look, not touch. Her mood swings were frequent and extreme. One minute, she was offensive and insolent, the next irresistibly delightful. Christie, an obsessive people-watcher, suspected Katharine could also be dangerous. Fortunately, Katharine concluded that the quiet, pleasant novelist represented no threat to her status as Queen of the Dig, and Christie got on so well with the Woolleys that they invited her to come back again as soon as she could.

After returning to England in time for Christmas with Rosalind, Christie delivered the manuscript of a book called *Giant's Bread*, not a detective story but a mainstream novel about a gifted musician called Vernon Deyre. Notable for its untypically positive representation of Jewish characters, the book appeared the following year under a pseudonym, Mary Westmacott. Christie's authorship was kept secret even longer than the identity of Francis Iles. She said later that she felt guilty about departing from her usual sort of story, but she kept busy enough with detective fiction, writing short stories, a stage play, and a novel. She also bought a small mews house in Cresswell Place, Chelsea, and lent it during the summer to the Woolleys.

Christie returned to Ur in February 1930, and this time she met Leonard Woolley's assistant, who had been away during her previous visit, suffering from appendicitis. Max Mallowan was twenty-five years old, the Oxford-educated son of an Austrian father and French mother. She found him affable and self-assured.

Katharine Woolley became more domineering than ever. She was a bulimic who sent members of her husband's staff off to the *souk* to buy Arab confectionery, for her to binge on and then vomit up. Max and the other young men were often instructed to brush her hair, but if any of them found her tempting, they were doomed to disappointment. She shrank from any hint of sexual contact. Gossip on the dig was that the most intimate part of her relationship with her husband was that she allowed him to watch her bathe at night. There was even a bizarre rumour that she was actually a man. Perhaps this was inspired by Gladys Mitchell's debut novel, *Speedy Death*, which features a cross-dressing explorer.

Without meaning to, Katharine did Christie a good turn by insisting that Max escort her on a tour of local sights. He and Christie enjoyed each other's company, and when she was summoned back to England because Rosalind was ill with pneumonia, he offered to accompany her. Rosalind recovered, and Christie socialized with Max in London.

To her amazement, he proposed marriage. She was a divorced woman, fifteen years his senior, and he was a Catholic, but with him she felt 'quiet and safe and happy'. After agonizing long and hard, she accepted, and Max left the Catholic Church because it would not recognize the marriage. They kept their engagement secret because she was afraid of being harassed by the Press, and married on 11 September.

On their marriage certificate, they lied about their ages, stating that he was 31 and she 37. This kind of deception was popular with Detection Club members – Arthur Morrison pretended to be younger than he really was, while Ngaio Marsh took advantage of her father's four-year delay in registering her birth. During the honeymoon, the couple stayed in Venice, Split, Dubrovnik, and Greece before Max returned to work at Ur, a reluctant desertion that she teased him about in *Death in the Clouds*, where an archaeologist who abandons his wife for work is called a 'barbarian'.

Back at the dig, Max faced the wrath of Katharine Woolley. His marriage had inflamed her jealousy, and she reacted by forbidding Christie to return to Ur. Christie seemed to turn the other cheek, dedicating *The Thirteen Problems* to the Woolleys. But behaving badly towards a crime writer carries risks. Christie started plotting revenge.

Neither travel nor romance slowed Christie's productivity as a writer. Like so many of her colleagues in the Detection Club, she was a workaholic. The quality of what she wrote was mixed, but that was inevitable, partly because she was so prolific, but also because she was never afraid to take a risk and try something new. In 1930, she accepted a commission to write a short story for a competition designed to attract tourists to the Isle of Man. 'Manx Gold' launched a treasure hunt that anticipated by more than forty years the success of Kit Williams' *Masquerade*. In the same year, her first stage play opened in London. *Black Coffee*, a spy thriller, enjoyed only limited success, but even so, it was made into two films within the next couple of years. The play was turned into a novel by Charles Osborne after Christie's death, but his version was lifeless. Writing a novel in the Christie style, even with a ready-made plot, is not as easy as Christie made it look.

The Mysterious Mr Quin gathered a dozen stories blending romance, detection and the supernatural which experimented with an unusual version of a Holmes–Watson relationship. Mr Quin appears when crime threatens the happiness of lovers, and is assisted by one of life's spectators, the elderly Mr Satterthwaite. Sayers scoffed that the stories were not a very successful attempt 'to combine detection with sentiment' but she respected Christie's willingness to try something different.

Far more significant was *The Murder at the Vicarage*. This marked the first novel-length appearance of Miss Jane Marple, whose life in the quiet village of St Mary Mead had equipped her with all the worldliness and expertise needed by a Great Detective, because it gave her a deep understanding of human nature. Christie had tried Marple out in short stories before deciding that she was a strong enough amateur detective to take the lead in a novel.

In her very first outing, 'The Tuesday Night Club', Marple modestly denies being clever, but says experience of village life 'does give one an insight into human nature'. This was the secret of her success as a detective. Her very ordinariness made her a much more attractive character to many readers than the brilliant egotist Poirot. Her companions, including her nephew Raymond West, a trendy novelist, are sceptical. However, when the former Commissioner of Scotland Yard relates the story of a mysterious poisoning, Miss Marple, the ultimate armchair detective, puts aside her knitting and solves the puzzle, which reminds her of the story of 'old Mr Hargreaves who lived up at the Mount'.

In a pioneering full-length study of crime fiction, *Masters of Mystery*, H. D. Thomson recognized that Miss Marple was 'an entirely new kind of detective . . . an incorrigible Cranfordian, a spinster and a gossip'. Yet Thomson saw no long term future for her: 'Miss Marple can only hope to solve murder problems on her native heath. If Mrs Christie is planning a future for Miss Marple . . . she will be bound to find this an exasperating limitation.'

Like so many other people, Thomson under-rated Christie. She proved more than equal to the challenge.

Miss Marple's debut was followed by *The Sittaford Mystery*. The setting is a snowbound village on Dartmoor, and there are some parallels with *The Hound of the Baskervilles*, including the presence in each story of an escaped convict, and a good helping of spooky atmosphere. From childhood, Christie was intrigued by ghosts and the paranormal, but her fundamental outlook was always down-to-earth.

Apparently supernatural incidents supply red herrings in Christie's novels, but she never failed to provide a rational solution to her puzzles. At around this time, *Psychic News* claimed that five hundred societies were affiliated to the Spiritualist's National Union. People who, like Conan Doyle, had lost loved ones during the war often took comfort from spiritualism and séances, but for every believer there were plenty of sceptics, and many were members of the Detection Club. Berkeley featured a fake séance in *Cicely Disappears*, while Sayers' *Strong Poison* mocks psychical research. The Coles included a dubious séance in *Burglars in Bucks* (a murder-free novel about which the most baffling puzzle is why the American edition was called *The Berkshire Mystery* though set in Buckinghamshire).

In *The Sittaford Mystery*, a message from the spirit world during a séance announces that Captain Trevelyan has been murdered, and Trevelyan duly proves to have been bludgeoned to death. After a 'least likely person' culprit is unmasked, it emerges that a key clue was given in the first chapter, when the table-turners' conversation touches on crossword competitions and acrostics. This is a detective puzzle emphatically connected to the enthusiastic game-playing of the period, rather than the killer's psychology, which is left unexplored.

Another fake séance helps Poirot to get to the truth in *Peril at End House*. Christie's scepticism about 'messages from the other world' is demonstrated by the satiric choice of a reluctant Hastings to play the part of a phoney medium. The book offers one of Christie's cleverest 'least likely suspect' plots. As so often with her best ideas, it involved role reversal, a ploy she liked so much that she kept returning to it. While staying at a hotel on the Cornish coast, Poirot and Hastings learn that a pretty young woman has had three narrow escapes from death. Poirot fears that someone is trying to kill her and make it look like an accident. Murder duly follows.

The storyline includes a secret engagement, crucial to the plot, and possibly inspired by Christie's own engagement to Max. As so often in detective novels of the Thirties, cocaine is used by members of the 'Smart Set', and Christie cunningly exploits the ambiguity of terms like 'dearest' and 'darling'. Simple tricks of this kind did not rely on specialist expertise, and were among her favourite techniques of misdirection. Her ability to supply readers with all the information needed to solve the mystery, and yet spring a surprise in the closing pages, was matchless.

In *Peril at End House*, Hastings glances at the newspapers and concludes that 'The political situation seemed unsatisfactory, but uninteresting.' Even by his standards, this observation suggests a startling lack of awareness, but he was simply reflecting a widespread disgruntlement with politics. Christie herself was again concentrating on writing and married life. Yet between the date when the Detection Club first came into being and when it formally adopted its Rules and Constitution, a period of little more than two years, the political landscape changed out of all recognition.

The aftershocks of the Wall Street Crash led to political as well as economic turbulence. In Britain, the general election produced a hung Parliament, but Labour formed a government under Ramsay MacDonald. This was the 'Flapper Election' – for the first time, all women over the age of 21 were eligible to vote, and it was symptomatic of the increasing prominence of women in public life that eight of the founder members of the Detection Club were female. Strikingly, five of the seven founder members born in or after 1890 were women. Their energetic participation was crucial to the Club's social mix, and its success.

Labour fought the election on the slogan 'We Can Conquer Unemployment', but idealism proved incompatible with the reality of taking power and responsibility. Severe public spending cuts caused a schism in the Labour ranks, and MacDonald outraged his natural supporters by joining forces with the Conservatives and Liberals to form a National Government. He was widely regarded as a class traitor, and the Labour Party expelled him. Several of his associates were also thrown out – including one of the Detection Club's founder members, Lord Gorell.

In the general election of 1931, the National Government, dominated by Conservatives, won by a landslide. From then on, the real power rested with Stanley Baldwin (whose positive qualities included a passion for detective stories) and Neville Chamberlain. MacDonald remained Prime Minister, but was a figurehead, and much derided: R.C.Woodthorpe gave his name to a parrot in *Death in a Little Town*. Gorell continued to saunter around the corridors of power, and when he travelled to the USA, he was one of the first guests of the new president, Franklin Delano Roosevelt. Later, he became chairman of the Refugee Children's Movement, and as a result probably the first Christian to be legal guardian to Jewish children: 'In all I had, at one time, over 3,000 children legally mine.'

In contrast to Gorell and those incurable campaigners the Coles, Christie and Sayers concentrated on writing, and kept their distance from politics. Anthony Berkeley's love of an argument, on the other hand, meant he took a close interest. Looking back in 1934, he said: 'We really did think that a National Government, with a *carte blanche* from a desperate nation, might do something. For a time it looked as though they really would.' Soon his hopes evaporated, and in a state of deep disgruntlement, this unlikely activist set about devising an extraordinary new political agenda of his own.

Notes to Chapter 11

the noted criminologist Richard Whittington-Egan
His *The Riddle of Birdshurst Rise* is the outstanding account of the case.

a commission to write a short story for a competition designed to attract tourists to the Isle of Man
See Tony Medawar, 'Gold and the Man with Legs for Arms', *CADS* 13, February 1990. 'Manx Gold' was published in *While the Light Lasts*, a posthumous gathering of obscure Christie stories.

The play was turned into a novel by Charles Osborne after Christie's death
Osborne, a music critic whose *The Life and Crimes of Agatha Christie* reflects his love of her work, also adapted *The Unexpected Guest* and *Spider's Web* into novels.

Miss Marple was 'an entirely new kind of detective'
At about the same time, Patricia Wentworth (1878–1961) created Miss Maud Silver, a character often compared to Miss Marple, although she is a retired governess who has taken up a new career as a private detective. Wentworth, whose real name was Dora Amy Elles, was a prolific writer, and Miss Silver continued to investigate for more than thirty years.

12

The Best Advertisement
in the World

'Most authors are not intelligent enough to see it, but there is no advertisement in the world like having your work broadcast,' according to the playwright Rodney Fleming in *Death at Broadcasting House*. This detective novel, brimming with inside know-how about the making of a radio programme, was co-written by two BBC staff members, Val Gielgud and Holt Marvell. Marvell was the pseudonym of Eric Maschwitz, who also wrote the lyrics to 'A Nightingale Sang in Berkeley Square'. Gielgud, brother of the more famous John, and himself an actor as well as a radio producer, was elected to the Detection Club after the Second World War.

Like his fictional mouthpiece, Gielgud understood the power of the mass media. And when Sayers, Christie and Berkeley were approached by the BBC about the possibility of broadcasting a collaborative mystery together, they jumped at the chance. Publicity on this scale seldom came the way of detective novelists. The result was a pioneering enterprise linking the broadcasting and print media, and enabling detective story fans to participate interactively. People could listen to the story on the wireless, read it in *The Listener*, and then take part in a prize competition judged by Detection Club member Milward Kennedy.

The project was made possible by the creation of the BBC. The British Broadcasting Company, which became a corporation in 1927, was run by a Glaswegian control freak called John Reith, who insisted that announcers should wear a dinner jacket and bow tie, and speak in a standardized pronunciation. Then, as now, the BBC could not please everyone. Douglas Cole wrote in the *New Statesman*, shortly after the BBC was granted a Royal Charter, 'Whatever the BBC does is, of course, wrong.'

An early scandal embroiled Ronald Knox. People complained that the BBC schedules were dull and lacking in variety, so Knox, already recognized as a gifted satirist, was hired to liven things up. On January 15, 1926, he broadcast live from Edinburgh. The BBC's studio was located at the back of a music shop in George Street. The studio was small and cramped, but that did not matter with a one-man show. Knox gave the performance of his life – a parody of a news bulletin called 'Broadcasting from the Barricades'.

The BBC announced that this was a work of humour and imagination, enhanced by 'sound effects', still a novelty. Knox's script began innocuously, before moving to a news item about a demonstration in Trafalgar Square. One witty giveaway was that the protesters were led by a man called Poppleberry, secretary for the National Movement for Abolishing Theatre Queues. Music and cricket news were interspersed with reports of increasing violence. Listeners heard an explosion at the Savoy Hotel (created by smashing an orange box next to the microphone) and a dignitary named Sir Theophilus Gooch was 'roasted alive' on his way to the studio to talk about housing for the poor. 'He will therefore,' Knox solemnly informed his audience, 'be unable to deliver his lecture to you.' The clock tower of Big Ben was brought crashing to the ground, and the Minister of Traffic was hanged from a tramway-post on the Vauxhall Bridge Road. Finally, the BBC itself was stormed.

Knox's satire played on the widespread fear, months ahead of the General Strike, that British workers would follow their Russian comrades and overthrow the state. Many listeners took it as deadly serious. One called the Admiralty, demanding that the Royal Navy set off up the Thames to tackle the rioters. Twenty minutes after the programme finished, Knox sat down to dinner, unaware he had caused panic across the nation. About ten million people tuned in, and the impact was all the greater because heavy snow in London delayed the delivery of newspapers revealing that all was well. Knox's spoof was the first of its kind, possibly inspiring Orson Welles's legendary version of *War of the Worlds*, which terrified American listeners twelve years later.

The newspapers reacted with noisy outrage. 'People Alarmed All Week-End' wailed a headline in the *Daily Express*. Sir Leo Money, a former Liberal minister who had turned to socialism and writing for newspapers after losing his seat in Parliament, condemned the programme as 'utterly humourless'. The Lord Mayor of Newcastle complained that his wife had been seriously upset. Rumours swirled that Knox was 'blacklisted' by the BBC because of the furore he had caused, but he worked with the BBC again as soon as the Detection Club sprang into life.

Chastened by reaction to 'Broadcasting from the Barricades', the BBC struggled to come up with innovative new ventures before the Talks Department decided to risk a serialized detective story written by a team of writers. The 'round robin' story form had emerged in the nineteenth century, notable examples including *The Fate of Fenella*, a sensational story blending the irresistible ingredients of adultery, murder, and mesmerism. Two illustrious contributors were Arthur Conan Doyle and Bram Stoker, author of *Dracula*. But Golden Age detective novelists had never tried their hand at a round-robin story. The constraints of playing fair by listeners and readers were bound to prove testing.

Six leading authors were approached: Sayers, Berkeley, Christie, E. C. Bentley, Knox and Hugh Walpole. Over lunch at the Savoy, they discussed the project with Howard Marshall, an up-and-coming young man who later became a pioneering commentator at live broadcasts of state occasions and major sporting events. They decided that each writer ought to broadcast the instalment of the story that he or she wrote, and Walpole agreed to circulate a synopsis. The writers of the first three instalments – Walpole, Christie and Sayers – would move the story along 'according to their own several fancies'. Their successors were left to use their wits to unravel the clues left by the first trio.

Walpole was a celebrity. His fame, coupled with an excellent speaking voice, made him an obvious choice to take the lead, as writer and broadcaster. Sayers agreed to coordinate the project, liaising between her fellow authors and the BBC. The timescale for the project was strict. Each author was due to broadcast on a Saturday evening, with the 1,800-word script appearing in *The Listener* the next Wednesday.

So far, so good. The trouble started when Walpole announced he was not willing to write out his story word for word. A natural with the microphone, he preferred the spontaneity of reading from notes. This meant that the BBC had to hire two parliamentary reporters more familiar with working on *Hansard*. They had to make a full note of his words for typing on Sunday, and posting to the magazine printers for half past seven on Monday morning. It was all alarmingly tight.

The challenge for the writers – above all those like Christie, who were unused to broadcasting – was that, as the playwright and occasional crime writer Emlyn Williams said, 'British radio was still a momentous force.' To go live before an unseen audience of millions was terrifying, with the soundproof studio like a dungeon filled with microphones resembling a 'regiment of robots' with 'each dead eye turned bright red and staring at its victims'.

'Hate was the principal feeling in young Wilfred Hope's mind as he walked hurriedly down Sunflower Lane one wet and stormy evening.' Walpole's opening to *Behind the Screen* had a bleak tone typical of his occasional forays into crime fiction. The Ellis family, into which Wilfred hopes to marry, has taken in a lodger called Dudden who has 'acquired over all of them a most curious dominance'. When Wilfred calls at their home, he sees, behind a large, old-fashioned Japanese screen, the body of Dudden, 'horribly dead'.

'Look! Look! The blood!' cried Walpole as he ended his instalment with a melodramatic cliffhanger designed to make sure listeners tuned in the following week. In a single, short piece, he demonstrated the storytelling knack which had earned him success. He yearned to be one of the great and the good of the literary establishment, and an invitation to join the prestigious new Detection Club boosted his fragile ego. Yet throughout his life he remained an outsider.

Walpole was born in Auckland, New Zealand, where his father – later the Bishop of Edinburgh – was Canon of St Mary's Cathedral. The family was British, and Walpole's grandfather was the younger brother of the first Prime Minister. After they returned to England, he set his heart on establishing himself as a writer. His fierce ambition was not accompanied by a thick skin. He wanted everyone to love him, but in his drive to build a reputation and the right connections he sometimes trampled on the feelings of others. He even included a league table in his diary, ranking his friends in order. Yet he was easily bruised by criticism and incurably jealous. When Hilaire Belloc described P. G. Wodehouse as the best English writer of the day, Wodehouse thought it hilarious, but Walpole was hurt. His wealth provoked envy and he alienated people through trivial disagreements. One enemy wrote a vindictive anonymous obituary of him in *The Times*.

Walpole's sensitivity was compounded by the intense social pressure he felt to remain discreet about his homosexuality. For him, unlike Douglas Cole, writing and the intellectual life was not enough. At the end of his first year as a student, he noted in his journal, 'Meanwhile I still wait the ideal friend. . . . I'd give a lot for the real right man.' Suffering from loneliness during a holiday in Cornwall, he wrote in his diary that marriage 'really seems the only thing' and proposed to 'a ripping girl' from the house where he was staying. He wooed her by saying, 'I've always thought of you more as a man than as a woman.' She was not flattered, and turned him down.

His biographer, writing when homosexual acts were still illegal in Great Britain, made cryptic reference to visits to Turkish Baths which provided Walpole with 'informal opportunities of meeting interesting strangers'. Walpole's chief companion was Harold Cheevers, a married former constable in the Metropolitan Police and former police revolver champion of the British Isles. His role in Walpole's life so far as the outside world was concerned was as his chauffeur. Walpole and the Cheevers moved to the Lake District, background for the Herries Chronicles, his series of popular historical novels. In his private journal, Walpole set out a self-portrait: 'I adore to be in love but am bored if someone is much in love with me. I'm superficially both conceited and vain but at heart consider myself with a good deal of contempt.' His sexual orientation was very different from Berkeley's, but they were equally complex and contrary characters whose most personal work had a sado-masochistic flavour.

Julian Symons later contrasted the 'saccharine sweet' flavour of the Herries Chronicles with Walpole's sporadic ventures into crime, such as *Above the Dark Circus*, which were 'tart as damsons'. The dark emotions swirling in these novels suggest that Walpole – like other gay and lesbian novelists oppressed by the prejudices of the age – found an outlet through writing crime fiction that was denied to him in everyday life.

For readers, much of the pleasure of a round-robin story lies in the chance to appreciate the varied styles and approaches of the contributing authors. Collaborative stories which have not been planned out in advance lack the flow and structure of a book written by a single person. Seeing how each writer tackles the task of keeping the story coherent and appealing is at least as entertaining as the story itself.

So it was with *Behind the Screen*. With six short sections, it is no more than a novella, and scarcely a model of 'fair play'. But the quintet of writers who followed Walpole enjoyed themselves. After the bleak opening section, which contained no dialogue at all, Christie played to her strength, moving the plot forward with an almost unbroken stream of light, lively conversation. Unlike Walpole, she had little talent for descriptive writing, but she knew her limitations, and was accomplished at skipping around them.

Sayers followed, then Berkeley and Bentley. Finally, Ronald Knox wrapped things up. His contribution began with the pious reflection that 'there is kindliness even in the most warped natures' and concluded with a solution out of left field. The result was a flagrant breach of the rules he'd laid down in his Decalogue. But breaking the rules was more fun than obeying them.

Sayers kept in close touch with Berkeley about progress. At this point their relationship was strong, and she was frank in her comments about their colleagues. For Christie, back from the Middle East and contemplating a new life with Max Mallowan, the BBC project was not the top priority, and her delays drove Sayers to distraction. But she managed to persuade Christie to put the fatal wound in Dudden's throat rather than his midriff, since it made the trickle of blood described by Walpole more likely.

Knox panicked her by suggesting that, with so much blood spilled, Dudden might have suffered from haemophilia. She was working on a plot involving haemophilia, and few things depress crime writers more than learning that their latest brainwave has been anticipated by a rival. She told Berkeley that, thankfully, she had managed to head Knox off. Decades later, post-war Detection Club member Michael Innes recorded Knox's claim that Sayers heard haemophilia mentioned when the plot for *Behind the Screen* was being discussed, and 'was observed to make an entry in her notebook'. Knox was simply making mischief. There was little love lost between him and Sayers.

Milward Kennedy approached the round-robin game with his usual zest. Having seen a synopsis of the first four episodes, but without knowing what was in the final instalment, he posed a series of questions for contestants. Fearing that Knox would pull a rabbit out of the hat, he backtracked on *The Listener*'s claim that enough clues would be given by the time readers reached the middle of the story to enable them to guess the solution. He argued that it was enough for the clues to be in place by the end of the penultimate instalment.

The BBC received 170 entries to the competition and Kennedy supplied a detailed assessment of the answers to his question.

Nobody got every point right, and very few people identified the correct culprit, thanks to Knox's unlikely solution. Two mistaken guesses did indeed involve haemophilia. Very few solutions linked the actual murderer to the crime – not surprisingly since the culprit was a minor character in the story, and the motive was concealed. *Behind the Screen* had an unexpected legacy, through a line Berkeley gave to the despairing Inspector Rice, who finishes his notes about the suspects with the question: '*Are they all in it?*' Chance remarks often inspired Christie and perhaps this jokey, throwaway line lingered in her subconscious. She was to develop it into the stunning plot of one of her most celebrated novels.

The experiment was a triumph, although nerves frayed at the BBC because of the writers' unpredictability. The Talks Department was keen to run a follow-up as soon as possible, and the Detection Club members, bitten by the broadcasting bug, were happy to oblige. But tensions persisted. The editor of *The Listener* told Sayers that they had not had 'a very happy time in regard to publishing the previous story . . . owing to lack of prior collaboration' and he wanted to avoid this the second time around. Sayers was again willing to act as supervisor of the exercise, but cautioned that Christie, whose name was a big draw, was at present unavailable because she was out of the country.

J. R. Ackerley of the Talks Department wanted to keep an 'editorial eye' on the project, but Sayers was having none of it. Relations between them began to disintegrate. When Ackerley warned Sayers he would die of heart failure if she delayed again in supplying a synopsis, she slapped him down. And when he rashly complained that frantic colleagues were raining telegrams upon him, she hit back at once, deploring the BBC's extravagance in resorting so readily to telegrams.

Two strong and colourful characters, Sayers and Ackerley were never likely to be soulmates. Joe Ackerley was the illegitimate half-brother of the future Duchess of Westminster, and his fondness for sailors and guardsmen caused E. M. Forster to warn him to give up looking for 'gold in coal mines'. Like Walpole, he spent a lifetime searching for his 'ideal friend', but never found him.

The new round-robin story had a Fleet Street background and was called *The Scoop*. The plan was for six authors each to write two instalments. Walpole and Knox stepped aside, and were replaced by a pair of very different writers, Freeman Wills Crofts and Clemence Dane. This time, the sextet fashioned their story from elements of a grisly real-life crime.

In May 1924, the police called Bernard Spilsbury (who had been knighted the previous year) out to a remote beach house on the Crumbles, a shingle beach in Sussex. He arrived, immaculate as usual in morning dress, black tailcoat, grey spats and black silk top hat, to encounter the most gruesome crime scene of his career. A human being had been burned, boiled, chopped up, and pulverised. Body parts were found in parcels and a hat-box, but the head was missing. Bits of human bone were mixed with ashes in the fireplace. More than nine hundred fragments needed to be sifted through and identified, along with other remains. Taking off his tailcoat (but not his spats), Spilsbury put on a large apron and a pair of rubber gloves and got to work. Comparing his painstaking task to work on a jig-saw puzzle, he concluded that the deceased was 'an adult female of big build and fair hair'. Milk could be squeezed from the breasts, and he concluded that the dead woman was between three and four months pregnant.

The deceased proved to be a pleasant, hearty shorthand typist in her late thirties called Emily Kaye, and her murderer a Liverpool-born commercial traveller. Patrick Mahon was handsome and persuasive, but forever short of money, a gambler and womanizer whose conquests included the wife of the literary editor of the *Daily Express*. He seduced Emily and raided her savings, but her pregnancy was an unwanted complication. Having bought her an engagement ring with her own money, as part of a 'love experiment' he invited her to the bungalow at the Crumbles. She wrote to her sister, saying,

'Don't worry, old sausage. I know I shall be very happy,' and set off to join him.

Mahon killed her and dismembered the corpse over a period of days, during which he had sex in an adjoining room with a woman called Ethel Duncan. Presumably Ethel lacked a strong sense of smell, but Mahon had unwisely left at his home a ticket to a railway left-luggage office. This aroused his wife's suspicions, and she hired a private detective. The ticket led the detective to Waterloo, and discovery of a Gladstone bag containing bloodstained clothing, a cook's knife, and a tennis racquet cover bearing Emily Kaye's initials.

There was no question of the Detection Club delving into the horrific detail of the Crumbles murder in *The Scoop*. Public taste simply would not have tolerated it. But the story Sayers' team concocted is lively and entertaining, as the *Morning Star*'s journalists investigate the stabbing of a young woman in a lonely bungalow at the 'Jumbles' in Sussex.

Given her hatred of putting herself in the public eye after the disaster of her disappearance, Christie's willingness to make a live radio broadcast reading her part of the story was unexpected and brave. It was equally an act of courage to expose herself to relentless correspondence from Sayers. Never afraid to badger people when the need arose, Sayers was an irresistible force. However, as the weeks passed, Christie proved adept at keeping out of her way. She flitted between houses and even countries, always seemingly one step ahead.

Sayers was more than a match for Ackerley, and her other colleagues offered strong support. Bentley was reliable, while Crofts, a thoroughly decent man with strong spiritual values, was always eager and industrious. Sayers described Berkeley as 'his own bright self as usual', which contradicts the widespread view that dealing with him was always hard work. Ackerley and the BBC, on the other hand, infuriated her. She was driven to distraction by errors in the illustrations that appeared in *The Listener*. At one point, a character was pictured out of doors in November without a hat or coat and 'apparently wearing a chemise'. Skirts were now longer, Sayers protested. Later she asked the 'crazy artist' to draw the death scene as 'an exercise in perspective'.

Quite apart from these irritations, she had to contend with the structural challenges of a jointly written story. At one point during the plotting process, Freeman Wills Crofts telephoned her to warn about a problem with a crucial alibi concerning a train journey. The soft Irish voice trembled with dismay. 'I'm afraid the 9.48 may have to get in late,' he confessed: a former railwayman's worst nightmare.

For her part, Sayers feared the alibi problem might ruin a scene in the newspaper office. The answer was to arrange a lunch meeting of the collaborators, in the hope of pulling the threads together. Unfortunately, the arrangements were confused by a mix-up about the precise time they were due to get together. Given this level of ineptitude, it is as well that the authors never tried to carry out in real life any of the ingenious and elaborate schemes favoured by their villains.

Christie fled to Switzerland with daughter Rosalind, chased by a frantic letter from Ackerley. In an early example of the mismatch of expectations between broadcasters and authors, he was unsympathetic to the demands of a classic whodunit, and kept worrying that listeners would lose the plot. Alarmed by the number of characters who appeared in the first two instalments, he warned: 'It has to be written almost as if for children.'

Sayers broadcast the first instalment of *The Scoop* on 10 January 1931, with Christie to follow a week later. At this point, the second half of the story still had not been written. Suffering from a cold, Christie asked the BBC to allow her to record the episode from Devonshire. Full of foreboding, Ackerley agreed, but begged her not to overrun her allotted time.

Max was digging away in Ur, but he promised not to miss his new wife's broadcast. The challenge was to find a radio with a sufficiently strong signal. Riding a horse for the first time in his life, he galloped across the desert to Nasriyah, so that he could listen to her on a wireless belonging to a major who was the political officer based there. He was delighted with Agatha's efforts, but his letter of congratulations took weeks to reach home.

Back in London in February, Christie completed her part in the project and wrote to Sayers of her joy at having finished it. She praised Sayers for taming the BBC, and invited her round for tea at Cresswell Place. A natural diplomat, she made a habit of dodging any hint of controversy. If she was annoyed that Sayers had taken such a close interest in her disappearance in 1926, she never showed it. Similarly, she seems never to have had a cross word with Berkeley – quite an achievement, given his provocative nature.

The Scoop is a stronger story than *Behind the Screen*, showing the benefit of better planning as well as the powerful raw material supplied by the Mahon case. Again, the varied styles of the different chapters are part of the charm. Clemence Dane focuses on the character of the attractive secretary Beryl Blackwood whereas Freeman Wills Crofts ignores life in the newspaper office, a background vividly established by Sayers in the first chapter, and keeps to his comfort zone, focusing on the investigations conducted by Scotland Yard. Christie, Berkeley and Bentley write with their usual lightness and deftness of touch, while Sayers finishes what she started.

This time, rather than run a competition, Ackerley conducted a survey to seek audience feedback – one more example of the project being ahead of its time. He received nearly 1,500 appreciations and only 60 criticisms. For all its flaws, the programmes proved a triumph. Unfortunately, the stress of the collaboration with the BBC deterred Sayers and her friends from repeating the experiment. Ackerley tried to tempt Christie into writing original stories for broadcast and subsequent publication. On Edmund Cork's advice, she declined. It paid better to publish in print first.

Christie was Ackerley's favourite detective novelist. He regarded her persistent lateness in delivering her contributions as tiresome, but found her 'surprisingly good-looking'. Yet he did not rate her highly as a broadcaster. Nerves caused her to gallop through her instalment almost as fast as Max had ridden across the desert. But anyone, Ackerley admitted, 'would have seemed feeble against the terrific vitality, bullying and bounce of that dreadful woman Dorothy L. Sayers'.

Notes to Chapter 12

An early scandal embroiled Ronald Knox
I have drawn on many sources, including the biographies of Knox
and the BBC website, for my account of the broadcast

the Talks Department decided to risk a serialized detective story
written by a team of writers
See Alexis Weedon, '"Behind the Screen" and "The Scoop": a cross-
media experiment in publishing and broadcasting crime fiction in
the early 1930s', *Media History*, vol. xiii, no. 1, 2007; Greene, Doug,
'Murder by Committee', *CADS* 1, July 1985, and Reynolds, William,
'Collaborative Detective Publications in Britain, 1931–39', *Clues*, vol.
9.1, Spring/Summer 1988, as well as contemporary correspondence
now held in the Marion E. Wade Center and by various collectors
and dealers.

Walpole's sporadic ventures into crime . . . were 'tart as damsons'
Walpole relished macabre fiction on the borderline of the crime and
mystery genre. He and Dane admired the work of Claude Houghton,
real name Claude Houghton Oldfield (1889–1961), author of novels
such as *I Am Jonathan Scrivener* (1930). They were responsible for
Claude Houghton: Appreciations by Hugh Walpole and Clemence
Dane with a Bibliography (London, Heinemann, 1935).

The BBC received 170 entries to the competition and Kennedy
supplied a detailed assessment of the answers to his question
Competition stories have continued to appear from time to time, an
interesting example being Kingsley Amis' *The Crime of the Century*,
which was first published in the *Sunday Times* in 1975, as a serial
in six episodes. After the publication of the fifth part, readers were
invited to send in their own solutions to the murder mystery, and
the winning entry was published alongside Amis' own (and quite
different) solution. Amis was like his friends, detective novelist
Edmund Crispin and poet Philip Larkin, an admirer of Golden Age
fiction. His 1973 novel, *The Riverside Villas Murder*, pays homage
to the Golden Age, and even contains Amis' variation on the theme
of the cluefinder.

the police called Bernard Spilsbury

The books about Spilsbury mentioned in the Select Bibliography range from the admiring (Browne and Tullett) to the sceptical (Rose). The variations reflect changing attitudes to the role of the expert witness. Spilsbury's evidence helped to hang Patrick Mahon, but that was not enough for him. After the execution, he conducted the post-mortem himself, perhaps hoping to find evidence of criminal abnormality in Mahon's brain tissue. He was becoming notorious for displays of forensic showmanship, and the Home Office turned down his request to remove parts of Mahon's fractured vertebrae, fearing he would use them for anatomical demonstrations. But sensitivities change as time passes. Sixty years after Emily Kaye's death, a radio broadcast about her murder by the true crime expert and occasional novelist Edgar Lustgarten was sampled by the Australian band Severed Heads in their song 'Dead Eyes Opened'. It became their first chart hit.

Part Three

Looking to Escape

THE
ANATOMY
OF
MURDER

DOROTHY L. SAYERS
HELEN SIMPSON
JOHN RHODE
FRANCIS ILES
E. R. PUNSHON
MARGARET COLE
FREEMAN WILLS CROFTS

The Anatomy of Murder, the third Detection Club book, published by The Bodley Head in 1936.

13

'Human Life's the Cheapest Thing There Is'

Science and technological advance dominated crime detection long before anyone dreamed of genetic fingerprinting and CCTV surveillance. Dorothy Sayers applied that 'terrific vitality' to studying what we now loosely call 'forensics'. She admired the expertise of Bernard Spilsbury, name-checking him in *Clouds of Witness*, and prided herself on accurate depiction of scientific homicide investigation. One of her strongest Wimsey short stories was inspired by a murder on Guy Fawkes Night in 1930.

Two cousins returning home in the early hours after a Bonfire Night Dance in Northampton were walking along a country lane in bright moonlight when they saw a bizarre apparition. A smartly dressed but hatless man was clambering out of a ditch. Moments later, the men saw in the distance a bright red glow. 'Someone must be having a bonfire!' the stranger called, and went on his way. The cousins headed for the scene of the blaze. As they drew near, they saw a Morris Minor motor car had gone up in flames. The police were called, and put out the fire. Inside the vehicle, they found a charred corpse.

The car was traced to Alfred Arthur Rouse, and the cousins identified Rouse as the man from the ditch. Like murderer Patrick Mahon, whose crime inspired *The Scoop*, Rouse was a salesman and compulsive philanderer. After he made a casual and very unwise reference to his personal 'harem', the police investigated his private life, and discovered that it was in such a tangled state that he had a strong incentive to fake his own death and start again. The body in the car was so badly burned that it was only identified as male thanks to the discovery of a fragment of prostate gland. Spilsbury examined the minimal burned remains carefully to establish the cause of death with his customary authority, while a vehicle expert testified that someone had tampered with the car's carburettor. Rouse was found guilty and confessed to the crime shortly before being hanged. He had given a lift to a man who remains unidentified to this day, killed him, and set fire to the car in the hope of starting a new life. His scheme had only careered out of control because he climbed out of the ditch at precisely the wrong moment. And there was a clue in his appearance: in 1930, a smart man's failure to wear a hat was a sure sign that something was amiss.

Sayers adapted the Rouse scenario for 'In the Teeth of the Evidence', exploring forensic dentistry in the case of a criminal who has 'studied Rouse' but still fails to outsmart Wimsey. Supposedly unindentifiable corpses found in blazing cars enjoyed a vogue both in fact – Rouse's cunning plan was similar to ones carried out by two German murderers around the same time – and in fiction. The best 'blazing car' novel was probably J. J. Connington's *The Four Defences*, a complex puzzle involving forensic analysis and 'rail fence ciphers' untangled by Mark Brand, a radio columnist with a taste for detection. Brand was Connington's attempt to update the amateur sleuth, but not until Eddie Shoestring arrived on the television screens in the 1970s did the idea of a radio presenter as gumshoe find popular success in Britain.

Sayers and Connington admired the meticulous scientific detective stories of an older Detection Club member, Richard Austin Freeman, although Sayers complained when Freeman spiced up his stories with 'love interest'. This paradox should have aroused her detective instincts, especially since one of his finest mysteries stressed the paramount importance of sex. Preoccupied with keeping her own life private, she never guessed that the sub-plot of Freeman's finest novel presented a fictional version of a real-life secret passion.

Freeman's precise literary style, like his calligraphic handwriting, suggests a dry, painstaking man, more comfortable with microscope and test tube than the ebb and flow of human emotions. In fact, he was a romantic whom women found highly attractive, but his personable manner concealed a streak of ruthlessness. Like Robert Eustace, Sayers' collaborator in *The Documents in the Case*, Freeman exploited his technical know-how in his fiction, inspiring writers who were fascinated by the potential of scientific progress, if occasionally appalled by the dangers it posed.

Eugenics, one of Freeman's hobby horses, provoked fierce debate. Detection Club members had strong opinions on every subject under the sun, and had deeply held, and conflicting, views about whether eugenics represented a threat to humanity. Eugenicists advocated improving the population's genetic composition. In practice, this meant identifying 'fit' members of the community and separating them from the 'unfit'. The 'fit' would be encouraged to reproduce, but not the 'unfit'. There was nothing new about this – Plato favoured secret state control of human reproduction – but in the early twentieth century the eugenics movement gained strong support from figures as diverse as John Maynard Keynes (a director of the British Eugenics Society), George Bernard Shaw, D. H. Lawrence, and Marie Stopes. Among the most vocal was Dean Inge of St Paul's Cathedral; he was called 'the gloomy Dean' because of his dire warnings about the dangers of over-population, but he and his wife cheered themselves up a little by reading detective stories.

G. K. Chesterton hated eugenics, but Freeman was prominent in the opposite camp. In *Social Decay and Regeneration,* Freeman argued that eugenic reform was necessary if human life were to continue to progress. Unlike some fellow eugenicists, he rejected compulsory sterilisation and restrictions on marriage, but advocated the voluntary segregation of the 'fit' in a League from which 'defectives' were excluded. League members would

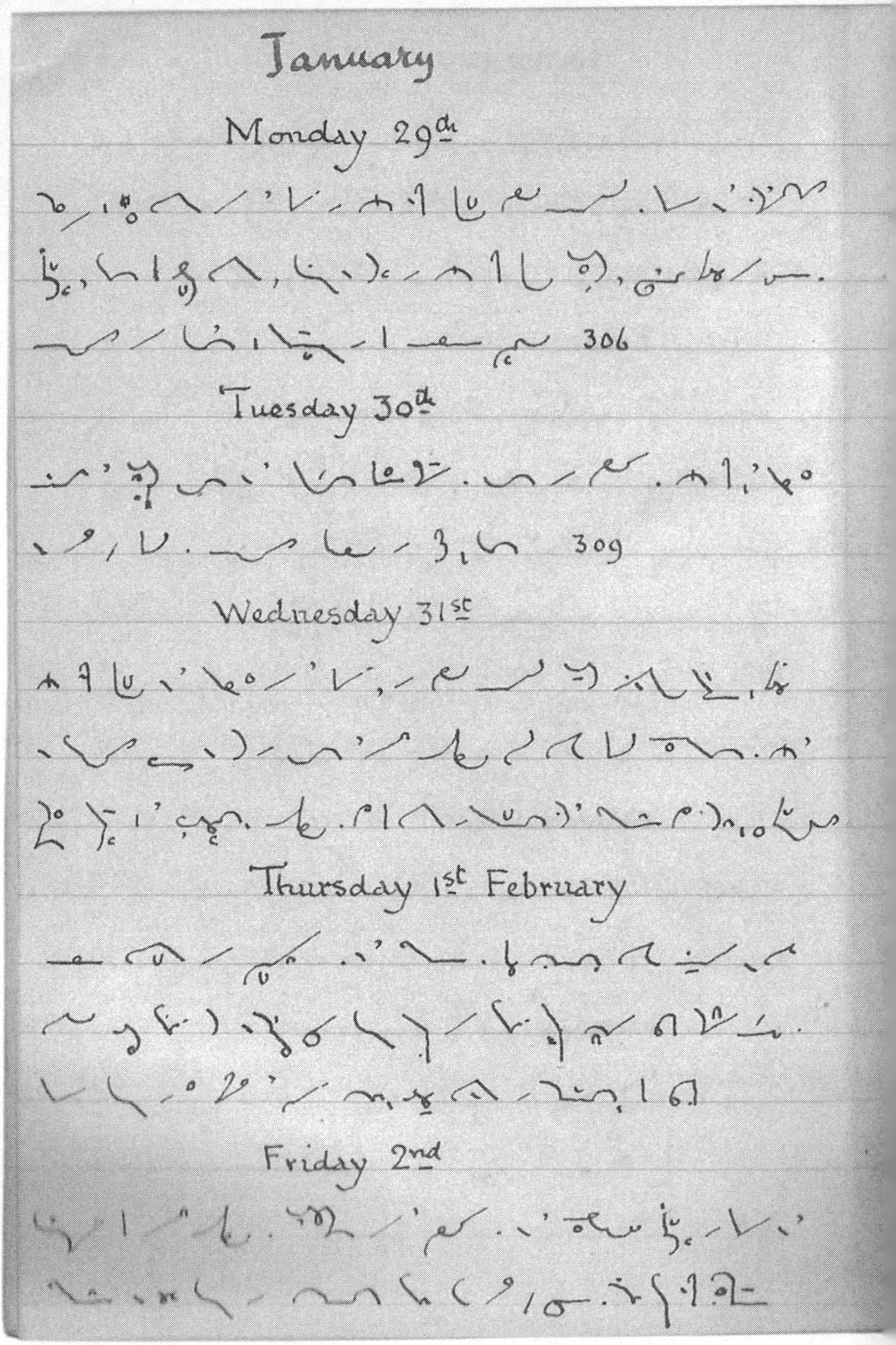

January

Monday 29th

[shorthand text] 306

Tuesday 30th

[shorthand text] 309

Wednesday 31st

[shorthand text]

Thursday 1st February

[shorthand text]

Friday 2nd

[shorthand text]

Pages from Richard Austin Freeman's coded diary (by permission of David Chapman).

February

Saturday 3rd

[shorthand text]

Sunday 4th

[shorthand text]

Monday 5th

[shorthand text]

Tuesday 6th

[shorthand text]

Wednesday 7th

[shorthand text]

pursue a utopian existence whose members concentrated on farming and skilled craftsmanship. The renowned sexologist Havelock Ellis, another enthusiastic eugenicist, contributed a foreword rhapsodizing about Freeman's vigorous mind and penetrating judgement.

Freeman found few kindred spirits in the Detection Club, even though its members wrote hundreds of books about the disposal of unattractive people. His fellow scientist J. J. Connington had some sympathy for eugenics, but writers with strong Christian beliefs were hostile. In *Gaudy Night*, Sayers makes fun of the American Sadie Schuster-Slatt, a leading figure in the League for the Encouragement of Matrimonial Fitness, while a scientist asking what would happen if only intelligent people were allowed to breed provokes Hercule Poirot's scorn in *Dead Man's Folly*: 'A very large increase of patients in the psychiatric wards, perhaps.' Ronald Knox mocked a family doctor in *Still Dead* with a passion seldom found in his fiction: 'He was all for sterilization and for lethal chambers; not only the feeble-minded, by his way of it, but the cripples, the topers and the idlers would be all the better for a swift end and a home in the ugly cemetery on the hill-side.'

Freeman was prouder of *Social Decay and Regeneration* than any of his mysteries, a wild misjudgement but not untypical. Detection Club members presumed their crime fiction would soon be forgotten. They could be as dismissive of their own mysteries as their snootiest critics, and just as wrong.

Freeman's hidden depths were hinted at by his 'dark, mesmeric eyes'. This phrase was Dorothy Bishop's. She was the daughter of Alice Bishop, who before the First World War typed Freeman's manuscripts and helped to check his proofs. Freeman and Alice were both married to other people, but there is a hidden picture of their relationship in one of his finest books. According to her daughter, Alice believed Freeman was a man of destiny: 'My conviction is that almost from the beginning she saw him as an extraordinary man, someone at whose feet she could sit, yet someone she could direct and dominate.'

'Did they become lovers in the usual sense?' Dorothy wondered. 'Or was sex overruled, sublimated to the making of a new writer? I am quite sure she saw him as famous long before Fame arrived. I am almost equally sure that underneath his magnetic personality was a cold and calculating mind. For in my mother's hand was my father's cheque book. A strange eternal triangle. And yet a partnership (let us acknowledge it) that enriched three lives, for in the end my father also basked in the reflected fame of Richard Freeman.'

Richard Austin Freeman was born in London in 1862, the son of a tailor. Like slum-life author and fellow Detection Club member Arthur Morrison, he later became embarrassed by his humble background. Having qualified as a physician and surgeon, he married the daughter of a master plumber, and they had two sons. Unable to afford to buy a practice, he joined the Colonial Service. He served on the Gold Coast, and succumbed to blackwater fever. Invalided back to Britain, he tried to make a living out of medical practice. During that time he published a book about his travels in Ashanti, and began his relationship with Alice Bishop. He dedicated two books to her, including *Social Decay and Regeneration*, and one to her apparently complaisant husband, Bernard.

Under the pen name Clifford Ashdown, and in collaboration with John James Pitcairn, a medic with whom he worked for a time at Holloway Prison, Freeman published two collections of short stories about Romney Pringle. Pringle is a villain who masquerades as a 'literary agent' – a concept which might strike a chord with some writers. Five years later, *The Red Thumb Mark* introduced the character who made Freeman's name, Dr John Thorndyke. As Raymond Chandler (an unlikely fan of Freeman's work) said, Freeman had produced 'a story about a forged fingerprint ten years before police method realized such things could be done'.

Failing health prompted Freeman to give up his medical practice and create his Great Detective. Handsome and brilliant, Thorndyke is not only a doctor but also a fully-trained lawyer. He has 'a scientific imagination . . . the capacity to perceive the essential nature of a problem before the detailed evidence comes into sight'. Above all, his method 'consists in the interrogation of things rather than persons'. Thorndyke seldom ventured out without his green travelling research case, packed with tiny reagent bottles, test tubes, spirit lamp, dwarf microscope and 'assorted instruments on the same Lilliputian scale'. His chambers housed a laboratory and workshop occupied by his assistant Nathaniel Polton.

Freeman prided himself on the integrity of the scientific methods he described. He even conducted his own laboratory experiments to validate his hero's detective work, and as his biographer said, 'collected and photographed marine shells and industrial dust; built see-behind spectacles and periscope walking-sticks, all so that his characters could engage in realistic activities'. This obsessive devotion to accurate detail set him head and shoulders above American contemporaries such as Arthur B. Reeve, creator of Professor Craig Kennedy, and the brothers-in-law William McHarg and Edwin Balmer, whose plot devices veered towards technology – such as the lie detectors which Chesterton despised.

The Eye of Osiris, the second Thorndyke novel, mixed ingredients ranging from Egyptology to the appearance of fragments of a skeleton in a number of fish ponds and watercress beds, and a lecture on the life-cycle of the liver fluke. The narrator is a young physician who falls for Ruth Bellingham, niece of a missing man, just as Freeman had become entranced with Alice Bishop.

'The one salient biological truth is the paramount importance of sex,' Thorndyke insists. When he adds that 'the love of a serious and honourable man for a woman who is worthy of him is the most momentous of human affairs,' it is clear he is Freeman's proxy, speaking to Alice.

One researcher has suggested that Freeman was the father of Dorothy's brother, Gerald. Certainly, for a time his wife Annie left him and moved to Broadstairs. She was a Catholic, and divorce was out of the question – a scenario providing a motive for murder in dozens of Golden Age novels. In the Freemans' case, the answer was compromise. Freeman rejoined Annie, and eventually they moved to Gravesend, where the Bishop family lived.

Freeman anticipated real-life events when writing *The Cat's Eye*, which appeared in 1923 with a preface explaining that an episode in the story, in which a poisoned box of chocolates is sent to two characters (Thorndyke persuades them not to tuck in), was written *before* a similar incident in real life. Sir William Horwood, the Metropolitan Police Commissioner, had made the extraordinary mistake of treating himself to chocolates from a mysterious parcel of walnut whips sent to him at New Scotland Yard. He thought they were a birthday present from his daughter, and decided they would be the ideal way to finish off a hearty lunch of pork and apple sauce, bread and butter pudding and Guinness.

In fact, the sender was Walter Tatam, an insane horticulturalist from Balham. He had laced the chocolates with arsenic, and Horwood became so ill that he was lucky to survive. Tatam said voices coming from the hedges in his garden had urged him to send poisoned chocolates – mostly chocolate eclairs – to senior police officers. The Horwood case, and Freeman's story, created a fashion in fictional homicide. The arrival of a mysterious box of chocolates became a recurrent hazard in the lives of Golden Age characters, but the concept of talking hedges was too strange for fiction.

Freeman's relationship with Alice Bishop cooled, and he became involved with an accomplished watercolourist called Bertha Fowle. Bertha was more than thirty years his junior, which suggests that, whatever else he lacked, it was neither charm nor stamina. Despite her husband's waywardness, the long-suffering Annie was willing to keep the marriage going. She and Freeman continued to live together in Gravesend until his death.

Freeman wrote a story for Isaac Pitman, 'The Man with the Nailed Shoes', in Pitman's shorthand, and this prompted him to invent a shorthand system of his own. He kept a diary, which contained a few commonplace entries in longhand, mainly

about his tax return, a subject always apt to vex authors. The
rest of the diary is written in his unique shorthand, and in effect
encrypted. It does not take a Thorndyke to deduce that Freeman
was trying to ensure that nothing he wrote would destroy
his marriage if Annie laid her hands on the diary. Was Alice
Bishop the subject of his private musings, or Bertha Fowle, or
both? Lord Peter Wimsey would have relished the challenge of
cracking Freeman's ingenious code. So far it has defeated the
attempts of lesser mortals to break it.

Freeman dedicated his 1931 novel *Pontifex, Son and
Thorndyke* enigmatically to Bertha 'in commemoration of many
industries and pleasant labours'. In the same year, Sayers wrote
seeking permission to include one of his stories in her new
anthology. He thanked her for asking about his health, 'which is
slowly improving and may, if I live long enough, return nearly
to normal. Some day I hope to turn up at a "Detection Club"
dinner and give myself the pleasure of making the acquaintance
of some of my fellow sleuths. The club seems to be a triumphant
success and promises to develop into a really important insti-
tution. It does very great credit to the organizing power and
initiative of those who, like yourself and Mr Cox, saw it through
its perilous infancy.'

With a humility that gives a clue to a self-deprecating charm,
he expressed gratitude for Sayers' kind words about his books:
'The quality of your own work makes a compliment from you
specially gratifying and encouraging; particularly to an aged
Victorian who is none too confident of his powers to maintain
a respectable standard of achievement.' Despite his ailments
and advancing years, the aged Victorian continued to write, and
eventually the oldest member made it to the Detection Club's
dinners.

Sayers interest in chemistry is illustrated by the repeated
appearances of Sir James Lubbock in her books. Lubbock is
the Home Office Analyst, and his prowess is reminiscent of
both John Thorndyke and Bernard Spilsbury. The Detection
Club boasted its own eminent chemist in Alfred Walter Stewart,

alias J. J. Connington. A Scot, he studied chemistry at Glasgow University, and his publications included a successful textbook, *Recent Advances in Organic Chemistry*.

Connington became engaged in his mid-twenties, but his wife-to-be 'died suddenly, after the wedding presents had come in'. Although eventually he did marry and had a much-loved daughter, the trauma of bereavement may have hardened his attitudes. Scorn for softness and sentimentality is a recurrent theme in his books, and his Great Detective is the most ruthless of all. Not for nothing was the American edition of one of his novels entitled *Grim Vengeance*.

A small and unassuming man, Connington had a biting sense of humour. Never starry-eyed about scientific fame, he wrote in *The Boat-House Riddle*: 'In science, an international reputation implies merely that an author's papers are read by a handful of specialists, half of whom probably disagree with the conclusion.' After enjoying success with a successful dystopian 'pseudo-scientific thriller', *Nordenholt's Million*, he was inspired by Freeman's example to tackle the challenges of detective fiction.

That dependable hate figure, the selfish financier, regularly crops up as a victim in Golden Age stories. In many other books, the corpse belongs to a blackmailer who had threatened victims with exposure and disgrace – a powerful motive for murder at a time when most people yearned for respectability. With the economic slump causing much suffering, any unpleasant old miser with a host of impoverished family members was unlikely to survive long in a crime novel, and anyone who called in their solicitor to change their will was signing their own death warrant. An unappealing victim was an easy way of supplying plenty of suspects. It also prompted questions about the nature of right and wrong. Connington agreed with Berkeley that the conventional legal system sometimes failed to deliver true justice. His answer was to create a detective who sometimes operated above the law, and sometimes allowed murderers to escape punishment for their crimes. But this man was not a private detective, like Holmes, or a journalist like Sheringham. He was a Chief Constable.

By 1927, T. S. Eliot reckoned that Connington had joined 'the front rank of detective story writers'. That year saw the first appearance of Sir Clinton Driffield, a surprisingly youthful Chief Constable, and his friend, 'Squire' Wendover, in *Murder in the Maze*. Connington's publishers proclaimed the book as 'one of the half-dozen masterpieces' of the genre. Two brothers are found murdered in the maze, poisoned by darts tipped with curare. Despite his official position, Driffield arranges for poisoned gas to be pumped into the maze when the killer is trapped inside it. Conversely, he allows a happy ending to a character who commits theft and forgery in a 'not a penny more, not a penny less' retribution against a swindler prefiguring the plot gimmick of Jeffrey Archer's debut novel.

Driffield proves equally uncompromising in *Mystery at Lynden Sands*, where he and Wendover find their seaside holiday interrupted by the death of an elderly man, apparently of cerebral congestion. Connington exploits the beach, quicksand and curious rock formations of the resort – not to evoke atmosphere, but to provide crime scenes, clues from footprints in the sand, and a dramatic climax. When one villain, who has threatened to inject a young woman hostage with rabies, is trapped and facing an agonizing death, Driffield is in no hurry to rescue him: 'This isn't a case where my humanitarian instincts are roused in the slightest.'

The Case with Nine Solutions again demonstrates a harsh worldview. A scientist says to a doctor friend: 'Still got the notion that human life's valuable? The war knocked that on the head. Human life's the cheapest thing there is.' The doctor goes out in the fog to visit a patient, calls at the wrong house, and discovers a young man's corpse. When he, Driffield, and Inspector Flamborough contemplate the crime scene, he reflects: 'All three of them were experts in death, and among them there was no need to waste time in polite lamentations. None of them had ever set eyes on the victim before that night, and there was no object in becoming sentimental over him.'

The elaborate storyline boasts two separate killers and four murders, even before a climactic explosion leaves another character dead. One character makes use of hyoscine as a 'date rape' drug, in an attempt to have sex with a woman who would not remember what he had done to her. In real life, Dr Crippen may have tried something similar, and Connington explains how Crippen might have become confused over the dosage.

Premeditated rape is an astonishing plot element for a Golden Age mystery, but criminal psychology preoccupied Connington less than plot and playing fair by the reader. In *The Eye in the Museum*, he includes a 'cluefinder'. Cluefinders reflected the notion of 'fair play'. When the solution to the mystery was given, references were appended (in this book, by way of footnotes) to point out the pages where clues to the puzzle had been given. This device was borrowed by other British writers, notably Freeman Wills Crofts, Ronald Knox and Rupert Penny, and most flamboyantly by the American C. Daly King.

Sayers extolled Connington's next book, *The Two Tickets Puzzle*, in her novel *The Five Red Herrings*, which elaborated upon his trick concerning a train ticket and an alibi. Perhaps her story grew out of a conversation with Connington at a dinner hosted by Berkeley. Her culprit, a detective fiction fan, has read Connington's book, and hidden his copy from Lord Peter Wimsey to prevent discovery of his cunning scheme. Unfortunately for him, Wimsey had already read *The Two Tickets Puzzle*. This typifies the way Club members referenced each other in their fiction, and was reinforced by Milward Kennedy's mention, in *Death to the Rescue*, of Sayers' and Connington's 'tricky way with train tickets'.

For many people, gambling offered escape from the drab everyday world, and the chance to dream of something better. Football pools, invented in the Twenties, were immensely popular, along with betting on horse- and dog-racing. Financial ruin suffered by gamblers who never knew when to stop was a common motive for murdering rich relatives in Golden Age mysteries. Crofts' puritanical distaste for betting surfaces in *Fatal Venture*, which features a luxury floating casino sailing outside British territorial waters. Christie, herself a competition addict, made crafty use of the craze as a motive for murder in *The Sittaford Mystery*. And a betting syndicate was at the heart of Connington's *The Sweepstake Murders*, which combines a clever puzzle with a sardonic glance at the changing face of rural England. Driffield's sidekick Wendover, a traditionalist with 'an inherited prejudice in favour of agriculture', deplores 'the new trades and factories which were springing up like mushrooms', producing 'flimsy articles' ranging from fancy brands of enamel to toffee or office gadgets.

The Sweepstake Murders is an early 'who will be next?' whodunit featuring a rationally motivated serial killer. Nine men, including Wendover, decide to have a flutter in a coming sweepstake, and draw a horse which comes second in the Derby, making their ticket worth almost one quarter of a million pounds. One syndicate member dies in an air crash, and a court action by his estate delays the payout. The survivors agree to share the winnings between those who remain alive at the time of payment – an unwise deal promptly followed by the apparently accidental death of another syndicate member, who falls into a chasm known as Hell's Gape.

Wendover's fellow syndicate members 'cared nothing for the countryside or the country people', and their attitude to the sweepstake reflects their innate greed. They are such an odious bunch that critics reckoned it was a pleasure to see them gradually eliminated. Connington humanizes Wendover by saying that he saw victims and suspects as human beings, rather than chess pieces – but overall, most of his characters *do* resemble chess pieces. A striking example is Thomas Laxford, a supposed left-wing idealist, in *The Ha-Ha Case*. Laxford's apparently well-meaning socialism makes an unconvincing contrast with his cynical deceptions. Connington had no time for ruthless businessmen, but he was equally contemptuous of idealists.

A tantalizing mystery of Victorian Scotland inspired *The Ha-Ha Case*. Alfred John Monson was hired as a private tutor to the Hambrough family, who owned the Ardlamont estate in Argyll. Monson, his friend Edward Scott and his wayward pupil Cecil Hambrough went out hunting one day in 1893, and after estate workers heard a shot, Cecil was found dead. Monson claimed the young man had accidentally shot himself in the head while climbing a fence. The death was regarded as a tragic accident until it emerged that Cecil had taken out life insurance policies in favour of Monson's wife. It emerged that the day before his death, Cecil, a non-swimmer, had narrowly escaped drowning after taking a boat ride with Monson. When Monson was tried for murder, Dr Joseph Bell (whose deductive methods Conan Doyle borrowed for Sherlock Holmes) was a witness for the prosecution. Despite the weight of circumstantial evidence against Monson, a 'not proven' verdict was returned, and he walked free. He was jailed for insurance fraud, and also became involved in a matrimonial dispute with his wife, whom he accused of committing adultery with Cecil. When Madame Tussaud's exhibited a waxwork of Monson, carrying a gun, outside the Chamber of Horrors, he sued for libel. But his luck with the law had run out. The jury humiliated him by awarding only a farthing in damages.

The other ingredients of *The Ha-Ha Case* are pure Golden Age: a country house party, an obscure point of English inheritance law, a dash of medical science, and some tricky work with ballistics – illustrated by a diagram. Connington plays a trick on the reader through an unorthodox use of narrative viewpoint before Johnnie Brandon goes out in a rabbit-shooting party. The young man is duly found shot dead in a sunken ditch (or 'ha-ha'), in a chapter with one of the most wonderful titles to be found in any Golden Age novel – 'The Ha-Ha of Death'.

Notes to Chapter 13

blazing cars enjoyed a vogue . . . in fiction
Forgotten blazing car novels include Francis Everton's intriguing *The Young Vanish* (1932), in which one character announces that 'it is the first occasion on which metallurgical and spectographic analysis has been called in the aid of the Law'. Everton was the pseudonym of Francis William Stokes (1883–1956), whose technical expertise matched that of Crofts and Rhode, but who had too much flair to be classed as humdrum. A note in *Murder May Pass Unpunished* (1936) describes him as a 'distinguished engineer who has been largely responsible for the development of the special process for making castings under centrifugal pressure'.

he and his wife cheered themselves up a little by reading detective novels
When Inge's wife sent Freeman Wills Crofts a complimentary post-card, he responded with his customary good manners, and she preserved his letter in a copy of his village mystery, *Enemy Unseen*.

his personable manner concealed a streak of ruthlessness
The research of Norman Donaldson and Oliver Mayo has helped to develop my understanding of Freeman's life and work, and I am especially indebted to two Freeman enthusiasts, David Chapman and Mark Sutcliffe, for information about his life and work.

The rest of the diary is written in his unique shorthand
David Chapman has been kind enough to show me extracts from the diary, and I share his hope that one day Freeman's code can be cracked.

Alfred Walter Stewart, alias J.J. Connington.
The most detailed account of Connington's life and work is to be found in Curtis Evans' *Masters of the 'Humdrum' Mystery*.

That dependable hate figure, the selfish financier, regularly crops up as a victim in Golden Age stories.
Examples include *Death of a Banker* (1934), an 'impossible crime' story by Anthony Wynne. Wynne was the pseudonym of Robert McNair Wilson (1882–1963), a doctor with an interest in economics

and a friend of Ezra Pound. In the same year, McNair Wilson published *Promise to Pay: An Inquiry into the Principles and Practice of that Latter-Day Magic Sometimes Called High Finance*. Wynne's detective Dr Eustace Hailey, the snuff-taking 'Giant of Harley Street', often investigated locked room mysteries, perhaps the most ingenious being *Murder of a Lady* (1931).

notably Freeman Wills Crofts, Ronald Knox and Rupert Penny, and most flamboyantly by the American C. Daly King
For examples, see Crofts' *The Hog's Back Mystery* (which Sayers mistakenly said in a review of King's novel was the first book to feature a cluefinder), Knox's *The Body in the Silo*, Penny's *She Had to Have Gas*, and King's *Obelists Fly High*. Rupert Penny was the pen name of Ernest Basil Charles Thornett (1909–70), who wrote eight ingenious whodunits in a short space of time at the tail end of the Golden Age. Thornett, like many other detective novelists, undertook intelligence work during the war, as well as writing a thriller under the name Martin Tanner. He never returned to the genre, and was best known in later years as a doyen of the British Iris Society, and editor of its yearbook.

A tantalizing mystery of Victorian Scotland
Discussed, for example, in Francis Grierson, "The Ardlamont Mystery" in *Great Unsolved Crimes*, and in "The Ardlamont Mystery: Tragic Mistake or Calculated Evil?", *The Scotsman*, 9 December 2005.

14

Echoes of War

Connington's cynicism in *The Case with Nine Solutions* was understandable – human life did seem all too cheap, especially during the war. Sayers' husband Mac Fleming knew this better than most. As the first battle of the Somme raged, Mac had been posted to France. His brother was killed in action, and the conditions Mac faced as a member of the Army Service Corps haunted him: 'Roads vanished under a sea of mud, guns got bogged down . . . ammunition lorries got stuck . . . what about the poor devils who – many times – worked forty-eight hours on end, at least half the time under shell-fire, plunging and wallowing in and out of shell-holes . . . no lights, and very often no food, and not the slightest protection . . . when the road was under fire.'

Nobody can understand the Detection Club without understanding how the war affected its members. Shadows cast by the conflict darkened Sayers' life with Mac, and the lives of most of her colleagues. To his dying day, Berkeley suffered from the effects of the Germans' use of chemical weapons of mass destruction. Ronald Gorell and Henry Wade were wounded in action, as were Agatha Christie's brother and Gorell's. Jessie Rickard's second husband was killed in the battle of Aubers Ridge, while Ned Bristed, the only man for whom Ngaio Marsh seems to have entertained romantic feelings, died fighting in Belgium. Marsh treasured the ruby ring he gave her for the rest of her life.

Close encounters with death so far outside the experience of present day novelists as to be almost unimaginable left many people with mental as well as physical scars. Mac Fleming and Monty Miller, like Berkeley, were tough to live with, but for all their faults, they were not just survivors of war, but its victims.

The war impacted on detective fiction, at first in an unexpected way. Violent death is at the heart of a novel about murder, but Golden Age writers, and their readers, had no wish or need to wallow in gore. They had already encountered enough to last a lifetime. The bloodless game-playing of post-conflict detective stories is often derided by thoughtless commentators who forget that after so much slaughter on the field of battle the survivors were desperately in need of a change. For a decade or so, detective fiction offered not so much cosiness as a form of convalescence, until people were ready to write and read about terrible events on the field of battle.

Consequences of war drove Sayers' *The Unpleasantness at the Bellona Club*. Remembrance of those who died is crucial to a time-of-death puzzle after the body of General Fentiman is discovered on Armistice Day, while his officer grandson rages at the senseless of war: 'A man goes and fights for his country, gets his inside gassed out, and loses his job, and all they give him is the privilege of marching past the Cenotaph once a year and paying four shillings in the pound income tax.'

Through Mac, Sayers gained a first-hand insight into the nightmarish world of the trenches, and her novel reflected the prevailing mood. The same period saw memoirs such as Robert Graves' *Goodbye to All That* and Erich Maria Remarque's *All Quiet on the Western Front*, as well as *Journey's End*, R. C. Sheriff's play set in an officers' dug-out. Sheriff's drama was rejected countless times by theatres who said the public hated to be reminded of the war and would not watch a play without a leading lady. When it finally reached the West End, with Laurence Olivier in the lead, it caught the moment, earning a long run, widespread translation and a film adaptation. The British public did not forget the 'glorious dead', but people were at last ready to face up to war's horrors.

The former military man was a staple of everyday life and traditional detective fiction. This is why Colonel Mustard features in the Golden Age-inspired board game *Cluedo*. At first sight, Colonel Mustard had real life counterparts in the Detection Club, but there was more to the men in question than met the eye. Henry Wade, John Rhode, Milward Kennedy and Christopher Bush formed a quartet of former soldiers who turned successfully to detective fiction in the Twenties. Clever and hard-working, they published almost two hundred and fifty novels between them and enjoyed a good deal of success. One of the mysteries of the Golden Age is – why have they been airbrushed out of its history so completely that it is often seen as the exclusive territory of the 'Queens of Crime'?

Wade seemed, at first glance, a Colonel Mustard lookalike. Tall, moustached, and with a commanding presence, he might have marched straight from a parade of the Grenadier Guards. His real name was Henry Lancelot Aubrey-Fletcher, and he had served in the Grenadiers with distinction. Unlike his Detection Club colleagues, he was a member of the landed gentry, with an insider's knowledge of life in an English country house. The family title dated back to the eighteenth century, and his father became fifth baronet, moving to Chilton House in Buckinghamshire. After Eton and Oxford, Wade joined the Grenadiers. Twice wounded during the war, he earned both the Distinguished Service Order and the Croix de Guerre.

Following the Armistice the Grenadiers had to march through Belgium towards Cologne, where British troops formed part of the force occupying Germany. On the way, at Fosses-la-Ville in Namur, Wade attended a talk on 'Detective Fiction' given by Valentine Williams, a former war correspondent who had been blown up while fighting at the Somme. Whilst recovering, Williams had begun a thriller, *The Man with the Clubfoot*, which launched a long career as a popular novelist. His talk stuck in Wade's mind, and when Wade published his first detective novel, *The Verdict of You All*, he inscribed a copy of the book in memory of the talk, and presented it to Williams.

Wade, like Mac, could not scrub out of his mind the blood

he had seen shed on the Front. A decade and a half after the Armistice, in *Mist on the Saltings*, he created the artist John Pansel, who was seriously wounded in battle: 'Officially "cured" and pensionless, John Pansel's digestion had been ruined by the jagged sliver of shell-case, the ripping knives, the draining tube, the cat-gut, and all the pains and paraphernalia of healing.' When Wade says that 'the years of merciless destruction had killed – so he thought – the power, even the desire, to create', he was talking about himself. But once he adjusted to peacetime, and found fresh creative energy, he explored the lasting damage done to men by the war, and the way English society had changed forever.

On leaving the army, Wade set about building a new life. A cricketing all-rounder talented enough to play regularly for Buckinghamshire, he became a Justice of the Peace, County Alderman, and High Sheriff. When he published *A History of the Foot Guards to 1856*, he listed his recreations, with tongue in cheek, as 'hunting, shooting and fishing'. Perhaps it is because he was a card-carrying member of the Establishment that the excellence of his crime fiction has often been overlooked. But his work reveals a keen awareness of the responsibilities that accompany the privilege of leadership, within the police or anywhere else, and his storylines were sometimes poignant, and often strikingly original.

At first, his writing was influenced by Freeman Wills Crofts – but Wade had one crucial advantage over Crofts, as a result of holding public office, which gave him a close personal understanding of how professional detectives worked. He was not the first insider to write police stories. Sir Basil Thomson, a former Head of CID at Scotland Yard whose eventful career also included spells as assistant prime minister of Tonga and governor of Dartmoor and Wormwood Scrubs, wrote several mystery stories, including a series charting the rise through the ranks of a policeman called Richardson. Thomson worked with the intelligence service during the war, conducting an interrogation of Mata Hari, the Dutch exotic dancer and spy subsequently executed by a French firing squad. In his mid-sixties, Thomson gained first-hand experience of the criminal justice system when he was charged with an act of indecency in Hyde Park with a woman who gave the name of Miss Thelma de Lava. Thomson claimed he was talking to her for the purpose of researching vice in London, prior to meeting a confidential source in the Communist Party at Speaker's Corner. His defence was not helped by the fact that Miss de Lava was a prostitute, or by his having misled a police constable about his identity. Thomson was a controversial figure, and it is conceivable that he was 'fitted up' by enemies in the police or political classes, but he was found guilty and fined five pounds.

Wade, a more accomplished writer than Thomson, became the first major crime novelist to blend police procedure and strong plots with exploration of the relationships and, sometimes, rivalries between police officers of all ranks. Far from being a backward-looking reactionary, he developed into one of the Golden Age's most ambitious innovators. The quality of his work has been underestimated, in part because of its variety, and perhaps also because Julian Symons, whose rare lapses of critical judgment were not quite so rare when it came to the Golden Age, ranked him alongside Freeman Wills Crofts and the Coles as a 'humdrum'. At his best, Wade was anything but.

Speaking very broadly, detective stories fall into one or more of five categories: puzzle, psychological, police/legal, playful/ ironic and medical/scientific. *The Verdict of You All* contained all these elements, with an early example of courtroom drama at its heart. The victim, as in *Trent's Last Case*, is a financier. Sir John Smethurst seems amiable, but proves to have been a bully. Wade believed in the status quo and class hierarchies, but his books display a fierce contempt for people who misuse their money and power. Sexual betrayal and the consequences of the war contribute to a conspicuously unsentimental story. Just like Berkeley, this pillar of the establishment showed cynicism about the machinery of justice, dedicating his novel 'in all sympathy to the innocent and still more to the guilty'.

Another financier dies in Wade's third novel, *The Duke of York's Steps*, when his aneurysm bursts after an assailant bumps into him. The aneurysm is a helpful condition for detective novelists seeking unpredictable ways to kill off their characters, as Anthony Berkeley later demonstrated in *Trial and Error*. In Wade's story the investigation is led by Inspector John Poole, first of a series of 'gentleman cops' created by Detection Club members. They include E. R. Punshon's Bobby Owen (who graduates from Oxford with a pass degree and finds that the only available job during the 'economic blizzard' of the slump is as a police constable, though he soon rises through the ranks), Ngaio Marsh's Roderick Alleyn, John Rhode's Jimmy Waghorn, Michael Innes's John Appleby, and, decades later, P. D. James' Adam Dalgleish. Wade is at ease in describing the atmosphere of London's gentlemen's clubs, and charts the effects of war on a wide range of characters, including a German Jew, embittered by the persecution he suffered during the conflict.

Corruption in local government has a timeless quality, and it provides the backdrop of *The Dying Alderman*. The book also boasts a 'dying message' clue, of the kind often found in Golden Age fiction. A murder victim on the point of death gives a tantalizing hint about the killer's identity. Dying messages soon became clichéd, but Wade's is neatly contrived, its meaning revealed in the very last line of the book.

Wade's books reflect his pessimism about the state of Britain as it entered the Thirties. Questions of family dishonour and the decaying state of the ruling classes dominate books such as *The Hanging Captain*. Ferris Court, the Tudor home of twelve generations of Sterrons, is crumbling. Inside, the decor is faded, outside the shrubberies are overgrown. Sir Herbert Sterron, brought low by gambling and poor investments, has squandered his inheritance, and is now trying in vain to sell the family heirlooms to one of his guests. His younger wife Griselda is pursued by a former adventurer who has become the county's High Sheriff, and also by an erratic priest who has taken to calling himself 'Father', just possibly a dig at Ronald Knox. Sterron's sexual impotence (delicately hinted at when the police question his doctor) symbolizes the collapse of the old order.

The Chief Constable in this book is a former soldier who 'having no qualifications for civilian employment other than the somewhat vague phrase "experience and control of men" . . . naturally thought of the police'. Wade's sarcasm was shrewdly targeted. In the aftermath of war, people on the left of politics had been afraid that the authorities had a covert plan to militarize the police, a fear fuelled by the recruitment strategy of Brigadier General Sir William Horwood, the police commissioner who survived eating poisoned walnut whips only to become known as 'the Chocolate Soldier'. Horwood's tenure had been marked by a series of calamities, including an alleged cover-up involving Sir Leo Money, the Italian-born economic theorist who had served as Lloyd George's parliamentary private secretary (and had subsequently criticized Knox's hoax broadcast for the BBC).

In an echo of Sir Basil Thomson's indiscretion, Money was accused of indecent behaviour with Miss Irene Savidge, a radio valve tester. Once again, the alleged misbehaviour took place in a leafy corner of Hyde Park. Money claimed he was merely offering Irene career advice, although what he knew about test-ing valves was not reported. The two of them were acquitted amidst complaints of a conspiracy to protect the establishment which led not only to a public inquiry but to a controversial five-hour interrogation of Irene by male officers. Their efforts to uncover the truth somehow led them to ask her to show them her pink petticoat. Police corruption and misbehaviour were all too common. The recruitment of university-educated detectives like John Poole was part of a drive to clean up the Metropolitan Police after a string of scandals, often involving officers bribed by bookmakers and brothel-keepers.

Encouraged by Sayers and other Detection Club colleagues, Wade became adventurous, trying something new with almost every book. The war continued to haunt him, and a soldier's act of cowardice formed the core of a bleak and effective novel published almost two decades after the Armistice. In *The High Sheriff*, a lengthy prologue conveys the grimness of life in the trenches, and explains why Robert D'Arcy, the High Sheriff of Brackenshire, has something to fear. A proud man, he once succumbed to a cowardly impulse when facing almost certain death, and dread of exposure has tormented him ever since.

Wade's experience as a high sheriff helped to ensure authenticity. Yet for all his preoccupation with the war, he later made a confession to a friend. 'Unbelievably', he groaned, he had overlooked a fundamental error in the dust jacket artwork. This shows D'Arcy presiding in court – but despite his wartime service, he is not wearing his medals.

John Rhode's life too was shaped by military service. A big, bluff heavyweight with an astonishing capacity for beer and an intensely practical cast of mind, he became a soldier before the outbreak of the war. After a spell as chief engineer of the Lyme Regis Electric Light and Power Company, he returned to the army and was promoted to the rank of major. His battery was often quiet, due to the need to conserve ammunition, and he relaxed by scribbling stories in his field message book. When his observation post was shelled, he woke up in the casualty clearing station to find the book had vanished.

Wounded three times, he was awarded the Military Cross before another artillery strike left him unfit for active service. Since anything was preferable to being 'relegated to some impossible camp, charged with the duty of teaching recruits the art of loading a howitzer without dropping the shell on their toes', he moved to Military Intelligence and worked on press propaganda. 'Our business was to glorify ourselves and our Allies, and to disparage our opponents by every means in our power. . . . The patron saint of Propaganda was the Father of Lies.'

This was an excellent training ground for a writer of fiction, and after a couple of wartime memoirs and other factual books, in 1924 he published a thriller under the name of John Rhode. By the end of the decade, he had established himself as a prime candidate for founder-membership of the Detection Club. His engineering skills enabled him to wire up Eric the Skull, so that in his role as Skullbearer, he could switch on the batteries lighting Eric's red eyes at just the right moment during initiation rituals. Sayers admired his ingenuity, as well as the fact that he was 'a perfect elephant for work'.

Rhode helped Sayers with *Have His Carcase*, but like her, he had reason to keep his personal life private. He was popular among his peers, and Lucy Beatrice Malleson, writing as Anthony Gilbert, dedicated her autobiography to him. Yet one anonymous obituarist (probably his Detection Club colleague Edmund Crispin) said that 'he was not an easy man to know'. The American Howard Haycraft regarded Rhode as one of the most secretive detective novelists – in a very competitive field.

His real name was Cecil John Charles Street, and he was born in Gibraltar. His father, a general in the British Army, was serving on the Rock, but the family soon moved back to England. Although Rhode had already reached the age of forty by the time of his debut as a crime writer, he went on to produce a staggering 143 novels. After two thrillers, he turned to detective fiction with *The Paddington Mystery*, which introduced his Great Detective, Dr Lancelot Priestley.

E. R. Punshon, a Detection Club colleague and crime fiction reviewer, helpfully described Rhode as 'Public Brain-Tester No. 1' and Collins Crime Club happily blazoned that slogan in publicizing Rhode's books. He possessed enough scientific, medical and practical know-how to set in motion an almost never-ending conveyor belt of ingenious methods for committing murder. Occasionally, they were inspired by real-life cases; remembering the death of the nineteenth-century chemist Adolph Gehlen helped Priesley to solve an ingenious puzzle in *The Corpse in the Car*. Rhode's most outlandish M.O. was, however, unlikely to have been employed in practice: it involved homicidal use of the spines of a hedgehog painted green.

Rhode's early books touched on interesting ideas – an altruistic murder in *The Davidson Case*, and the murderer's deliverance from justice in *Shot at Dawn*, for instance – that Berkeley and others developed in greater depth. But he lacked a gift for characterization, and it takes a reader with stamina to piece together Priestley's life story. A tetchy, cerebral mathematician, the doctor is a widower, with a daughter called April. In his first case, he clears April's husband-to-be, Harold Merefield, of suspicion of murder, but April is hardly ever mentioned again. Families were an inconvenience to Golden Age detectives; in the same way, the wife of John Dickson Carr's Dr Gideon Fell soon vanished from the accounts of her husband's exploits.

Harold, however, becomes a fixture as Priestley's long-suffering secretary and right-hand man. In *Shot at Dawn*, a corpse is spotted one morning, sprawled across the top of a motor cruiser's cabin. After studying the tidal stream in the estuary, Priestley tells Harold: 'The best way of representing the observations will be by a graph. I have brought some squared paper with me and it will be a pleasant occupation for you to draw the curve after dinner.' Harold dutifully converts 'the velocities, as observed, into the probable velocities at spring tides. For this purpose he multiplied Dr Priestley's figures by the factor four over three. Thus the velocity observed at eight-fifty, .42 knots, became .56 knots.' When his task is completed, his employer calls it 'quite a creditable piece of work' – high praise by Priestley's standards. Rhode thoughtfully reproduces the graph for the benefit of readers drowning in the flood of technical data.

In 1928, the year Berkeley produced *The Silk Stocking Murders*, Rhode also published a detective novel featuring a serial killer. *The Murders in Praed Street* begins with a sequence of apparently motiveless murders. Each victim receives a bone counter bearing a Roman numeral shortly before his death. Only when six men have died, and a seventh has received a numbered bone counter, does Inspector Hanslet take over the investigation and call in Dr Priestley. The great man has cut himself off from the outside world while absorbed in writing *Some Aspects of Modern Thought*, 'a book which was to enhance his already brilliant reputation . . . [and] to shatter the majority of the pet theories of orthodox science'.

Priestley rapidly identifies the motive for the crimes. The connecting link between the victims became such a cliché in detective fiction that Julian Symons bemoaned its dreary familiarity, so it is easy to forget that Rhode was breaking fresh ground. The killer's murder methods exploit Rhode's technical know-how. One crime involves the use of 'a remarkably virulent synthetic alkaloid', and another sees a man lured into a cellar and killed by prussic acid, released into the atmosphere by an electric current. An even more ingenious weapon is a metallic potassium bullet tipped with the broken end of a hypodermic needle and fired from an air gun. Priestley is the killer's final designated victim. To a modern reader, the whodunit twists are obvious, and Priestley is so slow to see through a villainous disguise that his negligence is almost criminal. At the time, however, the book represented something fresh in detective fiction.

The historic backdrop to the crimes is a mercy killing, but Rhode ignored the ethical implications. Christie, at her best, integrated the concept of justice into her plots, while Berkeley played ironic games to demonstrate the fallibility of justice. Rhode's interest lay in the mechanics of murder, not the moral questions it prompts. In one book, remarkably, a child-killer is allowed not only to get away with his crime, but to inherit a fortune. This was *Heir to Lucifer*, written as by Miles Burton, published in 1947 but bearing the hallmarks of traditional inter-war Golden Age fiction. The novel is a country house murder mystery, complete with amateur detective, Desmond Merrion, but the outcome is far from conventional. Merrion finds himself unable to prove the murderer's guilt, and dismisses out of hand his wife's despairing suggestion that the culprit will at least be troubled by a guilty conscience: 'The death of one small boy is not likely to disturb the philosophic calm of a student of Lucretius.' Merrion even goes so far as to maintain, 'Really, taking the broad view, things haven't turned out too badly.' The killer's psychology is not explored, and his extreme callousness is hard to reconcile with the way in which he is presented earlier in the story. Intriguingly, he shared a forename with the author.

Like Henry Wade, Rhode made sure that his work reflected changing times within the police service. Hendon Police College was established in May 1934 to train a new breed of 'officer class' cadets, and the following year Rhode published *Hendon's*

First Case, a clever and topical whodunit which contrasted the traditional working methods of Superintendent Hanslet with the more imaginative approach of Hendon (and Cambridge) man Jimmy Waghorn. Despite this nod to up-to-the minute authenticity, however, both men continue to consult Dr Priestley when faced with the trickiest murder puzzles. Rhode remained unpretentious about his writing. 'What could be more soul-destroying than re-reading one's own tripe?' he once asked Sayers.

The origins of the modern serial killer whodunit, a sub-genre impossible to avoid nowadays, seem to date back to 1928. That year saw the appearance of the books by Rhode and Berkeley, and S. S. Van Dine's *The Bishop Murder Case*. Earlier, Marie Belloc Lowndes' *The Lodger*, inspired by the Jack the Ripper killings and filmed by Hitchcock, had emphasised suspense rather than detection. After Berkeley, Rhode and Van Dine led the way, other Golden Age serial killer mysteries soon followed, most famously Christie's *The ABC Murders*.

Like Berkeley and Christie, Rhode ran into marital difficulties. He and his wife separated and he started living with Eileen Waller, although they did not marry until 1949, shortly after he became a widower. By the standards of middle-class respectability this was an unconventional personal life, and no doubt accounted for the secretiveness mentioned by Howard Haycraft, but Rhode was a generous and broad-minded companion. His closest friends in the Detection Club, Anthony Gilbert and John Dickson Carr, were significantly younger than him. He and Eileen lived in the countryside, and shared Freeman Wills Crofts' love of holiday cruises. Village pubs often feature in Rhode's books, and a recurrent theme is the absurdity of restricted licensing hours. In *The Charabanc Mystery*, a Miles Burton book, a character remarks: 'Wonderful how the smell of beer seems to pervade this case.'

Even when personal tragedy struck, Rhode's reaction was not to mope but to redouble his productivity. As with Sayers and others, writing and involvement in the Detection Club offered a brief escape from misery - in his case, grief over the death of his daughter Verena. The bereavement probably explains why he abandoned April Priestley – he simply could not bear to write about his detective's daughter any more.

Military service and rank were a source of great pride in the years between the two world wars. Sayers' husband insisted on being called Major Fleming, although Sayers confided to her cousin that she thought he was only entitled to the rank of captain. It was a sensitive issue, and she dared not provoke his temper by questioning him about it.

Christopher Bush liked to be known as Major Bush. His real name was Charlie Christmas Bush, and he grew up in Norfolk, one of a family of ten. His father was a radical Methodist and also a poacher. Bush won a scholarship to a grammar school and did some poaching himself to help pay family bills. After taking a degree he married, and worked as a school teacher before and after a spell in the army. Photographed in uniform, he cut a dashing figure, complete with military moustache. In 1920, a teaching colleague called Winifred Chart gave birth to his son, Geoffrey, but Bush never had anything to do with the child. After Winifred's death Geoffrey wrote to his father, but the letter was returned. This is sad, for Geoffrey Bush, who became a successful musician, also developed a taste for detective fiction. He wrote a Wimsey parody, and co-authored an excellent story, 'Who Killed Baker?' with Edmund Crispin, a talented post-war Detection Club member.

Christopher Bush wrote his first novel for a bet, rather like Christie and Douglas Cole. Soon he followed Berkeley and Rhode in writing about serial murders. Inspired by the letters supposedly sent by Jack the Ripper to Scotland Yard, *The Perfect Murder Case* set the template for whodunits in which a killer plays a game with the police. The Press and New Scotland Yard receive a letter from 'Marius' which opens: 'I am going to commit a murder.' The fair-play ethos lies behind the announcement: 'By giving the law its sporting chance I raise the affair from the brutal to the human.' Marius gives the date when the murder will occur, and says it will take place 'in a district of London north of the Thames', and describes his proposed crime as 'the Perfect Murder'.

This is a superb device for a detective story, imitated count-less times. Two more Marius letters follow, giving more clues as to the location of the killing, and causing a popular sensation which Bush captures vividly: 'Flapperdom arranged murder parties at hotels. The Ragamuffin Club had a special dance gala and a gallows scene painted for it. . . . Medical students organ-ised a gigantic rag. An enormous fortune must have been laid in bets. . . . What Marius had intended to be the sublime was likely to become the gorblimey.'

The authorities prove powerless to prevent the stabbing of wealthy and unscrupulous Harold Richleigh, and are left with a locked room mystery that does seem to amount to a perfect murder. All the likely suspects possess alibis. Much of the unofficial detective work is done by Ludovic Travers, the company's financial wizard and author of *Economics of a Spendthrift*, 'a work not only stupendous in its erudition but for the charm of its style a delight in itself'. Travers is widely regarded as a wealthy dilettante, but a clue he picks up proves crucial to the solving of the case.

The Perfect Murder Case boasted plentiful Golden Age trim-mings, a plan of the crime scene, maps showing the prime suspect's whereabouts, and a coded letter. A key element of the culprit's plan anticipates the murderous scheme in Christie's *Lord Edgware Dies*, published four years later. Travers eventu-ally became a private inquiry agent, and his career in detection continued until the late Sixties. Bush was elected to the Detection Club two years before war broke out again. A publicity photo-graph taken of him in middle age shows a dapper man in a trilby, resembling a suave private eye.

Milward Kennedy's bespectacled, serious appearance was mis-leading. A witty, affable man who served with distinction in the war, he received the Croix de Guerre before becoming the youngest male founder member of the Detection Club. Sayers had Lord Peter Wimsey praise his second novel, *The Corpse on the Mat*, and in the early Thirties Kennedy seemed destined to become one of the genre's leading lights.

Kennedy was educated at Winchester and Oxford, and his real name was Milward Rodon Kennedy Burge. He served on the British delegation to the Paris Peace Conference and in the Egyptian Ministry of Finance before joining the International Labour Organisation in Geneva. The ILO was an agency of the League of Nations, set up following the Treaty of Versailles, which focused on achieving social justice in labour relations, and in 1924 Kennedy became director of the London office. His publisher, Victor Gollancz, shared his radical political sympathies, but the strength of their friendship was severely tested before the end of the Thirties.

His first crime novel, *The Bleston Mystery*, published under the name of Robert Milward Kennedy and co-written with A. G. Macdonnell, was a romp concerning a treasure hunt for a missing legacy. He was taken on by Gollancz, and adapted his pen name to Milward Kennedy for most of his subsequent work. *Murder in Black and White*, however, was published under another pseudonym, Evelyn Elder, and contains a 'challenge to the reader' in the style of Ellery Queen. An amateur artist takes a holiday in the south of France and becomes involved in a seemingly impossible crime. His sketches are reproduced, so that readers can try to solve the puzzle by studying them. Another Evelyn Elder book, *Angel in the Case*, included one of the most elaborate maps found in any Golden Age novel. Kennedy's love affair with maps (and his tendency to complain about books lacking them) prompted John Dickson Carr's jokey grumble: 'I don't see how he can carry his own copy to the newspaper office without a large-scale diagram of Fleet Street. That man could get lost in a telephone-box, and a journey by Underground would kill him.'

In 1931, Kennedy dedicated *Death to the Rescue* to Berkeley, drawing on conversations they and Sayers had at Detection Club dinners: 'We have sometimes discussed the future of the Detective Novel. You, I believe, discern a new road – the "inner history" of the murder itself. You and Miss Sayers and others have given us masterly glimpses of that new road. But – will it not lead you away from Detection? . . . Can Detection in itself be the whole motive of a story? I suggest that you can write a novel which will prove that the answer is "yes".' The book offers something unique – if unrepeatable – in the genre. One aspect of it was, however, familiar, as Kennedy drew plot material from a controversial recent case.

On a Saturday evening in June 1929, Annie Oliver left her sixty-year-old husband Alfred, an expert on cigars, alone in their tobacconist's shop in Reading. After taking her little Pekingese dog out for a walk, she returned to find Alfred lying in a huddle on the floor of the shop. He was holding a handkerchief to his mouth, and it was saturated with blood. Rushing over to him, she asked what had happened. 'I don't know,' he murmured, and lapsed into unconsciousness. He had been beaten badly, and died twenty-four hours later. The crime had more than one victim. The tobacconist's shop was close to the County Theatre, where a creaky melodrama called *The Monster* was enjoying a brief run. Actor Philip Yale Drew, who played a detective, came under open suspicion from the coroner conducting the inquest. The jury, refusing to accept that anyone's guilt was proved, returned a verdict of murder by person or persons unknown. Nobody was ever charged with the crime, and the coroner's abuse of his power provoked a public outcry which led to a change in the law.

With Alfred Oliver's murder as his starting point, Kennedy fashioned a complex story. Most of it is narrated by Gregory Amor, a rich and conceited middle-aged bachelor with an unhealthy interest in young women. When his new neighbours slight him, he embarks on a lengthy investigation into their past, and chances upon a link with an unsolved killing of an old woman more than two decades earlier. An actor called Garry Boon emerges as a prime suspect during the inquest, but Amor comes up with a succession of increasingly elaborate theories about the case. He hits upon the truth, but is too clever for his own good. A 'locked room murder' is committed, and the cleverness of the method defeats the agent of justice, who satisfy themselves that it is a case of suicide. The ending is powerfully ironic.

But in his quest for something fresh and dazzling, Kennedy overreached himself. The publication of *Death to the Rescue* led, a few years later, to catastrophe. Philip Yale Drew had not killed Alfred Oliver, but the actor came close to destroying Kennedy's career as a novelist.

Notes to Chapter 14

Wade seemed, at first glance, a Colonel Mustard lookalike.
My account of Wade's life and work has drawn on correspondence
from Wade in my possession, Charles Shibuk's 'Henry Wade: a
Tribute' in *The Armchair Detective*, vols. 1.4 and 2.1, and an essay
about Wade by Curtis Evans, kindly shared with me prior to its
publication.

Valentine Williams, a former war correspondent
George Valentine Williams (1883–1946), a journalist who was
awarded the Military Cross, reported on major events such as the
Versailles Peace Conference and the opening of Tutankhamun's tomb
before leaving his job as the Foreign Editor of the *Daily Mail* to
write full-time. Late in his life, he worked for the Special Intelligence
Service, vetting potential new recruits ranging from Malcolm
Muggeridge to Kim Philby

He was not the first insider to write police stories.
A contender for the title of first professional police officer in Britain
to establish a separate career as a detective novelist was Frank
Froest (1858–1930), who was Walter Dew's superior officer in the
Crippen case, and who rose to become a Superintendent at Scotland
Yard. Froest's strength earned him the nick-name 'the man with
iron hands' and he was said to be capable of tearing a pack of
cards in half, and snapping a sixpence 'like a biscuit'. During his
retirement, he published several crime novels, notably *The Grell
Mystery* (1913), which was filmed. Some of his books were officially
co-authored by a journalist, George Dilnot (1883–1951), and it may
be that Froest provided story ideas, and Dilnot wrote them up.

John Rhode's life too was shaped by military service.
My outline of Rhode's life and work has drawn on the researches
of Tony Medawar and Curtis Evans, including the latter's *Masters
of the 'Humdrum' Mystery*.

*Marie Belloc Lowndes' The Lodger, inspired by the Jack the Ripper
killings and filmed by Hitchcock, had emphasised suspense rather
than detection.*
Even before the dawn of the twentieth century, serial killing was

not unknown in crime fiction. John Oxenham's *A Mystery of the Underground*, serialised in Jerome K. Jerome's magazine *To-Day*, frightened readers with its account of a Tube-travelling serial killer with so much success that passenger numbers slumped. Oxenham was a pseudonym used by William Arthur Dunkerley (1852–1941) and later borrowed by his daughter Elsie, a popular author of children's fiction.

Christopher Bush liked to be known as Major Bush.
I am indebted to Chris Garrod and Avril McArthur for sharing with me their researches into Bush's life.

Edmund Crispin, a talented post-war Detection Club member
Crispin's real name was Bruce Montgomery, and he also composed music for the *Carry On* films. He created the Oxford academic and amateur sleuth Gervase Fen, and dedicated his most famous novel, *The Moving Toyshop*, to his friend John Dickson Carr. Another influence was Michael Innes, whose novel *Hamlet, Revenge!* features a character called Gervase Crispin. Crispin published eight novels in the Golden Age tradition before he was 32, but like Carr he was a heavy drinker, and Fen did not return for a quarter of a century. By then, the Golden Age was a distant memory, and Crispin's touch had deserted him.

in the early Thirties Kennedy seemed destined to become one of the genre's leading lights
Surprisingly little has been written about Kennedy's life and work; a thorough study is overdue.

co-written with A. G. Macdonnell
Archibald Gordon Macdonnell (1895–1941), a journalist and playwright, was most celebrated for his humorous novel *England, their England* (1935). He wrote a handful of detective novels under the pseudonym Neil Gordon, one of which borrowed a notable plot device from John Rhode's *The Murders in Praed Street.'*

15

Murder, Transvestism and Suicide during a Trapeze Act

The Detection Club's initiation ritual appealed to members with a theatrical streak. Many of them loved acting – and pretending to be someone else was a way of guarding their secrets. Sayers, in particular, found herself leading a double life. To the world at large, she was a childless celebrity, an intellectual eccentric. In private, she was the mother of an unacknowledged illegitimate son, and trapped in an increasingly unhappy marriage.

Her performance became increasingly extravagant as she grew into the public persona she had created for herself. During her student days, she once watched five Gilbert and Sullivan operettas in a week while rehearsing for a play in which she took the lead role, and she yearned to become a playwright. Money was an added incentive. In an age when going to the theatre was, for many, as much a social obligation as attending church, a West End smash could earn a fortune for the playwright.

The power of the screen was less clear. Though countless television and cinema adaptations have since shown his concerns to be misplaced, Alfred Hitchcock thought Golden Age novels lacked emotion, and complained that 'all the interest is concentrated in the ending'.

It is a pity Hitchcock was never invited to one of the Detection

Club's theatrical initiation rituals – he would surely have relished a close encounter with Eric the Skull. Apart from infuriating Berkeley with his mangling of *Before the Fact*, his closest link was perhaps through Frank Vosper, a playwright and actor whose suave good looks meant he was apt to be cast as an urbane villain. In Hitchcock's first version of *The Man Who Knew Too Much*, Vosper appeared as Ramon, the assassin. Later, he not only adapted Christie's short story 'Philomel Cottage' into a play that was later filmed, *Love from a Stranger*, but also took the lead role of Bruce Lovell.

Vosper's interest in criminology matched Anthony Berkeley's, and he enjoyed attending trials at the Old Bailey. Venturing where Hitchcock feared to tread, he wrote a play based on the case of Edith Thompson and Frederick Bywaters, both executed in 1923 for the murder of Edith's husband. *People like Us* had a brief run at the Strand Theatre, but the daring subject matter was too much for the Lord Chamberlain's office, a haven for prejudice until the late Sixties, and further performances were banned. *People like Us* did not resurface until long after Vosper died – a death that posed a real-life Golden Age puzzle.

Berkeley's own ventures into the theatre achieved only modest success, whereas A. A. Milne had a West End hit with *The Fourth Wall* as well as several plays not in the crime genre. But the leading dramatist among the Club's founder members was Clemence Dane, whose flair for visual writing proved ideally suited to film. She received an Academy Award for *Vacation from Marriage*, released in the UK as *Perfect Strangers*, the first Detection Club member to win an Oscar.

A book co-written by Dane and another Detection Club member, Helen Simpson, provided the basis for a rare Hitchcock whodunit movie. Dane was not primarily a crime writer, but she and Simpson shared a love of the stage, and this led them to co-write a mystery set in the world of the theatre. The book was called *Enter Sir John*, but while he was shooting a film version, the Master of Suspense opted for a title needing no explanation: *Murder!*

Murder! represented a milestone in crime films. Hitchcock's third talking picture, it demonstrated his daring as a director. Despite his reservations about cinematic whodunits, the theatrical background and melodramatic potential of the storyline led him to experiment. As François Truffaut said in conversation with Hitchcock, *Murder!* is in essence 'a thinly disguised story about homosexuality' – complete with transvestism, and suicide during a trapeze act.

Hitchcock gave Herbert Marshall, playing the amateur detective, a stream-of-consciousness monologue about his role as a juror in a trial which seems destined to result in a beautiful woman being sent to the gallows. Familiar in the theatre, the monologue was a novelty in film, and Hitchcock showed his genius in a scene geared to the techniques of sound. Marshall is shaving while listening to music on his radio set. Since it was impossible to record the music later, Hitchcock had a thirty-piece orchestra in the studio, behind the bathroom set, playing the Prelude from *Tristan und Isolde*. The film did well in London, but flopped in the provinces, and suffered a long period of critical neglect. Although some of the acting is hammy by modern standards, this is one of the better movies Hitchcock made before moving to Hollywood. After the Second World War, he filmed *Under Capricorn*, a costume drama set in nineteenth-century Australia, and based on a book Simpson wrote alone. But by then she was dead.

Clemence Dane and Helen Simpson were the Detection Club's oddest couple. Dane, whose real name was Winifred Ashton, studied art in London and Dresden, and spent a few years acting under the name Diana Portis. When she turned to writing, she adapted her pseudonym from the name of a church in the Strand, St Clement Danes. Teaching in a girls' school during the war furnished the background for her novel *Regiment of Women*. Dane's book was an inspiration for Radclyffe Hall's lesbian classic *The Well of Loneliness*, although, constrained by the mores of the time, Dane settles for a heterosexual 'happy ending'. When Dane tried her hand as a playwright, *A Bill of Divorcement* made a topical contribution to the debate in the early Twenties about a legislative proposal to allow women to divorce if their husbands were alcoholics, insane or in prison.

She often wrote for radio, and Emlyn Williams, cast in a play she wrote about Shakespeare, described her as 'an outsize author with a handsome generous face topped by hair as over-flowing as her talent . . . in a cascade of black to the floor, with a corsage of big happy flowers which accentuated her size.'

Dane kept any turbulent passions she may have felt hidden beneath her apparently naïve façade. Her friend Noel Coward later based the bumbling medium Madame Arcati in *Blithe Spirit* upon her. She entertained Coward and others in their circle with her regular – and supposedly unintentional – *faux-pas*; she liked to describe herself as 'randy', when meaning to convey her liveliness and energy. On one occasion, this promi-nent feminist described the different sides to a person's nature: 'Yes, every man has three John Thomases – the John Thomas he keeps to himself, the John Thomas he shares with his friends, and the John Thomas he shows to the world.'

Simpson named her daughter Clemence, in tribute to Dane. The pair shared a publisher, and a plot idea donated to them by C. S. Evans, their editor, led them to write *Enter Sir John*, featuring actor and theatre manager Sir John Samaurez (born Johnny Simmonds) as amateur detective. Samaurez marries the woman he has saved from the gallows. Although he resumed his detecting career, it proved short-lived.

After they had written three novels together, Dane's interest in detective fiction waned, but Simpson's grew. Tall and pale, with thick dark wavy hair, Helen de Guerry Simpson was an astonishingly high achiever, who seemed to dedicate her life to proving that a woman could have it all. Convent-educated, she was a keen snuff-taker with a love of fencing and witchcraft. She played the piano and the flute, and was a keen horsewoman, as well as a gifted cook who enjoyed making home-made wine according to ancient recipes. After broadcasting a series of talks about cooking on the BBC, she was deluged with fan mail, and her popularity led to lecture tours in Australia and the United States, where she spoke on subjects ranging from literary impostors to how cheesecakes were made in the time of Samuel Pepys. When she stood for Parliament as Liberal candidate for the Isle of Wight, for a general election that never took place because of the war, she campaigned by travelling around in a donkey-cart.

Sydney-born, Simpson was the daughter of a solicitor and granddaughter of a French marquis. After her parents separated, she moved with her mother to France, and then to England, where she decoded messages in foreign languages for the Admiralty. She studied music at Oxford, but her love of drama brought mixed fortunes. She helped found the Oxford Women's Dramatic Society, but was sent down for breaking the ban on male and female students acting together. Undaunted, she threw herself into a literary career, publishing poetry, plays, translations and short stories as well as novels, starting with *Acquittal*, written in five weeks to win a bet. She contributed dialogue to Hitchcock's *Sabotage*, and married fellow Australian Denis Browne, a surgeon.

A journalist interviewed her at her London home whilst she was in the midst of writing three books at the same time as bringing up her young daughter, Simpson confessed to a secret passion for a good cigar. 'I love going to the gasometer-shaped reading room of the British Museum and digging out history,' she said. Each day she wrote a thousand words in pencil, usually while the nursery wireless was at full blast in the next room. The journalist was struck by her determination not to waste time. During the interview, she kept stitching a chair cover.

Sayers and she became close friends – although she was not told about John Anthony's existence – and Sayers borrowed from *Enter Sir John* to create the storyline of *Strong Poison*. But not even Helen Simpson could have it all forever. She died young, leaving Sayers, never a woman to gush, to say: 'I have never met anybody who equalled her in vivid personality and in the intense interest she brought into her contacts with people and things'.

Notes to Chapter 15

Frank Vosper . . . adapted Christie's short story 'Philomel Cottage'
To be precise, Vosper adapted *The Stranger*, Christie's unperformed stage version of her story.

Emlyn Williams . . . described her as 'an outsize author with a handsome generous face topped by hair as overflowing as her talent'
The description comes from Williams' memoir *Emlyn* (London, Bodley Head, 1973). Williams (1905–87) was an actor and playwright whose work occasionally touched on crime. He also wrote a semi-fictionalized book about the Moors murders committed by Ian Brady and Myra Hindley.

Helen de Guerry Simpson was an astonishingly high achiever
See Philip L. Scowcroft, 'Detection, History and Australia: The Literary Experience of Helen Simpson', *CADS* 16, May 1991, and Liz Gilbey, 'To Hitchcock and Beyond: Australian Author Helen Simpson', *CADS* 58, June 2010, which suggests that Simpson's short story 'Mr Right' influenced Sayers' *Strong Poison*.

She contributed dialogue to Hitchcock's Sabotage, *and married fellow Australian Denis Browne*
Browne's uncle wrote the nineteenth-century classic *Robbery under Arms* using the pen name Rolf Boldrewood. Denis Browne later became an eminent paediatric surgeon at Great Ormond Street Hospital and earned a knighthood.

16

A Severed Head in a Fish-Bag

Detection Club members were escapists, just as much as their readers. The Twenties and Thirties supplied plenty of reasons for people to yearn for a break from their everyday lives. Playing a part, on stage or off it, was one solution, and so was going to the theatre or watching a film. Travelling around, at home or abroad, was another way of getting away from it all. For writers, holidays provided fresh backgrounds for their novels. For readers, the chance to read a mystery set somewhere unfamiliar added to the pleasure of discovering whodunit.

Douglas and Margaret Cole enjoyed walking holidays. One fine summer's day in Lyme Regis, Margaret was striding ahead of her husband when she caught sight of a vast and unmistakable figure seated on the steps outside a Georgian hotel. It was G. K. Chesteron. He and his wife liked the Three Cups Hotel – a favourite of Jane Austen, Tennyson and Tolkien – so much that they had become close friends of the landlord. The Coles were delighted by the unexpected encounter with the Detection Club President. Chesterton's views often chimed with theirs, and they regarded his poem 'The Song of the Wheels', ferocious in its denunciation of the exploitation of labour, as the best ever written in defence of striking workers. The Coles spent the evening captivated by the cheeriness of this huge yet somehow child-like man, who fidgeted with his fingers and had a squeaky, gurgling laugh. His latest hobby horse was the difficulty of capturing the nuances of his writing when translating it into foreign languages. 'How,' he demanded, 'would you put the phrase "the child she-bear so beloved of hymnologists" into idiomatic and intelligible French?'

That day proved memorable for a much less happy reason. During their walk, Douglas fell behind Margaret, instead of outpacing her as usual. He simply had no energy. They put it down to a touch of the sun, but a few months later they went walking in Kent, and again Douglas could not keep up. He abandoned his plan to stand for Parliament – and so avoided becoming one more statistic in the rout of the Labour Party at the next general election. Margaret fell dangerously ill with pneumonia, and completed her convalescence with a month as a guest of a doctor friend at a villa on an island off Portofino. For her, it was 'an enchanted April' in the sun, although when Victor Gollancz came to stay, he kept on his city suit, and spent most of his time indoors, playing billiards in a stuffy room with Douglas.

As Margaret recovered, Douglas found himself plagued by drowsiness and a raging thirst. Diabetes was diagnosed, and an attempt to treat him without recourse to insulin turned him into a living skeleton, while the Coles' house stank with the stench of 'biscuits' made from seaweed which were intended, along with 'a revolting kind of aerated cottonwool' to replace bread in a brutally restricted diet. Eventually he was put on insulin and his condition improved. But he was never the same man again, and attacks of hypoglycaemia affected him mentally as well as physically. This resulted in what Margaret described as a 'heightened nervous tension'. He was more feverishly prolific than ever, but became deaf to constructive criticism.

Clumsiness weakened their detective novels, and this did not go unnoticed by colleagues in the Detection Club. Nicholas Blake, whose politics were close to the Coles', praised the dialogue and setting of *Scandal at School*, but felt the plot resembled 'a clockwork mouse: erratic in direction, and requiring too frequent winding-up'. Berkeley liked the Coles, but was disappointed by *Death of a Star*, which had a solution so painfully obvious that the police's delay in discovering it caused him to lose patience. At least he enjoyed 'the admirable opening', in which the severed head of a popular and glamorous film star is discovered in a fish-bag on the Embankment.

Douglas Coles' poor health seemed like a metaphor for the damaged state of the country. The National Government, re-elected with a resounding majority to the Coles' despair, presided over a sick economy. The medicine of job losses, means testing and higher income tax was harsh, and recovery a long time coming. For people with little or no money, borrowing detective novels from libraries offered respite for an hour or two. The better-off were forced to make economies, and Detection Club members felt strong commercial pressure to write what their readers wanted most.

In the Hungry Thirties, men often walked long distances in search of work. The romance of the road quickly faded, and the 'passing tramp' became a scapegoat for many a fictional murder, although the real culprit invariably proved to be someone else. Walking was cheap, and 'the right to roam' became a hot topic. The formation of the Ramblers' Association was followed by a mass trespass on Kinder Scout in Derbyshire in 1932, a protest echoed three years later in *Death in a Little Town* by R. C. Woodthorpe. Local people take 'direct action' to tear down a fence blocking a public right-of-way, and soon the unpleasant landowner responsible is found dead, but Woodthorpe's narrative offers a leisurely ramble rather than a brisk march to the solution of the mystery.

The wintry economic climate, and a deteriorating exchange rate, meant that people became desperate to get away from it all, though even those who could afford a holiday mostly stayed in Britain. A generation earlier, Chesterton had rhapsodized about the detective story reflecting 'the romance of the city', but during the Golden Age, hundreds of mysteries were set in country villages.

Mac Fleming, a keen fisherman and artist, was fond of south-west Scotland. He loved speeding at eighty miles an hour along the Kirkcudbright-to-Gatehouse road, much to the horror of his wife, trapped in the passenger seat. Their Scottish holidays prompted Sayers to set a novel in an artistic community in Galloway, where Wimsey stumbles across a murder during a fishing trip. *The Five Red Herrings* was a 'pure puzzle story', not Sayers' strong suit, but at least Gollancz equipped it with a better map than Freeman Wills Crofts was allowed for *Sir John Magill's Last Journey*. Sayers thundered that Collins had supplied her luckless friend with 'the most mean, miserable, potty, small, undecipherable and useless map, scrimshanking, feeble and unworthy to the last degree'.

She combined writing her own detective stories with supervising the round-robin mysteries and compiling anthologies. Frenetic activity took her mind off domestic worries: tax demands, Mac's poor health, and his continuing lethargy about fulfilling his promise to adopt her illegitimate son John Anthony. She took over from Berkeley as Honorary Secretary of the Detection Club, and returned to form in *Have His Carcase*.

The story opens with Harriet Vane on a walking tour around the south-west coast of England. On such a holiday, the Coles had bumped into Chesterton, but Harriet encounters a corpse on a rock known as the Devil's Flat-Iron. The dead man's throat has been cut from ear to ear, and the wound bleeds on to her. Harriet sets about breaking a seemingly impregnable alibi, and describes to Wimsey how different fictional sleuths solve elaborate puzzles, name-checking Inspector French, Dr Thorndyke and Roger Sheringham.

The victim, a Russian gigolo supposedly of noble birth, had worked at the Resplendent Hotel – 'one of those monster seaside palaces which look as though they had been designed by a German manufacturer of children's cardboard toys' – dancing with guests like the rich but lonely widow Mrs Weldon. Harriet is scathing about men who expect women to be submissive, and women who are content to depend on men. She had become a mouthpiece for Sayers.

Like *The Five Red Herrings*, the book owed a debt to the Detection Club. Sayers picked Robert Eustace's brains about a means of causing confusion about the time of death, and also consulted Crofts and John Rhode. Rhode thought the codes typically used in detective fiction were too easily broken and therefore unsatisfactory. He made this point to Sayers, and encouraged her to use a much trickier cipher by sending her an explanation (running to five pages) of how to encode and decode a Playfair cipher, together with a sample message for encoding. In a prefatory note, she acknowledged Rhode's help with 'the hard bits', and during the novel Wimsey mentions Rhode's *Peril at Cranbury Hall*, which devotes a whole chapter to explaining how to decode the cipher. Unravelling the cipher in *Have His Carcase* also requires pages of yawn-inducing explanation. Obsessive accuracy of detail was a strength of Sayers (unlike the Coles, who in *Last Will and Testament* had a character mauled by a tiger in Africa) but once in a while it caused her to become as dull as Douglas Cole on a bad day.

Sayers and Henry Wade both loved the atmospheric East Anglian landscape, and rendered it superbly as a setting for murder. The small fishing community at Bryde-by-the-Sea in Wade's *Mist on the Saltings* is a world away from the thatched cottage and village green stereotype associated with Golden Age novels by people who seldom read them. Bryde is nominally a harbour, but separated from the North Sea by 'a wide expanse of weed-grown mud, intersected by a maze of channels which at high tide are full to the brim of salt water and at low are mere trenches of black and treacherous ooze'. The dreary and desolate Saltings obsess the troubled war veteran and artist John Pansel, while his wife's loyalty is tested by Dallas Fiennes, a lecherous novelist camped in a hut on the sand dunes. In the taproom of the local pub, a sick and unemployed singer and an out-of-work engineer join Pansel in bemoaning the state of the nation – 'We encourage enemy aliens and put our own heroes on the dole' – and worry about whether Mussolini will provoke another war. Pansel concludes, 'We may not be too proud to fight, but we're too damn poor.'

Fiennes is found dead in the mud of the Saltings. Did he lose his footing in the fog, or did someone kill him? In the final scene, a small boat rocks on the sea, its occupant lost in the water, a suitably bleak conclusion to a book closer in spirit to the modern crime novel than almost anything previously written by members of the Detection Club. Sayers praised the originality of *Mist on the Saltings*, but teased Wade about his depiction of the novel-writing Casanova: Fiennes, she said, 'plans a seduction like Napoleon – and executes it like the famous Duke of York'. Perhaps this served Wade right after his complaint two years earlier that Harriet Vane was 'the least real of your characters. At times she is a rather common tom-boy, at others she is ravishing Wimsey.' However, Sayers admired the characterization of John Pansel, noting that his sullen behaviour was 'convincingly true to life'. Perhaps she was thinking of Mac.

Reviewing attracted her because in those days newspaper and magazine editors allowed plenty of space to consider the form seriously. Torquemada was the most renowned crime fiction critic, but Berkeley, Margaret Cole, E. R. Punshon, Nicholas Blake and Milward Kennedy all tried their hands. So did T. S. Eliot and other poets such as Herbert Read, Edward Shanks and Dylan Thomas. Thomas's fascination with the Detection Club influenced an abortive mystery novel of his own that was never published in his lifetime, partly for fear of libel actions by the fellow poets whom he satirized, partly because the story was feeble. Other notable Golden Age reviewers included Virginia Woolf's husband Leonard, Arthur Ransome (under the pseudonym William Blunt), and the feminist writer Rose Macaulay. Charles Williams, a friend of Sayers, was one of the 'Inklings', the Oxford literary group led by C. S. Lewis and J. R. R. Tolkien, and also an enthusiastic critic of crime whose own novels occasionally veered towards detective fiction.

Nobody brought more energy and expertise to criticism of detective novels than Sayers. For more than two years she reviewed three books each week, reading – but possibly not always finishing – at a rate of more than one book each day. She singled out Punshon for high praise, but her commitment to intellectual integrity meant that not all her Detection Club colleagues were so lucky. She was as dismissive of the Coles'

The Affair at Aliquid as she was generous to the early novels of other writers with radical sympathies such as R. C. Woodthorpe, Nicholas Blake and Christopher St John Sprigg. Occasionally, she added a postscript to her column, featuring 'The Week's Worst English'. Sayers being Sayers, one postscript was devoted to 'The Week's Worst Latin'.

She also covered books by American novelists, but readers, and therefore publishers, showed limited interest in crime fiction from further afield. This was the nature of the times; as Bertolt Brecht said: 'The crime novel, like the world itself, is ruled by the English.' Yet during the Golden Age, writers who enjoyed and wrote detective fiction were as diverse, and as geographically scattered, as Argentina's Jorge Luis Borges, New Zealander Miles Franklin, Australia's Paul McGuire and Arthur Upfield (an Englishman who emigrated at the age of twenty), and Europeans such as Karel Čapek, Friedrich Glauser, Stanislas-André Steeman, and the creator of Maigret, Georges Simenon. Brecht planned to co-author crime novels with another fan, the philosopher and critic Walter Benjamin. The rise of Hitler halted their project, depriving us of detective fiction written by two German Marxists entranced by the possibility of playing games with the genre. Nazis saw little need for the self-indulgence of literary escapism.

At Benson's advertising agency, Sayers learned about offering added value, and she realized the worth of an atmospheric context for a murder mystery. Having popularized the workplace-based mystery with *Murder Must Advertise*, she wrote a book combining a memorable setting with esoteric background information. Today, a blend of fact and fiction is a key part of the appeal of novels by writers as diverse as Dick (and now Felix) Francis and Patricia Cornwell, but the pattern was set by Sayers. *The Nine Tailors* told readers everything they needed to know about campanology but were afraid to ask. Bell-ringing even supplies an unusual cryptogram, the key to which is a specific peal written out in change-ringing notation.

The Fenland backdrop, lovingly depicted, gives the book

depth. On New Year's Eve, Wimsey is stranded when his car breaks down at the village of Fenchurch St Paul, and before long he finds himself acting as a substitute when one of the church's bell-ringers falls ill. Next morning the local squire's wife dies, and when her husband expires the following Easter, the family grave is opened and a mutilated body discovered. The cause of death, brilliantly integrated into the storyline, was as original as those in *Unnatural Death* and *The Documents in the Case*, and equally controversial. Sayers drew on her knowledge of life in her father's parish in creating Fenchurch St Paul and its imposing church, and the closing pages show Sayers' powers of description as she conveys the drama of a flood with fatal consequences for a character who, like Wade's killer in *Mist on the Saltings*, is tormented by a guilty conscience.

Christie's love of travel meant Hercule Poirot spent a good deal of his time holidaying at home and abroad, although his attempts to get away from it all were constantly interrupted by cunningly contrived murders. *Peril at End House* is set in St Loo, 'the Queen of Watering Places', which like Loomouth in *Three-Act Tragedy* is a thinly-disguised Torquay. Despite all her gallivanting in the Middle East, Christie's love for Devon was undimmed. The Art Deco hotel on Burgh Island, which is cut off from the mainland at high tide, was a favourite retreat, and the potential for a 'closed circle' murder mystery were not lost on her. She fictionalized Burgh in *Evil under the Sun*, although it is too easily accessed to justify claims that it was also the inspiration for the island on which a group of disparate characters find themselves trapped in *And Then There Were None*.

For readers who could not afford holidays, detective novels featuring foreign travel held the appeal of a magic carpet. On a trip back to England for Christmas, bad weather led to a series of mishaps when Christie was on the Orient Express together with an extraordinary assortment of passengers, including the soon-to-be-assassinated King Alexander of Yugoslavia, his wife and a swarm of detectives. Others included an elderly American woman, an archaeology enthusiast from Smyrna, a large Italian, and a bald German. Christie was disconcerted by a Turk who wore an orange suit and gold chains and who spent the night trying to open the door between their two compartments, possibly in the mistaken belief that it led to a bathroom. At Sofia, three feet of snow had fallen, and the passengers found themselves marooned. Christie arrived home two days late, but the whole bizarre experience gave her a marvellous backdrop, along with several characters, for one of her most famous novels. To these ingredients she added a plot derived from the most notorious kidnapping of the age.

On 1 March 1932, the twenty-month-old Charles Lindbergh Jr, son of the famous hero of aviation and his wife Annie Morrow Lindbergh, was abducted from his nursery on the second floor of the family's luxurious mansion in New Jersey. An illiterate note was found on the nursery windowsill demanding a ransom of $50,000. The kidnapping caused a sensation, and President Hoover said he would 'move Heaven and earth' to recover the child. The legendary gangster Al Capone said he would help if he were released from prison, but this proved to be an offer the authorities were happy to refuse.

An elaborate game of cat-and-mouse between the family and police on one side, and the kidnappers on the other, led to complicated negotiations and a host of further ransom demands. A go-between eventually handed over the money, and was told that the child could be found in a boat called *Nellie* near Martha's Vineyard. After an unsuccessful search, the child's body was found by accident, partly buried and badly decomposed, less than five miles from the Lindbergh's house. The head was crushed, there was a hole in the skull, and some parts of the body were missing.

The FBI suspected an 'inside job', and among those questioned was Violet Sharp, a British woman who worked for the Lindberghs as a servant. Due to be questioned for a fourth time, Violet killed herself by swallowing a silver polish that contained potassium cyanide. Eventually, the police arrested a German immigrant called Bruno Richard Hauptmann, who was tried for

extortion and murder. He never wavered in protesting his innocence, but the weight of circumstantial evidence against him
led to his conviction. Still refusing all inducements to confess,
on 3 April 1936 he was executed in 'Old Smokey', the electric
chair at the New Jersey State Prison. Controversy still rages
over whether he was guilty.

Christie was struck by the collateral damage inflicted by the
crime on people in the Lindberghs' circle, notably Violet Sharp,
who had an alibi for the kidnapping but was worn down by
police questioning and feared the loss of her job. Christie came
up with a plot in which an American gangster suspected of a
similar kidnapping and murder is found stabbed to death on
board the Orient Express. With the train halted by a snowstorm,
Poirot has to find out who was responsible. Ultimately, he comes
up with two competing theories, one orthodox, the other bizarre
but (and this is Christie's skill) logical. The reader is left in no
doubt that Christie thought justice best served by allowing the
murder to go unpunished. Raymond Chandler hated the solution, saying, 'only a half wit could guess it'. In other words, he
failed to pick up the clues. Sayers, like most people, admired
the daring of the plot. Christie said Max Mallowan gave her
the idea, but Anthony Berkeley deserves credit too. He tossed
out the same notion in a line that surely lingered in Christie's
subconscious.

Trains and boats and planes carried Christie's characters
around throughout the Thirties. Readers with no chance of
experiencing first-class international travel for themselves relished the picture of life on a luxurious cruise presented in *Death
on the Nile*. But as always, what mattered with Christie was
the mystery, and she came up with an ingenious form of alibi.
Torquemada and E.R. Punshon wrote glowing reviews, and the
book became a genre classic. In contrast, when Freeman Wills
Crofts used a Mediterranean cruise as the setting for *Found
Floating*, published in the same year as *Death on the Nile*, he
drifted into travelogue mode, even including a chapter devoted
to a description of the ship. Until old age caught up with her,
Christie never allowed herself such self-indulgence.

In *Death in the Clouds*, another 'closed circle' puzzle, a blackmailer is killed while flying on the airliner *Prometheus* from Paris to Croydon. Among the suspects is Lady Horbury, a glamorous former chorus girl, whose tastes run not just to collegian hats and fashionable fox furs, but also to gambling and cocaine. Christie hides a clue in plain sight, within a lengthy list of contents of passengers' luggage. Detection Club members found countless ways to distract readers' attention from vital plot information. John Dickson Carr's favourite technique was to plant a clue and then follow it immediately with something graphic – a method he called 'blood on a white bandage'. Sayers agreed that, as readers pictured the vivid image, they forgot the clue. In *The Five Red Herrings*, the *absence* of an item that should have been present at the scene of the crime alerts Wimsey to the fact that an artist did not die in an accident but was murdered.

One of the passengers on the *Prometheus*, Daniel Clancy, writes detective fiction featuring a popular sleuth who 'bites his nails and eats a lot of bananas'. Poirot points out to him the benefits of crime writing as therapy: 'You can relieve your feelings by the expedient of the printed word. You have the power of the pen over your enemies.' This seemingly throwaway remark suggests an idea taking shape in Christie's mind. It supplies a clue to the mystery surrounding a first-edition copy of *Murder in Mesopotamia*, which Christie inscribed enigmatically to an unnamed friend: 'With love from one who may have done crimes unsuspected, not detected!?'

The Nine Tailors sold nearly one hundred thousand copies in seven weeks, and Sayers' fame kept growing. Ezra Pound wrote to her, inviting her to turn her attention to the larger crimes in the world of economics and government. She replied that she did not think they offered enough mystery. Interviewed by the *Daily Express* 'in her comfortable book-lined flat in Bloomsbury', she smoked innumerable cigarettes through a long holder, and informed the journalist she was a scholar gone wrong. For the BBC programme *Seven Days*, she was the only woman speaker in a group of contributors including Winston Churchill, David Lloyd George and George Bernard Shaw.

The more success a writer enjoys, the fiercer the criticism he or she attracts. Sayers' writing provoked hostility as well as admiration. The American critic Edmund Wilson could not imagine why readers might be interested in the detail of bell-ringing. He found Margery Allingham 'completely unreadable', Ngaio Marsh's books 'unappetizing sawdust', and Christie 'impossible to read', although he was marginally more sympathetic towards John Dickson Carr's *The Burning Court*.

Wilson's rants about Golden Age fiction included the essay 'Who Cares Who Killed Roger Ackroyd?' This was an excellent title, but a foolish question; Golden Age books had their faults, but when it came to popular fiction, Wilson's judgments were on a par with Captain Hastings' detective work. Not content with rubbishing detective novelists, he applied his critical genius to H. P. Lovecraft's short stories, derided as 'hackwork,' and *The Lord of the Rings*, which he considered 'juvenile trash'.

Sayers' next collection of short stories, *Hangman's Holiday,* featured a cheery travelling salesman in wines and spirits. Montague Egg was a far cry from Wimsey. He didn't wear a monocle or fall in love, and when he dropped quotations they weren't from the classics but from *The Salesman's Handbook*. Gollancz liked Monty Egg, but readers were lukewarm, and he never appeared in a novel.

Sayers also created a female sleuth, contradicting complaints about her snobbery. Jane Eurydice Judkin, a parlourmaid, appeared in 'The Travelling Rug', a story intended to lead into a series. Sayers wrote from the point of view of a working-class woman who moves from job to job, from 'situation' to 'situation'. It was an interesting idea, and Judkin was another polar opposite of Wimsey, but neither plot nor concept was strong enough. 'The Travelling Rug' was not published until almost half a century after Sayers' death.

Her married life, meanwhile, was falling apart. Mac had given up regular journalism, but he liked writing about food and drink. He published an illustrated *Gourmet's Book of Food and Drink* and dedicated it to his wife, 'who can make an Omelette'. The text also complimented her on her tripe and onions. His over-indulgence in whisky, his jealousy of her success and his continued unwillingness to adopt her son were undermining their relationship. Each of them was getting on the other's nerves. The strain became too much for Sayers, and her doctor advised three weeks of complete rest.

Where to go to get away from it all? No cross-Continental train trip for Sayers, no exotic cruise, no flying off to the sun. Instead, she embarked on a motoring holiday in the English shires with an old friend from Somerville, Muriel St Claire Byrne. At one point they stopped at Ivy Shrimpton's cottage in Oxfordshire, and Muriel met John Anthony. When they left the cottage, Sayers was crying. Muriel was bewildered, but Sayers did not reveal that she was the boy's mother, and Muriel only discovered the truth after her old friend died. Trying to be a good mother in secret and from a distance was not the only pressure bearing down on Sayers. As she and Muriel roamed around rural England, she wrestled with the dilemma of whether to walk out on her husband.

Notes to Chapter 16

how to encode and decode a Playfair cipher
The Playfair cipher was devised by Charles Wheatstone (who also invented the Wheatstone bridge, which measures electrical resistance) and was named after Lyon Playfair, 1st Baron Playfair of St Andrews, whom Wheatstone introduced to the technique in 1850. Put simply, the Playfair cipher encrypts pairs of letters (digraphs) rather than single letters, as in the more straightforward 'substitution ciphers' favoured by Edgar Allan Poe, Arthur Conan Doyle and other crime writers. For a detailed account of the help Rhode supplied to Sayers, see Peter Ibbotson, 'Sayers and Ciphers', *Cryptologia* 25 (April 2001).

other poets such as . . . Edward Shanks
Edward Shanks (1892–1953), first winner of the Hawthornden Prize, earned acclaim as a war poet, literary critic and journalist. He wrote a biography of Poe, and occasionally veered towards an unorthodox brand of mystery in his fiction, notably with *Old King Cole* (1936).

an abortive mystery novel of his own that was never published in his lifetime
The Death of the King's Canary, co-written with John Davenport, eventually appeared in 1977. Thomas wanted the book to be 'the detective story to end detective stories, introducing blatantly every character and situation – an inevitable Chinaman, secret passages, etc. – that no respectable writer would dare use now'.

Virginia Woolf's husband Leonard
The Woolfs ran the Hogarth Press, and occasionally published novels of crime and detection, including *The Case is Altered* (1932), the most memorable book by William Plomer (1903–73). Plomer based the story upon a wife-murder committed in a London boarding house where he happened to be living. As well as writing novels and poetry, Plomer was a literary editor, and Ian Fleming dedicated *Goldfinger* to him. The Woolfs also published Clifford Henry Benn Kitchin (1895–1973), a barrister, stockbroker, pianist, bridge and chess player, rare book collector, greyhound owner, and gambler with a private fortune. Kitchin's early work attracted comparisons with Aldous Huxley, but today he remains known mainly for his

mysteries; like Chesterton and the Coles, he would never have anticipated such a fate. His finest novel in the genre is, arguably, the unaccountably neglected *Birthday Party* (1938), and he was considered for considered for membership of the Detection Club shortly after war broke out. Kitchin's *Crime at Christmas* (1934) ends with a 'Short Catechism' in which the stockbroker sleuth Malcolm Warren says: 'The excuse for a detective story is two-fold. First, it presents a problem to be solved and shares, in a humble way, the charm of the acrostic and the crossword puzzle. But secondly – and this, to my mind, is its real justification – it provides one with a narrow but intensive view of ordinary life, the steady flow of which is felt more keenly through the very violence of its interruption.'

the feminist writer Rose Macaulay
Dame Emilie Rose Macaulay (1881–1950) enjoyed a distinguished literary career. *Mystery at Geneva. An Improbable Tale of Singular Happenings* (1922) is a minor work set in the near future, and is as notable for its social commentary as the mystery element.

Charles Williams, a friend of Sayers
Charles Williams (1886–1945), a British novelist, not to be confused with an American thriller writer of the same name, was a poet and theologian. Although *Many Dimensions* (1931) was published in a green Penguin paperback edition, it was barely a 'crime novel'. Williams' sympathetic reviews of Golden Age fiction display his knowledge and love of the genre more obviously.

The Nine Tailors *told readers everything they needed to know about campanology but were afraid to ask.*
Professor B. J. Rahn's 'Dorothy L. Sayers' The Nine Tailors: Detective Story or Christian Allegory or both?' (written in 2014 but unpublished at the time of writing) argues that the book's main underlying structure 'is that of the poetic romance – with the conventions of detective fiction superimposed upon it – because of the reliance on religious allegory to resolve conflict'.

Argentina's Jorge Luis Borges
Jorge Luis Borges (1899–1986) wrote several detective stories, most famously 'Death and the Compass', first published in 1946. Chris Power says in 'A brief survey of the short story part 27: Jorge Luis

Borges', *The Guardian*, 22 July 2010, that his key influences include 'Poe, Kafka and, perhaps more surprisingly, Chesterton. . . . The investigative element of Borges's writing, which excites readers' natural curiosity even as it withholds detective fiction's customary satisfactions, instils a tension in his work that is rare in experimental literature.'

the New Zealander Miles Franklin
Miles Franklin (1874–1954) is now remembered for her novel *My Brilliant Career*, which was filmed in 1979. *Bring the Monkey* (1937) was a spoof mystery that enjoyed much less success.

Australia's Paul McGuire and Arthur Upfield
Paul McGuire (1903–78), a prominent Catholic who served as Australian Ambassador to Italy, set most of his mysteries in England. Arthur Upfield (1890–1964) was a prolific writer whose series detective, DI Napoleon Bonaparte, has Aborigine origins.

Bertolt Brecht said: 'The crime novel, like the world itself, is ruled by the English.'
See Brecht, 'On the Popularity of the Crime Novel' (trans. Martin Harvey and Aaron Kelly), *The Irish Review*, 1986, vol. xxxi, and Wizisla, Erdmut, *Walter Benjamin and Bertolt Brecht: The Story of a Friendship* (Yale: Yale University Press, 2009).

Europeans such as Karel Čapek, Friedrich Glauser, Stanislas-André Steeman
The Czech writer Karel Čapek (1890–1938), noted for his science fiction, and for popularizing the word *robot*, was also an early writer of and commentator about detective fiction. Friedrich Glauser (1896–1938) was a Swiss writer addicted to morphine and opium who spent much of his short life in psychiatric wards, mental hospitals and even (after being convicted for forging a prescription) prison. Nevertheless, his novels featuring Sergeant Studer have stood the test of time. Stanislas-André Steeman (1908–1973) was a prolific Belgian crime writer whose *Six Dead Men* (1931), like *The Invisible Host* (1930) by the American husband-and-wife team Gwen Bristow and Bruce Manning, boasts plot elements anticipating aspects of Christie's *And Then There Were None*.

the creator of Maigret, Georges Simenon
Georges Simenon (1903–89) occupies such a significant place in the history of the genre that Julian Symons devoted a whole chapter to his work in *Bloody Murder*. Simenon influenced numerous detective novelists writing in the English language, including Alan Hunter, W. J. Burley and Benjamin Black (the crime-writing *alter ego* of John Banville).

Sayers drew on her knowledge of life in her father's parish in creating Fenchurch St Paul and its imposing church
She also acknowledged the influence of J. Meade Falkner's vivid melodrama *The Nebuly Coat* (1903), a book admired equally by A. N.Wilson. In 'The Nebuly Coat', *The Daily Telegraph*, 5 January 2004, Wilson says: 'It would be much too heavy to read it as an allegory of England, its faith and its aristocracy on the verge of collapse. If not an allegory, however, it is certainly a mirror of these things.'

a method he called 'blood on a white bandage'
Carr's granddaughter Shelly Dickson Carr has recalled his use of this term on her website, www.ripped-book.com

Ezra Pound wrote to her
The poet and critic Ezra Weston Loomis Pound (1885–1972) was a detective story fan who collaborated with his mistress, the violinist Olga Rudge (1895–1996), on an unpublished and perhaps never completed detective story called *The Blue Spill*.

Wilson's rants about Golden Age fiction included the essay 'Who Cares Who Killed Roger Ackroyd?'
The essay appeared in the 20 June 1945 issue of *The New Yorker*.

17

'Have You Heard of Sexual Perversions?'

'Time and trouble will tame an advanced young woman, but an advanced old woman is uncontrollable by any earthly force,' remarks the lawyer Sir Impey Biggs in Sayers' *Clouds of Witness*. In the same book, Mary Wimsey, Peter's sister, demands, 'Why should the one always be the breadwinner more than the other?'

Sayers loathed being labelled a feminist, but that is what she was. Her conviction that women should not be subordinate to men resonates throughout her writing and the way she conducted her life. She believed women should have sexual freedom, and despised sex discrimination. There was certainly no controlling Harriet Vane. She became a model for the strong-minded, independent and sexually active young women commonplace in detective fiction today, but almost unthinkable before Sayers created her.

Christie's feminism was less demonstrative. She never experienced a torrid affair like Sayers' with John Cournos, and her women protagonists are not as feisty as Harriet Vane. Nevertheless, Tuppence Beresford and Jane Marple are more than a match for any man. Writing detective novels had become an eminently suitable job for a woman, even those who occasionally disguised their identity by taking a masculine or gender-neutral pseudonym.

With Sayers, Christie, Margaret Cole and Helen Simpson prominent, women were taking centre stage in the Detection Club. When Clair Price of the *New York Times* produced the first feature article about the Detection Club, she described the hunger for detective fiction as 'colossal'. According to her estimate, there were five hundred British crime writers but only one in twenty met the rigorous standards imposed by Berkeley and Sayers.

Price reported that Britain, the home of both Scotland Yard and Sherlock Holmes, was the only country in the world with a huge export trade in detective fiction and only a small import trade. As ever when supply struggles to meet demand, quality control was under threat. Price applauded the efforts of the Detection Club – 'a small and permanent communion of the faithful' – who wanted the detective story to be 'the most strenuously exacting of all literary forms'.

A candidate for membership needed two sponsors, and the founders were joined by three new members elected in 1933. E. R. Punshon and Anthony Gilbert were sponsored by Berkeley and Margaret Cole, and when the death of Victor Whitechurch in May created a vacancy, Berkeley and Helen Simpson put forward Gladys Mitchell. The following year saw the election of Margery Allingham. Mitchell had studied at University College, London, but the other three were not university-educated, and the elections diluted the Club's Oxbridge bias. Allingham came from a literary family, but none of the newcomers were born with a silver spoon.

Ernest Robertson Punshon had worked in a London office from the age of fourteen before heading for Canada and taking up farming without success. Penniless, he worked his way back to Britain on a cattle ship, and tried to make some money from writing. After winning one of the earliest literary prizes ever offered for open competition, he embarked on a long career as a novelist. He wrote mainly under his own name, but also as Robertson Halkett, whose *Where Every Prospect Pleases* is a thriller set in Monte Carlo and the Riviera which features a sadist with a taste for crucifixion and murder by whipping. Punshon's first book appeared in 1907, but his best work belonged to the Golden Age. Before creating Police Constable Bobby Owen, he wrote about Sergeant Bell and Inspector Carter, a duo portrayed with a sardonic touch that seems ahead of its time. Bell is a smart detective, but his publicity-seeking boss likes to grab all the credit. Punshon's fans included Bertie Wooster, who in *The Code of the Woosters* enjoys *Mystery of Mr Jessop* – another clue to Wodehouse's love of whodunits.

Punshon's novels were occasionally punctuated by dark and macabre scenes, but in person he was bald, affable, and popular with his colleagues, who invited him to become Honorary Secretary of the Club. In his early sixties, he was the odd man out in the quartet of new members. The other three were women aged under thirty-five. If, as Sayers joked in an unpublished essay, 'there is no profession so freely open to men and women . . . as that of murder,' it is also true that reading detective fiction is an equal-opportunities occupation. Women readers borrowed detective novels in large quantities from libraries, whereas men often preferred to read or write thrillers. Even the great male detectives, Wimsey, Poirot, and Father Brown, were not remotely macho compared to John Buchan's Richard Hannay and to crude action men such as Sapper's Bulldog Drummond and Sydney Horler's Tiger Standish. For all the innovations of Berkeley, Wade and Kennedy, for all the industry of Rhode, Connington and Punshon, the Thirties would eventually be remembered as the decade of the Crime Queen.

Anthony Gilbert was the main writing name of Lucy Beatrice Malleson, whose actor cousin Miles Malleson played the hangman with a taste for poetry in *Kind Hearts and Coronets*. She was born in London, although when explaining her careful attitude to money she described her origins as 'Yorkshire, with a dash of Scotch'. The real reason for her prudence was the financial hardship her family suffered after her stockbroker father lost his job. She took up shorthand typing to earn a living, and started publishing poetry.

Gilbert never married, and seems not to have had a long-term intimate relationship. She was very sociable – perhaps too much so, because even her friends thought she talked too much. Behind her cheerful chattiness lurked a deeply felt anguish: 'When you know what loneliness is like, you cease to laugh at the solitary women who make gods of their pets . . . when you find them writing letters to themselves or even posting boxes of violets to their own address in time for Valentine's Day. They're not mad or even peculiar. They are desperately lonely people trying to keep sane.'

During the Twenties, she was afraid of sexism blighting her career. Her first two books appeared under the sexless *nom de plume* of J. Kilmeny Keith, and she submitted the third under the name of Anthony Gilbert, in the belief that 'there were still plenty of people who didn't believe in women as writers of crime stories'. When she was asked for publicity material, she invented a phoney biography and had her photograph taken disguised as an old man with a beard. The snapshot disconcerted her agents, as her publishers thought they had signed up 'a new, vigorous young author' and that 'to present them with an elderly gentleman with one toe feeling precariously for the rim of the tomb might have unfortunate effects on future contracts'.

Collins conjured up publicity by dropping hints to the Press that the name 'Anthony Gilbert' concealed the identity of someone in the public eye – possibly 'a well-known amateur airman . . . who has played a fairly prominent part in the political world for many years'. Even after the next Gilbert book appeared, Collins remained ignorant of her sex. One commentator thought the *nom de plume* might belong to Hugh Walpole.

The slump led to Gilbert losing her American publishing contract and she rejected her agent's suggestion that she should write about Young Love: 'I had no experience of young love, and the love that you learn after thirty is quite a different kind, and certainly not suitable for bestsellers. Anyway, love stories must have a conventionally happy ending.' This is as much as she gave away about her love life in her autobiography. Christianna Brand, who disliked her, later claimed that Gilbert lusted after

John Dickson Carr, but Brand was an unreliable gossip. Years later, Gilbert wrote sensitively about abortion in two short stories, but there is no evidence that she based them on her own experience.

She became confident enough to adopt a female pen name, Anne Meredith, for a book marking a major departure. Dostoevsky was her model, although Berkeley's influence was also in play. *Portrait of a Murderer* opens as strikingly as the first two Francis Iles books, although the bleakness of the opening paragraph is not relieved by wit or irony: 'Adrian Gray was born in May 1862 and met his death through violence, at the hands of one of his own children, at Christmas, 1931. The crime was instantaneous and unpremeditated, and the murderer was left staring from the weapon on the table to the dead man in the shadow of the tapestry curtains, not apprehensive, not yet afraid, but incredulous and dumb.'

The victim was a half-crazed campaigner against all forms of immorality, and the culprit manages to throw suspicion upon Eustace Moore. Eustace, a shady financier, is Jewish, but is characterized with subtlety and a degree of sympathy. This was in sharp contrast to the grasping Jewish moneylender who is so often a depressing stereotype in Golden Age novels. Gilbert skilfully maintains suspense over whether there will be a miscarriage of justice, and as the story unfolds she offers biting social comment to accompany her account of the consequences of crime.

Portrait of a Murderer failed to transform Gilbert's fortunes, and was quickly – if undeservedly – forgotten. Yet it earned praise from Sayers and an American publishing deal. Gilbert said: 'It was clear that the effects of the slump were unlikely to be permanently offset by books modelled, be it ever so faintly, on the works of Russian genius, but on the whole it was as well that I had decided not to proceed with my original idea of writing thrillers, for, before *Portrait of a Murderer* was published, I had received an invitation to become a member of the Detection Club. . . . Everything snobbish in my system acclaimed this opportunity to hobnob with the Great. . . . I hold no particular brief for the aristocracy, but it is pleasant to be counted, once in a while, among their number.'

Gilbert trembled with excitement as she arrived for her first Club dinner in a Northumberland Avenue hotel, dressed in her best green georgette. She had fantasized about Sayers as 'slender and aloof – willowy' and was startled to find a 'massive and majestic lady' swimming towards her. Another shock swiftly followed. She pictured John Rhode as 'one of those young dark sardonic men with a black lock falling over his nose. Infinitely superior' – only to discover he was older than her and weighed seventeen stone. Chesterton, a magnificent giant in a flowing black gown, presided over her initiation, putting the questions 'in a voice that might have come from the abyss'.

'Hang your head a little, can't you?' Margaret Cole whispered fiercely during the ritual, 'You are only a neophyte.' Gilbert's green georgette was the only splash of colour in the darkness until Eric the Skull's red eyes lit up. She had not been given advance warning of the dress code. For Gilbert, 'It was a glorious experience; I felt as though I were marching to my wedding in the condemned cell.'

The instant the ceremony was over, everyone rushed to the bar, and Rhode came over to put her at ease. Genial and kind, he became a close friend, and she dedicated her autobiography to him. The title, *Three-A-Penny*, came from Sayers, who in her usual brisk way announced: 'You must remember, Anthony Gilbert, that although authors are three-a-penny to us, they are quite exciting to other people.'

Christie and Gilbert also became friends, and as a Detection Club in-joke Christie gave the name Anne Meredith to a woman in *Cards on the Table* who has committed murder and got away with it. Chatty and companionable, Gilbert loved the meetings, and soon became one of the Detection Club's stalwarts. So did Gladys Mitchell.

Mitchell was known to her close friends as 'Mike'. Although in old age she claimed she had only academic knowledge of romance or sex, she wrote unpublished Sapphic poetry and lived with another woman, Winifred Blazey. Christianna Brand, frank to the point of rudeness, thought Mitchell's appearance remarkably plain, but appreciated her engaging personality. She grew up in Brentford – where in her novel *The Rising of the Moon* a killer runs amok – and started teaching at St Paul's School a few years after Margaret Cole left to pursue socialism and her future husband.

Victor Gollancz, the great talent-spotter of the Golden Age, took on Mitchell as a first-time novelist when she was still in her twenties. *Speedy Death* opens in familiar Golden Age territory, with a country house party at Chayning Court, where Mrs Bradley is a guest. A corpse is discovered in a bath, as in *Whose Body?* But the body is that of a woman who has been masquerading as a man – a famous explorer called Mountjoy. Mountjoy had been engaged to be married to the daughter of the house, and sexual repressions are central to the murderer's psychology.

Mrs Bradley is introduced by a fellow guest as 'Little, old, shrivelled, clever, sarcastic. . . . Would have been smelt out as a witch in a less tolerant age.' In fact, she is aged fifty-seven and has already buried two husbands (the number rose mysteriously to three in later books). A strong believer in 'applied psychology', she discusses the murder with the splendidly named Inspector Boring, and his Chief Constable, and offers copies of her *Small Handbook of Psycho-Analysis* to the police at half price, post free. A typical Mitchell touch, just like the way she pokes fun at sexual prudishness.

'Have you heard of sexual perversions?' Mrs Bradley demands. The Chief Constable nods, and says gruffly, 'Not a nice subject.' Writers at this time were prevented by the obscenity laws, as well as the mores of the time, from writing explicitly about sex. D. H. Lawrence's *Lady Chatterley's Lover*, first printed privately in Italy in 1928, did not appear in full unexpurgated form in Britain until 1960 and the dawn of the Permissive Society. Yet despite the constraints of the law and the superficial prissiness of the times, Golden Age novelists repeatedly smuggled sexual references into their work. Berkeley, Connington, and Nicholas Blake all wrote novels with storylines involving kinky sex.

Mrs Bradley suggests that Mountjoy had formed 'a very real and . . . very strong attachment' to a woman. In order to prevent further loss of life, the detective commits an altruistic murder and is defended on a murder charge, in breach of every professional rule, by her son, Ferdinand Lestrange KC. Although guilty, she is acquitted, in a manner of which Berkeley surely approved. He was increasingly fascinated by the idea of the well-intentioned murder as a means of putting right injustices beyond the reach of the law.

Mitchell was as eccentric a novelist as Mrs Bradley was a detective. Nobody could have seemed more different from the glamorous and unquestionably heterosexual Helen Simpson, whom Mitchell extolled as 'brilliant, witty, charming and highly intellectual'. The contradictions in Mitchell's books mirrored those in her personal life. Her storylines were exuberant and packed with action, but often meandered far off track (even though she used the one-inch Ordnance Survey map as an aid to her writing). She admired Sigmund Freud and was addicted to the supernatural. A career teacher who spent a lifetime working in traditional schools, her interest in educational experiments was reflected in *Death at the Opera*. Her political instincts were conservative, and her passion for the traditions and folklore of all four corners of the British Isles are evident in dozens of her books, yet she loved to tilt against the establishment.

Mitchell, like Gilbert, loved the Detection Club from the moment of her election. In *Dead Men's Morris*, Mrs Bradley visits the Club rooms in Soho – she has been elected as an honorary member. The first victim in this book dies, apparently from natural causes, early on Christmas Day in rural Oxfordshire. Mitchell hurls disparate ingredients into the mix – pig farming (the second victim is savaged by a boar), Morris dancing, a secret passage, and a legend about a ghost. The verve with which she describes her cackling detective's investigation is matched by the wildness of the plot, in which the sexual adventures of two young women play a part. Despite her claimed lack of sexual experience, Mitchell was no prude.

*   *   *

Margery Allingham took longer to acclimatize to the convivial atmosphere of the Detection Club. She was a precocious literary talent whose first novel, the swashbuckling romance *Blackerchief Dick*, was published when she was a teenager. At the age of seventeen, she met Philip Youngman Carter, and they married six years later. A writer and illustrator, Pip designed many of Margery's dust jackets, as well as those for other Golden Age novelists. His contribution to his wife's books was greater than is often recognized, and they collaborated on *The Crime at Black Dudley*, in which her most famous detective, Albert Campion, made his debut. Allingham said: 'We argued over every word. It took us three months of hilarious endeavour. Never was writing more fun.' But Pip's role was subordinate to his wife's, and his name did not appear on the cover.

The Crime at Black Dudley has a country house party setting, like the first books by Christie and Berkeley. In Ngaio Marsh's debut, *A Man Lay Dead*, guests at the Frampton estate take part in a game of 'Murder', with the inevitable outcome that one of them finishes up stabbed through the heart by a Russian dagger. Similarly, when Allingham's characters re-enact an ancient family ritual, murder is done. Her story is a romp rather than a 'fair play' whodunit. The detecting is done by a pathologist, George Abbershaw, but he allows the culprit, whom he sees as 'both a murderer and a martyr', to escape to a new life in a monastery in Spain. Like so many fictional sleuths, Abbershaw finds that 'the old problem of Law and Order as opposed to Right and Wrong worried itself into the inextricable tangle which knows no unravelling.' Long before the days of *CSI*, Allingham envisaged her pathologist as a series detective, but the publisher preferred Albert Campion. As a result Allingham did not become a Golden Age forerunner of Patricia Cornwell, but her idiosyncratic and atmospheric books won a loyal following.

Campion is described to Abbershaw as 'a lunatic', but 'quite inoffensive, just a silly ass'. Allingham portrays him as an eccentric resembling Wooster and Wimsey, but with a shady side. He moonlights as a conman whose aliases include Mornington Dodd and the Honourable Tootles Ash. When the book was reprinted,

Allingham cut out a section describing his rascally conduct as Mornington Dodd, although Campion soon acquired a former burglar as a sidekick. Campion's background is illustrious, but his precise pedigree remains a mystery. His real name is supposed to be Rudolph, but Allingham once said that he gave up detection when he was crowned King George VI.

Allingham's writing became increasingly inventive, although *Police at the Funeral* borrowed a plot device from the casebook of Sherlock Holmes. Alongside the novels published under her own name, she dashed off a trio of thrillers as Maxwell March, which began life as magazine serializations. Like her colleagues in the Detection Club, she needed to earn money. As she said privately, 'Maxwell March is a first-class hack – he makes the cash. Margery Allingham thinks of her reputation.'

Following Sayers' lead, Allingham set up a long-running romance for Campion – Lady Amanda Fitton, who appeared as a precocious teenager in *Sweet Danger* and returned in *The Fashion in Shrouds* working as an aircraft engineer. Amanda's career choice, and the fact that she proposes marriage to Campion, reflected Allingham's embrace of Sayers' feminist values.

Like Anthony Gilbert, Mitchell, and Clemence Dane, Allingham was childless. She described occasional arguments with Pip on the subject of '*kid v. car*', which always ended with a decision in favour of buying a new car or something else for the house. In later years at least, Pip reckoned that 'sex was of minor importance' in their relationship. Allingham was attractive, with good bone structure, but her weight ballooned as the result of an under-active thyroid, which was not diagnosed for some time. To camouflage her size, she wore tight corsets and loose, comfortable dresses, but unhappiness about her looks, as well as the effect of her thyroid condition and worries about Pip's interest in other women, resulted in regular mood swings. Veering from exhaustingly energetic and jolly to nervous and depressed, she could become tongue-tied and self-conscious in the company of strangers. An early introduction to the great and the good of the literary world at a PEN Club dinner haunted her, as did her struggle to cope with questions such as: 'Have you been painted by Augustus John?'

Her first encounter with the Detection Club did not come at a good moment in her life. In stark contrast to Anthony Gilbert, she did not enjoy her initiation – probably because she'd made up her mind in advance that it would be an ordeal. Her private diary noted: 'Cut out my dress for club party which I dread', and 'Learnt ritual for party (almost)'. The event itself was 'awful'.

A glance at a photograph of the members and their guests, assembled in their finery for the annual black-tie dinner, shows why she felt overwhelmed. Chesterton's massive figure dominates the top table, with Sayers the epitome of calm magnificence at one end and Berkeley debonair and darkly handsome at the other. Allingham spotted Chesterton laughing as she swore her oath with a hand on Eric the Skull, but she did not get the joke, and she found Sayers terrifying.

Even more intimidating, the BBC oversaw an international broadcast of her initiation, with John Rhode credited as Skullbearer, and Freeman Wills Crofts and Edward Punshon as Torchbearers. Chesterton and Berkeley introduced the show by talking about the Club's origins. The broadcast was heard in the United States, enlivening the Sunday dinners of American listeners as well as an Englishman abroad, the thriller writer Valentine Williams, who was provoked to write from New York to *The Times* by the description of Soho as a 'red light district'. Soho was the Detection Club's home ground, but Williams deprecated 'such centres of honest trade as . . . Old Compton Street, with its spaghetti shops and wine stores . . . being depicted in American eyes as the happy hunting grounds of the "madame", the "louie", the "trigger-man" and the "strong-arm squad".' Could not someone 'who knows something of American conditions keep an eye on the script?'

Notes to Chapter 17

According to her estimate, there were five hundred British crime writers
Dabblers in the genre included C. P. Snow (1905–80) and T. H. White
(1906–64) who both published their solitary detective novels in 1932
while in their mid-twenties, long before becoming famous for their
respective novel sequences, *Strangers and Brothers* and *The Once
and Future King*. In the late Fifties, Snow was a guest speaker at
the Detection Club's annual dinner. Mysteriously, a typewritten list
of members from that period includes his name, but there is no
other evidence that he was ever a member.

John Wyndham Parkes Lucas Beynon Harris (1903–69), who
achieved fame in science fiction as triffid creator John Wyndham,
published one detective novel. This was an apprentice work, as were
several early mysteries by Winston Graham (1908–2003), who later
turned successfully to psychological suspense and a historical series
set in Cornwall, televised as *Poldark*.

More distinctive is *Death by Request*, published by the husband
and wife team Romilly and Katherine John in 1933 while they were
both still in their twenties. The story, a country house mystery with
a Christie-style twist, is told with enough zest and humour to make
it regrettable that the Johns deserted the genre. Romilly (1906–86)
was the son of the artist Augustus John, and his most notable book
was a memoir of his unconventional upbringing; Katherine later
established a reputation as a translator of Scandinavian literature.

the founders were joined by three new members elected in 1933
I have gathered material about Gladys Mitchell from numerous sources,
notably the Gladys Mitchell Tribute Site, www.gladysmitchell.com. The
main sources of information about Anthony Gilbert were her memoir
Three-a-Penny, written as by Anne Meredith, and the reminiscences
of her family members, who retain a great affection for her. As yet,
E. R. Punshon's life and work have been subject to little research,
although William A. S. Sarjeant's *Punshon's Policemen* is useful.

The following year saw the election of Margery Allingham.
Allingham's life and work are celebrated by the Society that bears
her name, and I have found its publications, the excellent biography
by Julia Jones, and research undertaken by Barry Pike to be of
considerable assistance.

18

Clearing Up the Mess

Soho made a perfect setting for the Detection Club's activities. Whatever Valentine Williams believed, the whiff of danger and excitement appealed to Club members. Sayers had longed for permanent meeting rooms in central London. Her idea was that she and her friends would go out for dinner and then return to their very own premises, and chat and drink in privacy all night long. These rooms would also house a reference library of books on criminology to assist members in their research. But where could they find the money? For writers, the answer was simple. Why not raise funds by producing a full-length round-robin novel?

Writing is notoriously a solitary occupation, and this makes the repeated group efforts of the Detection Club especially unusual. Sayers was undeterred by the frustrations of dealing with Joe Ackerley at the BBC, or by the unenviable task of herding her fellow writers into line, and insisted: 'There is no reason why a perfectly "correct" detective story should not be produced, even where the plot is not planned in collaboration at all.'

In a trial run, she produced an extended version of her opening chapter for *The Scoop*. The typescript still exists, but it was never published. Soon, a fresh idea was floated. Rather than expand an existing story, a dozen members would combine to write a brand new book. The result was a murder mystery widely regarded as the most successful chain novel, and the most popular collaborative crime novel, ever published. *The Floating Admiral* is a Golden Age classic, complete with a map showing the scene of the crime.

Sayers laid down two rules. Each writer must have a definite solution in mind, and must not add fresh complications without having any idea of how to resolve them. And each writer was expected to tackle the challenges set by earlier instalments. Never a woman to under-sell a new project, Sayers claimed the results cast light on fundamentals of human nature: 'Where one writer may have laid down a clue, thinking that it could point only in one obvious direction, succeeding writers have managed to make it point in a direction exactly opposite. And it is here, perhaps, that the game approximates most closely to real life. . . . Preoccupied by our own private interpretations of the matter, we can see only the one possible motive behind the action, so that our solution may be quite coherent, quite plausible and quite wrong.'

The scene was set by Canon Victor L. Whitechurch. Very early one morning, an elderly fisherman catches sight of the local vicar's rowing boat, drifting on the River Whyn. Inside the boat is the body of Admiral Penistone. This evocative description proved to be the Canon's last contribution to the activities of the Detection Club. He died shortly after writing his chapter.

The Coles wrote the second chapter, and were followed by Henry Wade (the first contributor to come up with a solution), Christie, John Rhode, and Milward Kennedy. The lack of advance planning showed when the latter pair's chapters were respectively entitled 'Inspector Rudge Forms a Theory' and 'Inspector Rudge Thinks Better of It'. By the time Sayers took up the baton, her four predecessors had come up with four different explanations for the mystery. Resisting any temptation to despair, she set about putting *The Floating Admiral* on an even keel, introducing new, vivid characters: a pushy journalist, a strong-minded working woman and a precise lawyer.

Knox's contribution, 'Thirty-Nine Articles of Doubt', sees Inspector Rudge list all the areas of uncertainty thrown up by the investigation. Knox was followed by Freeman Wills Crofts, Edgar Jepson (the brevity of whose contribution suggests that he struggled to cope with the challenge), and Clemence Dane. In a long concluding chapter pointedly called 'Clearing up the Mess', Berkeley showed great dexterity in resolving the tangled plot. After the book was complete, Chesterton wrote the Prologue, set in Hong Kong. It added nothing to the story, but his connection with the book made for good publicity.

Although several contributors got themselves into deep water, somehow *The Floating Admiral* managed not to sink. The book was well received by critics, and its period charm meant that a reissue almost eighty years later was equally successful. Sales were so healthy that the Club's coffers received a huge boost, just as Sayers had hoped.

But what happened to the cash? *The Floating Admiral* has been reprinted and translated several times over the years, and in an introduction to an American edition of 1979 Christianna Brand (reminiscing about her own membership of the Detection Club) claimed: 'The agent involved, having negotiated a most satisfactory deal – I'm *almost* absolutely certain that this was the book involved – then scarpered with the proceeds.' She also states that a majority of members, led by the relentlessly decent Freeman Wills Crofts, voted to take no action against the woman concerned, because of the financial distress that had led her to embezzle the money. This was at best hearsay, and as that *almost* suggests, Brand's entertaining anecdotes need to be taken with a massive pinch of salt. She was not elected until long after *The Floating Admiral*'s publication, and she was, above all, a storyteller.

John Rhode was either more discreet (not difficult in comparison to Brand) or more accurate when he said that the Club was able to establish and maintain its own premises because of the money it made from British and American sales of this book and its successor, *Ask a Policeman*. A different anecdote has surfaced over the years, that the Club premises were burgled shortly after they were acquired, and that the combined detective skills of the members failed to pinpoint the culprit.

The two small rooms rented by the Club were at 31 Gerrard

Street in Soho. This was indeed in the heart of the red light district, a stone's throw from the most legendary nightclub of the Roaring Twenties, at 43 Gerrard Street. The 43 Club was run by Kate Meyrick, 'Queen of the Nightclubs', and had its own literary connections. It occupied premises once home to John Dryden, while Meyrick was the model for Ma Mayfield of the Old Hundredth in *Brideshead Revisited*.

A suffragette turned entrepreneur, and supposedly the first Irishwoman to ride a bicycle, Meyrick was a prominent target for sporadic police crackdowns on the vice trade. At the 43, she catered to the whims of a dazzling roster of celebrity clients, including Tallulah Bankhead, Rudolph Valentino, Charlie Chaplin and Joseph Conrad. Politicians from all parties attended, along with assorted gangsters, as well as peers of the realm, the Crown Prince of Sweden, and the King of Romania. Meyrick's downfall came when she was jailed for bribing a policeman called Goddard who ran a protection racket, and her health was weakened by poor conditions inside Holloway Prison as well as in her clubs. She died at fifty-seven, shortly after publication of her memoirs was banned, and at around the time the Detection Club was moving in just down the road from her legendary club, by then renamed the Bunch of Keys.

Sleazy but seductive, Soho fascinated the younger members of the Detection Club. The cosmopolitan ambience offered rich pickings for a detective novelist, when nobody could tell what perils might lurk around the next corner. The dinginess of the neighbourhood during daylight hours vanished when darkness fell, and bright lights from the restaurants broke up the shadows between the gas lamps. Black jazz trumpeters and clarinettists played alongside Jewish dance musicians in claustrophobic basements beneath French and Italian cafés, hedonists of all kinds danced and drank the night away at 'bottle parties' flouting the licensing laws, and as the small hours beckoned, dope addicts and cross-dressers came out to play.

Despite relishing their close encounters with the *demi-monde*, the Club members were too respectable (or too timid) to be seduced. Sayers' portrayal of 'the de Momerie crowd' of revellers in *Murder Must Advertise* is an outsider's view. In Kate Meyrick's time, the 43 was reputed to be the centre for drug dealing in London, but Sayers kept a safe distance from the underworld. As she admitted to Victor Gollancz, the portrayal of drug-trafficking lacks realism because she 'didn't know dope'. What she did know was that idle rich good-for-nothings ought to get their just deserts. Dian de Momerie ends up with her throat cut.

The rooms were furnished with shabby chairs and tables that members no longer wanted, while prints on the walls displayed a suitably criminal preoccupation: John Thurtell's murder of William Weare, a portrait of William Corder, the Red Barn murderer, and a scene from the story of the killing of Lord Russell by his valet. The premises were handy for *L'Escargot Bienvenu*, a favourite restaurant of Sayers' in Greek Street, which offered exclusive use of an upstairs room for Detection Club members. For years, the price of a good dinner never varied from eleven shillings: five for the meal, five more for the alcohol, and a shilling for the waiter. Alcohol flowed freely: Sayers enjoyed a drink, although late in life she confessed to Michael Gilbert that, unlike Lord Peter Wimsey, she could not tell the difference between burgundy and claret.

The regular attendees were younger writers. Sayers, Berkeley, and Christie were usually there, along with Rhode, Kennedy, Wade, Crofts, Margaret Cole, Lord Gorell, Mitchell, Anthony Gilbert, and Punshon. Ronald Knox came along from time to time and so, after they were elected, did Margery Allingham and John Dickson Carr. Despite devoting little time to crime writing, Ianthe Jerrold often turned up, though Berkeley used to chide her for literary inactivity. Jerrold wrote a couple of detective novels featuring a Wimsey-lite sleuth, John Christmas, but she and the Irishwoman Jessie Rickard were the least renowned of the founder members. One puzzle is why this pair became members, whereas several more gifted and interesting writers, including Philip MacDonald and Josephine Tey, did not. MacDonald left Britain for Hollywood in the Thirties, which may explain his omission. Tey was a painfully shy single woman who only visited London twice a year, to see her sister by way of a break from caring for her elderly father at home in Inverness.

The hazards of life in Soho at night created an inevitable challenge for Detection Club members. When they were on their way back to the meeting rooms, staggering through the narrow streets after plenty to eat and drink, the women kept close to their male colleagues – Sayers and Margaret Cole forming a formidable guard of honour, determined to protect the men from the patrolling prostitutes whose favourite question was: 'Are you on your own, dear?'

Ask a Policeman followed a year after *The Floating Admiral*, the fourth collaborative mystery story produced in quick succession by Club members. The question was how to match the success of *The Floating Admiral*. The answer was to borrow a classic trope of detective fiction – members would impersonate each other. In other words, they agreed to exchange detectives. The gimmick gave them the chance to poke fun at the quirks of their colleagues' sleuths, and they seized it with relish.

The original dust jacket blurb captured the playful mood of *Ask a Policeman*: 'Here is something delightfully new in "thrills" – a story which combines the interest of detection with the fun of parody. A problem is propounded; ingenious, and, for the solvers, malicious, and in itself a parody of a thousand and one detective stories. A great newspaper proprietor dies in his study, and suspicion falls upon an Archbishop, a Secretary, a Police Commissioner, and the Chief Whip of the political party in power. There is, too, a Mysterious Lady. What, then, can the Home Secretary do but call in the Amateur Experts? There are four of them; each takes a hand and each produces a different solution.'

The story is introduced by an exchange of letters composed by John Rhode and Milward Kennedy. Rhode sets the scene by recounting the authorities' reaction to the murder of Lord Comstock at Hursley Lodge, a map of which is, of course, supplied. The death of Comstock, whose newspapers claim 'to be the real arbiters of the nation's destiny at home and abroad' is 'an event of worldwide importance'.

Rhode's characterization of the dead man is unusually

compelling. Wealthy and influential newspaper magnates were as feared and unloved in the Golden Age as are some media tycoons of the modern age. Shortly before *Ask a Policeman* was written, Viscount Rothermere, of the *Daily Mail*, and Lord Beaverbrook, of the *Daily Express*, had turned their fire on Stanley Baldwin, whose brand of Conservatism was not to their liking, and tried to use their muscle to remove him as Prime Minister. Baldwin poured scorn on his tormentors in a memorable speech that turned the tide in his favour: 'What the proprietorship of these papers is aiming at is power, and power without responsibility – the prerogative of the harlot throughout the ages.' This killer line, dreamed up by his cousin, Rudyard Kipling, resonated with the general public, and parliamentary democracy prevailed over propaganda. At least Rothermere and Beaverbrook lived to fight another day, unlike the fictional Comstock.

Rhode handed the baton to Helen Simpson, who portrayed Mrs Bradley with typical verve. Mitchell shared Sayers' admiration for the 'brilliant, witty, charming and highly intellectual' Simpson, and even allowed Simpson to bestow a second forename, Adela, upon her detective. Mitchell did a competent job with her parody of Sir John Samaurez, before leaving the story in the hands of the two stars of the show.

To parody Sayers' hero required chutzpah. Needless to say, Berkeley volunteered. His contribution captured Wimsey brilliantly, in one of the finest of all parodies of Golden Age detective fiction, while offering a clever solution to the problem posed by Rhode. As for Sayers, she rendered Sheringham effectively, with a neat joke when he overhears two employees of the late Lord Comstock being rude about him. Yet her solution is less compelling than Berkeley's. By now she was more concerned with the people she wrote about than the puzzle.

This time it was Kennedy's turn to clear up the mess. His solution does not 'play fair' with the reader, but *Ask a Policeman* oozes with period charm. John Rhode captured the genial mood of the enterprise when he inscribed a copy of the book to an unnamed recipient, possibly Kennedy, 'in memory of our violent onslaught on the Detection Club'.

Gladys Mitchell recalled in old age that 'Anthony's manipulation of Lord Peter Wimsey caused the massive lady anything but pleasure'. It seems odd that Sayers failed to appreciate the flair of Berkeley's rendering, for she did not lack either a sense of humour or the ability to make fun of herself. Yet shortly afterwards, when discussing potential contributors to a volume of Sherlockian pastiches to be edited by the American scholar Harold Bell, she dismissed Berkeley as 'too rough a parodist'. She spoke more highly of Simpson, Kennedy and A. A. Milne, as well as Bentley, by now a close friend.

This reflects a cooling of her friendship with Berkeley that had little to do with his parody of Wimsey or his portrayal of her as Isobel Sedbusk in *Before the Fact*, but was probably due to his desertion of his wife Peggy for Helen Peters. As Sayers came to know him and his writing better, she became aware of failings as well as strengths, and when she reviewed *Jumping Jenny* and *Panic Party* her admiration for his cleverness was tinged with distaste for his cynicism about humanity.

Baker Street Studies appeared with authors including Sayers and Simpson, as well as Knox, but no Berkeley. Sayers had warned Harold Bell that Knox was 'dreadfully slipshod', but admitted that with his track record in Sherlockian scholarship he was well qualified to contribute. When she expressed private doubts about whether Crofts and Rhode were talented enough writers, much as she liked them personally, Bell took the hint and did not include them.

Sayers became a founder member of the Sherlock Holmes Society of London, whose inaugural dinner was held, naturally, in Baker Street, at Canuto's Restaurant on Derby Day in 1934. As usual, Sayers had plenty to say. If Peter Pan could be honoured with a statue, why not Holmes and Watson – and, come to that, why not Mrs Hudson, 'the Happy Warrior of below-stairs'? Sayers' enthusiasm for Sherlockiana persisted, and she later took part in a one-act play for Detection Club members, written by John Dickson Carr and called *The French Ambassador's Trousers*. John Rhode made a suitably bluff Dr Watson, and the barrister Cyril Hare's profile proved a perfect match for Holmes's, while

Carr played the Gallic ambassador. Sayers could scarcely have played the glamorous Irene, but she made an unforgettable Mrs Hudson, dressed in a billowing red flannel nightgown.

Detection Club members seized almost any opportunity to socialize together and with professional crime investigators. Even Christie, the supposed recluse, turned out to support a Foyle's literary lunch devoted to crime writing, with Freeman Wills Crofts, John Rhode and the reviewer Torquemada among the speakers. Rubbing shoulders with the novelists were pathologist Bernard Spilsbury, now an established celebrity of the crime scene, and several of Scotland Yard's finest.

Gerrard Street remained the hub. Three photographs taken there appeared in a breezy and irreverent magazine called *Weekly Illustrated* under the heading 'Sleuths on the Scent', which was akin to John Le Carré and Ruth Rendell posing for *Hello*. The snaps were squeezed in beside a shot of Mussolini's grandson playing on an Italian beach, and beneath a picture of Baroness Platen, who was reputed to spend three thousand pounds a year on hats. Advertisements warned male readers not to spoil with rough, red hands the caresses that should be velvet-soft, and to make good use of snow fire glycerine jelly, while a promotion for a book called *The Hygiene of Life* insisted that 'knowledge of yourself is essential to married happiness'.

Punshon, Ianthe Jerrold and Anthony Gilbert, the latter pair looking as though in recovery from a good night out, were pictured as a seated group of 'eager sleuths'. E. C. Bentley, looming over Milward Kennedy's head, was described as 'investigating the mystery' of his colleague's 'bodyless head'. A wonderful shot showed Helen Simpson, dark, lean and elegant and wearing a pearl necklace, standing behind the seated figure of Sayers, resplendent in a wide-sleeved silk jacket embroidered with flowers. Each woman was lifting a tankard of beer. Sayers was gleeful, declaring it the best photograph she'd ever had taken. Simpson's expression of eager enjoyment was, she said, the thirstiest thing she'd seen for a long time.

SLEUTHS
ON THE
SCENT

DETECTION Club in Gerrard Street, West End, is favourite meeting-ground of detective-creators and literary crimesters. Above, a group of eager sleuths. Mr. E. R. Punshon, left, Miss Ianthe Jerrold and "Anthony Gilbert." Right, Miss Dorothy Sayers, seated, Miss Helen Simpson at back.

Bodyless head in lower half of picture belongs to author Milward Kennedy. Behind him, investigating mystery, is E. C. Bentley.

'Sleuths on the Scent' feature in *Weekly Illustrated*.

Notes to Chapter 18

Meyrick's downfall came when she was jailed for bribing a policeman called Goddard who ran a protection racket
A corrupt police force was seen in some quarters as the legacy of the hapless and unpopular Sir William Horwood, the Metropolitan Police Commissioner nicknamed 'the Chocolate Soldier' after his narrow escape from death by poisoned chocolate. Horwood supposedly retired on grounds of age, but his successor, Lord Byng, was six years older. Byng launched a clear-up operation, and Goddard and Kate Meyrick fell foul of it. Henry Wade's awareness of the realities of police work post-Horwood is illustrated in *Constable, Guard Thyself!*, where Inspector Poole reminds Sergeant Gower, 'They've cut us very close on our expenses since '31.'

Ianthe Jerrold often turned up
Ianthe Jerrold was the daughter of William Jerrold, a writer and deputy editor of *The Observer*. She dabbled intermittently in fictional crime, sometimes under the name Geraldine Bridgman, long after her election to the Detection Club. In 'Some Thoughts on the Least-Known Member of the Detection Club', *CADS* 10, July 1989, Doug Greene points out, that in combining a wealthy amateur sleuth (rejoicing in the name John Christmas) with a plodding professional policeman, Jerrold was adopting a method used by Sayers, albeit with less success.

the Irishwoman Jessie Rickard
Jessie Louisa Rickard, who usually published as Mrs Victor Rickard, was a prolific popular novelist, but her contribution to the detective genre was modest. Her most noteworthy crime novel, *Not Sufficient Evidence*, published four years before the Detection Club's foundation, was based on the Bravo case.

One puzzle is why this pair became members, whereas several more gifted and interesting writers, including Philip Macdonald and Josephine Tey, did not.
Not everyone invited to join the Detection Club over the years has accepted. For example, Georgette Heyer (1902–74), renowned for historical romances but also a detective novelist, declined to join, perhaps because her mysteries were largely plotted by her husband, the barrister Ronald Rougier.

The reasons for other surprising omissions from the membership list are debatable. Philip MacDonald (1900–80) may have been regarded as primarily a thriller writer. He wrote too much, too fast; even his friend Margery Allingham described *The Crime Conductor* as 'the lazy work of a clever mind'. Yet his novels featuring Colonel Anthony Gethryn included such successful mysteries as *Warrant for X* and *The List of Adrian Messenger*. Oddly, although Macdonald became a highly successful screenwriter (whose credits included the classic films *Rebecca* and *Forbidden Planet*) he did not write the screenplay for the film of either of these books. *Warrant for X* was filmed as *23 Paces to Baker Street*, with a script by Nigel Balchin (1908–70). Balchin was an accomplished mainstream novelist whose last published work, the television drama *Better Dead*, combined a Golden Age style storyline with a plot twist about transvestism; any plans he had to turn it into a series were ended by a fatal heart attack.

Josephine Tey was the principal pseudonym of Elizabeth Mackintosh (1896–1952), a highly accomplished writer whose *A Shilling for Candles* was transformed beyond recognition by Hitchcock when he filmed it as *Young and Innocent*. A biography of Tey by a member of her family, the present day Detection Club member Catherine Aird (a pen name of Kinn Mackintosh) has long been awaited, but is yet to be published.

Fryniwyd Tennyson Jesse (1888–1958), great-niece of Alfred, Lord Tennyson, wrote stories featuring Solange Fontaine, whose 'delicate extra sense' warns her of evil; as well as an outstanding fictionalised version of the Thompson–Bywaters case, *A Pin to See the Peep-Show* (1934). A beautiful but troubled woman, Jesse wrote a seminal book about motives for murder, and several introductions to *Notable British Trials*, as well as editing the English version of *The Baffle Book* by Lassiter Wren and Randall MacKay, a collection of detection-based parlour games. She worked as a war correspondent and playwright, but developed an addiction to morphia (following an accident which caused two of her fingers to be amputated) and alcohol. She had a more obvious claim to membership of the Detection Club than, say, Jessie Rickard. Perhaps she earned the disfavour of either Berkeley or Sayers.

Francis Beeding was the main pen name used by John Palmer (1885–1944) and Hilary St George Saunders (1898–1951), mainly for a long series of thrillers. Their occasional detective novels were, however, of high quality, and included *The House of Dr Edwardes*

(1927), filmed by Hitchcock as *Spellbound*, *Death Walks in Eastrepps* (1931), one of the best Golden Age serial killer whodunits, and *He Should Not Have Slipped* (1931), a variant of the 'altruistic crime' novel so popular with thoughtful Golden Age writers. A neat gimmick in *The Norwich Victims* (1935) is the inclusion of photographs of the main characters that contain a clue to the culprit's identity. Palmer and Saunders both worked for the League of Nations in Geneva; perhaps geography, rather than any other reason, made it impracticable for them to join the Detection Club.

the fourth collaborative mystery story produced in quick succession by Club members

The games played in *The Floating Admiral* and *Ask a Policeman* met with critical and financial success, and encouraged others to write round-robin mysteries. The first major American detective story of this kind was *The President's Mystery* (1935), in which a puzzle was posed by no less a detective fiction fan than Franklin Delano Roosevelt. S. S. Van Dine was among the contributors, and the story began life as a serialization, was published in book form, and was then adapted as a film, with a screenplay co-written by Nathaniel West, best known for *The Day of the Locust*. In Britain, the *Sunday Chronicle* serialized another round-robin mystery, to which Sayers and Crofts wrote the opening instalments. The story, originally called *Night of Secrets*, became *Double Death* when published in book form in 1939. Despite the participation of two of its leading lights, this was not a Detection Club venture, and Sayers felt it suffered because the other writers were not of the highest calibre. The chaotic nature of the enterprise is illustrated by the fact that although the book version contains authors' notes on the story, the contributors were not forewarned that these would be published. Their gloomy frankness is an entertainment in itself. F. Tennyson Jesse concluded that the two authors who followed her and had to make sense of the story should receive some kind of medal, while David Hume ended the book saying: 'May heaven preserve me from such a fate in future!' John Chancellor, whose serialized mystery had given Agatha Christie the chance to win a competition prize more than a decade earlier, was drafted in to give the story a better shape, and found that plenty of work was needed. Sayers did not give up entirely on round-robin mysteries, taking part in two later collaborations, one – *No Flowers By Request* (serialized in the *Daily Sketch* in 1953) – on behalf of the Detection Club.

one of the finest of all parodies of Golden Age detective fiction
The tropes of Golden Age mysteries have made them a perfect target
for parodies, ranging from a sketch in *Monty Python's Flying Circus*
to Anthony Shaffer's *Sleuth* and Tom Stoppard's *The Real Inspector
Hound*. Writers of the Thirties were equally aware of the parodic
potential of detective fiction. Rupert Croft-Cooke (1903–79), began
his long career as the detective novelist Leo Bruce with a parody,
Case for Three Detectives (1936). Sayers' publication of *Gaudy Night*
was soon followed not only by E. C. Bentley's story 'Greedy Night'
but also by *Gory Knight*, written by Margaret Rivers Larminie and
Jane Langslow and published by Gollancz; see Martin Edwards,
'The Mystery of *Gory Knight*', *CADS* 58, June 2010.

19

What it Means to
Be Stuck for Money

'The Slump had spread like the plague,' said Anthony Gilbert in her memoir of that time. By 1933, not only the labouring class was affected, but also 'black-coated workers with years of experience and good references found themselves adrift through no fault of their own.. . . . The cry of Too Old at Forty was becoming Too Old at Thirty or anyhow thirty-five. . . . No one had supposed an emergency like this.'

Money was desperately tight. One of the reasons Gilbert loved the escapism offered by Detection Club dinners was that she knew what it was like to struggle to earn a living. She decided to 'write a novel about a man who had committed a murder . . . from the point of view of the criminal.. . . Murderers were people like ourselves. . . . My central character committed his murder by accident, and couldn't feel himself a murderer on that account. . . . I realized that here I was, writing the story of the man who was the victim of the slump.' As she said, 'Charles, the coward of the title, was everything I most dislike in men, yet he is the only character of mine with whom I have ever felt completely identified.'

The Coward, again published under the Anne Meredith pseudonym, is an example of a Golden Age novel tackling the effects of the slump. The cliché that detective novelists routinely ignored social and economic realities is a myth. The trouble was that many readers were not in the mood for realism. They wanted to be entertained by light-hearted films and plays, and novels set in fascinating places. *The Coward* was applauded by critics but failed to become a breakthrough book. Gilbert was disappointed. 'Its sales remained obstinately under the two thousand mark. I was one of those authors who can please everyone except the public.'

Financial misery was everywhere, and people accustomed to having money were not exempt from the pain. Norman Urquhart, the solicitor in Sayers' *Strong Poison*, is typical, facing ruin due to the crash of the Megatherium Trust. The crushing effects of the slump on the middle classes are vividly presented at the start of Christopher Bush's *The Case of the Chinese Gong*. Four cousins have fallen on hard times and in the opening chapter Tom Bypass, a former soldier in poor health, rescues the depressed and unemployed Martin Greeve – whose toy business has failed – from an attempt to commit suicide. Martin has no hope of a job, Romney Greeve, an artist, cannot sell his pictures, and Hugh Greeve is short of pupils for his private school. The four men have an unpleasant uncle who relishes the financial power he holds. Even the dullest reader can predict his fate.

In theory, nobody was better qualified to solve the nation's financial woes than the brilliant economist Douglas Cole. Yet even his judgments were sometimes bewilderingly naïve. When ill-health forced him to pull out of a research trip to the Soviet Union, he was bitterly disappointed to lose a chance to see for himself how 'the Socialist Sixth of the World' had 'abolished unemployment'. At home, the Society for Socialist Inquiry and Propaganda dissolved itself, but Douglas was undaunted by the latest collapse of a cause close to his heart. He was convinced that the slump proved that the 'intellectual case against capitalism' was very strong. Capitalism's likely demise was linked, in his view, with a crisis in world civilization, and the mood of widespread despair was captured by Aldous Huxley's frightening vision of the future in *Brave New World*. Although the Coles kept writing detective novels in which order was restored by good old Superintendent Wilson, everywhere Douglas looked he saw chaos. Naturally, this gave him an idea for another book.

He persuaded Victor Gollancz to publish *The Intelligent Man's Guide through World Chaos*, which became known as 'Coles' *Chaos'*. Soon *The Intelligent Man's Review of Europe Today* followed. Douglas also edited *What Everybody Wants to Know about Money*. Facetious reviewers expressed dismay that the latter book did not answer the most important question of all – how readers could *make* money.

Ellen Wilkinson, a good friend of the Coles, was among the casualties of the Labour Party's landslide defeat in the election. A former Guild Socialist and Communist, the fiery 'Red Ellen' was a class warrior who organized the Jarrow Hunger March. After losing her seat at Middlesbrough East, Wilkinson published *The Division Bell Mystery*. The mystery surrounding a rich financier's murder stems from a supremely incompetent police investigation of the crime scene, but in the vivid writing, background colour and characterization there is ample compensation for a lack of 'fair play'. The book's enduring appeal is underlined by unexpected parallels between the society Wilkinson describes and British life in the twenty-first century. When she returned to Parliament, politics' gain was detective fiction's loss.

Capitalism got a bad Press in Golden Age fiction, whatever the political instincts of the author. Contempt for shady financiers and businessmen, at least as fierce in the Thirties as scorn for greedy bankers today, was a recurrent theme, starting with Bentley's denunciation of the murder victim Sigsbee Manderson in *Trent's Last Case*. Members of the board of directors of the ruthless corporation Hardware Limited are eliminated, one by one, in John Rhode's *Death on the Board*, while the conservatively inclined Freeman Wills Crofts became a persistent critic of business mores. Crofts, like Rhode, understood industry better than most detective novelists, and his descriptions of how businessmen (they almost always were men) operate are as convincing as any of the period. *The 12.30 from Croydon* describes how a factory owner facing ruin because of the slump is driven to contemplate murdering his wealthy uncle. All goes well until he has the misfortune to attract the attention of Inspector French.

A dramatic board meeting opens the Coles' *Big Business Murder*. Kingsley Manson, the managing director of Arrow Investments, reveals to his colleagues that the business is founded on a swindle, which seems likely to unravel unless they all support his attempts to dodge the problem. An honest director called Gathorne objects, but the others go along with Manson. The scene is set for a first-rate book, but after Gathorne's predictable murder the story falls apart. The business scam might have enabled the Coles to flay corporate greed, or to chart the unbearable pressures that drive people to crime. Instead, they came up with the feeblest of plots, and Wilson solves the mystery by proving the guilt of the most obvious suspect. A large chunk of the book pursues the ramifications of a false confession. Quixotic confessions to protect a loved one were a familiar feature of Golden Age novels, but this one is among the most tediously protracted. Christie was much cleverer, subverting the trope of the false confession in *The Murder at the Vicarage* by turning it into a double bluff.

In the hands of an innovative writer, as Bruce Hamilton showed in his occasional novels, Golden Age detective fiction was capable of reflecting a radical agenda, but the Coles were content with satire so gentle that it made Sayers look like Hogarth. The couple's sheltered existence in academe meant they had no experience of earning a living in business, big or small, and little insight into the corporate world they deplored as a matter of principle.

In stark contrast, Sayers' years at Benson's ensured the authenticity of her portrayal of office life in *Murder Must Advertise*. Wimsey assumes a false identity to take a job at Pym's Publicity so that he can investigate the death of an employee and the apparent link between the firm and a gang of drug-smugglers. The puzzle is perfunctory, but the depiction of office politics is highly entertaining. Sayers amuses herself by having Wimsey invent a campaign to promote Whiffles cigarettes that is a forerunner of the Air Miles type of scheme; tongue firmly in cheek, she has him describe it as 'the biggest advertising stunt since the Mustard Club' – which had been her own invention at Benson's, of course. The final sentence of the book is 'Advertise, or go under.'

Money and class are her key themes. 'You don't know what it means to be stuck for money,' the culprit tells Wimsey when making his confession. Wimsey did not – but Sayers did, and her empathy with people strapped for cash gives the novel its bite. Long before it became fashionable to critique the consumer society, she offers a picture of a world in which people are sold a dream of health and happiness, a world where they are gulled into thinking they can Whiffle their way to a fortune: 'If this hell's-dance of spending and saving were to stop for a moment, what would happen? . . . [Wimsey] had never realised the enormous commercial importance of the comparatively poor.' Sayers writes with a fierce sympathy about 'those who, aching for a luxury beyond their reach and for a leisure for ever denied them, could be bullied or wheedled into spending their few hardly won shillings on whatever might give them, if only for a moment, a leisured and luxurious illusion.'

Money was not everything. Social status still counted for a great deal. Sayers made her detective an aristocrat, which has prompted accusations of snobbishness. This criticism, like so many made of Golden Age writers, is simplistic and unfair. Similar complaints are never directed at the Coles, who wrote six books about the Honourable Everard Blatchington. Once, when Sayers and Gladys Mitchell discussed the initiation ritual, Sayers said that the member whose participation would most amuse her would be Lord Gorell, but she knew he would be far too dignified for such nonsense. She had no time for pomposity.

Sayers' snobbery, such as it was, resembled the Coles', and focused on intellectual, rather than social, elitism. Like the Coles, she appreciated 'the intelligent man' – and intelligent women. As for the arch-conservatives Wade and Connington, they were scathing about police officers and others who condescended to subordinates or ordinary working people. There was no short-age of class prejudice during the Golden Age, but it was not a defining feature of the Detection Club. That said, the attempts of members of all political persuasions to render the dialogue of working class people phonetically make a modern reader cringe, if not as much as recurrent examples of casual racism and sexism. But it is striking that, although Agatha Christie strove to separate her writing from her emotional life, one of the rare moments of deeply felt passion in her whodunits comes when Miss Marple is reduced to tears of pity and rage by the cruel murder, not a member of the genteel middle class, but a gullible, ill-educated housemaid.

One writer ferociously hostile to snobbery was Roy Vickers, who after a long writing career was elected to the Detection Club in the Fifties. William Edward Vickers, to give his real name, was educated at Charterhouse and Oxford, but left without taking a degree, and although he qualified as a barrister he soon turned to journalism. Despite his apparent advantages, the smooth progress of his career seems to have been hindered by lack of money and a supportive social network. Vickers' output includes a novel and a short story with different plots, both called *Murder of a Snob*. *The Judge's Dilemma*, written under the name of Sefton Kyle, has a chapter called 'Class Prejudices' in which the near-impossibility of a young barrister succeeding in his chosen career without money behind him is described with what seems like personal anguish. Vickers' writing simmers with resentment towards the 'haves' who patronized the 'have-nots'. He recognized, as did many others in the Detection Club, that England in the Thirties was not a meritocracy, nor a country at ease with itself.

Anxiety about the state of the economy went hand in hand with dread of another war. On 9 February 1933, a few days after Adolf Hitler became Chancellor of Germany, a student debate was held by the Oxford Union Society. The Gothic grandeur of the debating chamber was familiar to many members of the Detection Club, including Knox and Bentley, two former

Presidents of the Union. The motion was that 'this House will in no circumstances fight for its King and country' and the proposer argued: "It is no mere coincidence that the only country fighting for the cause of peace, Soviet Russia, is the country that has rid itself of the war-mongering clique.'

Douglas Cole spoke in favour of the motion. When an opponent demanded to know what he would do if a German tried to rape his wife, he replied, 'I would get in between.' This answer, according to one witness, 'brought the house down'. What Margaret thought about Douglas' jaunty riposte is unknown, since she chose not to mention the debate in either her own memoirs or her biography of him.

The pacifists won the day, with the motion passed by 275 votes to 153. Even in 1933, the Oxford Union was scarcely a microcosm of British society, but the outcome caused a furore. The *Daily Express* was incensed: 'There is no question but that the woozy-minded Communists, the practical jokers, and the sexual indeterminates of Oxford have scored a great success.' Someone sent the Union a box containing 275 white feathers, one for each vote for the motion, but this condemnation of cowardice lacked sting, given that the sender did not have the courage to give his or her name. Pacifism was a popular cause, and plenty of voices were raised in support of the students who voted for the motion.

Among them was A. A. Milne's. Although he had fought during the war, his health had suffered, and over time his long-held pacifist views hardened. In 1934, he published *Peace with Honour*, a passionately argued attack on the value and inevitability of war. He misread Hitler and Mussolini, but although his idealism was misplaced, he had personal experience of the horrific nature of fighting in battle, and did not want others to go through what he had endured. In the same year, the canon of St Paul's Cathedral, Dick Sheppard, invited men (not women) to send him postcards containing the pledge: 'I renounce war, and I will never support or sanction another.' This initiative resulted in the formation of the Peace Pledge Union, which soon attracted more than one hundred thousand supporters.

At Westminster, Baldwin struggled with the question of rearmament, which was hugely expensive and deeply unpopular. Churchill, a voice crying in the wilderness, said the government was 'decided only to be undecided, resolved to be irresolute, adamant for drift, solid for fluidity, all-powerful to be impotent. So we go on, preparing more months and years – precious, perhaps vital, to the greatness of Britain – for the locusts to eat.'

'Supposing I had gone to the country and said that Germany was rearming and we must rearm,' Baldwin retorted. 'Does anybody think that this pacific democracy would have rallied to that cry at that moment? I cannot think of anything that would have made the loss of the election from my point of view more certain.' Churchill thought this a 'squalid confession', but it was at least frank. When Mussolini invaded Abyssinia, Britain probably could not have stopped him, even had the political will to do so existed.

Trouble overseas was mirrored by despair at home. Berkeley was wracked by self-doubt in many areas of his life, but – like Douglas Cole – supremely confident that he knew what was best for others. He published *O England!* under his real name, A. B. Cox, and his publishers trumpeted it as 'an examination of the causes of our present discontents, social and political: a book which affects every citizen personally.' As a manifesto for sweeping reform, it is typical Berkeley: often disagreeable, sometimes ridiculous, but at times startlingly visionary.

Berkeley was lucky, never having known the financial hardship suffered by Sayers and Anthony Gilbert in their younger days. However, he announced he was writing out of 'indignation', a characteristic state where he was concerned. People who knew him must have blinked at his claim, 'I am a fairly typical ordinary English citizen'. He struck a populist note, lashing out at 'temperance cranks' and 'anti-gambling cranks', and insisting that 'England is a land of very special flavour. . . . Her national character is, without any exception at all, the best.' Yet he was quicker than many to understand the vile nature of Hitler's Germany: 'In the last two years, we find one great nation reverting to hooliganism and medieval Jew-baiting.'

Berkeley argued that professional politicians were incapable of making the changes needed, and people must be wary: 'Fascism and Communism, the twin autocracies, await us. . . . Italy, in a precisely similar dilemma, chose Fascism and Mussolini. Are we to choose Sir Oswald Mosley?' For Berkeley, a much better option was a European pact. 'Personally, I have no faith left in the League of Nations. It is too cumbersome, too political and too weak. . . . What I should like to see would be a League of European Nations. . . . It is bound to come one day.'

As ever, his views on women were mired in contradiction. On the one hand, he believed that 'if the Governments of all countries were in the hands of women, there would be no wars; and that in itself would almost justify the revolution.' Yet for him, the female mind had 'too great a preoccupation with human relationships', and the fact that he saw this as a weakness speaks volumes. He identified areas of unfairness towards women that should be put right: the power of a husband to disinherit a faithful wife; restrictions governing the employment of women; and unequal pay for equal work. His solution was a Women's Charter and a minimum adult wage for everyone over twenty-one.

Each political party was flayed in turn, but he reserved most of his vitriol for Labour, arguing that if they won the next election, there would be civil war within three years. Yet he highlighted the decency of Ellen Wilkinson, and mused, 'To a man such as Mr G. D. H. Cole the country might be prepared to trust itself. But these men, not being the shouters and the unscrupulous, or Trade Unionists, are lost.'

Berkeley was infuriated by 'the wretched little whipper-snappers and jacks-in-office who, inflated like blimps with their own arrogance, treat the public like dirt'. Presumably not feeling in the least arrogant, he made the memorable pronouncement: 'Undoubtedly the best as well as the most useful period of the human mind is from 35 to 45. (I am 40 myself, and have no doubt at all on the fact.)'

He criticized unfair business competition through use of 'the huge resources of the chain-store to sell at a deliberate loss, until the one-man shop has been put out of business'. Decades before it became fashionable to condemn multinationals which indulge in elaborate tax avoidance schemes, he insisted that the greater the size of a business, the greater the responsibility to the whole community. His manifesto proposed a temporary National Government excluding professional politicians, and the abolition of all 'petty restrictions that serve no adequate purpose'. He wanted legislation in plain English, a Ministry of Justice and a Public Defender, statutory protection of all workers from exploitation by employers and from unhealthy conditions of work, improved state education, and the reform of social security law to eliminate individual hardship. But he concluded gloomily by asking if there was any hope that his programme could be put through. The answer he gave himself was 'no'.

His publisher included a slip at back of book which 'can be removed without defacing your copy', noting that 'little or no help can be expected from the Press for obvious reasons' and inviting those who agreed with Berkeley to spread the word. But this was long before viral campaigning, and few people became aware of Berkeley's manifesto for saving the nation. Even fewer could be bothered to promote them. The dust jacket of *O England!* promised a follow-up volume. The title, *You and I and All of Us*, suggests a rallying cry along the lines of 'we're all in it together'. But the book never appeared.

Berkeley lost heart. The years of frantic, constant writing, coupled with failure to find happiness in his personal life, were taking a toll. At a time when Christie and Sayers were finally blooming with self-confidence, Berkeley's disgruntlement was in danger of turning into something much more harmful.

Note to Chapter 19

'The Slump had spread like the plague,' said Anthony Gilbert
My understanding of life in the Thirties has been aided by Gilbert's memoir, and by Julian Symons' thoughtful book about the decade.

20

Neglecting Demosthenes
in Favour of Freud

Sayers celebrated her forty-first birthday as guest of honour at top table in the opulent, wood-panelled dining hall of Somerville College. Expectant faces gazed up at her as she levered herself to her feet. A few years earlier, such an occasion would have filled her with dread – a college gaudy, a reunion of alumni. Hanging on her words were dons and former students, people she liked and respected but also feared. She had refused invitations to return to Somerville, terrified that John Anthony's existence might become known and expose her to ridicule and contempt. Success had restored her self-esteem, and from the moment she arrived she found herself made welcome. As she proposed a toast, she brimmed with happiness, delighting her audience with her witty explanation of the value of a university education in the advertising world: a scholar's way with words 'is as useful in writing a slogan as in writing a sonnet'.

In the weeks leading up to the dinner, she had wrestled with two dilemmas. The simpler challenge was what to wear on returning to her *alma mater*. She was now very large, and very conscious of it. Buying a black coat and skirt didn't appeal to her, so she consulted her old Somerville friend, Muriel St Claire Byrne. Would a very dark blue-grey coat and skirt be suitable in combination with academic dress? Muriel duly reassured her.

The second problem was more taxing. She had reached her peak as a detective novelist, admired equally by reviewers and readers. Yet she was working all hours, and Mac was a constant source of worry. He suffered from liver trouble and high blood pressure, and she confided that his behaviour was 'queer and unreliable'. The damage the war had done to his morale and temper was, she felt, at the root of their marital problems. His outbursts of rage were unpredictable, and were compounded by jealousy of a wife who was achieving far more success than he could ever hope for. Yet after her motoring tour with Muriel, Sayers had decided to stick with him. She felt some residual affection for him, and feared that he would go downhill even faster if they divorced.

She gave herself as much of a hard time as Mac did, beginning a fictionalized autobiography which amounted to an exercise in self-flagellation. She never finished it, perhaps because her mood lifted once she decided where to go next with Wimsey and Harriet Vane. Working on her speech for the gaudy – where Somerville would celebrate the scholarship of a don she admired, Miss Mildred Pope, who was leaving Oxford for Manchester – she stumbled on the answer.

Why not write about the intellectual integrity that for her was 'the one great permanent value in an emotionally unstable world'? This provided a theme that would be integral to plot and character, and bring Peter and Harriet together at last. She might have struggled to find love in her adult life, but her novel would celebrate love. Love of learning, love for the city that inspired her, and love between her detective and the woman he adored.

Sayers' scholarly leanings were shared by Detection Club colleagues, several of whom taught at school or university. Some were loyal establishment figures, others were sceptics who mocked the status quo. The close-knit communities found in private schools and Oxbridge colleges, very familiar to most writers of the time, made ideal settings for 'closed circle' whodunits, and the Golden Age saw a host of mysteries set in the world of education. The books were mostly read by people who had attended neither Eton nor Oxford – and that was the point. The glimpses offered by Sayers and others into privileged lives disrupted by murder provided as much entertaining escapism as mysteries set on the Nile or on the Orient Express.

Leading the subversives were two men who, like Sayers, had abandoned teaching as soon as they could. As a form of catharsis, they set their debut novels in a school. Ralph Carter Woodthorpe, one of the Detection Club's most elusive figures, was the former English master of Margery Allingham's husband, Philip Youngman Carter. A chess-playing Glaswegian, Woodthorpe joined the staff of Christ's Hospital in West Sussex, and set about improving the boys' cultural education. A shy, gawky man, he was described by Pip as 'a raven with awkwardly clipped wings. He had no gift for discipline and could therefore teach only the sycophantic or eager few. But he could inspire.'

Woodthorpe used Christ's Hospital as the model for Polchester in *The Public School Murder.* 'Think of the great work he is doing with his drills and parades and marches,' says one teacher sarcastically of his colleague in charge of the Officer Training Corps, 'sowing a hatred of militarism in our Polchester children at an impressionable age. The O.T.C. does more for the cause of peace than the League of Nations and all the anti-war movements rolled into one.' Events are seen from the perspective of Smith, a likeable history master, who routinely solves Torquemada's crosswords. When the culprit is identified, he obligingly jumps off the side of a steamer. As a result, Polchester's reputation is not besmirched. The murderer had, Smith says with bitter irony, 'played the game at the end. A plucky thing to do. A sporting thing. . . . He put the School first and played the game.'

Nicholas Blake's first book boasted the added ingredients of gleeful adultery and sexual repression as a motive for murder. Blake was the pen name of Cecil Day-Lewis, an Irishman who went on to become Poet Laureate. His first collection of poetry was privately published in 1925, and two years later he met W. H. Auden, who was addicted to whodunits. Auden wrote a poem called 'Detective Story' as well as a post-war essay, 'The Guilty Vicarage', which helped to embed the notion of classic detective fiction as a sort of mythic Quest for the Grail. Auden found Day-Lewis a teaching job which enabled him to pay the bills, and in the years that followed, they wrote political and polemical verse reflecting dismay at the economic malaise of the Thirties and the rise of fascism in Europe.

Day-Lewis was widely admired. At a country house party that would have made an excellent setting for a detective story, Winston Churchill bumped into T. E. Lawrence and bemoaned the lack of great men in the country, 'present company excepted'. If a gossip column story in the London *Evening Standard* is to be believed, Lawrence of Arabia replied, 'There is one great man in this country and his name is Cecil Day-Lewis.'

At around this time, Day-Lewis joined the Communist Party. His 'communistic leanings' were mentioned by Sayers when he was mooted as a candidate for election to the Detection Club, but did not deter her from supporting his membership or enjoying his company. Tall, fair, and slender, he was described by Rebecca West as 'a Greek Apollo', and his good looks and charm were inherited in due course by his Academy Award-winning son, Daniel Day-Lewis.

While writing poems and espousing revolution, he taught the offspring of the privileged. At one point he demonstrated his credentials as a common man by dropping the hyphen from his surname, although he soon repented of his daring and reinstated the controversial bit of punctuation. Supposedly to pay for the repair to a leaking roof in his Gloucestershire cottage, he produced his first detective novel pseudonymously, using his mother's maiden name, Blake, and a first name picked at random.

Julian Symons later described his shock, when he had first read Nicholas Blake's debut, at finding a quotation from T. S. Eliot on the second page: 'In those years before the war, the detective-story writers in the ascendant gave the impression that although they might have heard Eliot's name they would not have cared to be found reading his poems.' But Symons did his predecessors an injustice. Many admired Eliot, as Eliot admired them, and Agatha Christie took the title of her Mary Westmacott novel *The Rose and the Yew Tree* from a line in 'Little Gidding', the final poem of Eliot's *Four Quartets*. Misjudgements like this by critics as renowned as Symons (and many who are much less distinguished) have fostered misunderstandings and prejudices about Golden Age fiction that endure to this day.

The first part of *A Question of Proof* is seen from the viewpoint of Blake's alter ego, the left-wing English master Michael Evans. He is having an affair with Hero Vale, the gorgeous wife of the head of a preparatory school. Evans cavorts with Hero in a hay-rick before the start of sports day, but their timing proves catastrophic. The body of an unpopular pupil is found in the same hay-rick shortly afterwards. The Reverend Percival Vale, 'a great stickler for the more flashy manifestations of discipline', blames the crime on a vagrant, and attributes 'the wave of violence which has lately been sweeping the country to the disastrous policy of the late Labour Government'. Inevitably, the cuckolded Vale becomes the second victim, murdered during the course of a cricket match. The police suspect Michael and Hero, and Nigel Strangeways is brought in to look after the school's interests.

Strangeways, 'after a brief stay in Oxford, in the course of which he had neglected Demosthenes in favour of Freud' is a successful private investigator. He benefits from having an uncle who is Assistant-Commissioner of Police at Scotland Yard, and bears a distinct resemblance to Auden, with one or two additional quirks such as an excessive fondness for drinking tea. He duly unmasks a culprit unwise enough to keep a candid diary revealing his sexual hang-ups. As a solution, it is scarcely conventional Golden Age.

The storyline panicked Lord Lee, chairman of the governors at Cheltenham College, where Day-Lewis taught. Lee raised his concern with Dick Roseveare, the Canadian headmaster, who duly called in Day-Lewis. Lee was afraid that *A Question of Proof* provided a clue that Day-Lewis was having an affair with Mrs Roseveare. Fortunately for his short-term career prospects, the Roseveares were an amiable couple with a sense of humour. Day-Lewis, a man intensely attractive to women, certainly had a wandering eye, but when it did wander, it wandered in other directions.

A classic Oxford mystery predating *Gaudy Night* was *An Oxford Tragedy* by J. C. Masterman in which the Senior Tutor at St. Thomas's College acts as Watson to an engaging amateur sleuth, the Viennese lawyer Ernest Brendel. After the crime is solved, order is restored in the form of an argument between dons over the redecoration of the college rooms left unoccupied by killer and victim. Masterman took twenty-four years to write a follow-up, even though he was far from indolent. He represented England at lawn tennis and hockey, toured Canada with the Marylebone Cricket Club, and later became Vice-Chancellor of Oxford University and earned a knighthood. During the Second World War he worked for the intelligence service, chairing the Twenty Committee which supervized the day-to-day operation of double agents and which took its name from the Roman numeral XX – that is, 'double cross'.

John Cecil Masterman joined the Detection Club after the Second World War, as did the much more prolific Michael Innes, the Oxford academic John Innes Mackintosh Stewart writing under a pen name, responsible for urbane detective stories published over a span of half a century. The first Innes novel, *Death at the President's Lodging*, renamed *Seven Suspects* in the US to forestall connotations of foul play in the White House, introduces Inspector John Appleby, whose lengthy murder-solving career eventually sees him knighted. But the definitive detective novel set in academe had already been published.

This was *Gaudy Night*, Sayers' *magnum opus*.

Gaudy Night, like Sayers herself, divides opinion. Admirers are passionate, detractors merciless. As she said, presumably of a conversation at the Detection Club, 'I was once challenged, in a circle of writers, to account for the sales of *Gaudy Night*. I had not the honesty to say that I thought it sold because it was a good book.' When Muriel St Claire Byrne suggested the book was autobiographical, Sayers denied it fiercely. She was pro-testing too much; there is a good deal of her in Harriet. A key difference, though, is that Harriet's scandalous involvement in a murder case is public knowledge; nobody at the gaudy dinner where she proposed the toast knew about Sayers' secret, the existence of John Anthony.

The book is long, yet the detective plot slight. Not a single murder is committed. Sayers was transforming the detective novel into a novel of manners. Harriet's previous reluctance to return to Oxford resembles Sayers' own unwillingness to attend a gaudy. Harriet's feeling that her life has been tainted by being tried for the murder of her lover mirrors Sayers' secret sense of shame about having sex outside marriage and giving birth to an illegitimate child. In the novel, as in Sayers' life, the lure of Oxford eventually proves irresistible.

Back at Shrewsbury College for a gaudy dinner, Harriet finds that despite the old scandal she is warmly welcomed. The Dean of Shrewsbury seeks her help; the College is awash with poison pen letters, and a manuscript that Miss Lydgate (based on Mildred Pope) was working on has been defaced. The vindictive campaign intensifies, and Harriet almost loses her life whilst trying to bring the culprit to justice. With the mystery solved, Wimsey and Harriet at last find themselves on equal terms. This being an Oxford novel written by Dorothy L. Sayers, the great detective's proposal of marriage captures his acknowledgment of Harriet's strength in their relationship whilst being couched in formal Latin.

Sayers saw *Gaudy Night* as the pinnacle of her achievement as a novelist. Yet the conflicts lying at its heart are not those of a conventional whodunit, but clashes between principles and personal loyalties. Slender as the plot was, it did complement her characters and theme. Wimsey had evolved from a sleuth-ing Bertie Wooster into a three-dimensional character, but more convincing was Harriet's journey towards self-confidence and self-respect as a scholar, writer and human being.

Gaudy Night so powerfully reflects Sayers' belief in equality between the sexes that the book is often called the first major feminist mystery novel. However, Julian Symons dismissed it as a 'woman's novel', and Sayers is often patronizingly accused of 'falling in love with her hero'. The truth is that Sayers' unrelenting focus on female independence influenced many other women novelists, ranging from P. D. James to the American feminist and author of *Reinventing Womanhood*, Carolyn G. Heilbrun, who wrote detective fiction as Amanda Cross. Jessica Mann, a Secretary of the Detection Club in the Eighties, said she was one of many schoolgirls who have been inspired to apply for Oxford or Cambridge Universities 'because of reading *Gaudy Night* at an impressionable age'.

This is a legacy of which any writer could be proud, and *Gaudy Night*'s fans often cite Sayers' erudition and literary style as particular strengths. Conversely, in an essay for *Scrutiny*, Q. D. Leavis, whose venom could be as dangerous as any poison unknown to science, said Sayers 'performed the function of giving intellectual exercise to readers who would very much dislike that kind of exercise if it was actually presented to them'. Symons, although a more sympathetic judge of detective fiction than Leavis, complained that there was a 'breathtaking gap' between what Sayers intended and what she actually achieved.

Agatha Christie was not an ivory-towered academic like Queenie Leavis, and she was no intellectual elitist either. Writing a novel of manners held no attraction for her. Given her unrelenting focus on entertainment, she remained sceptical about Sayers' ambitions for the genre. Christie felt the best Wimsey books were the early ones, and regarded Harriet as tiresome. With rare brutality, she said: 'Lord Peter remains an example of a good man spoilt.' Fortunately for harmony within the Detection Club, she was wise enough to confine these opinions to an article written for readers in Russia, which was not published in English until long after both she and Sayers were dead.

Notes to Chapter 20

Ralph Carter Woodthorpe, one of the Detection Club's most elusive figures
Scant information is available about Woodthorpe, other than the remarks of Pip Youngman Carter in *All I Did Was This*, and the biographical note on the Penguin edition of *The Public School Murder*. The latter indicates that Woodthorpe's favourite among his own books was *London is a Fine Town*, which is not a crime novel. Despite his success with detective fiction, and his friendship with Allingham and her husband, his heart seems not to have been in the genre.

Blake was the pen name of Cecil Day-Lewis
Peter Stanford's biography is the principal source for my discussion of Blake's life. See also Tony Medawar, 'Serendip's Detections 2: Mr Nigel Strangeways and the Detection Club', *CADS* 9, July 1988.

W. H. Auden, who was addicted to whodunits
See Auden, 'The Guilty Vicarage: Notes on the Detective Story, by an Addict', *Harpers*, May 1948. When P. D. James, later a pillar of the Detection Club, was first published by Faber, a pleasing suggestion was made that Auden might write a few poems masquerading as the work of her detective, the police officer and poet Adam Dalgleish. Auden died before the plan came to fruition, but he enjoyed James' books as he had enjoyed Golden Age mysteries: see Kate Kellaway, 'Inside the Head of a Criminal Mastermind', *The Guardian*, 15 July 2012.

A classic Oxford mystery
'Exbridge', the setting of Victor L. Whitechurch's *Murder at the College* (1932) is clearly Oxford. *The Oxford Murders* (1929) by Adam Broome also pre-dates Masterman's book; Broome was the pseudonym of Godfrey Warden James (1888–1963), who worked in the Sierra Leone government and, unusually for the Golden Age, set several mysteries in Africa; so did Elspeth Huxley (1907–97), who remains better known for her memoir *The Flame Trees of Thika*. One of the finest Oxford detective novels was *The Mummy Case Mystery* (1933) by Dermot Morrah (1896–1974), a journalist who never returned to the genre but became Arundel Herald of Arms

Extraordinary. He wrote a speech for Princess Elizabeth shortly before she ascended to the throne which moved her and Churchill to tears; see Tom Utley, 'Grandad's words made the Queen and Churchill cry', *Daily Mail*, 8 June 2012.

in an essay for Scrutiny
See Q. D. Leavis, 'The Case of Miss Dorothy Sayers', *Scrutiny*, December 1937.

an article written for readers in Russia
The article, 'Detective Writers in England', is now widely available as a result of its inclusion as an addendum to the republication of the Detection Club's *Ask a Policeman* (London, HarperCollins, 2012).

Part Four

Taking on the Police

Six Against the Yard, published by Selwyn & Blount in 1936.

21

Playing Games with Scotland Yard

Crime detection in real life fascinated Sayers and her colleagues, and this led to a decision to offer membership, for the one and only time in the Club's history, to someone who was not a writer, but the head of the CID at Scotland Yard. Norman Kendal was elected in 1935, and knighted two years later, perhaps because his part in a Detection Club escapade in Soho went unnoticed by the powers that be.

Kendal risked professional embarrassment as a result of the practical incompetence so characteristic of many novelists. While everyone was gathering for the dinner at Grosvenor House and the initiation of R. C. Woodthorpe, it was discovered that part of the regalia used in the ritual had been left in the Club rooms at Gerrard Street. Every member had a key to the rooms, but frantic questioning revealed that nobody had brought their key along. Nobody had imagined that there would be any need to visit the Club premises that night, since many more guests had been invited than the Gerrard Street rooms could hold. The plan was to spend the whole evening at the hotel where the Dinner and ritual were to take place.

A taxi was summoned, and three members jumped into it, together with an apprehensive Kendal, who was pressed into service for good reason. There was no option but to break in to the Club rooms. Yet there was a risk of a heightened police presence, since the building had recently been burgled and other rooms ransacked, although the Club's premises were left mysteriously untouched. But the writers reckoned, as Gladys Mitchell put it, 'that Sir Norman's presence at the scene of the crime was essential in case any inquisitive copper came along at the wrong time and asked the unanswerable question: "What's all this, then?"' A constable could hardly arrest an Assistant Commissioner.

The cunning plan worked, and nobody was arrested. Speaking at the dinner that night was Sir Austen Chamberlain, the former Foreign Secretary (and half-brother to Neville) who described himself as a 'greedy, interested and passionate' fan of detective fiction, despite the number of Golden Age novels in which politicians were murdered. After the excitement earlier in the evening, the mood was exuberant, and alcohol flowed freely. Berkeley presided in Chesterton's absence, and Punshon made a jokey reference to a recent break-in at the Gerrard Street rooms. The amateur burglars had got away with it.

Norman Kendal had edited a practical textbook on criminal investigation, but his election seems partly to have been a publicity gimmick, and partly – as an inscription to him written by Punshon in a presentation copy of *Death of a Beauty Queen* indicates – a thankyou for his collaboration with the Gerrard Street break-in. Punshon was interested in punishment as well as crime, and *Information Received*, the debut of his policeman hero Bobby Owen, contains a powerful passage – quite irrelevant to the plot – condemning a legal clerk's insistence that burglars should be deterred by 'a good dose' of the cat o'nine tails: 'What really roused his enthusiasm . . . was a primeval love of cruelty lurking in his subconsciounesss. . . . What moved him was the pleasure and excitement it gave him to think of a naked body, its flesh torn and bloody and scarred with the strokes of a whip.'

This book, which earned Sayers' admiration, contradicts the glib assumptions of critics who claim that social comment is absent from Golden Age detective novels; innumerable other examples are to be found in Punshon's work, and that of many of his colleagues.

The Club's developing relationship with Scotland Yard led to an unorthodox collaborative book of detective fiction. According to the dust jacket of *Six against the Yard,* the instigator of the project was 'lying idly in his bath' one day, contemplating murder: there existed someone whom he wished dead, and it occurred to him that most people, however Christian, 'knew of one of whom they harboured a similar wish'.

This sparked an idea. Six writers would be invited to write a story about a perfect murder, and then a senior police officer would review the scheme and judge whether it was really foolproof from a detective's point of view. A recently retired superintendent, G. W. Cornish, had published his memoirs. Sayers praised the book in a review, and Cornish agreed to participate in the game.

Margery Allingham opened proceedings with 'It Didn't Work Out', a strong story told by a music hall singer. Knox's 'The Fallen Idol' blends topical political satire, classic detection and a word puzzle linked to psychometric testing. Berkeley's 'The Policeman Only Taps Once' parodied the hardboiled American crime story.

Sayers wrote 'Blood Sacrifice', its theatrical background reflecting her current absorption in a stage play she was working on with Muriel St Claire Byrne. Her themes were ambitious: good and evil, innocence and guilt. Cornish was keen to show that, however neat the plan, the police would always make sure that justice was done, but Sayers, taking her work as seriously as ever, was irked by his comments. To research blood transfusions, integral to the plot, she had consulted Helen Simpson's husband, the surgeon Denis Browne, and she refused to accept Cornish's verdict that the killer's plan was not watertight.

When her agent David Higham, prompted by the *Daily Mail*, had the temerity to wonder if she might revise what she'd written, she refused with a vehemence which would have impressed a strong-minded Somerville graduate of a later generation, Margaret Thatcher: 'No, no! I will not alter a word. . . .' In psychological terms, Sayers regarded the story as one of the best she had

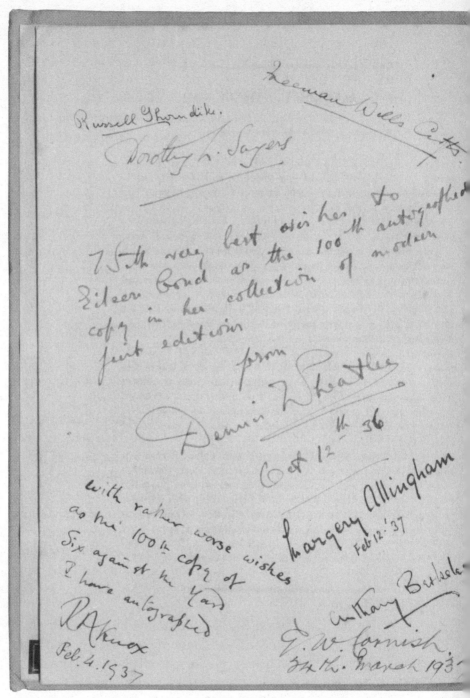

Russell Thorndike.

Freeman Wills Crofts.

Dorothy L. Sayers

With very best wishes to
Eileen Bond as the 100th autographed
copy in her collection of modern
first editions

from

Dennis Wheatley

Oct 12th 36

with rather worse wishes

Margery Allingham
Feb 12.'37

as the 100th copy of
Six against the Yard
I have autographed

R.A. Knox
Feb. 4. 1937

Anthony Berkeley

E.W. Cornish.
Sixth. March 193-

Six against the Yard, a copy inscribed by the authors and presented by
Dennis Wheatley to socialite and book collector Eileen Conn.

SIX AGAINST THE YARD

In which

Margery Allingham
Anthony Berkeley
Freeman Wills Crofts
Father Ronald Knox
Dorothy L. Sayers
Russell Thorndike

Commit the Crime of Murder which

Ex-Superintendent Cornish, C.I.D.

is called upon to solve

SELWYN & BLOUNT, PATERNOSTER HOUSE,
PATERNOSTER ROW - - LONDON, E.C. 4

written, and she said Cornish should speak to Denis Browne if he was not convinced.

A few hours later, as if afraid she had not made herself clear, Sayers wrote a second letter to Higham, repeating her views and saying that she had told the *Daily Mail* to withdraw a pointless change to one of her character's names. Nor was that all. Cornish's comments were good-natured, if not insightful, and he mentioned that he had not had the chance to discuss the case with Lord Peter Wimsey. Sayers promptly drafted a letter in which, surprise, surprise, Wimsey endorsed her view that 'Blood Sacrifice' did tell the story of a perfect murder. Higham was told that the *Daily Mail* could publish Wimsey's letter alongside Cornish's critique.

The playfulness of the project – for all Sayers' earnestness – appealed to readers. *Six against the Yard* is a unique book, a harmless piece of entertainment arising from one man's urge to murder an enemy. Harmless that is, assuming the cautionary remarks of the retired superintendent deterred anyone genuinely harbouring murderous intentions from putting any of the story ideas into practice. But an idea about murdering someone he knew lingered at the back of Berkeley's mind.

During the Golden Age, detective novelists usually kept their readers in the dark about the solution to the crime. The climax of the story was the revelation of whodunit, or occasionally how it was done. But there was another way to maintain suspense, and reader interest, a method similar to that in *Six against the Yard*. A writer could show readers the carrying out of an ingenious and apparently foolproof crime, and then describe how the detective solved the case – an 'inverted' detective story.

As well as leading the way with scientific detection, Richard Austin Freeman devised the 'inverted' story of crime. Four groundbreaking stories of this type were collected in *The Singing Bone* in 1911. Freeman was less interested in whodunit than 'how was the discovery achieved?' He was set thinking by Edgar Wallace's offer of a prize to a reader who identified the criminal in his 1905 novel *The Four Just Men*, a scheme which proved financially ruinous because too many people hit on the right answer. Freeman wondered if he could write a detective story which took the reader into his confidence from the outset. The result was 'The Case of Oscar Brodski': 'Here the usual conditions are reversed; the reader knows everything, the detective knows nothing, and the interest focuses on the unexpected significance of trivial circumstances.' That first story was split into two parts: 'The Mechanism of Crime' and 'The Mechanism of Detection'. A burglar murders a man in order to steal a packet of diamonds. His sole mistake is to leave his victim's felt hat at home before carrying the body away to be left on a railway track. He burns the hat, but in vain; Dr Thorndyke is able to solve the crime.

Here, once again, was a groundbreaking detective story with its roots in real life. One Saturday in November 1866, a Nottinghamshire rent collector called Henry Raynor set out for a cottage he owned in the village of Carlton. He and John and Mary Watson, a couple who occupied part of the building, were engaged in a long-running dispute about who had the right to vegetable produce from the cottage garden, and Raynor meant to put a stop to their activities. But that night, his body was found on a nearby railway line. He had been battered with a poker, and his money and watch were missing, as well as his hat.

The eminent toxicologist Professor Alfred Swaine Taylor was called in, and spotted marks of dragging between the cottage and the railway line which corresponded with Raynor's boots. A search of the cottage revealed a cindery substance on an iron rake which after heating and treatment with alcohol produced a shellac resin. This proved to be very similar to a substance obtained from a felt hat like Raynor's. The Watsons claimed that bloodstains on their clothes came from killing a pig, and luckily for them Taylor was unable to prove otherwise. They were found not guilty, although Freeman's fictional murderer was not so fortunate.

At first, inverted stories received scant attention. Freeman abandoned the form before the start of the First World War, which Sayers found regrettable. Berkeley's approach in *Malice*

Aforethought was different, as he presented the whole story from the murderer's point of view rather than, in part, from the detective's. Encouraged by Sayers, both the Coles and Freeman Wills Crofts wrote inverted detective novels, while Roy Vickers wrote excellent short inverted stories featuring Scotland Yard's Department of Dead Ends. The appeal of the form has endured, and in the television age, the inverted stories in *Columbo* achieved enormous popularity.

The outstanding inverted crime novel was *Heir Presumptive*, by Henry Wade. Eustace Hendel is alerted by a newspaper item to the fact that he might be line for an inheritance that will solve all his financial problems. He sees a possible route to becoming the next Lord Barradys, but unfortunately some family members stand in his way. The storyline anticipates aspects of the classic Ealing comedy *Kind Hearts and Coronets*, which appeared more than a decade later.

George Orwell had no doubt: ' Our great period in murder, our Elizabethan period, so to speak, seems to have been between roughly 1850 and 1925, and the murderers whose reputation has stood the test of time are the following: Dr Palmer of Rugeley, Jack the Ripper, Neill Cream, Mrs Maybrick, Dr Crippen, Seddon, Joseph Smith, Armstrong, and Bywaters and Thompson.'

Was it mere coincidence that Orwell's Golden Age of real life murder came to an end as the Golden Age of fictional murder was gathering steam? Orwell argued that, leaving aside the Ripper killings, the other eight cases had a good deal in common: six were poisoning cases, and all but two of the ten criminals came from the middle class. Sex provided a powerful motive in most of the cases, while 'respectability', such as the urge to avoid the scandal of divorce, was a recurrent factor in the culprit's mindset.

Crucially, as Orwell pointed out in 'The Decline of the English Murder', the context of almost all the classic cases 'was essentially domestic; of twelve victims, seven were either wife or husband of the murderer.' The Thompson–Bywaters trial, and the other cases Orwell highlighted, inspired Detection Club members and other Golden Age writers to produce much of their finest work. But it was a case that dominated the head-lines for weeks in 1931 that gave Sayers the chance to display her own skills as a detective.

Notes to Chapter 21

Six against the Yard *is a unique book*
Opinions vary as to whether it is accurately described as a product
of the Detection Club. Its originality is characteristic of Club members,
but the Club was not named on the first edition. Five of the six
crime writers were members of the Club. The exception was Russell
Thorndike (1885–1972), brother of the actor Sybil Thorndike. He
wrote popular novels featuring Doctor Syn of Romney Marsh, and
has occasionally been described as a member of the Club, although
that can only be the case if (as is not impossible) all trace of his
membership has vanished.

classic Ealing comedy Kind Hearts and Coronets
The film was based on a superbly ironic and inexplicably neglected
1907 novel, Roy Horniman's *Israel Rank*, a masterpiece of murder
subtitled *The Autobiography of a Criminal.*

22

Why was the Shift Put in the Boiler-Hole?

At 8.45 pm, on a dark January evening in 1931, the Johnsons, a couple who lived in Anfield, Liverpool, heard someone knocking at their neighbours' back door. Going outside to see what was the matter, they encountered William Wallace, who lived next door. 'Have you heard anything unusual tonight?' he asked. When they said no, Wallace said, 'I have been round to the front door and also to the back, and they are both fastened against me.' He tried the back door again, and it opened quite easily. While the Johnsons waited, he went inside. They heard him call out twice before he came hurrying back.

'Come and see,' he said. 'She has been killed.'

The body of his wife Julia lay in the parlour, stretched out on the hearth rug, with her feet close to the gas fire. Her skull had been smashed with such fury that her brains had spilled out. Blood spattered the room, on the carpet, the wall, an armchair and on Wallace's violin case. She had been beaten to death with a poker.

William Herbert Wallace, an insurance agent working for the Prudential Assurance Company, moved to Liverpool with his wife Julia a year after their marriage in March 1914. In his youth, Wallace worked as a salesman in India and China, but a kidney illness forced him to return to England, and he became the Liberal Party's election agent in Ripon, Yorkshire. There he met Julia, a former governess, whom he later described as 'dark haired, dark eyed, full of energy and vivaciousness'. He claimed to be devoted to her, while acquaintances described him as placid, honest, and 'an absolute gentleman in every respect'.

To all appearances, the Wallaces were a typical bourgeois couple of their time. Julia was a capable pianist, and Wallace learned the violin, so he could accompany her when they hosted musical evenings at their modest home in Anfield. They nursed a secret that never came out during their lifetimes. On their marriage certificate, Wallace was said to be aged thirty-six, and Julia a year older. In fact, she was fifty-three, and had falsified information about her date of birth and origins in answering questions on the census four years before the wedding. But there was nothing so unusual in outwardly respectable people lying about their age, their background and other aspects of their private lives. Several members of the Detection Club did the same. Respectability, as scores of Golden Age novels demonstrated, was often only skin deep.

Wallace helped to found the Central Liverpool Chess Club, which met in the basement of Cottle's City Cafe, in North John Street, and he played there each Monday night. On the evening of Monday 19 January, 1931, Wallace was on his way to the Club for a tournament game when a telephone call was put through to a waitress in the cafe. The caller wanted to speak to Wallace, and she handed the phone to the Club captain. The caller gave his name as R. M. Qualtrough, and said he particularly wanted to see Wallace at 7.30 p.m. the next day to discuss taking out some insurance as a present for his daughter. He gave his address as 25 Menlove Gardens East, Mossley Hill. The message was passed to Wallace, although he said he was not familiar with either Qualtrough or that address.

According to Wallace, the next evening he went out to keep the appointment, but could not find the address he had been given. A police constable told him there was no such road as Menlove Gardens East, although there were several addresses with similar names. In the end he admitted defeat, and returned home to make his horrific discovery in the parlour.

Wallace, the prime suspect, insisted he was innocent. The case against him was purely circumstantial. Charged with murder, he stood trial at Liverpool Assizes. The case caused a sensation, and after an hour's deliberation, the jury found him guilty. He was sentenced to death, but the Court of Criminal Appeal took the unprecedented step of ruling that the verdict was 'not supported by the weight of the evidence' and set him free. The disasters that had befallen Wallace were not over. After his release, he was dogged by a hostile whispering campaign, and found it impossible to return to work selling insurance. His kidney problems returned, and he died only a couple of years after his wife's brutal killing. Nobody else was ever charged with the crime.

The Wallace mystery has tantalized generations of true crime experts, along with novelists ranging from Sayers and Raymond Chandler to P. D. James. Margery Allingham wrote an essay about the private mock trial of Wallace by his peers, 'The Compassionate Machine', but it was not published until long after her death. Agatha Christie toyed with a plot idea based on the case when planning *Mrs McGinty's Dead*, while the story has supplied ingredients for several novels, including two written by John Rhode: *Vegetable Duck* and *The Telephone Call*, the former a strong candidate for any award for Least Likely Title of a Murder Mystery.

When members of the Detection Club cast around for a fresh idea for a fundraising book, Sayers, Berkeley and John Rhode favoured putting together a collection of essays re-examining real-life cases, and Helen Simpson agreed to take on the spade work. The cast of contributors was completed by Freeman Wills Crofts, Margaret Cole, and E.R. Punshon. With the Wallace case still fresh in people's memories, Sayers decided to explore it in depth. The book became *The Anatomy of Murder: Famous crimes critically considered by members of the Detection Club*.

Sayers' 'The Murder of Julia Wallace' is a masterpiece of armchair detection. Quoting the judge's summing-up, she points out that the question in a murder trial is solely whether the accused committed the crime, whereas the detective novelist wants to know whodunit, whether or not it was the accused. She argues that the Wallace case was a perfect subject for a detective novelist to study: if he was guilty, 'then he was the classic contriver and alibi-monger that adorns the pages of a thousand mystery novels; and if he was innocent, then the real murderer was still more typically the classic villain of fiction.'

At a time when Berkeley kept coming up with multiple solutions to fictional crimes, Sayers argued that such ingenuity was not as unrealistic as it seemed. In the Wallace mystery, there was 'no single incident which is not susceptible of at least two interpretations, according to whether one considers that the prisoner was, in fact, an innocent man caught in a trap or a guilty man pretending to have been caught in a trap.'

Sayers speculated about the Wallaces' relationship, noting how difficult it is 'to be certain how far an appearance of married harmony may not conceal elements of disruption'. She probably had her own life with Mac in mind. The extent of the age difference between the Wallaces was not public knowledge, and Sayers wondered whether it was significant that there were no children. She also asked herself whether Wallace's reference to his wife's 'aimless chatter' implied that he found her companionship trying. When looking at his low-key diary entry recording their fifteenth wedding anniversary, she found it stoical rather than cheery, but not the work of a man so exasperated that he was driven to madness.

For Sayers, character and psychology were crucial, and she felt there was a psychological stumbling-block in the case against Wallace. The killing could not have resulted from a 'momentary frenzy', because the evidence suggested careful planning, and the ferocity of the attack was probably due to panic. She felt Wallace's character was incompatible with his having committed the murder: 'One can only say that, if he was a guilty man, he kept up the pretence of innocence to himself with an extraordinary assiduity and appearance of sincerity.' Although she described the mystery as 'insoluble', one correspondent impressed her by saying that if Wallace had been guilty, it would have made more sense for him to arrange a genuine appointment on the night of the killing rather than a bogus one.

Research undertaken long after her death suggests she was on the right lines. In 1980, radio presenter Roger Wilkes, building on research undertaken earlier by criminologist Jonathan Goodman, pointed the finger of guilt at Richard Gordon Parry, a young colleague of Wallace's. The theory is that, having got Wallace out of the way, he burgled his house in the hope of stealing insurance money, only to be discovered by Julia, whom he then battered to death. But nothing is settled forever when it comes to classic cases of true crime, and in 2013, P. D. James argued that, although Parry made the telephone call as a prank, Wallace did kill Julia. Others suggest Wallace hired Parry as a contract killer, but struggle to come up with evidence of a motive.

So was Wallace the decent and trustworthy man his fellow chess players thought they knew, and as much a victim as Julia? His stoical demeanour seemed like callousness, although after the trial he tried to explain himself in a newspaper article: 'For forty years I had drilled myself in iron control and prided myself on never displaying an outward emotion in public. . . . My griefs and joys can be as intense as those of any man, but my rule has always been to give them expression only in privacy.' Wallace owed his destruction to an old-fashioned British insistence on maintaining a stiff upper lip.

No one is named as editor of *The Anatomy of Murder,* but Helen Simpson took responsibility for organizing the contributions. Sayers sent her the Wallace essay (describing it as a 'ghastly great tome') and apologized for the delay in submitting it: 'John Rhode and Anthony Berkeley were very fierce with me at the last meeting when you are not there to protect me!'

Given the strength of Sayers' personality, few people would imagine that, even in flippant mood, she might feel the need of protection, let alone contemplate looking to a younger woman to offer it. But Simpson was, in her elegant way, as forceful as Sayers. Even Berkeley and Rhode might have quailed at the prospect of confronting an Australian as forthright as she was good-looking. The reason Berkeley was infuriated by Sayers' delay was that he had already written his essay for the book, and it risked being superseded by a semi-official account in the *Notable British Trials* series. Rhode simply expected others to match his own astounding productivity. But Sayers, as they well knew, was not idle. Her tardiness was simply due to her perfectionism and obsessive attention to detail. It is this relentless commitment to quality in everything she wrote that has helped her reputation as a writer to survive.

After years of dinner meetings, the Club's members knew each other well. Formality had given way to familiarity. Friendship groups and alliances were emerging, and people were no longer always on their best behaviour, especially when the drink flowed. Sayers was finding Berkeley's provocative nature tiresome, and was displeased when he gave *Gaudy Night* a mixed (but not unfair) review. She also seems to have thought that he was responsible for a clerihew actually written by Bentley in a book of parodies to which Berkeley contributed a teasing skit of Hugh Walpole. In '*Greedy Night*', Bentley wrote:

> *Lord Peter Wimsey*
> *May look a trifle flimsy.*
> *But he's simply sublime*
> *When scenting out crime.*

She retaliated in a private letter to Helen Simpson (referring to an Oxford boulevard familiar to them both):

> *Mr Iles*
> *Should be debagged in the middle*
> *Of St Giles*
> *For calling Peter Wimsey*
> *Flimsy.*

Simpson's own essay focused on a nineteenth-century case, the killing of a Sydney bank teller called Henry Kinder, and

Margaret Cole also wrote about a Victorian mystery, the case of Adelaide Bartlett. Adelaide's husband died of chloroform poisoning after the couple had become involved in a *ménage a trois* with a vicar called George Dyson. She was charged with murder, but found not guilty. Margaret Cole's account is more of a polemic than an investigation, sympathizing with Adelaide and scoffing at the judge's prejudices against extramarital sex. The eminent surgeon Sir James Paget was more cynical, saying: 'Now that she has been acquitted for murder and cannot be tried again, she should tell us in the interest of science how she did it.' Instead, Adelaide disappeared permanently from sight, and so did the Reverend Dyson.

The serial killer Henri Landru was the subject of E. R. Punshon's essay, while Freeman Wills Crofts chose the Lakey murder case on the North Island of New Zealand. The key elements of the story are worthy of Inspector French: 'detective work of an extremely high order, involving persevering research, precise observation and deduction, magnificent team work and the use of the latest scientific methods'. As for Berkeley, twelve years after that the trial of Edith Thompson and Frederick Bywaters a similar case caused a sensation, and provided him the chance to explore his obsession with murder provoked by adultery.

The *Bournemouth Daily Echo* carried an advertisement in September 1934 for a 'willing lad . . . Scout-trained preferred' to do housework at a house known as the Villa Madeira. A fresh-faced eighteen-year-old called George Stoner applied for the job. He was not a Scout, but he was prepared to drive a car, and was recruited by Francis Mawson Rattenbury, a retired architect, and his wife Alma, as a chauffeur–handyman.

Rattenbury, depressive and ill-tempered, occasionally talked about committing suicide. Alma was his second wife; he was her third husband. She was attractive and almost thirty years younger; he was impotent. She was a talented musician whose courage working for the ambulance service during the war had earned her the Croix de Guerre, but she also had a fragile, addictive personality. Their relationship had become sullen and unhappy. During their most serious quarrel, Rattenbury blacked Alma's eye, and she bit his arm. The willing lad they hired proved to be a quick worker. Within a couple of months of his arrival at the Villa Madeira, he and Alma began an affair.

Rattenbury, who slept on his own downstairs, turned a blind eye to Stoner's nocturnal visits to Alma's room, which she shared with her six-year-old son. The young man became increasingly possessive, and she took him to a London hotel, showering him with gifts including three pairs of *crêpe de chine* pyjamas and silk handkerchiefs. She bought them at Harrods with money her husband had given her because she had said she needed an operation. A couple of days after their return, she suggested to her husband that they go on a trip to Bridport to cheer him up. Did she want to make Stoner jealous? Berkeley thought so. The young man refused to drive the Rattenburys to Bridport and borrowed a wooden mallet from his grandparents, saying that he meant to put up a screen in the garden.

That evening, Rattenbury was found, alive but badly beaten. He had been hit about the head with the mallet. Alma, who had drunk a lot of whisky, tried to kiss a police constable who came to the house, and said she had attacked her husband. Rattenbury died of his injuries, and both the lovers were charged with murder. They pleaded not guilty, and although Stoner was convicted and sentenced to death, Alma was acquitted. As she left the Old Bailey, a large crowd booed her.

A few days later, she took a train to Christchurch, walked across the meadow until she came to a riverbank, then thrust a knife into her left breast five times before dropping into the water. The stab wounds punctured the heart she thought was already been broken beyond repair. Unable to face the prospect of living without Stoner, she died as impulsively as she had lived. Although Stoner's appeal failed, his sentence was commuted to penal servitude for life. Berkeley estimated that if his conduct was good, he would be 'back among us' in about fifteen years. In fact, Stoner was released after just seven years, and lived until 2000.

Berkeley was spellbound by the Rattenbury and Stoner trial. Not, he insisted, because he was morbid, but because he was 'a student of character' with 'a sneaking passion for the truth'. He admitted, however, to a touch of voyeurism: 'Nothing outside fiction so effectually knocks down the front wall of a house and exposes its occupants in the details of their strange lives as does a trial for murder.'

His long essay about the case turned into an extended rant about the hypocrisy and irrationality of the English legal system, above all the presumption that a woman capable of committing adultery was capable of committing murder. He argued that Florence Maybrick had been sentenced to death for a single instance of adultery, coupled with suspicion (but not proof) that she had murdered her husband, while Edith Thompson had been 'executed for adultery'. And he went further, pouring scorn on the conventional bourgeois mores of his time: 'To say that respect cannot exist between a man and woman whose relations are legally improper is just as silly as to say that respect invariably exists between married couples.'

As usual, Berkeley's views were double-edged. His sympathy for Alma Rattenbury was humane, more in keeping with modern social attitudes than those prevalent in the Thirties. Yet Berkeley was no feminist. He lashed out so often against women who torment their lovers that it is hard to resist the impression that, as in so many of his novels, he was venting his feelings about the way he had been treated by a woman he adored. A woman who, like Edith Thompson or Alma Rattenbury, 'was incapable of seeing through the fog . . . to the real, selfish, petty core within'.

The final contributor to *The Anatomy of Murder* was John Rhode, his subject Constance Kent, the sixteen-year-old whose young half-brother Saville was murdered at the Road House in Wiltshire in June 1860. The story is a classic of detection which has fascinated writers ranging from Wilkie Collins in the nineteenth century and Agatha Christie in the twentieth to Kate Summerscale in the twenty-first. Summerscale's book, *The*

Suspicions of Mr Whicher, became a bestseller which sparked a television series.

Rhode had previously been responsible for *The Case of Constance Kent*, an entry in the *Notable British Trials* series. Five years after her brother's body was found, Constance confessed to the crime, and the trial resulted in her being sentenced to death. Given her age, and the fact that she had made a confession, the punishment was commuted to a sentence of penal servitude. She spent twenty years in prison, and after her release in 1885 she vanished from sight. At the time Rhode was writing, nobody knew what had happened to Constance.

Months after the book appeared, Rhode received an anonymous letter from Sydney, Australia, challenging his views on the case. He believed it had been written by Constance, but a handwriting expert disagreed. Not until further research took place in the Seventies was Rhode's theory vindicated. Constance had emigrated to Australia, where she worked as a nurse for many years. After retiring in 1932, she ultimately reached the age of one hundred, quite an achievement for someone condemned to the scaffold at the age of twenty-one. She was the author of the letter.

'The Sydney document' shaped Rhode's essay, as he explored Constance's 'elusive personality', showing greater interest in psychology than he did in his novels. He donated the original letter to the Detection Club's library, although depressingly this unique item of criminal history, like the Club's Minute Book, went astray during the Second World War, and has never turned up since.

Sayers' own fascination with the case dated back to her interest in Collins's borrowing of elements from the story to fashion *The Moonstone*. She acquired a copy of Rhode's book, and the trial transcript so intrigued her that she decided to do some investigating of her own. She pored over the evidence, and annotated the text of the book with thoughts on different aspects of the mystery. Her comments range from analysis of the evidence given at the trial to corrections of printing errors. Although she was writing only for her own entertainment, her remarks are fascinating.

The psychology of the characters, above all the culprit, enthralled her. When Rhode discussed the 'nerve' of the murderer, she compared the *sang froid* of the killer in the case that inspired *The Scoop*: Patrick Mahon had not only invited a woman back to the bungalow where he had killed his duped lover Emily Kaye the night before, but had sex with her there while his victim's corpse lay in the next room.

Sayers tackled the forensic evidence in the Constance Kent case with the zeal of a born detective. Several blank pages at the back of the book are crammed with carefully reasoned observations in her neat hand under the heading 'Notes on the blood-stained shift', divided into sections with headings such as 'Why was the shift put in the boiler-hole?' Her notes, totalling more than seventeen hundred words, are characteristically incisive. She was aiming to use her analytical skills to clarify aspects of the case which remained unclear. She mused over points such as the ownership of the garment, its precise nature – was it a nightdress or not? – and whether the blood that stained it was menstrual (she concluded that it was). As in the Wallace essay, her meticulous reasoning and close attention to detail make it a shame that she did not apply her gifts to more unsolved mysteries.

Sayers' interest in true crime was strong as Berkeley's. She explored real-life puzzles with such zeal and energy that Wimsey would have applauded. Had she not abandoned true crime for her other passions, she would surely have established herself as the outstanding true-crime writer of the twentieth century.

Notes to Chapter 22

a collection of essays re-examining real-life cases
The previous year saw the publication of *Great Unsolved Crimes*,
with a list of contributors dominated by present and future Detection
Club members and their associates, including E. M. Delafield
(discussing the Thompson–Bywaters case) and ex-Superintendant
Cornish. Berkeley wrote two essays (one as Iles), while Margaret Cole,
Crofts, Freeman, Val Gielgud, Kennedy, Helen Simpson and Wade
were also in the line-up. Sayers' essay, 'The Murder of Julia Wallace',
was an early version of her contribution to *The Anatomy of Murder*
and had originally appeared in the *Evening Standard*. The fashion
for asking detective novelists to solve real-life puzzles spread to *The
Star* in 1937, and Carr, Rhode and Punshon were among those played
the sleuth for the newspaper; see Tony Medawar, 'Serendip's Detections
XIII: Detective Writers' Detection', *CADS* 53 February 2008.

*a strong candidate for any award for Least Likely Title of a Murder
Mystery*
Rival contenders include *The Stoat* (1940) by Lynn Brock and *Twenty-
Five Sanitary Inspectors* (1935) by Roger East. The East pseudonym
concealed the identity of Roger d'Este Burford (1904–81), a poet
and diplomat who wrote film and television scripts as well as infrequent but interesting detective novels.

in 2013, P. D. James argued that . . . Wallace did kill Julia
See 'P. D. James on Britain's most compelling unsolved murder –
and how she finally came to crack it', *The Sunday Times Magazine*,
27 October 2013.

the Notable British Trials *series*
This, the first volume of which was published in 1905, developed
into an extensive library of historical and criminal trials embracing
the most famous British *causes célèbres* from the case of Mary,
Queen of Scots onwards.

*She pored over the evidence, and annotated the text of the book
with thoughts on different aspects of the mystery.*
Her unpublished annotations are to be found in a copy of the book
in my possession.

23

Trent's Very Last Case

1936 was a pivotal year in British history, and also in the story of the Detection Club. On 21 May, Sayers was one of ten people who attended a private dinner to celebrate a landmark in detective fiction. This was the kind of scenario which in fiction provided irresistible opportunities for murder, especially behind locked doors. In the event, the steak was not garnished with strychnine, and there was no cyanide in the champagne. The occasion was 'the Trent Dinner', marking the long-awaited return in a novel of Philip Trent, whose 'last case' twenty-three years earlier was the catalyst for the Golden Age.

The arrival of *Trent's Own Case* was greeted with much fanfare. Constable had acquired the publishing rights, thanks to the enthusiasm of one of the company's directors, Michael Sadleir, that old Oxford friend of Sayers and the Coles. But this was very different from *Trent's Last Case*. E. C. Bentley lacked the stamina and commitment needed for the long haul of a novel, and the book was a joint effort with Herbert Warner Allen. An old friend, Warner Allen had published detective novels featuring a wine merchant named, in Bentley's honour, Mr Clerihew, but they were never strong enough to merit his election to the Detection Club.

The Trent Dinner was attended by Henry Wade (who had established himself as Constable's leading detective novelist), Milward Kennedy, Sayers, Freeman Wills Crofts, Nicholas Blake

(Cecil Day-Lewis), Frank Swinnerton, and the two co-authors, together with Sadleir and his right-hand-woman at Constable, Martha Smith. This select gathering brought together most of Bentley's closest literary friends. Berkeley was absent, though not due to any form of snub, given that he had recently attended a cocktail party hosted by Bentley. He had probably retreated to Linton Hills. Christie was, as usual, on her travels. All those present – including Martha Smith – autographed copies of the new book as a memento of the great occasion.

A month earlier, Sayers had written to Bentley heaping praise on his new novel, and regretting that he had let two decades 'flow between the banks of Trent'. She took a dig at her friends in the Detection Club, comparing Bentley favourably to 'poor dear Berkeley and Crofts and Rhode' who worked 'so hard with their big machine-looms and make an intricate pattern, and then you come along and all your figures get cheerfully up and walk out of the tapestry and talk and eat and move about in three dimensions'.

Sayers' judgement was compromised by friendship, as well as by an increasing irritation with Berkeley, whose best writing was far superior to that of Crofts and Rhode. *Trent's Own Case* was striking only in its ordinariness. The story concerns the shooting of a sadistic philanthropist whose portrait Trent has been painting, and falters after a sound start. For all Sayers' attempts to bolster his morale, Bentley was haunted by a sense of failure, as if he had never quite fulfilled the brilliant creative promise of his younger days. This apparently aloof, complicated man never made a parade of his feelings, but a growing sense of frustration and inadequacy caused him to take refuge in alcohol. As a crime novelist, he was a one-hit wonder. *Trent's Own Case*, like his final novel, an unexciting thriller about amnesia called *Elephant's Work*, was all too forgettable.

The most notable absentee from the Trent Dinner was Bentley's boyhood friend G. K. Chesterton. Overweight and hopelessly unfit, the Detection Club's President suffered from assorted ailments for years although he continued to work hard and was a popular broadcaster on the BBC, taking book reviews as a starting point for digressions into whatever topics caught his fancy. His opinions remained as strong and idiosyncratic as ever, and his hostility towards imperialism strengthened his reservations about Fascism after Mussolini invaded Abyssinia.

As a writer, he fell into the same trap as Douglas Cole, sacrificing quality for quantity. *The Scandal of Father Brown*, the fifth and final collection of short stories about the little priest, received a muted reception. The old magic had gone and to prove it, when Chesterton wrote another Father Brown story, it was turned down by the *Storyteller* magazine, although his secretary managed to hide this from him.

Yet he had not lost all the old flair, as he showed in a radio debate with Bertrand Russell, the philosopher, on 'Who Should Bring up Our Children?' Russell said that poor parents could not give their children the food, clothing and space they needed, while rich parents spoiled their offspring. The progressive solution was for children to be cared for by doctors, nurses and teachers, in institutions. Chesterton regarded this as drivel. Parents were fitted by nature to bring up their children, and money would be better spent on improving living conditions for the poor. On the evening of the broadcast, Berkeley wrote from Linton Hills, 'with no human being within a couple of miles but with a glass at my elbow', to congratulate Chesterton on wiping the floor with Russell.

At the time of the Trent Dinner, Chesterton was coming to the end of a motoring tour of France, accompanied by his wife and secretary. He visited Lourdes, hoping his health might somehow recover. But he was now a sick man. There was to be no miracle cure.

Sayers and Mac were leading separate lives. The front room on the first floor of their house in Witham, Essex, was Sayers' library and study. Mac had a small room downstairs where he wrote or painted. They met for lunch and dinner, but seldom went out together. Mac – unlike Christie's husband Max Mallowan, or Clarice Dickson Carr – avoided meetings of the

Detection Club and remained a mysterious figure to most of her friends. Sayers' agent, David Higham, thought Mac 'completely idle and comfortable on the bottles she earned for him', but the couple established a *modus vivendi*. Sayers was an owl, getting up late and working into the small hours, so they spent less and less time with each other.

Mac preferred the company at the Red Lion, an eighteenth-century pub just along Newland Street, although when someone referred to him as 'Dorothy Sayers' husband', he stubbed out his cigarette and marched out in fury. He produced a book called *The Craft of the Short Story*, but the text ran to a paltry eighty-eight pages, perhaps because he had no track record of short story writing. Among words of wisdom offered to budding writers was the advice never to use 'a *nom de plume* . . . an author is well-advised to use his or her name fearlessly'. This makes it all the more peculiar that he published the book under the name of Donald Maconochie.

Mac finally agreed to John Anthony's adoption, and although Sayers found it difficult to discuss her son with her husband, the lawyers sorted things out. John Anthony was duly told he had been adopted by Cousin Dorothy and Cousin Mac. He could now call himself John Anthony Fleming. He continued to live with Ivy, who made sure that he kept quiet about his connection with Dorothy L. Sayers. Sayers remained terrified by the thought that the Press might get wind of the story and that the truth about his parentage would come out.

So John Anthony remained a secret she kept even from very close friends. When she sent a birthday present to Helen Simpson for her daughter Clemence, she made an elaborate fuss over becoming confused about the child's name, saying that such lapses accounted for her 'unpopularity with parents'. Simpson was trustworthy, but Sayers dared not risk the truth leaking out. In harping on her supposed childlessness, she was over-egging the pudding, but she got away with it. On other occasions she said that she disliked children, but this was part of a performance. She still burned with shame, and her tender feelings towards her son were overlaid with a characteristic briskness.

Yet the businesslike tone of her letters to John Anthony did not imply that she only looked after him out of a sense of responsibility. It was a detective novelist's strategy of deception, a technique for disguising her vulnerability.

She compensated for feelings of guilt with an increasingly terrifying public demeanour. Her plainness and obesity were exaggerated by her outlandish taste in fashion. When she came to stay at Henry Wade's country house Chiltons, one of his sons was thrilled to discover that she wore cuff-links in the form of a skull and crossbones. Her fondness for mannish clothes led some people to assume she was a lesbian. Sayers did not care, as long as they did not uncover her real secret. Ngaio Marsh's taste for menswear may have been a clue to her sexual orientation, but with both women, androgynous dress was first and foremost a form of self-defence. Clothes became a disguise, assumed to create distance and preserve privacy.

Just as Bentley hated the early film versions of *Trent's Last Case,* so Sayers cringed when Lord Peter Wimsey appeared on the silver screen in *The Silent Passenger*. She hated the lack of creative control that is an author's fate when screen rights are sold, and rejected a lucrative offer from Metro-Goldwyn-Mayer to film *Murder Must Advertise*. When the movie of *Busman's Honeymoon* was screened at the Whitehall Cinema next door to her house in Newland Street, she refused to go and see it.

The theatre appealed to her much more, but she worried about her lack of experience in writing drama, and asked Muriel St Clare Byrne to collaborate on a stage play featuring Wimsey. Sayers wanted the play to be a comedy, a break from the seriousness of *Gaudy Night*, and also a 'fair play' detective mystery. She devised a murder method and storyline, while Muriel helped with dialogue and sharpening the moments of drama. Much of 1936 was spent in search of financial backing for the play, which they called *Busman's Honeymoon*. Eventually, the money was found, and the main parts cast, with Dennis Arundell playing Wimsey.

When the play went on tour, she delighted in travelling with the company around the provinces. With evident pride, she wrote from Birmingham to John Anthony, describing life on the road. She would arrive at the theatre at eleven to watch rehearsals for a couple of hours, breaking for a snack before the afternoon's work. After that, she had an endless list of things to do: discussing rewrites; advising a tailor or dressmaker on costumes; talking to the Press; telling the management how to write the advertisements; dining with members of the cast and boosting their egos by admiring the brilliance of their performances.

The play finally reached London's West End, opening at the Comedy Theatre. Reviews were good, and it ran for nine months. To celebrate the one hundredth performance, the theatre management invited a group of allegedly reformed criminals to attend as a publicity gimmick. During the second interval, a couple of skilful pickpockets managed to remove Dennis Arundell's braces without his knowledge, adding an extra level of tension to his performance in the final act.

The publishing business was in a state of flux (its usual state, many writers might say). Readers had a huge appetite for detective fiction, but little money to spare for buying books. The present-day scarcity of many Golden Age first editions, and the sky-high values of books with dustjackets in excellent condition, is due to the fact that the main market for commercial fiction was the libraries. As well as public libraries, circulating libraries attached to chain stores such as Boot's attracted many subscribers throughout the Golden Age. Roughly three-quarters of the borrowers were women, and women's tastes and interests influenced detective novelists in their work. This helps to explain the distance that existed between Golden Age fiction and thrillers aimed at a masculine readership. During her disappearance, Christie borrowed books from the Harrogate branch of W.H. Smith's library, while William and George Foyle added a chain of twopenny libraries to their bookselling business in Charing Cross Road. The challenge for publishers was how to turn demand into high sales and increased profits.

Victor Gollancz, quick to recognise the hunger for cheaper books, set up a subsidiary called Mundanus which published paperbacks. *Malice Aforethought* was one of the first Mundanus titles, with a hardback edition produced for sale to circulating libraries, but the venture perished in the aftershocks of the Wall Street Crash. In Germany, a Hamburg publisher enjoyed success with Albatross paperbacks, produced for the mass market, and its marketing ideas were built upon in Britain by Penguin Books.

Penguins were the brainchild of Allen Lane, whose uncle John was Agatha Christie's first publisher. Allen met Christie when she called at the office to complain about the dustjacket of *The Murder on the Links*, having failed to realize that when a publisher asks an author's opinion of a jacket, the response required is rapture. Despite this, and her subsequent defection to Collins, she and Allen Lane became good friends, and he invented Penguin books after paying a weekend visit to her home in Devon. Finding himself at Exeter railway station with nothing worthwhile to read, he decided to set about selling well-produced paperback editions of popular books. They might cost sixpence, the price of a packet of cigarettes, and be sold from a vending machine.

A 'Penguincubator' book-vending machine duly appeared in Charing Cross Road, but although this radical innovation did not stand the test of time, the broader commercial strategy did. Another key to the success of Penguins was their iconic design: three horizontal, colour-coded bands, green and white in the case of crime fiction. The first ten Penguin titles included two detective novels. Significantly, they were *The Unpleasantness at the Bellona Club* and *The Mysterious Affair at Styles*, both written by members of the Detection Club.

The popularity of Christie's books – after the war, Penguin sold one hundred thousand copies of each of ten of her titles within months – contributed to the success of the imprint from the outset. Lane was the first to acknowledge this. Penguin became a separate company in 1936, setting up premises in the Crypt of the Holy Trinity Church on Marylebone Road. A fairground slide was used to receive deliveries from the street above. Within twelve months, Penguin had sold three million paperbacks. Lane could afford to give financial support to Max

Mallowan's expeditions, and each year he sent the archaeologists a Stilton cheese.

Gollancz had the right idea about paperbacks, but timing is everything. His next brainwave was timed to perfection.

Julian Symons identified 1936 as 'the heart of the Thirties dream. Consider: in this year, the Left Book Club was founded, the Spanish Civil War began, the Surrealist Exhibition was held, the Jarrow Crusade began. . . . Fascism in Britain became strongly arrogant and obtrusive.'

The Left Book Club sprang from a conversation between Victor Gollancz, Stafford Cripps (a future Chancellor of the Exchequer) and John Strachey, who subsequently popularized the concept of the 'Golden Age' of detective fiction. The concept of a book club for like-minded left-wing members was inspired by the success of the Collins Crime Club. Each month a panel highlighted one book as a monthly choice. The break-even target was 2,500 members, but 40,000 were recruited in the first year. Success brought occasional setbacks. Douglas Cole was furious when *The Condition of Britain*, which he had written with Margaret, was denied the honour of being picked as a monthly Choice.

With hindsight, Symons concluded that the Left Book Club's chief function was 'to serve as a propaganda machine for Communism', although he admitted his friend Gollancz would have regarded this as an outrageous slur. A dozen of the first fifteen Choices were vetted and approved by the British Communist Party, and in Symons' opinion, 'the typical attitude of Left Book Club members . . . [was that] any criticism of the Soviet Union was in essence pro-Fascist'.

The British Government kept out of the Spanish Civil War, but a couple of thousand Britons flocked to the Republican cause under the banner of the International Brigade. Among them was a talented poet and detective novelist called Christopher St John Sprigg. In contrast to the usual pattern among intellectuals, he wrote crime fiction under his real name, and more serious work under a pseudonym, Christopher Caudwell. In late

1936, he drove an ambulance to Spain, before training as a machine gunner. He was killed in action at 'Suicide Hill' on the first day of the battle of Jarama. Not yet thirty, he had already written seven detective novels. Symons' bleak verdict was that those, like Sprigg, who died with their illusions about the cause unshattered were the lucky ones. Others who survived, like Stephen Spender, became disillusioned and 'ashamed, shocked by the evidence of Communist ruthlessness around them'.

But that was the nature of the times. People on all points of the political spectrum found it hard to know what to do for the best. As Symons said, 'Those who condemn readily, without considering the social pressures that made otherwise intelligent people write such things, can never understand the Thirties.' This remains as true of Caudwell and Cole as it is of Connington and Crofts, Christie and Chesterton.

On 14 June 1936, less than a month after the Trent Dinner, a chaotic and remarkable life came to an end when Chesterton died of congestive heart failure. He had been invested by Pope Pius XI as Knight Commander with Star of the Papal Order of St Gregory the Great, and a requiem mass was held in Westminster Cathedral. Ronald Knox, delivering the homily, said: 'All of this generation has grown up under Chesterton's influence so completely that we do not even know when we are thinking Chesterton.'

In the same vein, writing privately to Chesterton's widow Frances, Sayers said that his books had formed a greater part of her mental make-up than those of any other writer. He had shown 'how to dignify a kind of literature which had fallen on very bad ways by restoring to it that touch with the greater realities which it had almost entirely lost.'

Chesterton's death caused shock and dismay to another admirer. This young American novelist had just been elected to the Detection Club, and had dreamed that the great man would preside over his initiation. The American had already modelled a detective hero on Chesterton, and news of this had gratified the older man. They both shared a passion for 'miracle problems', although their work was very different. The American was a specialist in macabre atmospherics, and establishing himself as the master of the 'locked room mystery', a man at whose ingenuity Sayers, Berkeley and Christie marvelled. His name was John Dickson Carr.

Note to Chapter 23

Among them was a talented poet and detective novelist called
Christopher St John Sprigg.

Christopher St John Sprigg (1907–37), a journalist who became a
prominent Marxist thinker, ran an aeronautics publishing company,
and his technical knowledge provided material for a textbook as
well as a mystery, *Death of an Airman* (1934). Sayers gave that
novel a rave review, and the pair corresponded briefly before Sprigg
became consumed by political activism. A young Communist, Margot
Miller (1912–80), earned brief celebrity during the Spanish Civil
War; a volunteer nurse who drove an ambulance for the International
Brigade, she was shot in the legs by machine gunners. More than
a decade later, as Margot Bennett, she wrote six acclaimed mysteries.
In 1958, her final crime novel, *Someone from the Past*, pipped
Margery Allingham's *Hide My Eyes* for the Crossed Red Herring
Award, now the CWA Gold Dagger, and earned her election to the
Detection Club. Julian Symons, who wrote her obituary for *The
Times*, compared her to Raymond Chandler, and said, 'She remained
a radical, at once disillusioned and optimistic.' Script writing paid
better, however, and she never wrote another crime novel, concen-
trating mainly on television series such as *Maigret* and the soap
operas *Emergency Ward 10* and *Honey Lane*.

24

A Coffin Entombed
in a Crypt of Granite

A chance encounter in the men's barbershop during an Atlantic crossing changed John Dickson Carr's life. It was the summer of 1930, a few days after the BBC broadcast the final instalment of *Behind the Screen*. Carr was twenty-three years old, and travelling back to New York on an ocean-going liner called *Pennland* after a visit to Europe. The trip was funded by earnings from his first detective novel, *It Walks by Night*, featuring a saturnine French detective, Henri Bencolin. The voyage took ten days and cost $125. Carr liked luxury, but he also liked spending money, and he had run too short of cash to be able to afford a more expensive passage on one of the modern ships that took less than a week to make the crossing.

A young Englishwoman called Clarice Cleave was also on board; her trip to visit friends in America was a twenty-first birthday present from her parents. Small and attractive, with blonde hair and blue eyes, she possessed the same quiet charm, and unexpected taste for adventure, that had attracted Archie Christie to Agatha. She decided to have her hair bobbed, so that when the ship landed, she would have the fashionable coiffeur of the day. The women's hairdresser was booked up, so she headed for the men's salon to ask if she could have her hair cut short. Carr was there, reading while he waited his turn, and offered to let her go ahead of him. That night, he asked her for a dance. He was smart, good-looking and sociable, so she said yes.

'Do you like detective stories?' he asked.

She shrugged. 'I've read a couple by Edgar Wallace.'

'What did you think?'

'Pretty poor stuff.'

If he was disappointed by her lack of enthusiasm, he didn't let it put him off. 'Actually, I've got a detective story I'd like you to try. Let me get it from my cabin. I won't be a minute.'

He disappeared before she had the chance to insist that she really didn't care for mysteries, and returned flourishing a copy of *It Walks by Night*, presenting it to her with a novice author's pride. So began a classic shipboard romance, which was not harmed when Clarice assured him she had enjoyed reading his book. As is the way with writers of fiction, whose insecurity is matched by their fondness for making things up, Carr bolstered his ego when he told friends back home about Clarice by embellishing the story: 'Guess what? When I met Clarice, one of the first things she said to me was that she'd just read this marvellous book called *It Walks by Night*.'

The couple married and moved into an apartment in New York, but when Clarice found she was pregnant, she persuaded Carr to come back with her to England. Britain's abandonment of the Gold Standard made it an attractive destination for people with American dollars, and they could live more cheaply there. Once they landed in London on Valentine's Day 1933, Carr's love affair with an Englishwoman became a love affair with England itself.

Carr was the son of a lawyer and congressman from Pennsylvania. His father was a heavy drinker, and so was Carr. It is no coincidence that on the first appearance of Gideon Fell, Carr's most memorable sleuth has been working for six years on *The Drinking Customs of England, from the Earliest Days*, and endlessly knocks back beer and whisky. Carr's sixth novel, *Hag's Nook*, introduced Fell as a Lincolnshire-based lexicographer with much the same physique and personality as Chesterton. Fell never actually bothers with dictionary-compilation; his real specialism is history. Like all the great detectives, he has a brain crammed with arcane knowledge that proves remarkably useful. He solves one case in part because he happens to know that Canadian taxidermists stuff moose heads with red sand.

Hag's Nook opens with a lyrical portrayal of England as seen through the eyes of a young American, Tad Rampole. Tad falls for a young Englishwoman, Dorothy Starberth, just as Carr had fallen for Clarice. Carr offers an 'impossible' problem, as well as a neatly conceived cryptogram, and cloaks his mystery with lashings of atmosphere, including a creepy prison that has stood abandoned for a century, and a legend that the Starberths die of broken necks – a fate duly suffered by Dorothy's brother. Are supernatural forces at work, or is the family affected by inherited madness? Gideon Fell comes up with a rational solution, and gives the culprit the chance to escape the gallows by shooting himself once he has written a statement explaining his crimes. Although Inspector Jennings is present, he proves extraordinarily accommodating: 'Our instructions from Sir William, sir, at the Yard, were to take orders from you.' But this murderer – unlike so many killers in Golden Age fiction – cannot bring himself to commit suicide.

The Hollow Man is a classic 'impossible crime' mystery, boasting a plan of the murder scene, a diagram of an illusion at the heart of one of the puzzles, and the famous 'Locked Room Lecture'. Fell expounds on his favourite topic, breaking the fourth wall with extraordinary bravura right from the start: 'We're in a detective story, and we don't fool the reader by pretending we're not.'

In his virtuoso analysis of how to commit murder in that apparently locked room, Fell highlighted the homicidal potential of quirky mechanical and scientific contraptions: 'The gun mechanism concealed in the telephone-receiver . . . the pistol with a string to the trigger, which is pulled by the expansion of water as it freezes. We have the clock that fires a bullet when you wind it and . . . the ingenious grandfather clock which sets ringing a hideously clanging bell on its top, so that when you reach up to shut off the din, your own touch releases a blade that slashes open your stomach. . . . There is death in every article of furniture, including a tea-urn.'

Fell waxes lyrical about weapons made of ice and the suitability of snakes and insects for murderous purposes: 'Snakes can be concealed not only in chests and safes, but also deftly hidden in flower-pots, books, chandeliers, and walking-sticks. I even remember one cheerful little item in which the amber stem of a pipe, grotesquely carven as a scorpion, comes to life a real scorpion as the victim is about to put it into his mouth.'

Part of the appeal of the 'locked room mystery' for Carr and many of his readers lay in its exotic artificiality. In real life, very few people have the misfortune to be murdered in locked rooms, but *The Hollow Man* was a *tour de force*, making Carr's election to membership of the Detection Club a formality. He was not quite thirty years old.

Carr's fascination with the occult resulted in a dazzling non-series novel, *The Burning Court*. Because his British publisher was worried that his love of grotesque settings and characters might alienate some readers, Carr came up with an unremarkable setting – a small town in Pennsylvania – and an apparently conventional set of characters. These ingredients he fashioned into an exotic mystery with a bizarre epilogue. An unofficial attempted exhumation in the dead of night reveals that the body of Miles Despard, a suspected victim of arsenic poisoning, has disappeared from its coffin, which had been entombed in a windowless crypt built of granite. A witness swears that she has seen a mysterious woman leaving the dead man's room through a door that cannot be opened and leads nowhere.

One suspect is a lookalike of a French woman poisoner who was guillotined long ago – has she returned to life and resumed her homicidal career? The detective is the elderly, eccentric and ugly Gaudan Cross, a murderer turned true-crime historian. His explanation of the mystery is rational and compelling, in keeping with Carr's facility for showing that the apparently possible was in fact all too possible. Then the kaleidoscope shifts in an extraordinary coda. The reader is presented with an alternative version of events which suggests supernatural forces are at work after all.

Carr, the devotee of fair-play detection, had broken the 'rules' in spectacular fashion. He never wrote another book in the manner of *The Burning Court*, saying that reader reaction to it had ranged 'from mildly shocked disapproval to puzzled wrath', but the following year *The Crooked Hinge* drew on his interest in Satanism. He dedicated the book to Sayers 'in friendship and esteem'. The story opens with an impersonation puzzle, and the circumstances are those of a classic impossible crime. Dr Fell announces that the case 'is what I've been half-dreading for a long time – an almost purely psychological puzzle. . . . There is an almost complete absence of material clues.' The most powerful image in this atmospheric book is that of the Golden Hag, an automaton as sinister as it is bizarre and based (like the key plot gimmick in *The Hollow Man*) on a device from the Maskelyne Mysteries magic shows.

Fell suggests a solution of the crime involving a gypsy throwing ball covered with fish-hooks, but this turns out to be a ploy to draw out the real culprit. The true explanation for the killing is dependent on a key character having been a legless circus performer. It could only happen in a Golden Age detective novel (or so one hopes). The use of two dazzling yet very different solutions to the puzzle is worthy of Berkeley, but Carr's method is that of the conjuror, and the story is founded on ingenuity of method rather than the psychology of the characters. But Carr allows the guilty to escape justice in a way that Berkeley surely approved.

Carr's novels focused on ingenious techniques for committing murder, rather than on the psychology of crime. Yet he understood that the appeal of murder is often linked to the mysteriousness of human behaviour, and was fascinated by real life murder – over the course of his career, his books referred to more than seventy different criminals. Above all, he loved playing the detective, and coming up with solutions to mysteries that had left the police baffled. At Christmas, he delighted in recounting the facts of a famous case and inviting family and friends to come up with their own solutions. *The Murder of Sir Edmund Godfrey* was his full-length account of a notable seventeenth-century crime presented in the form of a detective story, while in 1937 he was one of several writers (John Rhode was another) invited by *The Star* to contribute an article solving a notorious case to accompany a competition inviting readers to test their skills as armchair sleuths. Carr chose the murder of Caesar Young.

On 4 June 1904, the morning bustle of West Broadway in New York was disrupted by the sound of a gunshot. Startled passers-by thought someone had fired from inside a hansom cab. The cab pulled up at a nearby pharmacy, and everyone rushed over to see what had happened. They found inside a dying man and a pretty young woman. The driver headed straight for the Hudson Street Hospital, but Francis Thomas Young was found dead on arrival. Young, nicknamed 'Caesar', was a well-known 'turfman', a bookmaker and gambler with an uncanny knack for picking winners at the races. He had been married for ten years when he began an affair with Nan Randolph Patterson, a showgirl and member of the 'Florodora Girls'.

Young's enthusiasm waned when Nan pressed him to divorce his wife and feigned a pregnancy by way of encouragement. He offered to pay for her to go away to Europe, but when she refused, he booked a passage for his wife and himself. Young spent the evening before the ship was due to sail in Nan's company, but they started quarrelling. During a row at a restaurant, he shouted that he never wanted to see her again, but Nan told him he could not escape. Young spent the rest of the night with his wife Margaret, but crept out at seven in the morning, saying he wanted to buy a hat. Instead, he met Nan for a breakfast of whisky and brandy, before they set off in the hansom cab together.

'Caesar, Caesar, why did you do this?' Nan sobbed after arriving at the hospital. She claimed he had shot himself because he could not bear the thought of parting from her. He had begged her to forgive him for his cruelty, and resorted to suicide when she refused. The police were not convinced, and she was tried for murder. Her veteran lawyer, Abraham Levy, exploited her charming appearance with no great subtlety, playing on the sympathies of the all-male jury.

'Do you believe that this pleasure-loving girl could conceive the plot that would permit her at one second to kill and in the next to cover this act by a subtle invention?' he demanded. The courtroom drama proved too much for one juryman, who suffered a heart attack, and a mistrial was declared. Two further trials were deadlocked thanks to hung (or infatuated) juries. In the end, the judge ordered that all charges should be dropped, and Nan was cheered from the courtroom by admirers.

On her release from prison, Nan wrote a helpful article warning young girls about the perils of the stage, and, for good measure, 'idleness, fast-living, restaurant life, drink'. Unable to take her own advice, she soon appeared in a stage musical with modest success, before remarrying a man she had divorced as a teenager. After divorcing him for a second time, she slipped out of sight, though Alexander Woollcott reported an improbable rumour that she was 'living in Seattle a life given over to good deeds and horticulture'.

Carr's explanation for the mystery of the hansom cab was that Young drew out a gun and pretended to commit suicide. In a panic, Nan seized hold of the weapon and discharged it by accident. His scenario was typically inventive, if also typically far-fetched. He, like Berkeley, was susceptible to a pretty face.

Gideon Fell says in *The Crooked Hinge* that, of the questions 'who, how and why?' the most revealing, but usually by far the most puzzling, is why. 'Why did Mrs Thompson write those letters to Bywaters? Why did Mrs Maybrick soak the fly-papers in water? . . . Why did Julia Wallace have an enemy in the world?'

Carr owed his interest in the fate of Julia Wallace to Sayers. She was amazed when he admitted ignorance of the 1931 Liverpool case, and gave him a copy of a full account of it. He duly came up with his own theories, which focused on a single clue, that Julia's body was found in a room usually reserved for practising and playing music. This led him to suspect first a violin master, and then her piano teacher, although he failed to come up with a credible motive. In return for Sayers' gift, he sent her a book about the mystery of whether Lizzie Borden took an axe to her father and stepmother. To Sayers' delight, the book arrived in time to give her 'a happily blood-stained Christmas Day'.

Domestic murder in fact and fiction still preoccupied the Detection Club members, and their readers. But politically moti-vated crimes in Europe, as well as the behaviour of agitators at home, was already making a mark on the genre.

Notes to Chapter 24

A chance encounter in the men's barbershop during an Atlantic crossing changed John Dickson Carr's life
My account of Carr's life and work draws extensively on information supplied by Douglas Greene and on his biography of Carr.

a classic 'impossible crime' mystery
In discussing 'impossible crimes', I have benefited from the expertise and writings of both Douglas Greene and Bob Adey.

Part Five

Justifying Murder

25

Knives Engraved with 'Blood and Honour'

Agatha Christie met her first Nazi in the unlikely setting of a tea party in Baghdad. After finishing work on *Lord Edgware Dies*, she had been helping Max on a dig at a *tell* (the Arabic word used for a mound covering an ancient ruin) called Arpichiyah, near Mosul. Max directed the work on behalf of the British School of Archaeology in Iraq, and conditions were physically demanding, while the worsening political climate in the region added to the challenge. The excavations were a triumph for Max, yielding a large amount of the distinctive pottery of the Halaf period, and confirming Arpachiyah as one of the most important prehistoric sites in the region. The heat was cruel and unrelenting, and Christie was now a heavily-built woman, but she laboured for hour after hour, measuring the pieces of smashed vessels, and making calculations to guide the process of reassembling the scarlet, orange and black fragments. It was a form of detective work that she came to love. At the end of the season, the party returned to Baghdad. Max supervised the packing and shipping of his finds, a complex task which brought him into contact with the German Director of Antiquities, Dr Julius Jordan.

Cultured and charming, Jordan invited Max and Christie to his house for tea. He offered to play on his piano for them, and as she listened to Beethoven in Jordan's sitting room, Christie admired her host. He was a fine figure of a man, gentle and considerate. But in the course of conversation, someone mentioned Jews, and Christie saw a change come over his face, a change so remarkable that she'd never seen anything like it before.

'You do not understand,' he said. 'Our Jews are perhaps different from yours. They are a danger. They should be exterminated. Nothing else will really do but that.'

Christie was stunned. Soon she discovered that Jordan's wife was an even more ferocious Jew-hater than her husband. Jordan was a trusted representative of the Nazi government, and had been sent to spy on the German Ambassador in Baghdad. Even so, it took time for the reality of Nazism and Fascism to sink in fully with Christie, and millions like her who could scarcely believe that atrocities were happening across the North Sea. Depressing prejudices about Jewish people, and their supposed fondness for money and political influence, died hard. Even so, hints of anti-Semitism in Christie's books, and other novels of the period, became less frequent. A few years later, a character in *One, Two, Buckle My Shoe* was mocked as a member of the 'Imperial Shirts' who march with banners and have a 'ridiculous salute'.

Civilization was under threat, but few people had any idea how best to protect it. Sayers was one of many who at first saw Nazism as a form of unpleasant nationalism rather than anything more sinister. She instructed her literary agent that even if her German publishers insisted on cutting out 'one or two slightly acid references to Mr Hitler's policy, they must not alter these references into any expression of agreement with it'. Some of her Detection Club colleagues were more scathing, but Margaret Cole frankly admitted that even those who were dismayed when Hitler came to power failed to understand what it would really mean. Berkeley and H. C. Bailey were never in much doubt about the odious nature of Hitler and his regime, but it was the left-leaning E. R. Punshon who appears to have been first to heap scorn on Nazism in a detective story.

This comes towards the end of a novel which up to that point, like its title, *Crossword Mystery*, had reflected familiar Golden

Age values. In a wildly improbable police stratagem, Punshon's detective Bobby Owen is sent to stay at the East Anglian home of a retired businessman, George Winterton, who believes that his brother Archibald's death by drowning was no accident but is unable to provide worthwhile evidence to substantiate his claim. Winterton is equally fanatical about crosswords and the gold standard: 'Getting back to gold is the only thing that can save civilisation.' When he devises a crossword with 'gold' as the keyword, even an ingenuous reader may guess that it contains a cipher revealing the location of a hidden cache of gold. Unfortunately, long before Bobby pinpoints the only viable suspect, Winterton has been murdered, and so has his dog. Sharper than his plotting is Punshon's satire, with the decision to give the name of Dreg to an unappealing solicitor an inspired touch.

A striking climax makes up for the tedium of the crossword aspect of the mystery. A German analytical chemist with Jewish blood paints a graphic picture of life in his homeland as he describes how he tried to curry favour with the Hitler regime: 'When I saw a number of high-spirited young Storm Troopers kicking an aged Jew into a canal, and then pulling him out to kick him again, I gave the Nazi salute as I passed. Also, when the son of a friend of mine was baptized, I had sent, as a christening gift for the baby, one of the new youth dagger-knives with "Blood and Honour" engraved on the blade. . . . That weighed very much in my favour, and finally I was released on promising to hand over my business . . . to a real Nazi, who had distinguished himself greatly by his zeal against Jews, but who afterwards had the misfortune to blow up himself and my laboratory . . . chemicals caring, apparently, very little whether you are Jew or Nordic, if you do not mix them in the right proportions.'

Punshon was quicker than most to realise what was happening under Hitler. To add to his social insights and occasional shafts of wit, he had a flair for the macabre. The last scene of the book, where the culprit commits suicide in a shocking yet peculiarly appropriate way, so as to 'fall writhing and choked, a dreadful, disfigured thing no longer human', stuns the onlooking detectives, 'so held in stillness were they by the horror and the greatness of the deed'. This is one of the Golden Age fiction's darkest finales, and an astonishing end to an uneven but unjustly neglected book.

For most of the Thirties, British people were more concerned with the antics of Fascists in their own back yard than with Hitler's manoeuvres on the Continent. One of the more embarrassing occasions in the Coles' campaign to rebuild the divided Left saw them entertain Oswald Mosley and his wife Cimmie to dinner. A baronet from a family of wealthy landowners, Mosley was a gifted public speaker whose talents were eventually overwhelmed by aggression and arrogance. He had become a Conservative MP and married Lady Cynthia Curzon, daughter of the then Foreign Secretary and one of the wealthiest women in the country. Disenchanted with the Tories, Mosley became an Independent before joining first the Labour Party and then the Independent Labour Party. The Coles' other dinner guests included Mosley's ally John Strachey, who coined the phrase 'the Golden Age of detective fiction', and the Marxist academic Harold Laski and his wife.

Mosley wanted high tariffs to deter foreign imports, nationalization of public bodies, and an ambitious programme of public works to cut unemployment. The Coles sympathized with many of these ideas and were tempted to join forces with him. But the joint project was stillborn because shortly after the dinner he flounced out of the Independent Labour Party and set up the New Party. As Labour loyalists, the Coles felt they had no choice but to cut off the talks. This turned out to be a stroke of luck that saved their reputations. It would have been ruinous to become associated with a demagogue who soon adopted aggressive anti-Semitism as a strategy for winning popular support.

The New Party won backing from the *Manchester Guardian* and the *Daily Mail*, but was trounced in the election of 1931. Mosley responded by studying the methods of Mussolini and deciding that Britain would benefit from a dose of Fascism. He founded the British Union of Fascists, copying the black uniforms worn by Mussolini's supporters. Before long, the BUF claimed fifty thousand members, but the Fascists' brutality provoked a hostile response from the police and political opponents. They were also treated with contempt in novels written by members of the Detection Club.

Some writers fought against Fascism with the weapon of wit. Ronald Knox guyed Mussolini in 'The Fallen Idol', a story about the murder of Enrique Gamba, 'the Inspirer of the Magnolian Commonwealth', who had liberated his country on April Fool's Day, 'abolished the national debt, and exchanged a flood of telegrams with the League of Nations'.

The year before war broke out, Punshon's *Dictator's Way* mocked the dictator of Etruria, '"the Redeemer of his country"', in his characteristic country-redeeming attitude so strongly reminiscent of Ajax defying the lightning'. The book was yet another Detection Club product addressing the idea of the altruistic murder. A thrillerish narrative is interspersed with pot shots against Hitler and Stalin ('who have done so much to bring back prosperity to our world by inducing us to spend all our money on battleships, bombs, tanks, and other pleasing and instructive toys of modern civilisation'), as well as Mussolini, Oswald Mosley and the City financiers who gave them financial backing ('Money has no smell and money knows no loyalty either'). Mosley had 'always been a rich man and has a rich man's ideas all through' Punshon's contempt for brutal dictators and their apologists extended to the Foreign Office: 'They wipe their perspiring brows and say: ". . . Thank God for Hitler, he may want our colonies but at least he's fighting Bolshevism." I don't know if they thank God for Oswald Mosley too. Perhaps nobody could go quite that far.'

A post-war Detection Club Secretary, Richard Hull, subtly poked fun at Mosley in *Murder of My Aunt*. Edward Powell, whose parents have died in a mysterious accident, lives with his scary Aunt Mildred on the outskirts of Llwll in a remote part of Wales. Edward spends his time reading smutty French novels, patronizing the locals and concocting ways to kill Mildred and escape from Llwll. He admires 'the virile Mosley', while his aunt is a fan of Stanley Baldwin. Edward's political judgment proves to be on a par with his skills as a murderer.

R. C. Woodthorpe wrote two novels excoriating Fascists in the year the *Daily Mail* printed an article by Rothermere headed, 'Hurrah for the Blackshirts'. Having given up teaching for journalism, he joined the *Mail*'s left-wing rival, the *Daily Herald*, writing book reviews and music and drama criticism, while gathering background for his second mystery. *A Dagger in Fleet Street* blended social comedy with an authentic picture of working lives at a time when no job was safe. A newspaper editor, 'a petty Mussolini', has his throat cut, while another character owns an unpleasant dog called Hitler. A likeable secretary, who says, 'Thank God for the National Union of Journalists' and reveals herself to a newspaper colleague as a closet Communist, confides: 'You'd be staggered if you knew how many people in this jolly old stronghold of capitalism are communists.' Woodthorpe's next book confirmed that his approach to crime fiction was the polar opposite of Christie's. His interest lay in people and politics rather than puzzle and plot.

Silence of a Purple Shirt, acclaimed by Sayers as 'the most brilliant and humorous detective story of its season', satirized Mosley's followers in the shape of the 'Make Britain Free' movement, populated by the purple-shirted army led by the repellent Duke Benedict. One of Benedict's right-hand men, Henry Truscott, is bludgeoned to death, and the murder weapon is linked to a fellow Purple Shirt, Alan Ford. In a furious tirade, the novelist and amateur sleuth Nicholas Slade tells Ford, 'In spite of the best efforts of you and your fellow harlequins, this is not yet Russia or Germany or Fascist Italy. Let us have no more of this nonsense.' Whilst Slade is 'not overmuch in love with the established order of things. Indeed, he had satirised it in many of his books', he hates the prospect of a regimented life under the Purple Shirts. Slade dismisses a suggestion that Britain is 'a law-abiding country', saying, 'I cannot remember a time, except, perhaps, during the war, when laws were not deliberately flouted.' He refers to the Nonconformists, the

Suffragettes, and 'the army officers who mutinied in preference to coercing Ulster'. Truscott's murderer is allowed not only to remain unpunished, but to bask in public eminence and admiration, and Woodthorpe was fast-tracked into membership of the Detection Club.

Helen Simpson's *Vantage Striker* was a flawed novel, but intriguing and ahead of its time in that, as early as 1931, she portrayed a popular politician as a closet Fascist, and allowed him to be dealt with ruthlessly by extra-legal means. As the dangers posed by Hitler and Mussolini became clearer, colleagues in the Detection Club took up this theme, blending their entertainments time and again with a serious question seldom mentioned in most discussion of the Golden Age. Could there be such a thing as a *justified murder*?

Frightening political developments throughout Europe gave this debate increasing resonance. Through his role in the International Labour Organisation, Milward Kennedy stayed closer to corridors of power in the world's major capitals than anyone else in the Detection Club, even Lord Gorell. Kennedy was acutely aware of the threat to peace posed by Hitler and Mussolini, but no clearer than anyone else about how to deal with it. Wrestling with this dilemma prompted him to write an experimental novel, *Sic Transit Gloria*. James Southern discovers the body of glamorous Gloria Day in his London flat. Has she committed suicide or been murdered? Southern reflects on the morality of murder for political purposes. Can the assassination of a demagogue ever be justified? He ends up playing 'the part of justice . . . A jury could only have secured injustice. What did the law matter – if the law could not have secured justice? People talked of judicial murder: was not judicial failure to secure the just punishment of a murderer just as bad?'

This question of when murder can be justified is tackled so often – and so inventively – in books by Detection Club members that it was surely debated over drinks in Gerrard Street. Christie was so fascinated by the notion that it inspired three of her finest plots. She dropped a hint about one especially brilliant idea for committing the perfect murder in *Peril at End House*, and toyed with it for years before turning it into the book which brought Poirot's career to an astonishing end. *Curtain: Poirot's Final Case* was completed in the early stages of the Second World War, but not published until 1975.

Berkeley became obsessed by the idea of justified murder. He had already addressed the way 'civilized' people can cease to be bound by the norms of human behaviour in *Panic Party*, which is prefaced by a tongue-in-cheek riposte to the challenge Kennedy set him in *Death to the Rescue*: 'You once challenged me, in public print, to write a book in which the only interest should be the detection. I have no hesitation in refusing to do anything so tedious, and instead take the greatest pleasure in dedicating to you a book which is precisely the opposite, which breaks every rule of the austere Club to which we both belong, and which will probably earn my expulsion from its membership.'

Berkeley's claim was as perverse as ever. The novel does not break all the Club's rules, and detection plays a part, although it fails to solve the mystery in traditional fashion. Sheringham joins a yachting party organized by Guy Pidgeon, an Oxford don who has come into the money. The group finds itself marooned on a desert island, and Pidgeon announces that their party includes a murderer. He admits to borrowing the idea from J. M. Barrie's play *Shall We Join the Ladies?* and to inventing the story about the killer. This folly has a predictable outcome – Pidgeon is found dead in the sea, having apparently been pushed off a cliff.

Berkeley addressed the problem left unanswered by Barrie. As Sheringham put it: 'What . . . would a company of perfectly normal, presumably civilised persons do on learning that their numbers included an undetected murderer?' The set-up, with an assorted cast of characters and a murderer trapped on an island, anticipates the scenario of Christie's *And Then There Were None*. But Berkeley went further, tackling issues of human behaviour under pressure that were later portrayed with power and intensity by William Golding in *Lord of the Flies*.

The whodunit becomes a thriller as the veneer of civilization wears thin. Members of Pidgeon's party succumb to mass hysteria when they identify the person they think is the killer and set about lynching him. Roger Sheringham, no longer a caricature, morphs into a hero. He tries to save the victim, but is knocked unconscious for his pains. Only the arrival of a rescue ship saves an innocent man from a savage death.

Sheringham – making his final appearance in a novel less than a decade after his debut – continues to act as Berkeley's mouthpiece: 'A man is exceedingly foolish when a beautiful woman is concerned.' The woman in question, who is utterly self-centred, relishes the imminent killing of a fellow human being in way that chills Sheringham even more than 'the naked bloodlust' of her companions. She insists on the lynching because 'it is the law'.

In his portrayal of her, Berkeley again seems to be taking revenge for a disastrous entanglement of his own – but with whom? Even though he had succeeded in luring Helen Peters away from her husband, he was still unpredictable and often unhappy. The sourness that marred so many of his personal relationships had spread to his fiction. Sayers found *Panic Party* exciting and clever, but complained about 'the author's sneering hatred of his own puppets. . . . There is a point at which ruthless realism becomes not merely too unpleasant for popularity, but a little too bad for belief'. Yet there was more to his novel than that. *Panic Party* is forgotten, while *Lord of the Flies* is a modern classic, but Berkeley's dark vision of the way supposedly civilised people behave when normal constraints break down was perceptive. His pessimism was borne out in Hitler's Germany.

Hitler and Mussolini and their regimes seemed untouchable, and their quest for domination impossible to resist. With each passing year, the turmoil in continental Europe became more dangerous. Britain, meanwhile, was gripped by a constitutional crisis that had strange and unexpected consequences for Berkeley and Sayers.

Note to Chapter 25

a tongue-in-cheek riposte to the challenge Kennedy set him
Berkeley may also have been irritated by the claim of Kennedy's
American publishers, on the cover of *Corpse in Cold Storage*, that
Kennedy was 'President of the Detection Society of England', and
therefore all the more determined to put him in his place.

26

Touching with a Fingertip
the Fringe of Great Events

King Edward VIII's succession to the throne, following the death of King George V, led to an extraordinary sequence of events that changed Britain, as well as the British monarchy. Much less well known is that the Abdication provoked further crises, each of a strange and personal nature, for both Anthony Berkeley and Dorothy L. Sayers. As if unwittingly disrupting the careers of two popular novelists were not enough, Edward's lavish and self-indulgent lifestyle saw him become embroiled in a couple of sensational real-life murder cases.

As Prince of Wales, Edward was the most photographed celebrity of his time. He was handsome, gregarious and oozing charm, but also vain, petulant and reckless. He moved from one unsuitable mistress to another, with sultry and sloe-eyed French courtesan Marguerite Alibert an especially risky choice. Like so many unwise people who live to regret their indiscretions in detective stories, Edward wrote her a series of compromising letter. Marguerite recognized their value and kept hold of them, even after marrying a young and wealthy Egyptian 'prince' called Ali Fahmy.

It was scarcely a match made in Heaven: Marguerite was volatile and Fahmy sadistic. In July 1923, while staying in a suite at the Savoy Hotel in London, they had a violent quarrel and

Marguerite told the band leader that her husband had threatened to kill her. In the small hours, a porter heard three shots
fired from inside the suite. Fahmy's body was found sprawled
across the floor. Marguerite had shot him at point-blank range.
Earlier that evening, they had visited the theatre, to watch *The
Merry Widow*.

When she was tried for murder, Sir Edward Marshall Hall
secured an improbable acquittal. He argued that Marguerite
acted in self-defence when Fahmy, a sexually deviant Oriental
intent on degrading a beautiful Western woman, attempted to
strangle her. A recent theory suggests that the Establishment
contrived her escape from justice because of the fear that the
Prince of Wales' incautious correspondence would be made
public. The main evidence is a letter from the Foreign Secretary,
Lord Curzon, saying the authorities 'were terribly afraid that
[Edward] might be dragged in. It is fortunate that he is off to
Canada and his name is to be kept out.'

The near-disaster of the Fahmy case did not deter Edward
from his pursuit of dangerous liaisons, often with married
women. These culminated in a passionate relationship with Mrs
Wallis Simpson, an American divorcee whose second husband
was a wealthy shipping executive. The affair continued after
Edward became king, and although the British Press kept quiet
about the brewing scandal so that the public in Britain remained
in ignorance, newspapers in the United States and elsewhere
showed less restraint.

The lovers sailed off on a luxury yacht, the *Nahlin*, for a cruise
around the Adriatic that became the stuff of legend. Edward,
who made little secret of his regard for Hitler, was persuaded
by the Foreign Secretary not to stop off in Mussolini's Italy, but
he and Wallis soon found other ways of amusing themselves.
They introduced nudism to the island of Rab off Dubrovnik, and
drove three thousand golf balls into the sea while practising
their golf swings on deck. In Budapest, Wallis did a gypsy dance
in public, while Edward tended bar in the Ritz before shooting
out a row of street lights along the embankment in a drunken
demonstration of his skills as a marksman. Back on board, they

may not have found time to read detective novels, but Edward did try his hand at solving erotic jigsaw puzzles.

On returning to England, Edward segued smoothly from hedonistic playboy to man of the people. He toured the mining areas of South Wales and professed sympathy with people suffering extreme poverty. His visit produced a sound bite, long before there were sound bites: the King's message was that 'something must be done'. This spasm of social conscience might have been sincere, and it did no harm to his popularity. The *Daily Mail* contrasted his energy with the lassitude of the National Government led by Lord Rothermere's old enemy Stanley Baldwin.

Edward had probably made up his mind by this point to marry Wallis and give up the throne, leaving it to others to work out how to alleviate hardship in South Wales. After a flurry of alarm and excitement about a 'constitutional crisis', he abdicated on 11 December and was succeeded by his younger brother, who became George VI. Baldwin's patience with Edward's self-indulgence had run out, but he defused the crisis with tact and dexterity. Once George had been crowned, he retired as Prime Minister, handing over to Neville Chamberlain.

In the country at large, there was widespread sympathy for the man seen as sacrificing his royal destiny for the woman he loved. The new Duke of Windsor left Britain with Wallis, and displayed his flair for doing the wrong thing by paying a visit to Adolf Hitler's country retreat, where he gave a full Nazi salute. Later, the government installed him as the Governor of the Bahamas to keep him out of harm's way.

The plan failed spectacularly, as the Duke found himself embroiled in another murder mystery. His friend Sir Harry Oakes, a wealthy tax exile, was found battered to death in his mansion. Oakes' corpse had been burned and strewn with feathers from his pillow. His son-in-law, Alfred de Marigny, was charged with his murder, but although a rope was ordered for his hanging, he was acquitted. Not least because of the royal connection, conspiracy theories abounded. The killer was never brought to justice.

Sayers' immediate fear about the Abdication was that people would be too absorbed with the crisis to bother with the stage production of *Busman's Honeymoon*. Luckily, Edward stepped down while the play was in Leeds, before its all-important West End premiere. In gossipy correspondence, she reported stories that Wallis was hand in glove with the Nazi regime, and that Helen Simpson ('no relation', Sayers joked) told her that Edward was disliked at the Sandringham estate both for treating his staff badly and 'for running about the place with Mrs Simpson in an undignified manner in shorts!' Sayers had no time for rich and arrogant womanizers, and in her view Edward's younger brother was a much more suitable monarch. Before long, however, she realized that the Abdication had direct implications for the book she was writing.

Berkeley's reaction was very different. Contrary as ever, he launched a doomed campaign to save Edward from himself. He spent heavily on legal advice and hiring detectives to try to find 'bedroom evidence' that Edward and Wallis Simpson had committed adultery. Even after the Abdication, the earliest that Wallis's divorce could be made absolute was May 1937. Berkeley hoped to compromise the divorce proceedings, and prevent Edward from marrying her. He did not have a hypocritical objection to the couple's affair, but like a large proportion of the British public he believed Edward was the right man to lead the country.

He informed the King's Proctor that witnesses from a hotel in Budapest which the couple had visited during the *Nahlin* cruise would be willing to testify, provided their travel expenses were refunded. This proposal was rejected; it would have been improper to pay the witnesses. In any event, it was time to move on. Berkeley had to admit defeat, and it was just as well. Edward's flakiness would have destroyed the British monarchy and helped smooth Hitler's path to supremacy in Europe. For all his shyness and stammer, George was made of stronger stuff than his feckless brother.

Berkeley had wasted his time and his money, but his detailed private diary telling the story of his effort is held in the Royal

Archives at Windsor. He called it *Commoner and King*, and described it as the 'journal of an obscure and unimportant Englishman who nevertheless touched with a fingertip the fringe of great events'. At least one American literary agent handled the manuscript, but found it hopelessly unpublishable.

Berkeley's obsessive campaign over the Abdication was the most striking symptom of an increasingly troubled mind. His eccentricities were no longer amusing, and his love of contradiction was turning into irrational dogmatism. Years of overwork had caught up with him, and the flow of stories had slowed to a trickle. The death of his father, to whom he dedicated his first detective novel, came as a dreadful blow. His health was fragile, his temper uncertain, his emotions and mental state confused. The cost to him, and to those around him, was becoming hard to bear. At last he married Helen Peters, but a secret passion still tormented him. Then he suffered the humiliation of seeing his name appear in the Press for the stupidest of reasons.

The story began with one of those tiresome regulations which he derided in *O England!* A keen motorist, he was fined thirty shillings for ignoring a traffic sign. His defence was that it would have been more dangerous to stop than to slow down. 'I would rather go to prison than compromise my conscience by paying a fine,' he announced, despite pleading guilty. 'It is your duty to fine me, but I flatly refuse to pay.' He made what *The Times* wearily noted was 'a long statement to the Bench', but the magistrate wasted no sympathy on him, saying, 'If everybody took your attitude, life would be chaos.' Berkeley was forced to give in, but he was not quite finished. Having dodged a prison sentence, he assuaged his feelings by writing a short story based on the incident, with the appropriately childish title 'It Isn't Fair'. A motorist unjustly convicted of a traffic offence kills a Chief Constable sitting in an improperly parked car. Even though the exercise may have offered some form of catharsis, his story never made it into print.

Clues to the way he harped on at Detection Club dinners about the supposed injustice lie in E. R. Punshon's caustic remarks in

Dictator's Way about 'indignant motorists convinced that laws were only for the other fellow', and in *Diabolic Candelabra* about the way 'some motorists never forgave . . . what they held to be the uncalled-for insult to their driving ability'. These are surely in-jokes intended for fellow Club members weary of Berkeley's obsessive pontificating. He was in danger of becoming the Club bore, the traffic sign episode one more symptom of his self-destructive unhappiness.

Sayers was in much better spirits, although she did not know how to surpass *Gaudy Night*. She turned *Busman's Honeymoon* into a novel, and described it (worryingly, to whodunit fans) as a 'love story with detective interruptions'. Peter and Harriet set off for a honeymoon in the countryside only to stumble upon a man's body. The challenges of the detective novel were losing their excitement for her, and both plot and solution were substandard. P. G. Wodehouse, usually a Sayers fan, found it a let-down, while as Raymond Chandler said, a murderer needing so much help from Providence was surely in the wrong business.

Sayers' next idea for an original detective novel showed continuing ambition. The theme concerned the nature of married life. Perhaps the shortcomings of her own marriage tempted her to contemplate what might have been, through the idealized world of Peter and Harriet. She would integrate theme and plot by means of a contrast between the Wimseys' marriage and the marriages of two other couples. She wrote several scenes during the course of 1936, and went so far as to map out on paper how the characters would interact. In July, pleased that the emotional development of Peter's relationship with Harriet would lead to the solution of the murder mystery, she sent this detailed (and colour-coded) diagram to Helen Simpson. Significantly, she added that it now hardly seemed worth the bother of writing the story, though *Paradise Lost* had provided her with a title, *Thrones, Dominations*.

She never did finish the novel, although a version completed by Jill Paton Walsh saw the light of day more than sixty years later. A mix of reasons explained her failure to complete *Thrones,*

Dominations, including her increased focus on writing for the stage. But the key factor was Edward VIII's decision to give up his throne for Wallis Simpson. The drama of the Abdication, with its sub-plots of supposed self-sacrifice and complicated divorce, was bound to affect the way in which readers viewed the story and its analysis of the dynamics of marriage. Real life had overtaken the fiction, and this sapped Sayers' enthusiasm. She put the book aside, as she had put her biography of Wilkie Collins away, and never returned to it. Nor did she ever write another detective novel.

King Edward VIII had a lot to answer for.

Notes to Chapter 26

sultry and sloe-eyed French courtesan Marguerite Alibert
Andrew Rose's research about the Fahmy case is the principal
source for this account.

*a version completed by Jill Paton Walsh saw the light of day more
than sixty years later*
The novelist Jill Paton Walsh (born 1937) had previously written
four detective novels as well as children's stories and literary fiction.
The success of *Thrones, Dominations* has led to her writing three
more books featuring Wimsey.

27

Collecting Murderers

In the spring of 1936, Christie rejoined Max and his team at the dig at Chagar Bazar, not far from Mosul. One day, the local foreman told Max that he should take his wife into town the next day to witness a great event. A woman was to be hanged. Christie made it clear that she found the prospect repellent. Her reaction baffled the elderly Arab. The woman to be hanged had poisoned three husbands. To attend the execution of a female was a rare opportunity. Surely the famous crime writer would not want to miss such a drama?

All Christie wanted was to help her husband in his work. And the team's efforts were ultimately rewarded by the discovery of seventy cuneiform tablets which established a link between Chagar Bazar and the royal house of Assyria. Meanwhile, Christie gathered material which provided unusual background colour for books such as *Murder in Mesopotamia* and *Appointment with Death*, and after each trip she came back to England fresh and invigorated. While Berkeley and Sayers struggled to maintain their love of the game, she remained committed to entertaining an ever-expanding readership. In 1936, when neither Sayers nor Berkeley managed to bring out a single novel, Christie published three, including one all-time classic.

The ABC Murders became a landmark in detective fiction, and its central plot device has been imitated by countless other crime writers. Christie brought Captain Hastings back to London from his ranch in South America to narrate, and with customary understatement he says, 'It had been a difficult time for us out there. Like everyone else, we had suffered from world depression.' Hercule Poirot receives a series of anonymous letters signed 'ABC' which draw his attention in turn to Andover, Bexhill-on-Sea, Churston and Doncaster. In each place, a murder is duly committed, the victim's initials are the same as the crime scene's, and a copy of the *ABC Railway Guide* is left by the killer. Apart from the alphabetical links between the crimes, there is no apparent connection between the victims. A sequence of short chapters interspersed with Hastings' account of the case suggests that the culprit is a mentally unstable travelling salesman, and a serial killing story is brilliantly combined with a fairly clued whodunit.

The explanation is clever yet essentially simple, the hallmark of the best detective novels. Yet Christie produced her masterpiece through much trial and error. She flirted with the possibility of turning the story into another of her 'victim as killer' stories and only came up with the idea of the alphabetical sequence later. The creation of Alexander Bonaparte Cust may well have been inspired by the memorable initials of Anthony Berkeley Cox.

The story was serialized in the *Daily Express,* alongside a column of 'Readers' Guesses' about the solution, and one disgruntled train enthusiast complained that Poirot had not checked the *Guide* carefully enough. Freeman Wills Crofts would have taken pains over such minutiae, but he could never have written such a dazzling mystery. In the third chapter, Poirot suggests an idea for a murder puzzle: 'Four people sit down to play bridge and one, the odd man out, sits in a chair by the fire. One of the four, while he is dummy, has come over and killed him, and intent on the play of the hand, the other three have not noticed. Ah, there would be a crime for you!'

This became the premise of *Cards on the Table*. Mr Shaitana, the exotic foreigner who indulges in the risky hobby of 'collecting' murderers, and inevitably becomes a murder victim, is presented with a subtlety as characteristic as it is unobtrusive. Christie makes fun of the conventional English who sneer at Shaitana just as they condescend to Hercule Poirot. Mrs Ariadne Oliver, the detective novelist who aids and abets Poirot, is a satirical self-portrait; she bemoans the fact that she made her detective Finnish when she does not 'really know anything about Finns'. The contrast between Christie's light-hearted self-deprecation in her creation of Mrs Oliver, and Sayers' serious approach to characterizing Harriet Vane illustrates the difference between them not only as writers, but also as women. Yet they shared some opinions, including their views on the British government's limp response to the deepening crisis in Europe.

Christie became fascinated by the story of Akhnaton (often now spelt Akhenaten), an Egyptian pharaoh who was husband of Nefertiti and father of the boy king Tutankhamun. He has been described as 'the first scientist', 'the first monotheist' and even, in a bold claim, as 'the first individual'. He owes this celebrity status to his abandonment of Ancient Egypt's polytheism and his insistence that only the Sun God should be worshipped. His fatal flaw was a wish to appease aggressors. Christie found his story astonishingly topical, and decided to adapt it into a play.

Christie's Akhnaton is peace-loving and convinced of the goodness of men, but he lacks strength of character. He neglects the defence of his country, alarming his follower Horemheb, who still worships the sect of Amon, most powerful of the old gods. The people are angered by their ruler's attacks on the old religion, and the way his tax-gatherers relieve them of their money, but Akhnaton resists Horemheb's attempts to deal with insurrection, and continues to dream of a world with fewer sacrifices and with 'foreign countries given back to rule themselves'. This weakness leads to turmoil. Horemheb becomes convinced that the Pharaoh is mad, and causes his death. Afterwards, the old ways are restored.

Akhnaton was a thinly disguised attack on the belief that Hitler could be appeased. Christie was writing at a time when most people still hoped that a war could be averted, and her message was unlikely to be popular. Given that she had no talent for didactic writing, and no experience in writing histori-cal drama, it is hardly surprising that nobody wanted to stage her play. The fact that it required eleven scene changes and more than twenty speaking parts did not help.

She showed the script to John Gielgud, who made polite noises, but the play remained unpublished until shortly before her death and has seldom been performed. But she was not finished with writing about Egypt, ancient and modern. *Death on the Nile*, set mainly on board a river steamer, the *SS Karnak*, became one of her most successful titles and was later adapted for the stage. Seven years after the stillbirth of *Akhnaton*, she published *Death Comes as the End*, a murder mystery which broke fresh ground by being set in Ancient Egypt, and antici-pated a landslide of historical crime fiction that continues to this day.

Readers and theatre audiences thirsted for Christie whodun-its, but not for a preachy play about ancient history. Yet she was far-sighted in her criticism of appeasement, and unlike some vociferous critics of the 'guilty men' responsible for fruit-less attempts to appease Hitler she was not being wise after the event.

The Prime Minister was less astute, and also much less well travelled. Neville Chamberlain had never flown in an aeroplane before he set off for Germany at the age of sixty-nine, to meet Adolf Hitler at Munich and sign up to an Anglo-German agree-ment, a piece of paper that he waved in triumph on his return to England. Chamberlain's claim that Hitler was agreeable to 'peace for our time' was foolish, but his optimism was widely shared. Among many others, Virginia Woolf gasped with relief: 'What a shave!' President Roosevelt sent the Prime Minister a two-word telegram: 'Good man.'

Sayers shared Christie's robust attitude towards appease-ment, and believed that pacifism encouraged dictators. In her customary forthright manner, she said that the Germans had succumbed to 'persecution-mania' because they had been treated unfairly in the aftermath of war, but the only way to deal with people who behaved badly and would not see reason was 'to hit them extremely hard on the head and stop them'.

Around the time that Christie started work on *Akhnaton*, Frank Vosper's *Love from a Stranger* began a successful run in the West End. The first night performance was so tense that reports claimed members of the audience fainted with fright. *Love from a Stranger* remains one of the more successful stage versions by other hands of any Christie story, and was twice filmed. Less than a year after the excitement of the first night at the New Theatre, Vosper died in baffling and controversial circumstances. The mystery boasted a cast of characters worthy of a Golden Age whodunit, including a playwright, an actor, a beauty queen, a French marquis, a gay Jewish bullfighter, and a legendary American man of letters.

When *Love from a Stranger* transferred to Broadway, Vosper took the lead role, as he had done in London, but the play closed after a short run. Disappointed, Vosper sailed back from New York on the luxury liner *SS Paris*, but vanished during his last night on board before the ship arrived in Plymouth. A naked and badly injured corpse, minus a leg, was found washed up on the beach near Eastbourne sixteen days later. A make-up artist who knew Vosper, and was familiar with the shape of his profile and jaw, had the miserable task of helping to identify him. Medical evidence established that Vosper was alive when he went into the water.

He spent the night of his disappearance in the company of a former Miss England and a fellow actor called Peter Willes. Muriel Oxford, a 'blue-eyed, brown-haired beauty queen', had enjoyed a brief romance with a wealthy New York nightclub owner, and was returning home from a show in which she had been a chorus girl. Vosper and Willes, who were both homosexual, shared a cabin, and Muriel had invited them to come to her state room and drink champagne for what Press reports described as a 'gay party'. Nobody could explain how Vosper, at some point that evening, could have fallen into the water by accident. According to one report, at the time of his

disappearance he had twenty thousand dollars in his possession, and the money was never found. The journalists had a
field day.

The evidence of what happened that night was confused and
contradictory. Facts were obscured by gossip and innuendo.
Had Vosper caught Muriel with Willes on her divan, and been
pushed out of the window to his death during a fight fuelled by
jealousy and alcohol? Muriel insisted there was no question of
lovemaking – she and Willes had been lounging, rather than
lying, on the divan. Muriel denied rushing up on to the deck
crying that Vosper had committed suicide.

Willes said it was not true that he wanted to marry Muriel, or
that she had fondled him and stroked his cheek. A night steward
who had called into the state room told the inquest that Muriel
and Willes were merry, and Vosper's manner quite normal. In
response to a juryman's question, he had no comment to make
on the close friendship between Willes and Vosper. Stewards,
he said, took no interest in such things. The jury was plainly
dissatisfied with what they were told, but faced with so much
discretion and denial, found no evidence of murder and returned
an open verdict.

Anticipating the methods of *Crimewatch UK* by almost half a
century, Vosper's former lawyer, William Pengelly, conducted in
his London offices a re-enactment of the scene in Muriel Oxford's
cabin. He was assisted by Muriel, Willes and Vosper's father.
Willes claimed that he and Muriel 'were talking so earnestly that
Frank could have passed through the cabin without our seeing
him. I can't believe that he committed suicide. He wasn't the
type, and he seemed far too keen on his work.' But re-staging
the events of the fatal night cast no new light on what had really
happened. If Willes knew more about Vosper's death than he
admitted, he kept the secret for the rest of his days. Meanwhile,
Muriel Oxford married a stockbroker and faded from public
view.

The American novelist Ernest Hemingway had a walk-on role
in the *SS Paris* incident. His state room was across the passage-
way from Muriel's, and he had been at the party, though Muriel

recalled he had left by the time Vosper went missing. According to Hemingway, Vosper had quarrelled violently with 'one or two people' about Muriel during the voyage. He was scarcely a neutral witness, though: years later, Hemingway sought to impress a woman friend with his ruggedness by telling her that when Vosper approached him on the deck with a view to having a drink together, he smashed Vosper's glass, 'to indicate that I did not wish to drink with a pederast'.

Alfred Hitchcock never turned the mystery of the *SS Paris* into a film, but Christie must have been tempted to form a theory about the reason for her collaborator's death. In her quiet way, she always fancied herself as a real-life detective, just as Sayers did. In 1929 she had written a newspaper article about the Croydon poisonings of Grace Duff's husband, mother and sister. An unsolved Victorian domestic mystery, the Bravo case, intrigued her as much. At least three people are credible suspects for the murder of the wealthy lawyer Charles Bravo at the Priory, his home in Balham, but in her late seventies Christie wrote to *The Sunday Times Magazine* arguing that the family physician, Dr Gully, was the killer. Just as Wallace's psychological profile persuaded Sayers that he had not beaten his wife to death, so Gully's cool efficiency (coupled with the fact that he had had an affair with Bravo's wife) persuaded Christie that he was 'the right type' to commit murder.

Her personal connection with Vosper made her wary of public speculation about his death, but two books written more than a decade afterwards suggest she was still haunted by his ghost. In *Crooked House*, the actress Magda Leonides announces that a murder in the family provides the ideal opportunity to put on 'the Edith Thompson play', adding that 'there's quite a lot of comedy to be got out of Edith Thompson – I don't think the author realised that'. This line casts light on Magda's personality with elegant economy. The reference is to *People like Us*, revived at around the time Christie was completing her novel, once the Lord Chamberlain decided the theatre-going public no longer needed to be protected from Vosper's supposedly salacious version of Edith Thompson's story.

Christie later created Robin Upward, a flamboyant and implicitly gay playwright who is a major character in *Mrs McGinty's Dead*. The plot revolves around crimes of the past, and a thinly veiled version of the Crippen case is at the heart of the mystery. Robin is dramatizing a book written by Christie's alter ego, Mrs Ariadne Oliver, a process which she describes as 'pure *agony*'. The parallel with Frank Vosper is obvious, but the storyline bears no resemblance to events on the *Paris* – Robin is a suspect, rather than a victim.

Did Vosper kill himself, and if so, why? Did love from a stranger lead to real-life murder – and if so, who was in love with whom? There were as many possible scenarios as in an Anthony Berkeley novel. If Christie did play the detective, she took care never to reveal her conclusions. The risk of being dragged through the libel courts was too great.

Notes to Chapter 27

its central plot device has been much imitated
It was also anticipated by Chesterton in a Father Brown story, 'The Sign of the Broken Sword', and to some extent by Berkeley in *The Silk Stocking Murders*. *The 'Z' Murders*, published four years before Christie's book, was a serial killer thriller which took its central motif from the opposite end of the alphabet. The author was J. Jefferson Farjeon (1883–1955), a prolific novelist of whom Sayers said: 'Jefferson Farjeon is quite unsurpassed for creepy skill in mysterious adventures.'

Vosper died in baffling and controversial circumstances
My account of the death of Frank Vosper (1899–1937) and its aftermath is drawn largely from contemporary newspaper reports.

a fellow actor called Peter Willes
Peter Willes eventually became a successful television producer whose circle included the playwright Joe Orton, murdered by his lover in 1967.

The American novelist Ernest Hemingway had a walk-on role in the SS Paris incident.
Hemingway was on his way to report on the Spanish Civil War, and had partied with Muriel Oxford along with the Marquis de Polignac and Brooklyn-born Sidney Franklin, who acted as Hemingway's interpreter in Spain. Franklin's unlikely claim to fame was that he was the first successful Jewish-American bullfighter, and in *Death in the Afternoon* Hemingway drooled over his 'cool, serene and intelligent valour'.

28

No Judge or Jury
but My Own Conscience

The Crypt Bar, beneath the Royal Courts of Justice on the Strand, claimed to be the longest bar in England, and was a popular haunt for lawyers, police officers, journalists, and people ensnared in civil litigation as plaintiffs, defendants or witnesses. On 29 July 1937, a grey-haired American, a flamboyant actor who in his younger days played cowboys in silent films under the name 'Young Buffalo', bumped into a woman he knew as he came out of the court. She was a journalist and well aware that he liked to talk, and also to drink. The moment he knew that she was paying, he agreed to give an interview and they headed downstairs to the Crypt.

The woman was Phyllis Davies, and she was carving a reputation on the *Daily Mail* as one of Britain's first female crime reporters. Her interviewee was Philip Yale Drew, who eight years earlier had been the object of the coroner's open suspicion over the murder of tobacconist Alfred Oliver in Reading. Since that 'trial by inquest', Drew's acting career never recovered.

Phyllis Davies got to know Drew after the murder, and they ran into each other several times in London. He was down on his luck, and his behaviour was eccentric. Although he tried to turn on the charm, and liked to cadge drinks from her, it became increasingly clear that he was not going to impart any revelations about the fate of Alfred Oliver – probably because he had none to impart. A confession would have given her a scoop, but his repeated protestations of innocence became tedious. Her interest in Drew was rekindled by his decision to seek compensation for libel because of a thinly veiled portrayal of him in a detective novel.

The novel was *Death to the Rescue*, and the author whom Drew sued, along with publisher Victor Gollancz and printers Camelot Press, was Milward Kennedy. Drew argued that Kennedy had based the character of the actor Garry Boon on him. He had become aware of the book three years after it was first published, when Gollancz brought out a cheap edition. Gollancz had been bitten before by libel claims, and was no soft touch. The case reached the door of the court before frantic settlement negotiations resulted in a deal. After looking for £300 plus fifty guineas in costs, Drew accepted less.

Drew's life had been made a misery by wagging tongues and pointed fingers, he told Phyllis Davies as they sat drinking together in the Crypt Bar. Since Oliver's murder, he'd been 'the victim of poison-pen letter writers by the thousand'. He'd only had one week's work in the past eight years, and had been reduced to sleeping on the Embankment. The case against Gollancz and Kennedy felt like a vindication: 'I have been awarded substantial compensation and handsome apologies have been made to me.' But his tale of woe lacked a happy ending; three years later, he was diagnosed with cancer of the larynx. He died in poverty and was buried in an unmarked grave.

For Kennedy, the case was a disaster. A libel action is one of the worst fates that can befall an author, and for all his intelligence and diplomatic skill he had made a crass mistake. Kennedy's enthusiasm for true crime had returned to haunt him, as he used elements of a real-life mystery in his book but featured a character based on a man guilty of nothing. Even though Garry Boon committed no crime in *Death to the Rescue*, Kennedy portrayed him as a boastful drunk, and the resemblance between Boon and Drew was plain.

As so often happens when acrimonious litigation is compromised, a bland agreed statement was issued, in which Kennedy claimed that 'although he had used the circumstances of the inquest, he thought that he had so disguised the characters and the events as to prevent anyone thinking that Garry Boon referred to Mr Drew. He now appreciated that he had been wrong in so thinking.' The book was withdrawn from circulation. With hindsight, it seems astonishing that an intelligent and sophisticated man such as Kennedy should blunder into libelling a man who was never charged with a crime, but it is all too easy to be caught by the traps set by the law of defamation.

Taking Berkeley's lead, Kennedy had explored the nature of justice with irony and cynicism, using actual murder cases as a springboard for his mysteries to give an added touch of realism. Now he had been caught out, and so had Victor Gollancz. Kennedy's crime-writing career was derailed, even though Gollancz did not drop him from his list at that point. Before the case was brought, Kennedy published fourteen novels in nine years. Afterwards, he lived for more than thirty years, but produced just four more novels.

Prior to the court case, his books displayed touches of daring. *Poison in the Parish* begins with a scathing dedication to an unnamed 'friend' who has pointed out that the characters in Kennedy's novels are unpleasant, and it promises: 'Here is an attempt at something different.' The victim, an elderly woman resident in a village guest house whose exhumed corpse reveals that she was poisoned by arsenic, is typically unappealing, the suspects more attractive. The book opens innovatively, with a 'Prologue or Epilogue' which reveals the final act in the drama.

The narrator, a wealthy invalid who is asked to assist the police with their enquiries into life in the village, is called Francis Anthony. Kennedy borrowed the forenames from the two most celebrated pseudonyms of Anthony Berkeley Cox in a mischievous tribute to his friend. The story boasts a final twist which Berkeley surely enjoyed, with an unsuspected killer ultimately revealed thanks to a bizarre fluke. Kennedy came up with an original murder motive and Francis Anthony is unsentimental about British justice: 'I was tempted to remind him that before now innocent men had come to the gallows.' Again, we are a long way from cosiness, despite the village setting. An extra helping of irony, this time unintended, arises from the inclusion of an inquest, and veiled reference to Philip Yale Drew.

The novel Kennedy published in the year of the court case, *I'll Be Judge, I'll Be Jury*, included a libel disclaimer – an unfortunate example of shutting the stable door too late. He offers an alternative take on the theme of *Before the Fact*, but in his version the woman who fears that she is 'married to a murderer' is made of stronger stuff than Lina Aysgarth. Rather than succumbing to her fate, she resolves to 'watch and fight'.

The book opens boldly. Mary Dallas sneaks out from the hotel where she is staying with her husband very early one morning for a tryst in a beach hut. Under her short beach-coat, she is topless. Before encountering her lover, George Needham, she stumbles over the corpse of her guardian, while the murderer hides behind a curtain. In a panic, she and George contrive to make the death look like an accident, and their hurried interference with the crime scene succeeds in confusing the police. Soon Mary starts to suspect that her husband John committed the murder in order to benefit from the money she was due to inherit from her guardian. Her love turns to hatred, and she decides to act as judge, jury – and executioner. As so often with Kennedy, the book's concept is striking and original, and as with *Malice Aforethought* there is a cynical final twist. But Milward Kennedy could not match the success of Francis Iles, and the book sank without trace.

When the penalty for murder was death on the scaffold, miscarriages of justice had terrifying consequences. Anthony Berkeley was cynical about lawyers and the legal system, long before his confrontational antics in the magistrates' court. His prejudices were reinforced by close study of the cases of Florence Maybrick and Edith Thompson, and the unpredictable and sometimes unjust fates suffered by those accused of murder in real life.

He took a special delight in identifying with meek middle-class professional men who found themselves driven to murder. Herbert Rowse Armstrong, the model for Dr Bickleigh, was one example. Hawley Harvey Crippen, the mild-mannered American who ran businesses selling dubious homeopathic medicines and offering 'painless dentistry', was another. Crippen, like Armstrong, was an amiable, slightly-built man who was bossed about by a domineering wife. Cora Crippen, a brash extrovert who enjoyed a less-than-illustrious career as a music hall artiste under the name Belle Elmore, vanished from the couple's home at 39 Hilldrop Crescent, Camden, in January 1910. The subsequent discovery of human remains in the cellar of their house launched one of the most famous manhunts in history.

Crippen fled to the Continent, accompanied by his typist and mistress, Ethel Le Neve, who was disguised as a boy. Posing as father and son, they boarded the *SS Montrose*, heading for Canada, but the ship's captain became suspicious of them and communicated his suspicions to England by Marconi telegram. To the delight of journalists and a thrilled public worldwide, Inspector Walter Dew of Scotland Yard pursued the couple in a faster ship and eventually caught up with them. Crippen was tried for murder, despite doubt as to whether the flesh in the cellar could be identified as belonging to Cora. Bernard Spilsbury, in his first celebrated courtroom appearance, made his name as a pathologist by coming up with seemingly authoritative expert evidence supporting the prosecution case that Crippen had poisoned Cora with hyoscine had dismembered her corpse, and had buried some (but not all) of the remains in the cellar. Crippen was duly found guilty and hanged. Tried separately, Ethel Le Neve was acquitted after her counsel presented her as the innocent dupe of Crippen, who was inventively and inaccurately described as 'imperturbable, unscrupulous, dominating, fearing neither God nor man, and yet a man insinuating, attractive, and immoral'. Le Neve disappeared from public sight, although she travelled no further than Croydon, to spend the rest of her life in respectable suburban obscurity married to a man named Smith who went to his grave not knowing his wife's real identity.

Doubts persist about what really did happen at 39 Hilldrop Crescent, and the case has fascinated criminologists and crime writers ever since. Detection Club members often talked and wrote about it. J. J. Connington, the robust chemist, focused on Crippen's use of hyoscine to drug his wife for sexual gratification, while Sayers, who devoted so much of her life to an elaborate pretence, empathized with Ethel Le Neve's determined refusal to face up to the possibility that her lover had done away with his wife. Christie, after her experience with Nancy Neele, could never be starry-eyed about pretty young women who seduced married men, and suspected that Ethel knew much more about Cora's death than she (and Crippen, who remained besotted) would ever admit. Ethel had worn the dead woman's furs and jewellery – psychologically curious behaviour that intrigued Hugh Walpole as much as it had appalled Cora's friends. Berkeley, for his part, sympathized with the plight of Crippen, the affable adulterer with an inferiority complex.

As early as his second novel, Berkeley had Roger Sheringham side with Crippen – 'if ever a woman deserved murdering, Cora Crippen did' – and more than a decade later, he argued in an essay that Crippen did not have the right psychological profile to commit a savage killing. 'One does not remain gentle and kindly for 48 years and then reveal oneself as a fiend.' He agreed with Edward Marshall Hall, the legendary barrister known as 'the Great Defender', that Crippen overdosed Cora with hyoscine by mistake, wanting to keep her quiet while he had sex with Ethel in their home. On that view, his crime was not murder, but manslaughter.

Forever on the lookout for miscarriages of justice, Berkeley's weapon of choice when highlighting them was not passion or outrage, but irony. He led the way for a group of ironists who saw murder from the criminal's perspective, and derided the judicial process. As well as Raymond Postgate and Richard Hull, his disciples included C. E. Vulliamy, who wrote satires about vicars and dons becoming demented serial killers. The Marxist sympathizer (and godson of Arthur Conan Doyle) Bruce Hamilton followed up his scathing critique of the bourgeoisie in *Middle Class Murder* by adapting the *Notable British Trials* format into a fictional murder trial set in the near future. *Rex v. Rhodes: the Brighton Murder Trial* was not so much a novel as a polemic excoriating Fascism and eagerly anticipating the defeat of the established order by the workers.

Time and again in books by the ironists, murderers escape punishment for their crimes, although Fate often throws a spanner in the works just when they think they have got away with it. Kennedy was an early ironist, and Hull (Richard Henry Sampson under a pen name) was another. Miscarriages of justice were also central to books by traditionalists such as Agatha Christie. In *Five Little Pigs*, Caroline Crale dies in prison, sentenced to life for a crime she did not commit, while the real culprit escapes judicial punishment, suffering instead a meta-phorical kind of living death. Caroline is not the only Christie character wrongly convicted of murder and imprisoned. The widespread consensus that Christie and company never ques-tioned the status quo is wildly mistaken.

Richard Hull, a rare example of a chartered accountant with a gift for crime writing, became as bold an experimenter as Berkeley, specializing in trickery with story structure and point of view. Hull became the Detection Club's Secretary after the Second World War, but wrote his best books in the Thirties. Like Berkeley, and Kennedy, he loved creating unpleasant charac-ters. *Keep it Quiet* was set in a London club similar to the one in which Hull, a bachelor, lived for years. The members include a homicidal maniac and, in a touch of self-mockery, a fat man with the same initials as the well-upholstered Hull. A sub-plot involves a series of thefts of 'Dorothy Sayers' books. An amateur sleuth deduces that the culprit must be female, since Sayers' books appealed much more to women. After omitting Sayers' middle initial, and making such a sweeping generalisation, Hull was lucky to be elected to the Detection Club at all.

Forever exploring collisions between law and justice, this most creative of accountants came up with a superb plot in *Excellent Intentions*, which opens at the start of a murder trial. In a clever spin on the whodunit concept, the identity of the accused is kept hidden until the judge addresses the jury. The victim is a wealthy misanthrope with no redeeming qualities whatsoever, and five people had the means, opportunity and motive to commit the murder by lacing his snuff with cyanide. The action zips back and forth in time, between the trial and the events leading up to it, and the consensus is that whoever killed the old man had excellent intentions. 'To commit a murder because it was a Good Thing' is a new idea, Inspector Fenby reflects, and yet not entirely new: Hamlet regarded killing as a duty and Charlotte Corday, who assassinated French Revolutionary leader Jean-Paul Marat, was 'invariably . . . regarded as a heroine'.

Edgar Wallace had tackled well-meant murder in *The Four Just Men* thirty years earlier. Now the concept gained fresh resonance, as people decided the world would be a better place without Hitler or Mussolini. The judge's summing-up at the end of the trial is central to Hull's plot, and he quotes from the Thompson–Bywaters case as well as referring to G. K. Chesterton's love of paradox. The final pages deliver an original twist which sees the legal process manipulated to contrive an unorthodox but just result.

One unlikely admirer of Hull's novel was Argentina's Jorge Luis Borges, who thought this 'an extremely pleasant book. His prose is able, his characters convincing, his irony civilized.' Yet he had a typically Borgesian twist up his sleeve: Hull's solution was 'so unsurprising that I cannot free myself from the suspicion that this quite real book, published in London, is the one I imagined in Balvanera, three or four years ago. In which case, *Excellent Intentions* hides a secret plot. Ah me, or ah Richard Hull! I can't find that secret plot anywhere.'

When it came to altruistic murder, nobody did it better than Berkeley. In *Jumping Jenny*, a detective novelist organizes a fancy-dress party with guests representing well-known killers (including Crippen) or their victims. Berkeley seizes the chance to express his views about marriage and neurotic women, and even his obsession with spanking resurfaces: 'What Ena needs is to be married to a great big he-man who'd give her a sound thrashing every now and then. That's the only way to keep her in order.'

Sheringham makes a light-hearted offer to strangle the odious Ena Stratton, but someone else beats him to it. Berkeley plays a trick on the reader by appearing to show who is responsible for the crime, and most of the book is devoted to the efforts of Sheringham and his fellow guests trying to persuade the authorities that Ena Stratton committed suicide. The final sentence presents an alternative version of events. Both the actual and supposed culprits are appealing – the dead woman is appalling.

After publishing fifteen mysteries in ten years, as well as making major contributions to the round robins, Berkeley failed to produce a novel in either 1935 or 1936. He was under no financial pressure to write, but the root cause of this drop-off in productivity was mental turmoil. His ludicrous campaign against the Abdication, and the debacle of the motoring case, illustrate his troubled mental state, but whereas Margaret Cole published an excruciatingly detailed report on her husband's medical problems, no records confirm that Berkeley suffered some form of nervous collapse. He rallied, and his next crime novel was a masterpiece of wit and ingenuity. Returning to the theme of altruistic murder, again he based the plot on an actual murder. Unlike Kennedy, he took care to choose a case with dead protagonists.

On Boxing Day in 1864, a brawl in the bar of the Golden Anchor pub in Great Saffron Hill, London, led to murder. An Italian called Seraphini Polioni boasted to the landlord: 'I could kill six Englishmen like you,' and an associate called Gregorio Mogni struck the landlord. A fight started, a knife was brandished, and a man called Michael Harrington was stabbed to death.

Witnesses said that Polioni struck the fatal blow. He was charged with murder, found guilty and sentenced to death. But Enrico Negretti, a high-profile fellow Italian who had been one of the pioneers of photography, was not satisfied, and formed a committee to try to establish Polioni's innocence. A private prosecution was launched against Mogni, who admitted his guilt, claiming that he had acted in self-defence. Polioni gave evidence through an interpreter, and his first words to the court were memorable: 'I am now in Newgate under sentence of death.'

Polioni gave a convincing account of his limited involvement in the affray, and the jury found Mogni guilty of murder, with a strong recommendation to mercy. Polioni was set free, and Mogni sentenced to five years' penal servitude. A private prosecution had overturned the outcome of a state-backed trial, even though the judge who condemned Polioni had rashly said, 'I am as satisfied that you committed this murder as if I had seen it with my own eyes.'

As Berkeley summarized it, there were 'two men imprisoned at the same time, each of whom had separately been found guilty of the death of the same man; and the authorities clearly did not know what to do about it'. A situation so brimming with irony and paradox was tailor-made for Berkeley. He dedicated *Trial and Error* to P.G. Wodehouse, and opened it by echoing John Stuart Mill – 'The sanctity of human life has been much exaggerated.'

Lawrence Todhunter is told by his doctor that he is suffering from an aortic aneurism and only has a few months to live. Surreptitiously, he seeks advice from friends about the best use to which he may put his remaining time and finds himself 'advised, with remarkable unanimity, to commit a murder'. Todhunter contemplates the possibility of trying to do away with Hitler, Mussolini or Stalin, but decides on a more domestic form of altruistic crime, the murder of someone who is making life a burden for a small number of people.

He meets a popular author, Nicholas Farroway, who has fallen for a deeply unpleasant actress, Jean Norwood, and finds that the lives of Farroway and his circle are being ruined by Jean's vindictive behaviour. Todhunter decides to shoot her, but although he escapes arrest after carrying out his murderous plan, Farroway's son-in-law, another man ensnared by Jean, is charged with the crime and duly convicted. Todhunter admits his guilt – only to find that nobody believes him.

As the plot thickens, Berkeley keeps hurling satiric darts. Newspapers, politicians and the judicial system are targeted time and again. When Berkeley savages the judge presiding over Todhunter's trial – few judges refrain, he says, 'from the temptation to tell other people to live their lives in accordance with the law books' – he was taking revenge for his own brush with the law the year before. In the final paragraphs, Berkeley returns to the question that so preoccupied him, of whether 'it is better to preserve a pestilential nuisance alive rather than bring happiness to a great many persons by eliminating one'. In the very last sentence, with a breezy flourish, he reveals what really happened to Jean Norwood.

Jean's capacity to destroy the happiness of anyone with the bad luck to cross her path is as formidable as that of the women whom Berkeley savaged in *Panic Party* and *Jumping Jenny*. Nobody mourns Jean. 'There is such a thing as the fatal type,' Farroway insists. 'If you're lucky enough not to meet that type, your life goes on quietly, respectably, peacefully. If you do, it goes to pieces. You're done for.' He was surely speaking for Berkeley.

He contrived another variation on the theme of altruistic murder in *Not To Be Taken*. With hindsight, the opening sentence – 'Is it my imagination, or have other people noticed, too, that there is always something slightly sinister about the third of September?' – is bizarrely prescient. War broke out again on that very date the following year.

The story is told by Douglas Sewell, a fruit-farmer with a typical Berkeley inferiority complex. Sewell muses at one point: 'How many of us really know our own wives?' One character, a doctor's sister, is an Oxford-educated feminist who seems like a variant of Sayers, but with a different outlook on life. Berkeley allows himself a swipe at 'the bullying, hectoring, loud-mouthed, exceedingly unpleasant detective of American fiction' and introduces two minor characters who prove to be Nazis, satirizing their anti-Semitism.

Perverse as ever, Berkeley inserted a 'Challenge to the Reader' in the manner of Ellery Queen, whose books he disliked. Despite his interest in the mind of the murderer, he had not lost his love of the detection game. His challenge poses four questions, and notes that those who read the story in serial form failed to produce a single set of fully correct answers.

The culprit's explanation of the motive for murder reflects the concept that now obsessed Berkeley: 'I consider it a beneficial act to rid the world of a parasite and an incubus, which is what I intended to do. You may cling to the law if you like, with all your public-school mind. I admit no judge or jury but my own conscience.' But for Sewell, this is 'sheer Bolshevism'.

Once again, justice is satisfied by extrajudicial means. The killer endures an unbearable punishment for the crime that has nothing to do with the legal system, and, rather like the murderer in Allingham's *The Crime at Black Dudley*, departs the scene to become devoted to charitable work. The book ends in tantalizing fashion. Just as Berkeley seemed to yearn to do something utterly decisive to put an end to his emotional troubles, so Sewell is unsure whether to tell the authorities what he has deduced:

'I feel I really ought to do something.

But what ought I to do?'

Notes to Chapter 28

The Marxist sympathizer (and godson of Arthur Conan Doyle) Bruce Hamilton
Arthur Douglas Bruce Hamilton (1900–74) never created a series detective. This, coupled with the fact that he only published novels infrequently and kept varying his approach to crime writing, contributed to neglect of his work even during his lifetime. Bruce solicited a quote from his godfather to support his first novel, *To Be Hanged*, although the ailing Conan Doyle confided that not only had he forgotten the 'transaction' of becoming Bruce's godparent, but that he felt the book faltered after a good start. Nevertheless, Hamilton's books were unusual and interesting; *Middle Class Murder* is one of the better ironic novels influenced by *Malice Aforethought*. Bruce had a close but ambivalent relationship with his brother, Patrick Hamilton (1904–62), author of *Rope*, *Gas Light* and *Hangover Square*. Patrick's biographer, Sean French (himself one half of the crime-writing team Nicci French) has pointed out that Bruce's last, unpublished novel *A Case for Cain* 'culminates in a man rather like Bruce murdering a man rather like Patrick'.

Her interviewee was Philip Yale Drew
Richard Whittington-Egan's book about Drew is the main source of information about him. The settlement of his claim against Kennedy was reported in *The Times* on 30 July 1937. Phyllis Davies enjoyed a high profile while working for the *Daily Mail,* and was a prime mover in the Women's Press Club before succumbing to mental illness.

The case against Gollancz and Kennedy
Milward Kennedy was represented in the Drew litigation by Henry C. Leon, a young barrister who later became a county court judge. After the war, Leon was better known by his pen name of Henry Cecil, as a prolific author of light-hearted fiction, much of it with a mystery theme. Thirty-one years after Drew's libel claim, in the year of Kennedy's death, Leon too was elected to membership of the Detection Club.

a scathing dedication to an unnamed 'friend'
It seems clear from the content of the dedication that Kennedy was

not addressing Sayers. Yet when reviewing *Corpse in Cold Storage*, she said of *Death to the Rescue* that 'the hatefulness of his human beings reached the point of being actively repellent'. She was kinder about hard-drinking Sir George Bull and his attractive wife, appealing rogues who feature in two books including *Corpse in Cold Storage*.

more than a decade later, he argued in an essay
'Was Crippen a Murderer?', published as by Francis Iles in A. J. Alan, et al., *Great Unsolved Crimes*.

his disciples included C. E. Vulliamy
Colwyn Edward Vulliamy (1886–1971) was a Welsh historian, biographer and belle-lettrist whose early work in the Iles vein, notably *The Vicar's Experiments* (1932) appeared under the name Anthony Rolls. See Curtis Evans, 'Anthony Rolls (C. E.Vulliamy): Master of the Golden Age Crime Novel', *CADS* 68, August 2014, which contends plausibly that in *Bloody Murder*, Julian Symons 'underestimated both the quantity and quality of psychological crime novels published during the Golden Age of detective fiction'.

Gladys Mitchell and friends: Tyte (Margaret Tyte), Mike (Gladys Mitchell), Gunn (Muriel Gunn, afterwards Hall), Rene (Rene Woodgate, afterwards Fleming).

Part Six

The End Game

29

Playing the Grandest Game
in the World

As members of the Detection Club, following a splendid dinner, staggered back to Gerrard Street through the dark and dimly lit streets of sexy, seductive Soho, their young American colleague, swaying slightly from the effects of alcohol, urged them forward. 'Say, why don't we play a few games when we get back? There are paper and pencils in the room. . . .'

Sayers and John Rhode, his closest friends in England, talked him out of the idea. After consuming a great deal of rich food, and even more drink, the wits of the Detection Club's finest were blunter than usual. They simply wanted to spend the rest of the night chatting – and drinking. Gracious as always, John Dickson Carr admitted defeat. Subsequently, he brought along expensive bottles of whisky to make a change from the beer paid for from Club funds. Carr was excellent company, and even if he liked alcohol too much for his own good, in those early years it never dampened his high spirits. His wife Clarice Dickson Carr, pretty, vivacious and still in her twenties, was equally popular.

For Carr, playing games was a lifelong passion. Crime fiction became increasingly serious as the Thirties drew to a close, but he still saw detective stories as a contest between writer and reader. Even after the war, when tastes were changing, he wrote an essay celebrating traditional detective stories, 'The

Grandest Game in the World'. Inevitably, he became a mainstay of the Detection Club. The arrival of an energetic and American with a passion for the genre and its traditions gave the dinners a fresh infusion of vitality, and Carr was a natural choice as the next Honorary Secretary.

He loved the conviviality of the dinners and those late boozy evenings, putting the world to rights together with his literary heroes and heroines. They responded warmly to his generosity and enthusiasm. The bond between Carr and Sayers was strengthened by mutual admiration, though their lives and books had little in common. Presumably on Sayers' advice, Carr appointed David Higham as his British literary agent, and she also recommended him to the fiction editor of the *Evening Standard*. This led Carr to write the first Gideon Fell short story, and the evocative opening of 'The Wrong Problem' includes a slightly disguised reference to the Club: 'At the Detectives' Club it is still told how Dr Fell went down into the valley in Somerset that evening and of the man with whom he talked in the twilight by the lake, and of murder that came up as though through the lake itself.'

Carr was thrilled to meet Richard Austin Freeman, who turned up for the dinners when he could despite his frailty and advancing years. Carr escorted the older man up the stairs leading to the Club rooms – praying that Freeman would not collapse and die of a heart attack on the way to dinner. It was a wonder that John Rhode never broke his neck tumbling down that staircase. Carr claimed to have seen Rhode 'polish off ten pints of beer before lunch and more than that after dinner'. Given his drinking habits, it is amazing that Rhode managed to write almost one hundred and fifty novels. Physically he was much bigger than Carr – after G. K. Chesterton's death, incontestably the largest member of the Club – and coped much better with alcohol than Carr, who was five foot six and slightly-built.

Good-looking, with brown hair and large, dreamy grey eyes that Clarice adored, Carr liked women – and they liked him. After the war, both he and Anthony Berkeley carried a torch for the young and attractive Christianna Brand – according to

Brand – but romance never blossomed. Gladys Mitchell enjoyed Carr's sense of fun, while Anthony Gilbert nursed a hopeless passion for him – again, if Christianna Brand is to be believed.

Clarice took several portrait pictures at the Detection Club that survive to this day. Anthony Berkeley, very much in Dr Jekyll mode, looks dapper and good-humoured. The reserved E. C. Bentley seems a little uncomfortable, as if he found it rather un-English to pose for the camera. Sayers is shown holding Eric the Skull with as much delight as a mother cradling her newborn, and John Rhode smokes a pipe whilst flourishing a cushion on which Eric sits wearing a wicked grin. Rhode's insouciant expression struck Sayers as 'superbly characteristic'.

As Club Secretary, Carr kept coming up with bright ideas. He proposed a Viennese psychoanalyst as a guest speaker, and Sayers agreed, 'provided he was not embarrassingly earnest'. Carr was gratified that Baroness Orczy continued to make the trip to London from Monte Carlo for the main annual dinner. Clarice found her a 'small vivacious old lady with white hair and flashing dark eyes', and was amused when she said in a strong Hungarian accent, 'Oh Mr Carr, no one would ever guess, you know, that you're an American.' In contrast, the Irishman Freeman Wills Crofts sometimes seemed more English than the English. Crofts was invariably courteous – Gladys Mitchell compared him to a family solicitor – but his thoughts often seemed elsewhere, as if he were mentally unscrambling a complicated alibi concerning train timetables. To young Clarice, his white moustache made him look older than his years.

A. A. Milne's quietness baffled Clarice: 'He was a purely English type, nice-looking, almost film-starish, slim and small-boned, not short but not very tall either, with light brown hair. . . . He'd take himself to a corner and just sit there, talking to no one, looking at no one.' John Rhode told her that Milne was not standoffish, just naturally reticent in company, and Sayers too thought him a 'shy bird'. A. E. W. Mason, on the other hand, proved very amiable on the rare occasions he came to the dinners and had 'a grand presence'.

When they first moved to England, the Carrs lived in a

bungalow in Bristol, not far from where Clarice had grown up. Carr persuaded his wife to move to London, partly so as to be handy for Detection Club meetings. They found a flat on Haverstock Hill, where they entertained people from the world of literature. Guests included fellow novelists and Edward Powys Mathers, a poet and translator better known as the crime reviewer and crossword compiler Torquemada.

Agatha Christie also socialized with the Carrs. On her first visit to Haverstock Hill, the lift to the third floor got stuck, and Christie found herself trapped for half an hour alongside J. B. Priestley, a professional Yorkshireman who played up to his curmudgeonly persona. Conditions were cramped – Christie was putting on so much weight that later Sayers wrote: 'She is ENORMOUS – nearly twice as big as I am!' – and Priestley's wrath turned the air blue. Christie found the whole thing amusing. That night, since Carr was in charge of the entertainments, they played the Murder Game. Christie took the part of a suspect who claimed that the Archbishop of Canterbury would give her an alibi. Priestley, cast as the chief inspector, turned this claim on its head by inferring from it that she had murdered the prelate.

Clarice saw through the formidable manner that Sayers deployed as a protective shield. Bluntness and lack of diplomacy were part of Sayers' DNA, but she loved letting her hair down among trusted friends. One night at Gerrard Street, Sayers, Rhode and the Carrs were the last survivors of a convivial dinner. Having downed a large quantity of Scotch, Sayers 'arose like one addressing a Sunday School' and recited a ribald limerick about the young girl from Madras.

Carr's drive, and sheer likeability, enhanced the collegial ethos of the Detection Club. Margery Allingham was becoming increasingly ambitious as a novelist, and her publishers described *The Fashion in Shrouds* as 'a powerful modern novel which has something to say about the world in which we live', but Carr persuaded her to take a greater interest in the Club, and went to stay with her and Pip Youngman Carter in Tolleshunt d'Arcy. Later, they exchanged books with jokey inscriptions: Allingham's said Carr was 'the world's best detective story writer – EXCEPT ME!' As for Pip, Clarice was one of many women who felt the force of his charm.

Thanks to his encouragement, Margery Allingham stopped being intimidated by Sayers. She and Pip did not live far from Witham, although it was not until wartime that they started seeing Sayers apart from the Club dinners. At first, Sayers came over by bus, and Allingham decided she was 'a nice old duck really when you know her. Just determinedly belligerent.' Sayers was not yet fifty, but her demeanour, plain looks, and extravagant dress sense made her seem like a strangely exotic aunt with an erudite mind and an earthy sense of humour. Eight years were to pass before Allingham finally met Mac, 'the famous husband', when she and Pip were invited to Witham. Writing to her sister Joyce, Allingham even referred to her friend as 'Dot Sayers'. The mind boggles at the thought of her addressing the great lady as 'Dot'. Sayers' reaction would be worth travelling a long way to see.

Carr was probably responsible for talking Agatha Christie into becoming a member of the Detection Club's committee, along with Sayers, Simpson, Nicholas Blake, Anthony Gilbert, and Gladys Mitchell (who took charge of the Club's growing library of crime books). If it was Carr's doing, this was an astonishing feat of persuasion, even by his standards. Christie was exceptionally self-effacing, and the antithesis of a 'joiner', never mind a natural committee person. Her continuing enthusiastic participation in the Detection Club illustrates how much the Club still meant to her. She was now rich and successful, far more assured and contented than the broken woman whom Berkeley had invited to those early dinners in Watford, but she never became too grand to go to the Detection Club. Yet she remained reluctant to talk about her books. One of her successors as Club President, Harry Keating, recalled her being asked where she found her ideas – and her conversation-killing reply, 'At Marks and Spencer's stores.' Keating's wife, the actor Sheila Mitchell, found Christie hard work until they discussed the difficulty of travel, and Christie started chattering about the state of the motorways. Her preoccupation with the commonplace helps to explain the universality of her books' appeal. So does her intense curiosity. Julian Symons recalled arriving late at a Club dinner and not having time to wash his hands. His finger-nails were rimmed with dirt and he saw Christie eyeing them with fascination, as if wondering if he had just buried a body and was hastily attempting to establish an alibi.

A glance at the pre-war list of members' addresses reveals that everyone except for J. J. Connington and Baroness Orczy had a home in London or elsewhere in southern England. Geographical proximity at least made it easier for Club members to attend at Gerrard Street, helping to forge bonds between founder members and newer recruits, but the North and Midlands con-tinued to be massively under-represented among crime writers in general, as well as within the Detection Club. This only began to change when a new generation of writers, often educated at provincial grammar schools rather than fee-paying public schools, emerged in the Fifties and Sixties.

Despite all Carr's efforts, and even though veteran writers like Austin Freeman continued to produce books, the Detection Club needed new blood. Edgar Jepson died, while Morrison, Robert Eustace and Baroness Orczy gave up on detective fiction. Advancing years took their toll, and so did poor health. Connington, for instance, rarely managed to travel to London for the dinners. Cataracts formed in both his eyes, rendering him almost blind before surgery: at work on the later chap-ters of *In Whose Dim Shadow*, he could not read the words he was typing. The title of *A Minor Operation* was a mordant ref-erence to the risks of cataract surgery. Plot elements include love letters in a cipher created by a Braille-writing machine (Wendover suspects a clue to a Thompson–Bywaters type of intrigue) and Driffield secures the final evidence by drawing on what he 'learned at school by doing thiosulphate titrations'.

Connington suffered a heart attack before the book was pub-lished, and the quality of his later work dipped; *Truth Comes Limping*, Driffield's next case, was as lame as its title. *For Murder Will Speak*, which featured that reliable Golden Age plot device, an outbreak of poison pen letters, marked a partial return to form, but the scientific plot elements (including trickery with a wireless receiver, and X-ray treatment for a glandular disorder that has caused the luckless sufferer to become promiscuous) are very much of their time.

Fresh blood was needed – but whose? The members debated potential candidates long and hard, with Sayers and Berkeley adamant that standards must not slip. Along with Nicholas Blake and Christopher Bush, E. C. R. Lorac (a pseudonym for the prolific Edith Caroline Rivett, who also wrote as Carol Carnac) and Newton Gayle were elected in 1937. Gayle was the writing name chosen for an unlikely literary partnership between the American poet and equal rights campaigner Muna Lee and a Shell oil executive, Maurice Guinness; Gayle was her maternal grandmother's maiden name, and Newton his paternal grandmother's name. The strange title of the third of their five books, *Murder at 28:10*, refers to barometric pressure; it is surely the only crime novel to feature a series of barometric charts, a gimmick which helps to build tension in a story about a devastating hurricane in Puerto Rico.

In hard financial times, not every writer could afford the cost of the dinners. Doris Ball, who wrote as Josephine Bell, attended Blake's initiation at the Dorchester as the guest of Freeman Wills Crofts, who lived near her in Guildford. She was invited to become a member the following year, but reluctantly declined because she was short of money; she was ultimately elected in 1954.

John Dickson Carr exerted an unexpected literary influence upon the future Poet Laureate, who shared his pleasure in playing the detective game. *Thou Shell of Death*, Cecil Day-Lewis's second book as Nicholas Blake, is a splendid 'impossible crime' novel about a 'fantastic and paradoxical case . . . solved by a professor of Greek and a seventeenth century dramatist'. The famous airman Fergus O'Brien, a fictionalized T. E. Lawrence, has received messages threatening that he will die on Boxing Day, and calls on Nigel Strangeways' help. He is found shot – on the appointed day – in a hut surrounded by snow with only his own trail of footsteps leading to it. Good lines abound – a *femme fatale* is 'blonde as a Nazi's dream' – and Nigel meets his future wife, the explorer Georgia Cavendish.

Not long after Blake's book appeared, Carr and John Rhode devised a novel together. Carr had the idea of a murder committed in a sealed elevator, but he struggled with technical aspects of the murder method. Rhode came up with an ingenious and elaborate do-it-yourself weapon. Carr wrote most of *Drop to his Death*, with the pair collaborating on technical details when he made weekend visits to Rhode's home in Kent. A diagram of the murder weapon is provided, in classic Rhode style, but although the book sold well it fell far short of Carr's best work, and the outbreak of war put paid to their collaboration. Reflecting the co-authors' fondness for alcohol, the characters in the novel spend much of their time drinking – so much so that Carr's friend Torquemada told him that the book should have been called *A Drop Too Much*.

Carr's next detective, Colonel March, owed both his physique and his personality to Rhode, and was a large, amiable man weighing seventeen stone, with 'a very short pipe protruding from under a cropped moustache' and an extensive knowledge of trivia. He headed Scotland Yard's splendidly named Department of Queer Complaints. The March stories were later televised, with Boris Karloff, of all people, playing the Colonel. The resemblance to Rhode was lost, since Karloff was seventy years old, and wore an eye patch,

Sayers still loved the game-playing aspect of detective fiction, even though her interest in writing novels about Wimsey had waned. She had fun with a new pastime, as entertaining as delving into Sherlockiana, but more personal. Assisted by Helen Simpson, Muriel St Clair Byrne, and an expert in heraldry, Wilfred Scott-Giles, she explored the supposed history of the Wimsey family. The quartet produced a pamphlet, *Papers Relating to the Family of Wimsey*, with text written by Sayers and Simpson, whose flair for writing pastiche Sayers admired. Scott-Giles also organized a meeting at which the quartet delivered papers. Helen Simpson read extracts from an eighteenth-century Household Book kept by Mary Wimsey, whose descendants lived in New Zealand, while Sayers recounted the story of Lord Mortimer Wimsey, the Hermit of the Wash, who lived alone in a hut on the Norfolk coast, totally mute and eating nothing but shrimps and seaweed.

The fun and games of initiation into Detection Club membership continued. Sayers fine-tuned the wording of the ritual, and instructed Carr, as Secretary, that the promises to be made on Eric the Skull must be made by each new candidate individually. Richard Hull was among the potential new members, but ultimately the coming of war meant that he had to wait until 1946, when he joined along with Cyril Hare, the American Alice Campbell, and Christianna Brand.

John Rhode was tasked with compiling a volume of short stories on behalf of the Club. To his delight, A. A. Milne agreed to contribute a foreword, but some members, such as R. C. Woodthorpe, whose enthusiasm for the genre was fading, proved impossible to pin down. Many of the stories were reprints. Ianthe Jerrold, Arthur Morrison, Edgar Jepson and Baroness Orczy were among those who featured – but Berkeley, as Rhode said in his introduction to *Detection Medley*, was 'unfortunately . . . unable to contribute'. This seems odd, since Berkeley had written several short stories that would have been eminently suitable for inclusion. Possibly he had succumbed to the 'severe emotional strain' which, as he later confided in John Dickson Carr, was tormenting him. More likely, he was sulking over some imagined slight and opted out of the game like a moody child who takes his bat and ball home.

An unknown writer called Cameron McCabe played a unique and ingenious game with the Detection Club in *The Face on the Cutting-Room Floor*. A taut story, narrated by McCabe himself, grows rapidly in complexity following the discovery of an aspiring actress's body on a film studio's cutting room floor. In a lengthy epilogue, one of the characters, A. B. C. Muller (the initials are a nod to both Berkeley and Christie), apologises for his 'unwarranted intrusion into Mr McCabe's story' and proceeds to dissect it, with the help of quotations from a range of critics, include Sayers, Berkeley, Blake and Milward Kennedy.

The quotes, such as Kennedy's assertion that 'there is a world of difference between controlling your clues and interpreting those left by other people, and often, moreover, inadequately reported by other parties', are cunningly adapted to refer to McCabe's narrative. *Malice Aforethought* is discussed in this extraordinary segment, as is the fact that 'whistling in Germany is a sign of disapproval. It used to be, anyway, till Hitler came. Now it's all different, of course. There's no disapproval left. They've abolished it officially. You sure can't hear them whistle nowadays.'

Muller argues that 'the possibilities for alternative endings to *any* detective story are *infinite*', and the epilogue's finale is devised to demonstrate precisely that. The book winds up with a quotation from *Trent's Last Case*: 'As for attempts being made by malevolent persons to fix crimes upon innocent men, of course it is constantly happening. It's a marked feature, for instance, of all systems of rule by coercion. . . . If the police cannot get hold of a man they think dangerous by fair means, they do it by foul.'

In a pleasing twist of fate, Milward Kennedy was given the job of reviewing the book, and he loved it: 'If you are jaded from a surfeit of conventional detective stories or if you are persuaded that all detective stories are made from a conventional pattern, make haste to read *The Face on the Cutting-Room Floor*; and if you are neither, make haste to read it. . . . I have found it difficult to give any idea of it without spoiling it, and I would not do that for worlds.'

The McCabe pseudonym concealed the identity of Ernst Wilhelm Julius Bornemann, whose life was stranger than any fiction. A penniless teenage Marxist, he fled to England from Nazi Germany, and wrote *The Face on the Cutting-Room Floor* at the age of nineteen, as 'a finger exercise on the keyboard of a new language'. With the bravado of youth, he delivered his type-script in person to Victor Gollancz, because of his admiration for the Left Book Club, and Gollancz accepted it. After being interned as an enemy alien, Bornemann went to the United States, working as a jazz musician with Eartha Kitt, and in the film business for Orson Welles, before carving a reputation as a sexologist, whose credo was that 'you learn everything about life in bed with an interesting woman or – if you're gay – with a man.' At the age of eighty, he committed suicide with a cocktail of whisky and pills, following the collapse of an intense relationship with a beautiful woman less than half his age. None of his other books ventured into Golden Age territory, but Julian Symons judged *The Face on the Cutting-Room Floor* as a 'dazzling and perhaps fortunately unrepeatable box of tricks.'

Unrepeatable in that precise way, perhaps, but despite novelists' increasing focus on criminal psychology, many of them enjoyed playing literary games just as much as Carr and Bornemann. Writers like Richard Hull experimented with the form of the detective story throughout the Thirties, while Gollancz published Edward Powys Mather's *The Torquemada Puzzle Book*, which included *Cain's Jawbone*, a one-hundred-page detective story – with the pages printed in the wrong order. Each page was written so as to finish at the end of a sentence, and readers were invited to work out the names of the murderers and their victims, along with the correct page sequence. It sounds simple, but the idiosyncratic phrasing of the text makes solving the mystery fiendishly difficult. Despite offering a cash prize, Gollancz received only three correct answers.

Detective fans who loved playing games were spoiled for choice. The publishers Harrap produced 'jigsaw mysteries', while Collins promoted the Crime Club by marketing a card game dreamed up by Peter Cheyney, a Cockney who wrote hard-boiled thrillers in the American idiom. Another thriller writer, Dennis Wheatley, and J. G. Links, author of a renowned tourists' guide to Venice, carried the structural devices of *The Documents in the Case* and the Coles' *Burglars in Bucks* to their ultimate conclusion with four 'murder dossiers'. Each dossier was supplied in a cardboard folder with all the evidence and clues such

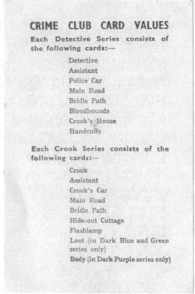

CRIME CLUB CARD VALUES

Each Detective Series consists of the following cards:—

Detective
Assistant
Police Car
Main Road
Bridle Path
Bloodhounds
Crook's House
Handcuffs

Each Crook Series consists of the following cards:—

Crook
Assistant
Crook's Car
Main Road
Bridle Path
Hide-out Cottage
Flashlamp
Loot (in Dark Blue and Green series only)
Body (in Dark Purple series only)

Examples from the Crime Club Card Game, devised by Peter Cheney.

ASSISTANT

ASSISTANT

JANET MURCH

ASSISTANT

ASSISTANT

SUPERINTENDENT BATTLE

CROOK

CROOK

Mr. EVANS

DETECTIVE

DETECTIVE

HERCULE POIROT

as 'poison pills', cigarette ends, used matchsticks and curls of hair. The solution was in a sealed section at the back of the folder. The dossiers, starting with *Murder Off Miami*, enjoyed a brief vogue, and Milward Kennedy called them a 'great game', although Howard Spring sneered, 'It is not for me to criticise *Murder Off Miami* any more than it would be for an art critic to criticise the artist's haystack'.

Three-quarters of a century later, we still love playing games. The structures of Golden Age detective fiction and the notion of 'rules of the game' inspire pastiche, parody, 'murder mystery parties' like those which John Dickson Carr hosted, and also hugely popular interactive games. Recent years have seen the arrival of mysteries that can be downloaded as apps, with viewers influencing plot developments via dedicated websites, receiving emails and mobile phone messages from characters in the drama, and being invited to attend 'events' in the story, which pop up in the calendar on their phones. It is only a question of time before cameras built into tablets read a viewer's facial expression, adjusting the story according to how they react to key dramatic moments in the plot. Back in the world of books, traditional whodunits have also inspired literary experiments from postmodernists such as Borges and Gilbert Adair. In *Who Killed Roger Ackroyd?* Pierre Bayard offered a dazzling alternative take on the Christie classic which, he argues, has fascinated the likes of Roland Barthes, Umberto Eco and Alain Robbe-Grillet, The detective story retains some claim to being, as Carr called it, 'the grandest game in the world.'

Notes to Chapter 29

he wrote an essay celebrating traditional detective stories, 'The Grandest Game in the World'
The essay was written in 1946, and a segment of it was published in an Ellery Queen anthology in 1963; the complete version finally appeared in a posthumous paperback edition of Carr's *The Door to Doom*.

Edward Powys Mathers
Edward Powys Mathers (1892–1939) translated *One Thousand and One Nights*, as well as love poems from Sanskrit. Some of his translations were set to music by the American composer Aaron Copland. He completed J. S. Fletcher's final novel, *Todmanhawe Grange*, after Fletcher's death, speaking in the introduction of his youthful enjoyment of the work of Fletcher and Austin Freeman. The prolific Fletcher (1863–1935) enjoyed a boost to his American sales when former President Woodrow Wilson said he was his favourite mystery writer.

J. B. Priestley, a professional Yorkshireman
John Boynton Priestley (1894–1964), a popular novelist, playwright and broadcaster, occasional dipped a toe in criminal waters: see Scowcroft, Philip, 'A Good Companion of Crime Fiction', *CADS* 10, January 1989.

her conversation-killing reply, 'At Marks and Spencer's stores.'
This resembles a remark in her introduction to *Passenger to Frankfurt*, a disappointing thriller written when her powers were fading, and Keating may have had that in mind.

the American poet and equal rights campaigner Muna Lee and a Shell oil executive, Maurice Guinness
Muna Lee was at this point married to Luis Muños Marin, a poet and politician who became known as 'the Father of Modern Puerto Rico'. A leading feminist, Lee contributed to the struggle for equal rights and was a founder of the Inter-American Commission of Women. Maurice Guinness was stationed in Puerto Rice when he met Lee. They became friends and decided to try collaborating on detective novels. Guinness thought up the plots and Lee did the bulk

of the writing. After five Newton Gayle novels, Lee gave up detective
fiction for good, while Guinness did not resume crime writing until
the Sixties, when he wrote three thrillers under the name Mike
Brewer. Perhaps he was inspired to return to the genre by a brief
acquaintance with Raymond Chandler, who at the time of his death
was engaged to Guinness's cousin, the literary agent Helga Greene.
In correspondence, Chandler and Guinness debated the pros and
cons of marrying off Philip Marlowe.

In Who Killed Roger Ackroyd? *Pierre Bayard offered a dazzling*
alternative take
Not to be confused with Edmund Wilson's essay 'Who Cares Who
Killed Roger Ackroyd?' Bayard, a French professor of literature, not
only cares, but seeks to demonstrate that the culprit identified in
Christie's original novel was not the true murderer.

30

The Work of a Pestilential Creature

Just before noon on a chilly June morning in 1937, a crowd of people at the barrier of Victoria Station watched as a group of latter-day pilgrims set off on a privately chartered train heading for Canterbury. Sayers had invited a party of guests, including Helen Simpson, Dennis Browne and Muriel St Clair Byrne to see the premiere of her new play. Lunch would be provided on the train. As usual, Sayers did not miss a chance to publicize her work. Because she was attending a dress rehearsal, she could not be present at Victoria to greet her guests. Sticking to her credo that murder must advertise, she asked her secretary, Dorothy Lake, to wait at the barrier with the tickets – flourishing a copy of *Busman's Honeymoon*. The shocking yellow dust jacket, with its vivid violet and black typography, was guaranteed to grab people's attention.

The play her guests would watch was not a work of detection. Religious dramas staged during the Canterbury Festival, notably T. S. Eliot's *Murder in the Cathedral* two years earlier, had enjoyed huge success, and although Sayers was not known as a religious writer, she had been commissioned to produce a new work for performance in Canterbury Cathedral. The result was *The Zeal of Thy House*, telling the story of William of Sens, a twelfth-century architect who rebuilt the central portion of the Cathedral after a devastating fire, but whose pride led to a fall when he crashed fifty feet from shoddily constructed scaffolding. Pride, integrity and the nature of creative imagination were among Sayers' themes. An amateur film-maker shot footage of characters in the play, and also of Sayers. For June, the wind was bitter, and the author was draped in furs, but she beamed for the camera, looking radiantly happy. She felt she had found her vocation.

Religion mattered to Sayers, and many of her Detection Club colleagues were regular worshippers. They had firm opinions about good and evil, though Christie devoted little space to spiritual reflection, even in *The Murder at the Vicarage*. Henry Wade and his family went to see *The Zeal of Thy House*, and Sayers introduced them to members of the cast – but there was one conspicuous absentee from the pilgrimage to Canterbury. Mac Fleming complained that Sayers was never at home, and spent his time in the Red Lion rather than at church. Sayers simply got on with her life without him. She invested time and money in organizing a provincial tour of the play at her own expense, and raised funds by writing advertising copy for Horlick's Malted Milk. When *The Times* teased her about this, she fired off an indignant letter in reply. Since the Church would not invest in the tour, she said, she had 'unblushingly soaked Mammon'.

The tour was a flop. People were too preoccupied with the gathering international storm to bother with the new play, and Sayers made a heavy loss. When overwork and disappointment left her in need of a break, she set off on a cruise of the Dalmatian coast with a woman friend, rather than her husband. The marriage continued to stagger along, without quite collapsing, and Sayers found relief from domestic unhappiness by exploring religious themes in her writing.

Her next drama was written for the Canterbury Festival of 1939. *The Devil to Pay* was a Faustian pact story about the battle between good and evil. The theme was perfectly in keeping with the preoccupations of the day. Yet the timing was disastrous, as the play's run coincided with the outbreak of war. Gladys Mitchell was among the few who managed to catch the play before it vanished from the stage, seldom to return.

The BBC commissioned a radio play from her, with Val

Gielgud as producer. John Rhode listened on the wireless in (where else?) his local pub on Christmas Day, and wrote to tell Sayers how much he and his fellow drinkers had enjoyed it. The plays' succcess encouraged her to write more, although she was still telling correspondents that she hoped to write another Wimsey story 'before long'.

Sayers formed a strong friendship with Val Gielgud, a man who packed a good deal into his life, including five marriages. A flamboyant figure who would have made an excellent suspect, or sleuth, in a detective novel, he had a goatee beard and often wore a cloak and carried a swordstick. He kept writing crime novels, on his own as well as with Eric Maschwitz, and after John Dickson Carr invited him to a Detection Club dinner, Gielgud encouraged Carr to start writing for radio. Carr, like Sayers, was soon bitten by the bug.

Despite the deaths of Canon Victor Whitechurch and G. K. Chesterton, the Detection Club still numbered among its members prominent Christians such as Sayers, Knox, Helen Simpson and Freeman Wills Crofts. Crofts identified with the Oxford Group, a loose association of the spiritually motivated, but Sayers rebuffed him when he tried to enlist her backing, telling him that 'as an English Catholic' she found some aspects of the Group's thinking distasteful. Years later, when Crofts published *The Four Gospels as One Story, written as a modern biography*, Knox, who did not approve of 'rearranging' the Gospels, confided in Sayers that he had refused to write a review. Christian faith could divide as well as unite.

With military preparations gathering pace, an American minister, Frank Buchman, who had formed the Oxford Group seven years earlier, declared that the time had come for *moral* rearmament. From this grew Moral Rearmament, an international movement now known as Initiatives for Change. Crofts concluded that Moral Rearmament was 'the only way of tackling the problem of crime at its root', and his detective novels increasingly reflected his beliefs, emphasizing that crime does not pay. *Antidote to Venom* was intended as a twofold experiment. First,

Crofts combined an inverted crime story with a straight account of police detection by Inspector French. Second, it was 'an effort to tell a story of crime positively'. Milward Kennedy was puzzled by the phrase, but Crofts meant he was writing a detective story with a clear moral purpose.

George Surridge is the respected Director of Birmington Zoo, but his marriage is unhappy and his precarious finances are compromised by a gambling habit. When he falls for a demure widow, he harbours thoughts of murdering an elderly aunt from whom he expects to inherit. The aunt dies of natural causes, but her solicitor has stolen her assets, leaving George in deep trouble. He finds himself sucked into a criminal conspiracy to kill someone else in order to recoup his losses. The zoo background is crucial to the plot, as the victim is killed by snake venom. But the precise method by which the murder is committed remains obscure until Inspector French – more receptive here than usual to 'psychology' – starts to investigate. A page of the book is devoted to diagrams clarifying the complicated means of murder.

The moral is that George faced a choice of doing right or wrong, and not, as George saw it, between two evils. At the end of the book, however, George finds redemption in God. Venom is to be found, as the chapter titles make clear, not only in snakes but in many different aspects of human life. For Crofts, the 'antidote to venom' is the love of God. George has sinned, but he is able to find redemption, and 'a peace he had never known before', despite having to pay the price demanded by the law for what he has done.

The story suffers from Crofts' limited skills of characterization. Nancy, the woman for whom George risks everything, is a cipher, and when George's haughty wife Clarissa mends her ways at the end of the book, the effect is unconvincing. Overall, *Antidote for Venom* was an ambitious but flawed attempt to write detective fiction with a religious message at its core. If Sayers had attempted something similar, the result might have been memorable, but the boldness of Crofts' unique experiment attracted less attention than it deserved.

Carr, Christie and Crofts were, like Wade, writing with as much energy as ever. But along with Berkeley, Sayers and Kennedy, some other Detection Club members were losing their love of the game. Life was becoming too serious for novelists whose only interest in crime lay in its possibilities for creating puzzles.

Evelyn Waugh, biographer of Ronald Knox, acknowledged that Knox 'had no concerns with the passions of the murderer, the terror of the victim, or the moral enormity of the crime'. His best novel, *The Body in the Silo*, was a quintessential country house mystery, complete with a map, a cipher based on an early form of shorthand, and clue-finder footnotes. The Bredons become involved in an 'elopement hunt', a variant of the 'scavenger hunts' popular in the Thirties, only for one of their fellow guests to be found dead in the hosts' grain silo. The culprit kills the wrong person by mistake, and eventually dies as a result of a further mishap while trying to target the originally intended victim. The paradoxes are reminiscent of Chesterton, but Knox was never able to write a detective novel matching the satiric brilliance of 'Broadcasting from the Barricades'. His career in crime ended with a whimper thanks to an incident on a Hellenic cruise.

Sailing the Mediterranean, Knox's most devoted admirer, Lady Acton, read the fifth and final Miles Bredon novel, *Double Cross Purposes*. She was so unimpressed that she hurled the book into the sea – together with her lipstick (Knox disliked women wearing 'paint'). Knox's bishop was equally dubious about his indulgence in criminal frivolity, and within a couple years Knox left the Oxford chaplaincy to become chaplain on the Actons' estate at Aldenham, where he concentrated on translating *The Bible* afresh from Latin. He remained incurably frivolous, and claimed that, in an audience with the Pope, they spent half an hour talking about the Loch Ness Monster.

Detective fiction darkened in tone, reflecting the mood of the nation. Yet even during the Twenties, a strong sense of evil had pervaded H. C. Bailey's writing. Bailey was that rare beast, a shy journalist, and he preferred to spend time at home with his wife and daughter rather than out carousing with Carr and company in the Detection Club. His stories were admired by Sayers and Christie, and reflected his powerful moral sense. In stark contrast to Ronald Knox, Bailey believed that 'if detective stories are concerned with crime, they are serious,' and although some of his short stories featuring Reggie Fortune were light-hearted, others were bleak and unforgiving of cruelty, especially where the victims were children or vulnerable adults.

Reggie is driven by humanity and sympathy for the underdog. According to Bailey, 'He holds by the standard principles of conduct and responsibility, of right and wrong, of sin and punishment. He does not always accept the law of a case as justice, and has been known to act on his own responsibility in contriving the punishment of those who could not legally be found guilty or the immunity of those who were not legally innocent. A cruel crime is to him the work of a pestiliential creature. . . . There is no more mercy for the cruel criminal than for the germs of disease.' This might equally have been Connington, speaking about Sir Clinton Driffield.

Shadow on the Wall, the first Fortune novel, elaborated on this theme. At a Buckingham Palace garden party, his friend Lomas, chief of the CID at Scotland Yard, tells Reggie about a vindictive letter sent to the child of a woman who has committed suicide, and strange events at a fancy dress party are followed by the death of a malicious gossip. Step by step, he uncovers a conspiracy of cruelty, occasionally wandering into his laboratory and using medical and scientific expertise to analyse doped champagne or a blood smear on wood, but more often relying on his supposedly 'simple mind' to examine the evidence. Bailey had much less faith in science than Austin Freeman or Connington.

The final scenes, as Reggie confronts a culprit riven with hatred, and Bailey draws a parallel between cruelty and cancer, are as compelling as any in a Golden Age novel. The comparison between the shadow on the wall that Fortune sees at the fancy dress party, and the shadow on the killer's lung, is unforgettable. Bailey's moral sense causes the murderer to be betrayed by a failure to allow for the fundamental decency of other people. 'That's the real force of progress,' Fortune says in the final paragraph, 'The common man's common virtues. Not the eminent expert.'

Bailey's loathing of cruelty is an enduring strength of his writing. The trouble with *Shadow on the Wall*, and his work as a whole, is that sound plotting and strong themes, intelligently explored, are shrouded in a fog of literary mannerisms. Fortune moans, murmurs and mumbles along, sighing regularly and harping on so much about his 'simple mind' that he risks becoming tedious. For awareness of his own brilliance, he ranks with Holmes and Poirot, but without some of their redeeming qualities. Bailey had a great deal of interest to say, but he became too ponderous about how he said it.

Crofts and Bailey, both born in the Victorian age, believed in moral absolutes. The younger generation of crime writers grappled with moral ambiguities. Nicholas Blake explored the obsessive nature of revenge and the working of a guilty conscience in *The Beast Must Die*, which offers both a study in psychological complexity and a crafty game played with story structure. This memorable book, later filmed by Claude Chabrol, echoes Henry Wade's *Mist on the Saltings* in its bleak mood and grim finale. The first section of the book is narrated by detective novelist Felix Lane, who pays due tribute to his 'colleagues in the thriller racket', John Dickson Carr, Gladys Mitchell and Berkeley. The opening paragraph is as striking as Berkeley's best: 'I am going to kill a man. I don't know his name, I don't know where he lives, I have no idea what he looks like. But I am going to find him and kill him.'

Lane's beloved son has been killed in a hit-and-run accident, and he sets about tracing the reckless motorist. In the second section of the book, written in the third person, Lane's scheme is discovered by his quarry, and in the third section, once murder has occurred, Nigel Strangeways is brought into the picture, with a view to establishing Lane's innocence. An ingenious plot is unravelled in the fourth section and, as with the culprit in Wade's novel, the murderer's conscience does not allow the punishment of someone innocent.

The Beast Must Die is one of the few Golden Age novels where a child is a key figure in the story, and the clever way Blake combines a kind of 'inverted' crime novel and traditional detection is complemented by compelling characterization. Like Christie in *The Murder of Roger Ackroyd*, and Richard Hull in *Murder of My Aunt* and *Murder Isn't Easy*, an interesting if flawed novel set in the world of advertising, Blake exploits the trust the reader places in a first-person narrator, in a classic example of tricky storytelling technique.

Along with Margery Allingham and Michael Innes, Blake was one of the 'young masters' acclaimed by John Strachey in his seminal article for *The Saturday Review*, 'The Golden Age of English Detection'. Describing himself as a 'steady student' of the detective novel, Strachey argued that 'some of these detective novels are far better jobs, on any account, than are nine-tenths of the more pretentious and ambitious highbrow novels'. Although he disliked Sayers' *Gaudy Night*, he thought *Murder Must Advertise* and *The Nine Tailors* 'glow with a vitality which, in spite of their absurdities, justified her vast success'.

For Strachey, like so many of his contemporaries, detective fiction offered much-needed escape from grim reality and dread about what the future might hold. Knowing that his name appeared on a Nazi death list, he had a suicide pill prepared. If Germany invaded Britain, he expected to be tortured before being killed, and suicide seemed preferable. These fears did not seem fantastic – they were shared by other left-wing intellectuals. His sister Amabel Williams-Ellis, wife of the architect who built the fantasy Italian-style village of Portmeirion in North Wales, also kept a suicide pill. Strachey and his sister never needed to kill themselves, but Brecht's friend, the German Marxist Walter Benjamin, took a fatal dose of morphine to avoid falling into the hands of the Nazis.

The late Lord Balfour was reputed to read one detective story a night, and Franklin D. Roosevelt was a fan, leading Strachey to wonder whether their literary taste was shared by Neville Chamberlain, and to add the withering comment that perhaps the Prime Minister never felt 'any need of escape from the world of which he is so largely the architect; for he sees nothing wrong with such a world'.

Two thriller writers who did see a great deal wrong with the world were making their mark, and both men saw the answers in terms of politics rather than religion or moralizing. Their attitudes were very different from the reactionary worldviews of popular contemporaries Sapper, Phillips Oppenheim and Dornford Yates. Both were elected to the Detection Club after the Second World War, when Sayers, Berkeley and their colleagues saw that everything had changed, including crime fiction.

Paul Winterton, a journalist who became well-known for thrillers written as Andrew Garve, started with *Death Beneath Jerusalem*, published under the pseudonym of Roger Bax. The story is set in a tense pre-war Jerusalem, with the British military struggling to contain the threat of Arab insurrection. Anyone reading the story with an open mind at the time would struggle to believe that the British Mandate for Palestine could be sustained.

Eric Ambler, the son of music hall artistes who ran a puppet show, dropped out of an engineering course, and joined an advertising agency – one of the few things, other than membership of the Detection Club, which his career had in common with Sayers'. He was only thirty when *The Mask of Dimitrios* appeared in 1939, but by then he had already published four novels, travelled widely, and become a fervent anti-Fascist. Ambler wrote short stories about an amateur sleuth called Dr Czissar, but he believed conventional detective fiction failed to reflect the darkness of Europe in the late Thirties. His protagonist, Charles Latimer, is a sort of Douglas Cole with added vim, a lecturer on political economy who becomes a detective novelist. On a visit to Istanbul, Latimer meets Colonel Haki, a detective story fan, who offers him a plot in which the butler did it, and who also provokes his interest in a real murderer – a shadowy villain called Dimitrios, whose corpse has just been pulled out of the Bosphorus.

Latimer has never either seen a dead man or a mortuary, and because 'every detective story writer should see those things', he persuades Haki to take him to inspect the body. Haki's dossier on Dimitrios has mystifying gaps, and Latimer becomes obsessed with the idea of 'an experiment in detection', in which he travels around talking to people who might be able to provide him with material for 'the strangest of biographies'. Soon Latimer is zigzagging across the Continent, encountering a string of sinister informants as his quest for the truth becomes increasingly dangerous.

The moral landscape is bleaker than the Fenland of Fenchurch St Paul, the neat solutions of the detective genre conspicuous by their absence. Latimer's friend Marukakis explains that a ruthless criminal like Dimitrios exists 'because big business, his master, needs him. International big business may conduct its operations with scraps of paper, but the ink it uses is human *blood*!' Latimer realizes that Dimitrios cannot be explained in terms of good and evil: 'Good Business and Bad Business were the new theology. . . . The logic of Michaelangelo's *David*, Beethoven's quartets and Einstein's physics had been replaced by that of the *Stock Exchange Year Book* and Hitler's *Mein Kampf*.'

With gloomy wit, Latimer imagines how a judge would condemn his meddling in affairs he does not understand. At the end of the book he returns to escapism, thinking about his next mystery: 'There was always plenty of fun to be got out of an English country village, wasn't there? . . . Summer, with cricket matches on the village green, garden parties at the vicarage, the clink of teacups and the sweet smell of grass on a July evening. That was the sort of thing people liked to hear about.'

The power and energy of Ambler's prose took readers' breath away, and he was one of the first British crime writers to tackle the fracturing of the moral certainties to which Christie, Crofts and others clung. Interestingly, Anthony Berkeley was among his early admirers. Yet Ambler's time passed, just like that of the dons who wrote detective stories for amusement. He was disheartened by the Nazi–Soviet pact, and his growing estrangement from the politics of the left culminated in tax exile in Switzerland. Eventually, his pessimistic world view became oddly reminiscent of the disillusionment that tormented Berkeley.

Notes to Chapter 30

the Detection Club still numbered among its members prominent Christians
Canon Whitechurch and Father Knox were not the only Golden Age novelists in holy orders. Cyril Argentine Alington (1872–1955), a former royal chaplain who became Dean of Durham in 1933, dabbled in the genre, and was a member of the panel tasked with selecting titles for publication by Collins Crime Club. James Reginald Spittal (1876–1951) was a vicar whose third, and regrettably final, whodunit, *Casual Slaughters* (1935), starts and ends with a meeting of a parochial church council.

the 'scavenger hunts' popular in the Thirties
'Scavenger hunts' take various forms, but typically involve a competition to see who can collect a set of specified objects the quickest. Knox was fascinated by games of this kind, and his *Double Cross Purposes* features a treasure hunt in the Highland countryside.

a strong sense of evil had pervaded H. C. Bailey's writing
My account of Bailey's life and work has benefited from the research of Barry Pike, author of a series of articles about the Reggie Fortune stories in *CADS* from May 2011 to date, and of Tom Schantz, whose Rue Morgue Press has reprinted some of Bailey's books. See also Nicholas Fuller, 'The Moral and Social Dramas of H. C. Bailey', *CADS* 54, July 2008. For a powerful example of Bailey's journalism, see 'Hitler's Grim Six-Year Record in Technique of Perfidy', *Daily Telegraph*, 4 September 1939.

For Strachey, like so many of his contemporaries, detective fiction offered much-needed escape from grim reality
The genre's unlikely fans included Ludwig Wittgenstein, who favoured American fiction but had a soft spot for Agatha Christie; see Josef Hoffmann, 'PI Wittgenstein and Language-Games from Detective Stories', *CADS* 48, October 2005.

31

Frank to the Point of Indecency

John Dickson Carr was as far apart from Ambler in his political sympathies as in his writing, but the brewing international crisis troubled every member of the Detection Club, and it cast a shadow over *The Reader is Warned*, published under his pen name Carter Dickson. The mysterious Herman Pennik claims to be a thought-reader who can kill without leaving any sign, external or internal, of murder. At a country house party, Pennik forecasts that the host, the husband of a mystery writer, will die before dinner – and the man's corpse is duly found, with no indication as to cause of death.

When Pennik predicts the death of the author, and she dies in similarly mysterious fashion, the concept of murder by 'Teleforce' is seized on by the newspapers and becomes an international sensation. People wonder if Hitler and Mussolini could be disposed of by thought waves, and if bombers can be knocked out of the air by the same invisible death-rays. Pennik's confidence that he cannot be convicted of any crime seems rash, but Carr's second-string sleuth, Sir Henry Merrivale, deduces that the man is a cat's-paw.

With Teleforce debunked, at the end of the book Merrivale strikes a positive and defiant note for the benefit of Carr's anxious readers: 'When you hear about these super-planes, these super-weaknesses on our side, think of Teleforce too. This tendency to believe anything puts a leerin' face on people. . .

there never was much room for Voodoo here.' Carr's treatment of racial issues – in a storyline touching on Bantu fetishism – is of its time, but steers clear of bigotry. Perhaps uniquely in Golden Age fiction, the catalyst for the crimes is the first victim's casual racism.

Carr captured the mood of fear as war loomed. Just as in 1914, Sherlock Holmes had told Watson that an east wind was coming, cold and bitter, so there was a chill in the air as the Thirties drew to a close. In February 1939, the premature death of Torquemada, whose reviews, crosswords and detective puzzle-novella reflected the game-playing spirit of the Golden Age, seemed to symbolize the end of an era. Unemployment had fallen from its peak, but poverty remained commonplace, and the bleakness of life for working-class people in the industrial north of England was evoked in the first half of George Orwell's *The Road to Wigan Pier*, published by the Left Book Club in 1937.

Perhaps the reason why working-class Northerners rarely featured in Golden Age mysteries was because little about their lives seemed either golden or mysterious. The second half of Orwell's book was a controversial essay, questioning attitudes towards socialism. When he could not persuade Orwell to cut out the second half of the book, Gollancz tried to subvert it by writing an explanatory introduction, This was an error of judgment, although not on the same scale as his choice of Josef Stalin as his 'Man of the Year'.

Unexpectedly, it was Henry Wade who explored the stresses felt by poor people encountering the forces of law and order at the sharp end. As a slice of social history, *Released for Death* is not in Orwell's league, but Wade's sympathy for people under pressure is not patronizing. He traces the misadventures of a cat burglar, Toddy Shaw, released from prison only to resume his criminal career with disastrous results. When Toddy is charged with a murder he did not commit, he realizes that he has been set up. At one point, the ambitious young PC John Bragg admits to his wife that as part of his duties he is trying to win the affections of a woman who has given the real culprit an alibi. The scene is superfluous to the plot, but Wade's willingness to show a junior officer juggling his responsibilities at work and at home signposted how the police story might develop in years to come.

Wade surpassed himself in *Lonely Magdalen*, making imaginative use of a downbeat storyline. The novel is an innovatively structured account of a police investigation into the strangling of a scarred prostitute on Hampstead Heath. The first section follows Inspector Poole's efforts to uncover the victim's true identity, while the second steps back twenty-five years, from the brink of one world war to the brink of another, describing the poignant sequence of events that cost her a life of privilege. The final section, returning to 1939, sees a culprit identified, but Wade does not flinch from showing police brutality, while an extraordinary last-paragraph tease hints that Poole mistakenly helped to send an innocent man to the gallows. The two-way journey in time is handled adroitly, and the portrayal of life in different strata of society, and the corrosive and never-ending consequences of war, is compelling. The result was not remotely cosy or humdrum. Wade had written the finest and darkest police novel of the Golden Age.

Christie's response to the gathering storm was to deluge her readers with escapist entertainment. Finding herself trapped in the lift at the Carrs' apartment block may have inspired her to devise an 'impossible crime' novel of her own, set at a homicidal country house Christmas party. At first, Christie called the book *Blood Feast*, and a key element is the double interpretation of the Shakespearean epigraph, 'Yet who would have thought the old man to have had so much blood in him?' The novel became *Hercule Poirot's Christmas*, and includes one of her slickest pieces of misdirection. When Poirot questions an elderly butler about a wall calendar, causing the butler to peer at it from close range, the reader assumes that this is a clue about a significant date, but in fact the crucial piece of information is that the butler is very short-sighted.

Leafing through the *Evening Standard*, Anthony Berkeley spotted a review of Christie's book by Howard Spring which gave away the ending. Outraged, he told Carr that Spring had spoiled the story for readers: 'You're Secretary of the Club. You must write to him and complain.' Carr readily agreed, but an unrepentant Spring retorted that books like Christie's were trash. Sayers was infuriated, possibly recalling that Spring had once compared her advocacy of detective fiction to an advertising man selling toilet rolls. She insisted that the question was not about literary merit, but about whether a reviewer was entitled to ruin a reader's enjoyment of a puzzle. Spring's attitude seems churlish, given that only four years earlier he had rhapsodized about detective fiction in a foreword to an anthology including stories by Christie and Sayers. Did he become jealous of their greater fame? Carr fictionalized this spat in *The Case of the Constant Suicides*, and the episode illustrated the solidarity between Detection Club members, and the genuine regard in which her friends held Christie.

The culprits in *Hercule Poirot's Christmas* and her next book, *Murder is Easy*, are splendidly unexpected. Christie had an unsentimental determination to outwit her readers and prove that in a detective novel *nobody* is ever above suspicion. Over the years, her murderers included a child, the person presumed to be the killer's intended victim, one of the apparent victims in a series of murders, the entire cast of suspects, a pillar of the British establishment, a police officer, a narrator, a Dr Watson figure, a spinster reminiscent of Miss Marple – and Hercule Poirot himself. It is striking how many Great Detectives were prepared to commit murder themselves – in order to do justice, in the widest sense, naturally.

The sunset of the Golden Age yielded the ultimate masterpiece of traditional detective fiction. *And Then There Were None*, published two months after the outbreak of war, is Christie's most stunning achievement. Ten people are invited by a mysterious stranger to a small island; one by one, they are killed, until no one is left alive. The murders followed the pattern of an old nursery rhyme, a conceit first used by S. S. Van Dine in

The Bishop Murder Case. This idea worked so well that Christie introduced nursery rhymes into several later novels, although never again did she integrate the device so perfectly with story-line and theme.

Christie was at the peak of her powers, and set herself twin aims – to test herself as a creator of ever more ingenious plots, and to enthral her readers by presenting them with a bewildering mystery. The solution, revealed in an epilogue, is dazzling. As in *Murder on the Orient Express*, Christie is using the classic whodunit form to explore how to secure justice for innocent victims when the conventional legal system fails to do its job. Yet the subtext never gets in the way of the story. Christie was not as cynical about the legal status quo as Berkeley, but she had a genuine passion for justice.

As for the Woman was the third and final book which Berkeley published as Francis Iles. 'I wrote the book at a time of severe emotional strain,' he confessed to John Dickson Carr. His relationship with Helen was disintegrating, and his powers as a novelist were failing. The last detective story published under the Berkeley name, *Death in the House*, was feeble. The ingredients of an impossible crime, a Challenge to the Reader, and a House of Commons setting were enticing, but the writing is lifeless. The man who for years wrote with imagination, ingenuity and industry was running out of steam. *As for the Woman* is in many ways a remarkable novel, but suffered because Berkeley prioritized paying off scores in his personal life rather than entertainment. There was no puzzle to solve, and few flashes of his trademark wit. Delivering a fatal blow to Berkeley's fragile confidence, Victor Gollancz stunned him by turning it down, saying: 'It is too sadistic.'

Jarrolds, a less prestigious imprint, agreed to publish the book. As if determined to give it the kiss of death, they supplied a dust jacket blurb which proclaimed that the novel was 'not a thriller', and added alarmingly that it was 'not intended to thrill'. The blurb, a case study in missing the point, continued: 'It is no more, and at the same time no less, than a sincere attempt to depict the love of a young, inexperienced man for a woman much older than himself, with all its idealism, its heart burnings, and its inevitable disappointments.' To make matters worse, the title page describes the book as 'a love story'. The copy might have been drafted by Berkeley's worst enemy. Perhaps he upset someone at Jarrolds.

The dismissive phrase 'as for the woman' had been used by the judge in referring to Edith Thompson shortly before he sentenced her to death. Berkeley returned to his theme that guilt and innocence are as much a matter of chance as of design. It was a subject that obsessed him. He wanted to show how a murder – like that of Percy Thompson – might happen almost by accident, as a horrifying form of wish-fulfilment.

Berkeley's protagonist, Alan Littlewood, is an Oxford undergraduate who, while convalescing from illness, becomes infatuated with a doctor's wife. Having won his sympathy by confiding that her husband makes her indulge in perversions, she proceeds to seduce him. In a weird and suggestive sequence, Alan is persuaded by his lover to disguise himself as a girl, and goes on the run in women's clothing. She has a masochistic streak, and that disturbing touch of inadequately suppressed violence towards women so characteristic of Berkeley surfaces once more. The book offers an insight into what passed for explicit sexual action immediately before the Second World War. Tame as the sex scenes seem in the age of *Fifty Shades of Grey*, the book was judged 'frank to the point of indecency' by author and critic J. D. Beresford, who twenty years earlier had recommended Collins to take Freeman Wills Crofts' *The Cask*.

Jarrolds announced the forthcoming publication of a book called *On His Deliverance*, and a Berkeley novel called *Poison Pipe* was also supposed to appear in 1941, but neither was published, and no trace of the manuscripts has been found. Berkeley had burned out. Like Sayers, he was finished as a detective novelist, but for a very different reason.

The times were changing. A terrifying novel by an illustrious founder member of the Detection Club showed the way forward for novelists of psychological suspense who wanted to explore the nature of evil. This groundbreaking novel was written not by Bailey or Blake or Berkeley, but by Hugh Walpole. The idea for the story obsessed him 'as no idea for a book ever has done' for three years before he wrote out a synopsis in 1937, the year he was knighted. With the unquenchable optimism of someone born, or doomed, to be a writer, Walpole thought the book 'will undoubtedly write itself and should be *my* best macabre and one of the best ever *if* it comes out right'. Yet like many brilliant ideas for novels, it proved challenging to execute, and he did not finish work on the book until the Luftwaffe was blitzing London. Ill health had taken hold, and a coronary thrombosis killed Walpole a few months before *The Killer and the Slain* saw the light of day.

The concept of *The Killer and the Slain* was simple but superb. A prissy novelist, John Ozias Talbot is driven to murder an old schoolfriend, but gradually metamorphoses, physically and morally, into his degenerate tormentor, James Oliphant Tunstall. Split personalities fascinated Walpole so much that he was surely intrigued by Anthony Berkeley. This probably explains why Talbot's finest book bears a striking resemblance to *Before the Fact*. Walpole, almost as much a true crime buff as Berkeley, drew on a real-life criminal case, the trial of one John Tunstall for attacking his wife's lover. On one level, Tunstall's crudity and character flaws reflect Adolf Hitler's, and in the final section of the book Walpole launches a searing attack on the cruelty of Nazism. Beyond the political message, there is a timeless aspect to this sexually charged riff on the Jekyll and Hyde theme, in which heterosexual and homosexual passions are conveyed subtly but with genuine power. Publication in wartime, with the author already cold in his grave, meant that *The Killer and the Slain* was destined for obscurity. The final tragedy of Walpole's life was that his posthumous masterpiece never received the acclaim it deserved.

Notes to Chapter 31

his choice of Josef Stalin as his 'Man of the Year'
Gollancz was invited to choose his Man of the Year by *Cavalcade* magazine in November 1937, and explained that Stalin 'is safely guiding Russia on the road to a society in which there will be no exploitation'. Gollancz was not alone in his misplaced enthusiasm for the Russian leader. Maxim Litvinov, a former Bolshevik revolutionary, accepted an appointment as Stalin's Commissar of People's Affairs in 1932; in the same year, Litvinov's London-born wife Ivy (1889–1977) published *His Master's Voice*, although her publishers advised her not to use the Litvinov name, since 'readers of detective fiction prefer an English author'. American publishers rejected the book, one reader saying: 'We advise Ivy Low to cut out the stuff about spring over the Kremlin, and put in another murder or two.' A couple of years later, Ivy entertained Margaret Cole to afternoon tea when a party of socialist thinkers visited Soviet Russia, following Labour's general election wipe-out, to learn how society ought to be run. Ivy wrote no more mysteries, and Margaret Cole justly described her solo effort as 'odd'. Maxim and Ivy both had Jewish origins, and after the war Stalin had Maxim killed when it suited him to indulge in a campaign of anti-Semitism. Maxim's last words to Ivy were, reputedly, 'Englishwoman, go home.'

As if determined to give it the kiss of death, they supplied a dust jacket blurb which proclaimed that the novel was 'not a thriller'
The jacket artwork itself, which featured a bland rural landscape, was utilized by Jarrolds for other books, an act of frugality uncommon among even the most parsimonious publishers.

J. D. Beresford, who twenty years earlier recommended Collins to take Freeman Wills Crofts' The Cask
John Davys Beresford (1873–1947) was a versatile writer admired by Orwell among others. He occasionally wrote detective fiction, although his best-known novel, *The Hampdenshire Wonder* (1911), is science fiction. His daughter Elisabeth, a children's writer, created the Wombles of Wimbledon Common. His son Marcus changed his name to Marc Brandel, had an improbable fling with the lesbian writer and later Detection Club member Patricia Highsmith, and went on to publish a handful of crime novels and to write screenplays for television series such as *Burke's Law*.

32

Shocked by the Brethren

As the threat posed by Hitler intensified, Sayers volunteered her services to the War Office. She was invited to join a committee tasked with briefing authors about how they could best help in the event of war. Other members included A. P. Herbert and the novelist and critic L. A. G. Strong, who later contributed dialogue to a film version of *Busman's Honeymoon* that Sayers refused to watch. The secretary to the committee was A. D. Peters, the first husband of Berkeley's second wife. Sayers became as frustrated by the inefficiency of the civil servants as by the BBC when masterminding *Behind the Screen* and *The Scoop*. The Ministry of Information, like Joe Ackerley, found her impossible to work with, and an internal memo described her as 'very difficult and loquacious'. Before long, she and the Ministry parted company.

The 'phoney war' following Neville Chamberlain's announcement that Great Britain was at a state of war with Germany was nicely evoked in Dorothy Bowers' *Deed without a Name*. Chamberlain had not only announced the beginning of war, but also, in effect, the end of the Golden Age of detective fiction, less than nine months after John Strachey introduced the term. Nothing would be the same again.

The BBC broadcast a series of plays by Berkeley and other members in 1940, the Detection Club's last significant venture for years. The Blitz meant dinner meetings were no longer feasible, and Punshon wryly dedicated *Ten Star Clues*, which he was composing at the time, 'to THE SIREN whose irresistible song so often lured the writer from his work'. Punshon remained in London, as did Anthony Gilbert, who told Sayers that she did not think Punshon would be 'put out by a bomb. I feel [the bomb] would go in another direction if it realised he was near by.' In October, Sayers wrote to Gilbert, saying she thought the Club's premises in Gerrard Street were still standing, if only because nobody had told her otherwise. She urged Gilbert to put the Minute Book and some of the prints that hung on the walls in a place of greater safety, but admitted that it was difficult to know where would be safer. It was a frightening time.

Sayers and the Club suffered a cruel blow with the death, at the age of forty-two, of Helen Simpson. Sayers had noticed her friend's face gradually 'getting smaller and smaller', a grim clue to an inoperable cancer. At the convalescent home where she died, Simpson told the sister how much she admired Sayers. Shocked by the loss of the vibrant and gifted Australian, Sayers wrote a poignant obituary for *The Spectator*. The death of the woman with whom she had discussed in depth her plans for *Thrones, Dominations* was the final nail in the coffin of that last projected Wimsey novel.

After Simpson's death, Sayers concentrated on translation and religious work, such as *The Mind of the Maker*, a study of creativity from a Christian perspective. *The Man Born to Be King*, a radio drama produced by Val Gielgud, was highly successful, although some conservative Christians disliked it, and some even suggested that the fall of Singapore was a sign of God's displeasure with the portrayal of Christ by a human actor. Sayers' personal view was that her finest achievement was her translation of Dante's *Divine Comedy*.

Club funds were severely depleted, causing a problem with the payment of rent to the landlord in Gerrard Street, 'J. P. Isaia, Human Hair Merchant, Importer and Exporter', who sounds rather like a shady character in a novel by one of the members. Emergency donations of two pounds per head were sought, although Margaret Cole improbably pleaded poverty. Thieves broke into the premises, but they did not bother to steal a motley collection of items including a chiffonier and other bits of furniture, together with saucepans, china tea, beer, and the Club library. Once the war was over, the Detection Club met again, but the miseries of war had taken their toll. John Dickson Carr found the occasion chastening: 'The brethren shocked me by looking much greyer and more worn.' He was dismayed that Sayers was devoting herself to Dante, but although he and Henry Wade tried to persuade her to write more detective fiction, their pleas fell on deaf ears.

Carr told Frederic Dannay, who now combined fiction with editing the highly influential *Ellery Queen's Mystery Magazine*, that the Club was finding it difficult to gain new members of distinction. In the United States, the private eye novels of Hammett and Chandler had overtaken elaborate whodunits in popularity, although Ellery Queen moved with the times. The Queen novels became less ornately plotted and artificial, but the Detection Club's influence persisted. The plot of *Calamity Town*, first of the more naturalistic Queen stories, was a remix of *Before the Fact*, with a hint of *Peril at End House* and a few drops of *Strong Poison*.

Carr told Dannay in 1946 that the Detection Club had ceased to function, but he was wrong. Seven new members were elected over the next couple of years, although Dorothy Bowers, widely seen as a worthy successor to Sayers, died young of tuberculosis. She learned from Sayers that she had been elected to join the remaining members (she was told there were twenty-two; there may have been unrecorded resignations, as well as deaths), and wrote a poignant letter to a friend, hoping – in vain, as it proved – that her health would recover to allow her to take part in her initiation ritual and resume her writing: 'Much as I'd welcome greater financial success for my books, I do appreciate still more this recognition by fellow craftsmen.' These sentiments have been echoed by many Club members over the years. Three other new recruits (Cyril Hare, Christianna Brand and Edmund Crispin) did become major figures in the genre,

Photos by Elisabeth Chat featured in *Picture Post*'s 'Behind the Whodunits' in 1952 featuring G.D.H. and M. Cole in their Flamstead home; Gladys Mitchell promoting sports training for schoolgirls at Brentford; Oxford men Michael Innes and Nicholas Blake; and railway enthusiast Freeman Wills Crofts demonstrating how signals were meant to imitate the action of the human arm.

and so did Michael Innes and Michael Gilbert, elected in 1949. Sayers recognized the need for an injection of youth and vitality, and became frustrated by Berkeley's cussedness in object- ing to candidates other than his own. He did not seem to care whom he offended, and wrote a rude letter to Punshon, now the Secretary, insisting that he had a right of veto over recruitment. This prompted the imperturbable older man to remind him to pay his subscription. As Sayers said to Milward Kennedy, 'We had better hasten to elect some new members before [Berkeley] Molotovs the lot!'

Sayers and Berkeley were not alone in falling out of love with writing detective novels. Shortly before the outbreak of war, Milward Kennedy found himself writing a mystery for chil- dren, *Who Was Old Willy?* The book featured a 'challenge to the reader', but the old zest had been killed off by Philip Yale Drew's libel action. After the war, Kennedy forsook pioneering detective fiction for thrillers. He could still come up with fresh ideas – the political assassination idea at the heart of *Escape to Quebec* broadly anticipates Frederick Forsyth's *The Day of the Jackal* – but failed to make best use of them. His final crime-fighting hero was a Canadian Mountie.

The Coles' last detective novel was written by Douglas. Halfway through their next effort, Margaret became so bored that she stopped work, and never resumed. For a while, she continued to turn up for Detection Club dinners, where her spiky manner irritated younger writers like Christianna Brand. After Douglas died, Margaret remained as keeper of the flame, and in her sev- enties she published his biography – under the imposing name of *Dame* Margaret Cole. Her final crusade was as a campaigner for comprehensive education; like Berkeley, her confidence that she knew what was best for other people never wavered. She died shortly after the nation elected as Prime Minister another Margaret equally untroubled by self-doubt.

E. R. Punshon published mysteries until he was eighty-three years old, but R. C. Woodthorpe lacked staying power. After the prophetically titled *Put out that Light* appeared in 1940, he lived for more than thirty years, but never published another book. He seems to have lost touch even with Allingham and Pip, while his failure to respond to a request for a story for *Detection Medley* irritated John Rhode. This reserved and very private man vanished so completely from the scene that his name has been almost completely airbrushed from the history of the genre, as well as from the Club's list of members.

Connington's poor health contributed to the variable quality of his later work. Henry Wade also suffered various ailments, but continued to craft enjoyable novels until the late Fifties. H. C. Bailey, another devoted family man, retired from *The Daily Telegraph* and moved to the idyllically situated house in North Wales where, decades earlier, he had first met his wife. His last novel, featuring the hymn-singing solicitor Joshua Clunk, appeared in 1950, but his great days were over long before then.

The same was true of John Rhode – although his production line continued to clank and whirr until the Sixties – and of Freeman Wills Crofts. Crofts prided himself on his scrupulous research, but all authors make mistakes. He and the librarian from Harrods were once invited to tea by two Mancunian businessmen, who challenged him about one of his books, where a quarter of a million pounds in single notes is carried in two suitcases. Did he realize that, even if tightly packed, they would occupy ten cubic feet and weight two hundredweight? In 1955, a couple of years before his death, Crofts included a rueful inscription in *Many a Slip*, a collection of his short stories: '*Now that I see these little tales in book form, I think they should have been further expanded, with more build up of the characters. Alas, that is now too late!*'

John Dickson Carr kept dreaming up tricky methods of killing people in locked rooms, but increasingly resorted to historical settings to disguise the essential lack of realism in his impossible crime scenarios. Clarice became so concerned by his binge-drinking, and his fondness for taking chloral hydrate to aid recovery, that she persuaded him to seek professional help. The drinking did not stop, and it wrecked his health. He was afflicted by hypochondria as well as an incurable distaste for the post-war world. On one occasion he was taken to hospital after overdosing on chloral hydrate when drunk, and the newspapers interpreted this as an attempt at suicide. Sayers' priority was – according to Christianna Brand – to protect the Club's reputation, and she told the Press that this was 'not *our* John Dickson Carr at all'.

Carr recovered, and resumed writing. His career ended with *The Hungry Goblin*, a weak effort featuring Sayers' old hero Wilkie Collins as a detective. The locked room mystery fell out of vogue, before enjoying a revival decades later, thanks to the popularity of television series such as *Jonathan Creek* and *Death in Paradise* in Britain and *Monk* in the US. The puzzle in Stieg Larsson's *The Girl with the Dragon Tattoo* is termed, in the English translation, a 'locked room mystery', though Larsson's scenario actually offers a 'closed circle'.

Christopher Bush and E. C. R. Lorac churned out books for the rest of their lives, and Anthony Gilbert, Ngaio Marsh and Gladys Mitchell were equally prolific. Nicholas Blake led his double life as crime writer and poet with distinction and boundless energy. During his first marriage, he pursued a lengthy affair with the novelist Rosamund Lehmann, before abandoning both wife and mistress to marry a young and beautiful actress, Jill Balcon. Their son Daniel became an admired actor, their daughter Tamsin a successful film-maker.

Margery Allingham died at the age of sixty-two after a long period of poor health punctuated by bouts of depression, which at one point led to her undergoing electroconvulsive therapy. Despite her private torments, she became one of the leading women detective novelists of the twentieth century. Pip Youngman Carter completed Allingham's last novel about Albert Campion and wrote two more by himself. He achieved posthumous notoriety when it emerged that he had fathered a child with the journalist, media celebrity and writer of humorous detective novels Nancy Spain. What made the affair startling was that she was also a lesbian of iconic status. Their son Tom was brought up by Spain's lover, Joan Werner Laurie, and his parentage was not publicly acknowledged until after the deaths of both Pip and Spain (who was killed along with Joan in an aeroplane crash as she was on her way to commentate on the Grand National). Spain was considered for membership of the Detection Club in the Fifties, but turned down – because of the flimsiness of her books, not because anyone knew the truth about Tom.

As for Ngaio Marsh, her long and successful career was belatedly marked in 1974 by her election to the Club whose initiation ritual had made such a lasting impression on her thirty-seven years earlier. The honour delighted her, but she was not well enough to travel from her home in New Zealand to attend.

Tastes were changing. Books in the Golden Age style continued to be written, and enjoyed, and several new writers of talent emerged. The dominant crime novelists, however, belonged to a generation preoccupied by the challenges of life in the Atomic Era. Traditional mysteries were perceived as past their sell-by date, and people who did not care to read them were nevertheless happy to make sweeping generalizations about them which contributed to the crude stereotyping of Golden Age fiction that persists to this day.

Sayers dominated the Detection Club to the end of her life, and continued to insist that candidates for membership must write books of quality. This requirement often gave rise to fierce debate, especially when Berkeley was in argumentative mood. She exploited her contacts in the hierarchy of the Church of England to find new premises for the Club, at Kingly Street, in a building owned by the Church. When Bentley, during a sad descent into alcoholism, gave up the Presidency at the end of 1949, she was his natural successor. Objections to the thriller writers were dropped, while the first Jewish member, Julian Symons, was elected on the strength of a handful of promising books, long before he became a master of the crime novel, which (to the continuing dismay of purists) he saw as a linear successor to the classic detective story.

Mac Fleming, whose heavy drinking contributed to prolonged ill-health, died of a stroke in 1950. For Sayers, motherhood continued to be a bittersweet experience. She was thrilled to see John Anthony follow in Peter Wimsey's footsteps, winning a scholarship to Balliol, and taking a first class degree. Her taste in clothes continued to be unorthodox – the only time she wore evening dress was for Detection Club dinners, and even then she never wore anything new, because 'excited torchbearers are apt to spill hot wax all over one while arguing about procedure' before the initiation ritual.

Michael Gilbert and his wife bumped into Sayers in London while shopping for Christmas cards in 1957. A few days later, the Gilberts received a card from her, but by that time she was dead. She was found at the foot of the stairs in the house in Witham, surrounded by Christmas presents. John Anthony was the sole beneficiary in her will. A few months before his own death, he told Sayers' friend and biographer Barbara Reynolds, 'She did the best she could.'

Sayers had seemed irreplaceable, but the Detection Club needed a new President. In conversations at her memorial service (with readings by Val Gielgud and Cyril Hare, and a panegyric by C. S. Lewis), Michael Gilbert urged fellow members to elect Agatha Christie. Christie was desperate to avoid joining organizations, let alone leading one, and made an unlikely figurehead. Nevertheless, she agreed to become President, demonstrating the depth of her continuing devotion to the Detection Club. At her initiation, Allingham, once so sceptical about the Club, took the role of Skull-Bearer, solemnly carrying Eric on his cushion.

Christie imposed one condition before taking office: that she should not be called upon to deliver any speeches. Lord Gorell (disrespectfully known by younger writers as 'Lord Sheep') agreed to undertake the public speaking, but insisted on being appointed co-President, and held that role until his death in 1963. After that, Christie continued in office alone for another thirteen years, with the legwork undertaken by Honorary Secretaries such as the lawyer Michael Underwood. Yet on one occasion never forgotten by those who witnessed it, she broke her own rule, and donned the President's red satin robe, filling it almost as amply as Chesterton had done. She read out her part of the ritual with unexpected *brio*, demanding of the initiate, 'Is there anything you hold sacred?' with a startling mixture of humour and solemnity. As Harry Keating said, the shrinking violet had transformed into 'trumpeting fierce-coloured African Queen Lily'. When in her last years she was too frail to attend dinners, she offered to stand down, but was persuaded to remain in office for the rest of her life.

Anthony Berkeley longed to be President of the Club, and felt it his due. The trouble was that he had alienated too many of his colleagues with his unpredictable moods and bad temper. At one point he even argued that the jokey title 'First Freeman' he awarded himself when the Club was set up gave him a right of veto over new members. A neat compromise would have been to ask him to act as co-President with Christie. Surely this solution occurred to a group of people with unrivalled gifts for unravelling complicated puzzles? Perhaps they feared Berkeley would become unbearable and the convivial atmosphere at Club dinners would be ruined. Berkeley's reaction was to sever all connections with the Club he had founded.

Notes to Chapter 32

the Detection Club's last significant venture for years
Correspondence between members during the war, and in years
that followed, with a focus on discussion about whether prospective
new members 'played fair' with their readers, is summarized in
Evans, Curtis, *Was Corinne's Murder Clued?*, the title of which comes
from debate about the merit of Douglas G. Browne's fiction. Browne
(1884–1963), grandson of Charles Dickens' illustrator Hablot K.
Browne, alias 'Phiz', also co-wrote a biography of Bernard Spilsbury.

Dorothy Bowers . . . died young of tuberculosis
My understanding of Bowers' life has been aided by information
supplied by Tom Schantz, whose Rue Morgue Press have reprinted
all her novels.

Bentley, during a sad descent into alcoholism, gave up the Presidency
Bentley's problems with drink are referred to in the memoirs of his
son Nicolas.

*Spain was considered for membership of the Detection Club in the
Fifties, but turned down*
See Nancy Spain, *Why I'm Not a Millionaire* (London: Hutchinson,
1956). Spain (1917–64) was a columnist for the *Daily Express*, which
boasted: 'They call her Vulgar; they call her Unscrupulous; they have
called her the worst-dressed woman in Britain.' She based her
amateur sleuth Miriam Birdseye on the actor Hermione Gingold,
who was at one time married to Val Gielgud's BBC colleague and
crime-writing collaborator Eric Maschwitz.

several new writers of talent emerged
They included Anthony Shaffer (1926–2001) and his brother Peter
Shaffer. The Shaffer twins collaborated on two entertaining novels
in the classic cerebral style in the Fifties. According to Anthony, he
provided the basic plots and the pair wrote alternate chapters, while
Peter had previously produced one solo effort with illustrations by
E. C. Bentley's son Nicolas. Later, they both earned fame separately,
writing plays as diverse (and successful) as *Sleuth* and *Equus*.
Anthony also worked on several screenplays based on Christie's
novels, and describes encounters with the Queen of Crime and with

Hitchcock in his breezy if perhaps not entirely reliable memoir *So What Did You Expect?* (London: Picador, 2001).

Michael Gilbert and his wife bumped into Sayers in London
See Michael Gilbert, 'A Personal Memoir' in *Dorothy L. Sayers: the Centenary Celebration.*

In conversations at her memorial service . . . Michael Gilbert urged fellow members to elect Agatha Christie
This emerges from copies of correspondence with the Honorary Secretary of the Detection Club, which also disclose Christie's offer to stand down as President and her reluctance to have the BBC film the ritual.

Agatha Christie and her publisher Billy Collins.

Part Seven

Unravelling the Mysteries

33

Murder Goes On Forever

How can we unravel the mysteries of the Detection Club? It is time to settle down in an armchair in the library, review the evidence, and do a little detective work. What, for instance, did Agatha Christie mean when she inscribed *Murder in Mesopotamia* 'with love from one who may have done crimes unsuspected not detected!?' Her light-hearted choice of words was a kind of false confession. She had not broken the law, but in writing the novel, she'd committed a social crime. After biding her time for years, she had paid back Katharine Woolley, domineering wife of the archaeologist Leonard Woolley, for reacting so poisonously to her marriage to Max Mallowan.

Christie emulated Anthony Berkeley, taking revenge through fiction as she drew on her experience of an archaeological dig for the novel's background. Several characters had real-life counterparts. Nurse Amy Leatheran resembles Christie, Max is represented by the amiable David Emmott, while Father Eric Burrows, a cleric who had specialized in the translation of cuneiform tablets, becomes Father Lavigny. The plot depends on an impersonation wildly unlikely even by Golden Age standards – Torquemada reckoned it 'near impossible'.

The biting portrayal of the murder victim is more memorable than the storyline. Louise Leidner is beautiful yet appalling, variously compared to *La Belle Dame Sans Merci*, the Snow Queen and a swamp creature. Poirot says she possesses a 'calamitous magic'. Like the killer in the story, Louise Leidner was impersonating someone. She was a very thinly disguised version of Katharine Woolley. Christie seldom unsheathed her claws, but this novel reveals her fury at Katharine Woolley's treatment of her. And that cryptic inscription provides an insight into Christie's nature. She did not simply love mysteries, she relished being mysterious.

One serious crime of which she *was* briefly suspected was treason. Early in the Second World War, MI5 speculated that she was guilty of disclosing national secrets. Agatha Christie, the Queen of Crime, a traitor? She was certainly the least likely of suspects. Time after time, however, Poirot and Marple demonstrated that nobody is above suspicion. Her novel *N or M?*, in which the Beresfords track Nazi spies, featured a suspicious character called Major Bletchley. Even more alarmingly, she had moved into the Isokon Building, the modernist block of flats in Lawn Road, Hampstead. This experiment in semi-communal living was the first building in Britain constructed with reinforced concrete – a safe haven that attracted as residents a number of Soviet spies, including the Kuczynski family and Eva Collett Reckitt. The authorities panicked. Was Christie a woman who knew too much? Was she taunting the establishment, by making Major Bletchley's name a clue to treachery? Would she betray the secret work undertaken at Bletchley Park to crack the German Enigma code?

Dilly Knox, brother of Ronald, was sent for. He was working on cryptanalysis at Bletchley, and knew Christie personally; presumably through guest visits to Detection Club dinners. When he was quizzed about how much she knew about Enigma, he found it impossible to believe either that she had stumbled upon the secret of Bletchley, or that she would give it away if she had. But his superiors feared there was no smoke without fire.

Dilly was asked to approach her and find out why she had mentioned Bletchley. The codebreaker duly invited the crime writer to meet for tea and scones. After the initial pleasantries, Knox led the conversation to the subject of *N or M?* At last he dared to put the question – why mention Bletchley? He studied her carefully. Would she lie or bluster, or even break down?

Christie responded with a gentle smile: 'My dear, I was stuck there for ages one day travelling on the train from Oxford to London. It was so dreadful, I took revenge by giving the name to one of the most odious people in the book.'

Dilly probably never realized that for Christie, the main attraction of the Isokon Building was not living cheek by jowl with spies (although there are hints of her acquaintance with the Kuczynskis in *N or M?)* but that it was also home to Stephen Glanville, the Eygptologist who helped her to research *Akhnaton* and the man to whom, after Max, she was closest. She treated him as a confidant when Max was away from home.

Sometimes coincidences are genuine. We need to temper our sleuthing instincts with realism when reading between the lines of a detective novel. Finding answers to the questions that persist about Christie's disappearance is a particular challenge. She hated talking about those missing days, and gave no explanation of them in her autobiography. So we have no neat and rational explanation of what happened, with all the loose ends tied up, in the manner of her books. Theories abound, ranging from the plausible to the playful. Kathleen Tynan's entertaining but far-fetched screenplay for the film *Agatha* saw Christie, played by Vanessa Redgrave, disorientated by electroconvulsive therapy. A witty episode of *Doctor Who* had her rendered unconscious by an alien in the form of a giant wasp.

Could she have engineered her disappearance to publicize her books, as a hostile Press believed? The evidence shows that in the first half of the Twenties she took part in promotional stunts, such as the mock trial presided over by G. K. Chesterton. In *The Secret Adversary*, Jane Finn faked amnesia – might Christie have adopted her own character's ploy?

Any detective who pays the slightest heed to the psychology of the suspect cannot believe the disappearance was designed to raise her public profile. Christie was far too self-effacing. Even at the time of publishing her breakthrough novel, *The Murder of Roger Ackroyd*, she did little or nothing to promote it.

She saw her job as to write. Selling books was emphatically the responsibility of her publisher. The mock trial is a red herring. She took part for the fun of it, and in any event she did so not to promote herself but *In the Next Room*, a play adapted by two other women, the now obscure duo of Harriet Ford and former actress Eleanor Robson, from the novel by Burton E. Stevenson.

Archie, and even the loyal Madge, suspected that she wanted her disappearance to result in publicity – but aimed at damaging him rather than selling more books. This is more credible. Long after her divorce, she wrote books which hinted at her preoccupation with Archie's infidelity, and it is tempting to believe that she meant to punish him for it. Her most autobiographical novel is *Unfinished Portrait*, published under the Westmacott name, which is not a detective story; the heroine is a woman who contemplates suicide in the aftermath of divorce. Among her mysteries, *Death in the Clouds* is one of several in which a seemingly attractive young man nurses a discreditable secret. Occasionally, she also let characters voice her own feelings.

'Men always approve of dowdy women – but when it comes to brass tacks, the dressed-up trollops win hands down! Sad, but there it is.' So says Sarah Blake in 'Triangle at Rhodes'. She was probably speaking for Christie.

'There is a horrid side of one,' Sarah adds, 'that enjoys accidents and public calamities and unpleasant things that happen to one's friends.' This reflects the response to Christie's disappearance, including Sayers' eager participation in the hunt for clues. Although Christie kept her counsel, years passed before the scars caused by Archie's adultery, and the public and Press hostility her disappearance aroused, began to heal. It may be no coincidence that, in one of her accounts of Bentley's initiation, Ngaio Marsh said Christie did not attend the dinner or ritual but turned up at Gerrard Street later in the evening. The Chief Constable of Surrey Police was a guest speaker at the dinner, although he had not been in post at the time of her disappearance. Remembering Superintendent Kenward's public pronouncements about her, Christie would be keen to avoid opening old wounds through an encounter with Surrey Police.

The truth about the disappearance is almost certainly chaotic and incoherent. Christie was desperate to run away from the horror of her marriage's collapse. Perhaps she hoped, in a confused way, that her flight would somehow bring Archie to his senses and enable them to salvage something from the wreckage.

The woman who planned her mysteries with such care, whose great detective was obsessed with logic and the need to use 'the little grey cells', exposed herself to public humiliation with no rational thought about the consequences of her actions, and no idea of what to do next. It was crazy and self-defeating, the result of unbearable emotional stress. Her determination to remain silent about the episode stemmed from a sense of guilt and shame, especially over her abandonment of her young daughter.

Christie was far too harsh on herself. She was a victim, but too strong to wallow in victimhood, and too proud to seek help before she cracked. Her extreme reaction to Archie's infidelity demonstrates more vividly than any psychiatrist's diagnosis the harm she suffered when her secure family life was destroyed. This left a mark on her writing. The 'ordeal by innocence' under-gone by ordinary people whose lives are disrupted by murder recurs in her writing as often as the 'wronged man' in the films of Alfred Hitchcock.

It does not take a Poirot to deduce that Christie was innocent, not guilty. The ordeal she suffered was greater and longer-lasting than Archie's short-term embarrassment when his matrimonial misdemeanours came under public scrutiny. She never commit-ted a real 'crime unsuspected not detected', and the passion for justice evident in her finest work was driven by her empathy for those who suffer injustice through no fault of their own.

Clues to the mysteries surrounding Dorothy L. Sayers lurk in the pages of *Murder Must Advertise*. A minor but memorable member of the supporting cast is Miss Meteyard, whose final words sum up Sayers' philosophy of business life: 'You have to advertise.' Meteyard is a self-portrait, a Somerville graduate and 'a funny woman' who shares Sayers' taste for vulgar limericks, her sardonic humour, and perhaps much more. For Miss Meteyard has in the past been threatened by the murder victim, Dean, with the exposure of a regrettable affair. 'You wouldn't think it to look at her, would you?' says an unimaginative man 'naïvely'. Her response to Dean was to say 'publish and be damned'.

A latter-day Wimsey might infer that a colleague at Benson's discovered the truth about Sayers' secret pregnancy, despite the lengths to which Sayers and Beatrice White went in constructing the charade of her supposed sickness absence. Sayers must have loved taking revenge on the mischief-making snooper by transforming him (if her enemy *was* a man – nothing can be taken for granted with detective novelists) into Victor Dean, an unpleasant blackmailer. Sayers implied that he was homosexual, and sent him tumbling to death on Benson's steep spiral staircase.

Sayers was too resilient to submit to the threats of a bully, but her strength came at a cost. The legacy of her treatment by her early lovers John Cournos and Bill White was that terror of emotion. The only way to protect herself was by building defences that nobody could destroy. The overbearing manner, the outlandish clothes, the relentless emphasis on passions of the intellect rather than of the heart, gave her as much security as a cast-iron alibi.

People thought her a battleaxe, but like Christie she was wracked by guilt and shame. Like Christie, she judged herself too severely. At first she kept quiet for the sake of her parents and her job. Later, marriage to a difficult man brought fresh complications. Why did she not insist that John Anthony come to live at Witham once she and Mac had adopted him? Mac was reluctant, and the boy seemed happy with Ivy, but Sayers never pushed the point. Given the moral climate of the Thirties, she feared humiliation if she admitted to an illegitimate child. Trapped in the web of lies she wove in desperation when she found she was pregnant, she could find no escape. Sticking to her story was the only safe option.

Why did she stop writing detective fiction, when her love of the Detection Club still burned bright? The Abdication may have killed off *Thrones, Dominations*, with its meditations on marriage, but devising a storyline that is overtaken by events is an occupational hazard for authors. Why did she fail to come up with an equally interesting mystery connected to the Wimseys' married life? The answer, in part, was that she felt that she could not surpass *Gaudy Night*. The slightness of *Busman's Honeymoon* (in content, if not in word count) supports this theory. Even P. G. Wodehouse, who admired her earlier books, told Anthony Berkeley privately that he was disappointed by it: 'I shuddered every time a rustic came on the scene.'

Sayers became more interested in *corpus christi* than Agatha Christie. Writing about religion gave her a deeper fulfilment than she could derive either from writing detective stories or from a marriage to a man whose personality had been damaged by the war.

The stress of keeping constantly on guard, unable to confide even in close friends such as Helen Simpson and Muriel St Claire Byrne, must have been hard to bear. So was her inability to take a mother's overt pride in her son's successes, and the inhibited, arm's-length nature of the relationship that the two of them maintained. A price also had to be paid in terms of public honour.

Following the success of her religious plays, the Archbishop of Canterbury offered her a Lambeth degree, an honorary doctorate in divinity. This honour would have filled Sayers with pride, but she turned it down. At first she said she did not deserve it. Later she maintained that a writer of commercial fiction might become an embarrassment to the Church, especially given that a section of the Press 'does not love me very much'. These were thin excuses. Her over-riding concern was that the Lambeth degree was incompatible with having given birth outside marriage. If she took the degree, and subsequently her secret came out, she feared her disgrace would be complete.

Like Sayers, Berkeley never wrote any significant detective fiction after the start of the Second World War. In 1941, Hitchcock's butchering of *Before the Fact* was matched by the miserable film version of *Trial and Error*. In *Flight from Destiny*, director Vincent Sherman turned Lawrence Todhunter into a university professor, moved the setting to the USA, and sacrificed irony for dismal solemnity. Even a man less cynical than Berkeley could be forgiven for despairing. A sign of how quickly his star fell is that, while Sayers' literary contributions to the war effort earned national attention, a story in which Berkeley revived Roger Sheringham in order to reinforce the message that 'careless talk costs lives' was published only in the *North Devon Journal*.

Pleasing speculation that he repeated the trick of *Malice Aforethought* by publishing a brand new novel under an undetectable pseudonym is not backed up by any evidence. Unlike Sayers, Berkeley did not take refuge in religion. His creativity was confined largely to producing raspberry-flavoured home-made wine, and writing limericks of dubious merit.

The damage the German army's gas had done to his lungs meant he was a martyr to asthma and bronchitis. As Francis Iles, he continued to review regularly, and his critical judgments mattered long after his books disappeared from the shelves. Julian Symons, a man capable of being as acerbic as Berkeley, said in an obituary, 'A whole generation of crime writers was in debt to Francis Iles.'

Even when he fell out of love with the Detection Club, Berkeley remained emotionally entangled with detective fiction. He supported the Crime Writers' Association – membership of which did not depend on a secret ballot – from its inception, contributing acerbic articles highlighting the shortcoming of publishers to the CWA's early newsletters. In the early Sixties, as a member of a panel judging the awards now known as Daggers, he condemned one shortlisted author's work as full of 'superior sex and sadism'. One might think these qualities would appeal to Berkeley, but he complained that the author in question did not deserve to be reviewed, let alone win a prize. As usual, he found it impossible to be philosophical when unable to get his own way, and resigned in a huff. Hard though he sometimes worked to cultivate friendships, they had to be on his terms.

As a reviewer, Berkeley was one of the first critics to laud the talents of gifted young writers such as P. D. James and Ruth Rendell. He corresponded for years with a prolific if minor crime writer, the Mancunian bank manager Harold Blundell, who wrote as George Bellairs. When they eventually met, Bellairs' wife cooked for them, and Berkeley heaped praise on her escalopes – the old charmer had faded, but not quite vanished. At one point, he offered shrewd advice to Bellairs on how to negotiate better terms with his publishers. To Bellairs, he made one of his most revealing remarks: 'You cash in on the gusto while you've got it. Believe me, it goes.'

But *why* did it go? The clues lie buried in Berkeley's writing. Corroboration can be gleaned from the work of the woman he yearned for. The fact is that Berkeley's career as a crime novelist began at around the time he met E. M. Delafield, and ended when she died. This was no coincidence. She inspired and obsessed him. Without her, he was finished as a crime writer.

Their relationship blossomed with those discussions about the tragedy of Edith Thompson, and is as intriguing as any between writers of the inter-war years. Yet it has been missed by everyone. The only evidence of it comes from coded references scattered throughout their writing. The couple played a secret game involving as many literary impersonations and hidden identities as could be found in any detective novel. Rather than portray their relationship directly in their work (as Sayers did in *Strong Poison*), they opted for subtlety, packing their books with nods and winks to each other, in characters' names and life stories. They revelled in their own ingenuity, finding a strange consolation for the fact they could not be together. Like Poe in 'The Purloined Letter', they were planting clues to their mutual devotion in plain sight.

Messalina of the Suburbs influenced Berkeley's use of actual crimes in his fiction, and he dedicated his second detective novel to Delafield. His description of her as the 'most delightful of writers' is slyly ambiguous. She returned the compliment, dedicating to him a book called *Jill*, in which the hero, like Berkeley, married in haste during the war. The stumbling-block was that Delafield was also married, with a young son and daughter.

In *The Way Things Are*, Laura Temple, a self-portrait, becomes obsessed with a male admirer, Duke Ayland, but tells him she cannot abandon her marriage, for fear of harming her children. Ayland writes music, as Berkeley did, while another character is a novelist whose first names have the same initials as Berkeley's. Laura is a detective story fan, and Delafield alludes to their shared interest in Edith Thompson. At one point Laura writes a long letter to Ayland expressing her feelings for him, before a recollection of correspondence featuring in murder trials prompts her to put a match to it. The book's ending is tantalizingly inconclusive, as if Delafield were teasing Berkeley, hinting that perhaps one day, things might be different. Yet Laura does not leave her husband. Neither did Delafield.

The soul-baring was mutual. Berkeley showed Delafield 'It Pays to Look Soulful: a Story for Cynics', in which he satirized social attitudes towards infidelity. He never published the manuscript, although Delafield commented on it approvingly. His main aim was to send her a message about the intensity of his feelings for her. One can picture him telling Delafield that his wife did not understand him. This was undoubtedly true, for Delafield was perhaps the only person who ever came close to understanding him.

Once Berkeley became involved with Helen Peters, Delafield knew she and he would never become a couple. She consoled herself, in the guise of her most famous character the Provincial Lady (a very thinly veiled self-portrait), with the reflection that 'writers are too egotistical to make ideal husbands for anybody'. The need to accept the inevitable influenced *Thank Heaven Fasting*, a biting study of what marriage meant for an upper-class woman. She reinforced the autobiographical subtext by giving her second forename to her protagonist, Monica.

Despite her spell as a Bride of Heaven, Delafield was not hostile to divorce. Her concern was about its consequences, and *Nothing is Safe* highlights the damage done to children after their parents split up. This was an age when woman divorced for adultery risked losing custody of her children. It was not a risk she could bring herself to take, yet she kept returning to the theme that it is a mistake to marry a person one has never truly loved. To live without one's true, passionate soulmate is to live without fulfilment.

Berkeley felt the same. But anger and an irrational sense of betrayal came easily to him. Delafield teased him from time to time in her books, and he retaliated with a series of dark portrayals of beautiful temptresses whose behaviour was monstrously inhuman. Read in this light, his books seem like howls of anguish, because he was besotted with a woman who had enslaved him yet refused to sacrifice her comfortable way of life to be with him.

In some respects, theirs was a love–hate relationship – but that intense mutual attraction persisted to the end. In 'They Don't Wear Labels', Delafield ventured into psychological suspense, with another nod to Francis Iles, as a wife staying in a boarding-house worries that her apparently adoring husband means to poison her. The resemblance to *Before the Fact* is unmistakable, while the notion of feeding someone shards of broken glass comes straight from the fantasy Edith Thompson shared with Frederick Bywaters.

A collection containing this seldom-noticed story was published in the same year that Berkeley's last novel appeared. He dedicated *As for the Woman* to Delafield with 'affection' and spoke of their 'long, happy and candid' friendship. That reference to candour speaks volumes. He and she could say things to each other in private that could never be revealed to anyone else. But did his story amount to a confession of a desire to commit murder?

Detective novelists love to test credibility to the limit. Laying false trails is seductive. Bluffs and double bluffs become a way of life. Berkeley's Roger Sheringham, more than any other fictional detective, demonstrated that apparently logical deductions can be wildly mistaken. Yet *As for the Woman* does imply that Berkeley harboured a homicidal fantasy driven by his infatuation with Delafield. Berkeley's alter ego in *Malice Aforethought*,

Dr Bickleigh, was a dreamer, and Berkeley's imagination was equally hyperactive. Given the endless tricks he played with character names, there can be no coincidence in the surname of the man who stands between Alan, based on Berkeley, and the woman he loves. It is Pawle – and it sounds exactly like the name of Delafield's husband, Paul.

Riven by jealousy, Alan contemplates murdering Pawle, and at one point believes he has done so – by accident. But Pawle survives, and so does the marriage. Alan is humiliated, and shamed by his own cowardice. He no longer knows whether Evelyn still loves him, and finishes up thinking only of himself. Pawle has 'destroyed his soul'.

Did Berkeley contemplate killing Paul Dashwood? If so, was this driven by jealousy, because Paul, like 'Pawle', had an unbreakable hold on the woman he loved? Perhaps, but Berkeley's overactive imagination may have led him to think that killing Paul would be an 'altruistic murder' of the kind he wrote about obsessively. A detective studying Delafield's fiction might deduce that she, like Evelyn, had been mistreated by her husband. If so, did she confide in Berkeley, and if she did, was she telling the truth? If Lina Aysgarth, the masochistic victim of *Before the Fact*, was a version of Delafield, was the seemingly charming but actually sociopathic Johnnie Aysgarth a savage caricature of Paul Dashwood?

Delafield drops delicate hints in books such as *Nothing is Safe* about husbands who make excessive and unpleasant sexual demands of their wives. Yet it is almost impossible to reconcile Delafield's gently humorous portrayal of the Provincial Lady's dull husband with the notion that Paul abused her – unless she was using fiction as way of masking the truth. Did she tolerate the intolerable simply for the sake of the children, or was Paul guilty of nothing worse than a lack of sparkle? No outsider can guess what goes on behind closed doors in respectable homes in the English countryside. Mental torture, perhaps, or simply mind-numbing tedium.

Berkeley may have devised the storyline of *As for the Woman* as a subtle metaphor for his dysfunctional relationship with

Delafield and her husband, with Anthony, Elizabeth and Paul represented by Alan, Evelyn and Pawle. Yet whatever the truth about Delafield's marriage, it would be a miscarriage of justice to convict Paul Dashwood of domestic abuse on fictionalized and equivocal evidence from a man who probably loathed him. Berkeley was depressed when he wrote *As for the Woman*, dissatisfied with his second marriage, and despairing because Delafield was out of reach. If he did fantasize about murdering Paul Dashwood, writing offered catharsis, and he committed no crime more serious than that minor motoring offence. He planned another book, in which Alan Littlewood married. Presumably this was to be another exercise in self-flagellating fictional autobiography. What stopped him from going ahead with it?

The answer surely lies in a series of disasters that befell Delafield in quick succession. Her son Lionel died at the age of twenty, from gunshot wounds in the armoury of the Infantry Training Service. An open verdict was recorded, but he may have killed himself. This shattering blow was followed by Delafield undergoing a colostomy. Cancer ravaged her beauty, as it had Helen Simpson's a couple of years earlier. She collapsed while giving a lecture, and died at the age of fifty-three. Her premature death explains why, for all her literary gifts, her name is no longer well known. Yet *The Diary of a Provincial Lady* continues to be reprinted, and its author resurfaced in the guise of Esme Delacroix in an episode of *The Simpsons* called *Diatribe of a Mad Housewife*. The ludicrous improbability of this would surely have appealed to her mischievous sense of humour.

Berkeley's career as a detective novelist began at the time of those criminal conversations with Delafield, and ended as her health failed. In her he found inspiration, and the grief caused by her death destroyed his creative impulse. The tragedy thickened the fog of misery that enveloped him during and after the Second World War. With the same obsessive persistence with which he pursued women and grudges, he stockpiled crates of 'Victory' stamps in the mistaken belief they would prove a shrewd investment. Seeking to outwit the taxman, he hid money under floorboards and stuffed family silver into false cupboards.

Berkeley's stepdaughter has miserable memories of the Forties, much of which she spent in rural isolation at Linton Hills while her brother stayed with their father. The large, lonely house was lit by oil lamps because there was no mains electricity or gas. In the teenage girl's eyes, Berkeley was a bully with a sadistic streak, a man who took pleasure in hurting women. He frightened her and was unkind to her mother, once 'la belle Helene'.

Helen's temperament was depressive, and she could not stand up for herself. Berkeley's attitude towards women was tainted by the conviction that they exploited men. He mourned Delafield openly, and spoke to his stepdaughter about her 'as if she were the love of his life'. He would shut himself away in his room every morning 'to write' – but never produced anything worthy of note.

When Berkeley's London house became habitable again after the war, the small, unhappy family returned there, but they lived separate lives on separate floors. Berkeley went back to Devon from time to time, but on his own. In 1951, Helen reverted to her maiden name, Peters, and moved out altogether. Berkeley never saw his stepdaughter again, and she was not sorry. 'He could be good company when he was in the mood, he was clever and entertaining,' she said, 'but ultimately the dark side dominated. I have never met anyone else like him, and I say that with profound thankfulness.'

Yet with Berkeley, there was always another twist in the tale. He entertained his niece, the daughter of his brother Stephen and Hilary, at Linton Hills after the war, and invited her to the Café Royal for a Detection Club dinner. To assist her recuperation from tuberculosis, he took her for a holiday in the Canaries and Madeira. She admired his wit and intelligence, and he treated her with generosity and respect. They got on well for the rest of his life, although his physical ailments and depressive streak sometimes made him challenging company. Hilary, who divorced Stephen Cox and married a soldier, was wary of Berkeley's avuncular interest in her daughter, and warned her about his reputation for womanizing. In fact, he behaved himself, even though one or two people they met on holiday jumped to the mistaken conclusion that the supposed 'niece' was really his mistress. Berkeley being Berkeley, he was not embarrassed, but amused.

The detective fiction of the Golden Age was as flawed as the human beings who wrote it. It does not take a Great Detective to find books awash with examples of homophobia, sexism and racism, along with other prejudices and faults. Even books written by progressives such as the Coles contain elements that a modern reader will find offensive. Equally, many successful books written today would have repelled readers in the Thirties.

Novels written by Detection Club members displayed the vices of their time, and sometimes a sloppiness falling far short of the standards to which the Club aspired. Theirs was popular commercial fiction, matching the demands of readers and publishers in the English-speaking world. Bucking the trend was fraught with difficulty. Yet Sayers, Berkeley and Christie dared to be different, time and again. The best books from the Detection Club did more than give readers enduring pleasure, in itself an honourable achievement. Their range, quality and inventiveness pointed the way forward for writers in the decades that followed.

An eccentric homage to the Detection Club appeared sixty years after its formation, when American writer Gaylord Larsen published *Dorothy and Agatha*. His novel featured Sayers, Christie and other members of the Club solving the mystery of a dead man discovered in Sayers' dining room. This pleasing concept was executed in such a slapdash way that Sayers might have been driven to murder had she read it. Larsen's book, hailed by the publishers as rendering 'every detail of character and place with uncanny accuracy', is a masterclass in howlers so extraordinary that the reader's initial astonishment turns into hilarity. Perhaps once she had recovered from Larsen's hapless rendering of English life and geography, Sayers would have seen the funny side. Berkeley might just have appreciated the irony of Larsen's belief that he succeeded Chesterton as President of the Detection Club.

Subtler tributes to the pioneering work of Berkeley and company have been paid time and again by their illustrious successors. The global success of *Inspector Morse* and its television spin-offs *Lewis* and *Endeavour* owes much to Colin Dexter's love of crossword puzzles and ability to craft whodunit mysteries as convoluted as those dreamed up in the Thirties. *Lonely Magdalen* has been followed by innumerable police procedurals, and *The Killer and the Slain* by endless dark novels of psychological suspense. Julian Symons' *The Man Who Killed Himself* and Simon Brett's *A Shock to the System* cleverly update *Malice Aforethought*, while P. D. James' *Original Sin* carries distant echoes of Nicholas Blake's *End of Chapter*, and her *The Private Patient* explicitly references Cyril Hare and his final novel, *He Sould Have Died Hereafter*, also known as *Untimely Death*. The central plot device in Lee Child's *One Shot*, filmed as *Jack Reacher*, recalls one of Christie's, while Amy in Gillian Flynn's *Gone Girl* plays a trick reminiscent of Felix Lane's in *The Beast Must Die*.

Nor is the appeal of plot lines beloved by Golden Age authors confined to the English-speaking world. Japanese crime novelists have often written stories in the Golden Age tradition, and an Agatha Christie Award is given annually for an unpublished mystery novel. Hans Olav Lahlum's Oslo-based mystery *The Human Flies* is a recent sample of Scandinavian *noir* that blends a seemingly impossible crime with a dash of Christie's trickery with plot.

A cult movie directed by Peter Greenaway, the enigmatic *The Draughtsman's Contract* is but one of many unlikely examples of the influence of Golden Age writing on popular culture. According to Greenaway, the story is 'not a thousand miles away from being an Agatha Christie story about a country house murder'; he compared the solution to that of *Murder on the Orient Express*.

The highly successful TV series *Sherlock* combines a twenty-first century version of the Holmes–Watson pairing with storylines borrowing from the Golden Age: Berkeleyesque multiple solutions, Christie's idea of a murder rehearsal, and Sayers' theory that Watson's middle name was Hamish (an ingenious means of reconciling Conan Doyle's use of both John and James as his forenames). J. K. Rowling's private detective, Cormoran Strike, may not resemble Lord Peter Wimsey physically, but like his predecessor he comes from a wealthy background (rock aristocracy in his case), went to Oxford, fought in battle and suffered grievously as a result, and is a man of innate decency. Rowling's fondness for Latin quotations echoes Sayers', although she has escaped the tedious complaints often directed at her predecessor's supposed snobbery. The enduring connection between past and present is reinforced by the Christie estate's commissioning of a brand new Poirot novel, *The Monogram Murders*, from Sophie Hannah, a poet, bestselling author, and member of the Detection Club.

Just as today's leading writers are – sometimes consciously, often not – influenced by the work of their forebears in the Detection Club, so do their storylines regularly re-work elements from real life crimes. The storyline of *A Place of Execution* draws on a case where the body of a convicted murderer's victim was never found. Ian Rankin's breakthrough book *Black and Blue* revisited the 'Bible John' serial killings, and the mysterious death of a radical Scottish lawyer provided a starting point for *The Impossible Dead*. Meanwhile, the ghosts of Edmund Wilson and Queenie Leavis continue to rattle their chains; Mary Gaitskill's lacerating review of *Gone Girl* begins with a giveaway admission typical of the genre's loudest critics: 'This is not a book I would normally read.'

Detective fiction remains deeply embedded in popular culture, and so overwhelmingly popular that 'literary' novelists more open-minded than Wilson and Leavis regularly draw on it for inspiration. A. S. Byatt's *Possession* and Eleanor Catton's *The Luminaries* embrace aspects of detection, while two more Man Booker prize-winning authors, John Banville and Julian Barnes, have written detective fiction under pseudonyms. Kazuo Ishiguro has noted that writers and readers of the Golden Age had 'seen the face of modern evil – rampant nationalisms, blood-lust, racism, dehumanized technological mass killing, chaos no-one could control. The 'Golden Age' detective novels . . . are filled with a pining for a world of order and justice that people had once believed in, but which they now know full well is unattainable. . . . It's escapism, but escapism of a particularly poignant kind.'

The Detection Club thrives to this day, holding three dinners each year, and publishing occasional books to supplement funds; the latest project is a round-robin novel whose title, *The Sinking Admiral*, gives a nod to the past. Each autumn sees the admission of newly elected members in a revised version of the initiation ritual which Ngaio Marsh witnessed, complete with Eric the Skull (although medical evidence suggests it should be re-named Erica). Members include such luminaries as P. D. James, Len Deighton and John le Carré, and the dinners are distinguished by the same sociable atmosphere that those strange literary bedfellows Anthony Berkeley and Dorothy L. Sayers prized so highly.

From the darkest days after her disappearance to the end of her life, Agatha Christie cherished the companionship she found in Detection Club. For almost half a century, the Club dinners were occasions where she could relax and feel she was among friends. When she was elected President, she was already a towering figure in popular fiction, but her lack of vanity and acute awareness of her limitations made her as popular with her fellow writers as with readers. Julian Symons was intrigued by the way she observed her companions, and speculated that she was making up stories about them in her head.

Unpretentious about her craft, but utterly committed to it, she became the most legendary of novelists. As a playwright, she fashioned from a modest talent a play which has run in London for over sixty years without a break and become the stuff of legend. The statistics of her success are bewildering, so far does she outstrip her rivals. Nearly five decades after her death, her detective stories continue to be devoured by vast readerships of all ages and backgrounds throughout the world. People do care who killed Roger Ackroyd.

The last word belongs to Christie. In 1940, at the height of the Blitz, when she could not know if she or her family and friends would survive for long, she inscribed a copy of *Sad Cypress*: 'Wars may come and wars may go, but MURDER goes on forever!'

Notes to Chapter 33

One serious crime of which she was briefly suspected was treason
See 'MI5 Fears and an Agatha Christie Mystery over Enigma "leak"',
Daily Telegraph, 4 February 2013.

She inspired and obsessed him.
There has never been any published study of the relationship
between Berkeley and Delafield, and my interpretation of it was at
first based solely on my reading of their work. Subsequently,
Berkeley's stepdaughter told me about her understanding that
Delafield was 'the love of his life', offering at least some confirmation for the general thrust of the theory advanced here.

American writer Gaylord Larsen published Dorothy and Agatha
A copy of the book was held in the Detection Club's extensive library.
After the Club ceased to rent premises, the library was kept at the
homes of Club officers, although H. R. F. Keating reported that only
one book was borrowed – by Julian Symons – during the time he
looked after the library. The library included books signed by members
as well as various criminological works, and many volumes contained
a special bookplate designed for the Club by Christianna Brand's
cousin, the artist Edward Ardizzone. The library was eventually sold
at auction to raise funds to subsidize future dinner meetings.

*According to Greenaway, the story is 'not a thousand miles away
from being an Agatha Christie story about a country-house murder'*
See Peter Greenaway, 'Murder he drew', *Guardian*, 1 August 2003.

Mary Gaitskill's lacerating review of Gone Girl
Mary Gaitskill, 'In Charm's Way: *Gone Girl*'s sickening worldview',
Bookforum, Sept/Oct/Nov 2013.

The Sinking Admiral
This new collaborative novel will be published by HarperCollins in
2016.

such luminaries as P.D. James, Len Deighton
Phyllis Dorothy White, Baroness James of Holland Park, (1920–2014),
an author of outstanding detective novels, died shortly before this

book went to press, having kindly offered me help and information in its earlier stages; she continued to attend Detection Club meetings to the end of her long and distinguished life. After Len Deighton (born 1929) read the manuscript of this book, he told me about two encounters with the then President of the Detection Club, the first as young man in the years before *The IPCRESS File* (1962) catapulted him to fame, the second at his initiation into membership of the Club:

'When Agatha Christie tired of travelling on the Simplon-Orient Express to Stamboul (a journey she made famous) and then by Taurus Express to Aleppo and Beirut, she went first class on British Overseas Airways. On the Lockheed Constellation airliner, with only First Class passengers aboard, she sipped the champagne I poured for her. I was a BOAC flight attendant. I then met Agatha at my skull session [in 1969]. She said politely: "I don't think we have met before." But I was able to correct her.'

TRENT'S OWN CASE

Dorothy L. Sayers

Henry Wade

Frank Swinnerton

E.C. Bentley

Martin Smith

Haxton Allen

Anthony Kennedy

Hudson Blune

Freeman W. Croft

Michael Sadleir

Trent June. 21.3.36

H. Warner Allen's copy of *Trent's Own Case*, signed by attendees at the Trent Dinner.

Appendices

Shown opposite and on the following pages is the original
Constitution and Rules of the Detection Club, adopted 11 March
1932 (from the Detection Club Archive).

CONSTITUTION
AND RULES
OF THE
DETECTION CLUB

1932

CONSTITUTION AND RULES
Adopted on 11th March, 1932

THE Detection Club is instituted for the association of writers of detective-novels and for promoting and continuing a mutual interest and fellowship between them. As every Member will, upon payment of his or her first annual subscription, become entitled to the benefits and privileges of the Club, so such payment will be considered as a declaration of his or her submission to the following Rules :—

1.

The Committee of Management of the Club shall draw up regulations to govern the election of Members and of Honorary Members. Such regulations must provide that a candidate for election as a Member shall be recommended by not less than two Members, and that the suitability of the candidate to promote the objects of the Club shall be fully and carefully examined, in order to ensure that he or she fulfils the following condition :—That he or she has written at least two detective-novels of admitted merit or (in exceptional cases) one such novel ; it being understood that the term " detective novel " does not include adventure-stories or " thrillers " or stories in which the detection is not a main interest, and that it is a demerit in a detective-novel if the author does not " play fair by the reader." As regards Honorary Members the regulations shall determine the method of election, the maximum number that there may be at any time and the maximum period of time for which an Honorary Member may be elected.

12.

The minute book of its proceedings shall be open to the inspection of any Member of the Club on the occasion of each General or Ordinary Meeting.

13.

If any measure not connected with the affairs of the Club for the past year shall be intended to be proposed to the Annual General Meeting, 21 days' notice shall be given of the same, and a copy sent to each Member as provided in Rule 10.

14.

The accounts of the Club shall be audited by a professional accountant or two Members who are not Members of the Committee, who shall be elected at each Annual General Meeting. A vacancy occurring in the office of auditor during the year shall be filled by the Committee.

15.

The Committee of the Club shall be elected annually by a postal vote of the Membership, held prior to the date of the Annual General Meeting. Any Members who have served continuously for two years shall thereafter be ineligible to serve for a period of one year. At least one month before the Annual Meeting the Committee shall send to every Member a ballot paper giving in alphabetical order the Names of the Members recommended by the Committee, and of any other candidates recommended by other Members ; the ballot paper shall declare by whom each candidate is recommended, and the date by which the ballot paper, duly completed by the Member to whom it is addressed, is to be returned. The Committee shall be responsible for the proper conduct of the ballot, and for the declaration of the result at the Annual General Meeting.

16.

In the case of the death or resignation of a Member of the Committee, one or more Members of the Club shall be nominated by the Committee to fill up the vacancy or vacancies.

17.

No Member shall on any pretence or in any manner receive any salary from the funds of the Club, under penalty of expulsion.

18.

The Committee shall be bound upon the requisition of ten Members to call an Extraordinary General Meeting, and shall be at liberty to do so of its own authority, specifying the object, and giving 14 days' notice of such meeting.

19.

The Committee shall take immediate cognisance of any infraction of the Rules of the Club, and if such infraction shall appear to have been direct and wilful, it shall be attended with the immediate expulsion of the offending Member. Every such expulsion shall be decided upon by a majority of the Committee present at a meeting of not less than three-quarters of its Members.

20.

If the conduct of any Member, either in or out of the Club shall, in the opinion of the Committee or a majority of the Members of the Club, who shall certify the same to them in writing, be derogatory to his or her station in society or injurious to the character and interests of the Club, he or she shall be subject to expulsion under the award of a General Meeting, which it shall be the duty of the Committee expressly to convene, for the purpose of investigating the charges brought against such Member.

The opinion of such General Meeting shall be taken by ballot when, if two-thirds of the Members voting shall decide that the offending Member has merited expulsion, he or she shall thereupon cease to be a Member of the Club.

21.

Any Members expelled, whether by the Committee or at a General Meeting, shall forfeit *ipso facto* all right to or claim upon the Club or its property, and any Member expelled under Rule 20 shall be for ever after ineligible.

22.

Every Member shall furnish his or her address from time to time to the Committee; and all notices and letters sent by post or otherwise to such address shall be considered as duly delivered.

23.

New Rules or repeal or alteration of existing Rules may be made from time to time by the vote of a majority of two-thirds of the Members present, and voting either at an Annual or Extraordinary General Meeting or by postal ballot arranged by the Committee, as the Committee deems suitable. In either case, at least one month's notice of the proposal must be given to every Member by the Committee before the date upon which the vote takes place.

INDEX TO RULES.

———

7

Select Bibliography

The primary sources for *The Golden Age of Murder* are the novels of the writers discussed, but a vast and eclectic literature deals with subjects touched on. These are some of the publications I found of particular interest and help.

The Detective Fiction genre

Adey, Robert, *Locked Room Murders* (London: Ferret Fantasy, 1979; rev. ed. 1991).

Bailey, H. C., et al., *Meet the Detective* (London: George Allen & Unwin, 1935).

Bargainnier, Earl. F., ed., *Twelve Englishmen of Mystery* (Bowling Green, Ohio: Popular Press, 1984).

Cooper, John, and B. A. Pike, *Detective Fiction: The Collector's Guide* (Aldershot: Scolar Press, rev. ed. 1994).

Craig, Patricia and Mary Cadogan, *The Lady Investigates: Women Detectives and Spies in Fiction* (London: Gollancz, 1981).

Evans, Curtis, *Was Corinne's Murder Clued? The Detection Cub and Fair Play,1930–1953* (*CADS* magazine supplement 14; Benfleet: *CADS*, 2011).

Foord, Peter, and Richard Williams, *Collins Crime Club: A Checklist of the First Editions* (Scunthorpe: Dragonby, 1987; rev. ed. 1999)

Gilbert, Colleen B., *A Bibliography of the Works of Dorothy L. Sayers* (Hamden, Connecticut: Archon, 1978).

Haycraft, Howard, *Murder for Pleasure: The Life and Times of the Detective Story* (New York: Appleton-Century, 1941).

Haycraft, Howard, ed., *The Art of the Mystery Story: A Collection of Critical Essays* (New York: Simon & Schuster, 1946).

Herbert, Rosemary, ed., *The Oxford Companion to Crime and Mystery Writing* (New York: Oxford University Press, 1999).

Hubin, Allen J., *Crime Fiction 1749-1980: A Comprehensive Bibliography* (New York: Garland, 1984).

James, P. D., *Talking About Detective Fiction* (Oxford: Bodleian Library, 2009).

Keating, H. R. F., *Murder Must Appetize* (London: Lemon Tree, 1875).

Keating, H. R. F., ed., *Whodunit?: A Guide to Crime, Suspense and Spy Fiction* (London: Windward, 1982).

Knox, Ronald, ed., *Best Detective Stories of the Year (1928)* (London: Faber, 1929).

Light, Alison, *Forever England: Femininity, Literature and Conservatism Between the Wars* (London: Routledge, 1991).

Lobdell, Jared, *The Detective Fiction Reviews of Charles Williams, 1930–1935* (Jefferson, North Carolina: McFarland, 2003).

Mandel, Ernest, *Delightful Murder* (London: Pluto Press, 1984).

Mann, Jessica, *Deadlier than the Male* (Newton Abbot: David and Charles, 1981).

Nevins, Francis M., ed., *The Anthony Boucher Chronicles*, vols. i–iii (Shreveport, Louisiana: Ramble House, 2001–2).

Overy, Richard, *The Morbid Age: Britain Between the Wars* (London: Allen Lane, 2009).

Panek, Leroy, *Watteau's Shepherds: The Detective Novel in Britain, 1914–1940* (Bowling Green, Ohio: Popular Press, 1979).

Pedersen, Jay P., ed., *The St James' Guide to Crime and Mystery Writers* (Chicago: St James's Press, 1991).

Queen, Ellery, *Queen's Quorum: A history of the detective-crime short story as revealed by the 106 most important books published in this field since 1845* (Boston: Little, Brown & Co, 1951).

Rhode, John, 'Foreword', *Detection Medley* (London: Hutchinson, 1939).

Routley, Erik, *The Puritan Pleasures of the Detective Story* (London: Gollancz, 1972).

Sayers, Dorothy L., ed., *Great Stories of Detection, Mystery and Horror* (London: Gollancz, 1928).

Sayers, Dorothy L., *Les Origines Du Roman Policier: A Wartime Wireless Talk to the French* (Hurstpierpoint: Dorothy L. Sayers Society, 2003).

Symons, Julian, *Bloody Murder: From the Detective Story to the Crime Novel* (London: Faber, 1972; rev. eds. 1985, 1992).

Symons, Julian, *Criminal Practices: Symons on Crime Writing 60s to 90s* (London: Macmillan, 1994).

Thomson, H. Douglas, *Masters of Mystery: A Study of the Detective Story* (London: Collins, 1931).

Turnbull, Malcolm J, *Victim or Villain: Jewish Images in Classic English Detective Fiction* (Bowling Green, Ohio: Popular Press, 1998).

Watson, Colin, *Snobbery with Violence: English Crime Stories and their Audience* (London: Eyre and Spottiswoode, 1971; rev. ed. Eyre Methuen, 1979).

Waugh, Evelyn, *Ronald Knox* (London: Chapman & Hall, 1959).

Winks, Robin W., ed., *Colloquium of Crime* (New York: Scribners, 1986).

Winks, Robin W., ed., *Detective Fiction: A Collection of Critical Essays* (Englewood Cliffs, New Jersey: Prentice Hall, 1980).

Authors

Barnard, Robert, *A Talent to Deceive* (London: Collins, 1980; rev. ed. 1990).

Bentley, E.C., *Those Days* (London: Constable, 1940).

Bentley, Nicolas, *A Version of the Truth* (London: Deutsch, 1960).

Brabazon, James, *Dorothy L. Sayers: A Biography* (London: Gollancz, 1981).

Brand, Christianna, 'Introduction', *The Floating Admiral* (Boston: Gregg Press, 1979).

Cade, Jared, *Agatha Christie and the Missing Eleven Days* (London: Peter Owen, 1998; rev. ed. 2011).

Carter, Philip Youngman, *All I Did Was This: Chapters of an Autobiography* (Nashville: Sexton, 1982).

Christie, Agatha, *An Autobiography* (London: Collins, 1977).

Cole, Dame Margaret, *The Life of G. D. H. Cole* (London: Macmillan, 1971).

Cole, Margaret, *Growing Up into Revolution* (London: Longmans, Green, 1949).

Curran, John, *Agatha Christie's Secret Notebooks: Fifty Years of Mystery in the Making* (London: HarperCollins, 2009).

Curran, John, *Agatha Christie's Murder in the Making: Stories and Secrets from Her Archive* (London: HarperCollins, 2011).

Dean, Christopher, ed., *Encounters with Lord Peter* (Hurstpierpoint: Dorothy L. Sayers Society, 1991).

Donaldson, Norman, *In Search of Dr Thorndyke* (Bowling Green, Ohio: Popular Press, 1971; rev. ed. 1998).

Drayton, Joanne, *Ngaio Marsh: Her Life in Crime* (Auckland, Collins, 2008)

Evans, Curtis, *Masters of the 'Humdrum' Mystery: Cecil John Charles Street, Freeman Wills Crofts, Alfred Walter Stewart and the British Detective Novel, 1921–1961* (Jefferson, North Carolina: McFarland, 2012)

Evans, Curtis, ed., *Mysteries Unlocked: Essays in Honor of Douglas G. Greene* (Jefferson, North Carolina: McFarland, 2014).

Ffinch, Michael, *G.K. Chesterton: A Biography* (London: Weidenfeld, 1986).

Fitzgerald, Penelope, *The Knox Brothers* (London: Macmillan, 1977).

Gorell, Lord, *One Man . . . Many Parts* (London: Odhams, 1956).

Greene, Douglas G., *John Dickson Carr: The Man Who Explained Miracles* (New York: Otto Penzler, 1993).

Hall, Trevor H., *Dorothy L. Sayers: Nine Literary Studies* (London: Duckworth, 1980).

Hart-Davis, Rupert, *Hugh Walpole* (London: Macmillan, 1952).

Hone, Ralph L., *Dorothy L. Sayers: A Literary Biography* (Kent, Ohio: Kent State University Press, 1979).

Johns, Ayresome, *The Anthony Berkeley Cox Files: Notes Towards a Bibliography* (London: Ferret Fantasy, 1993).

Jones, Julia, *The Adventures of Margery Allingham* (Pleshey: Golden Duck, 2009).

Keating, H. R. F., *Agatha Christie: First Lady of Crime* (London: Weidenfeld, 1977).

Kenney, Catherine, *The Remarkable Case of Dorothy L. Sayers* (Kent, Ohio: Kent State University Press, 1990).

Lewis, Margaret, *Ngaio Marsh: A Life* (London: Chatto & Windus, 1991).

Lougherey, John, *Alias S. S. Van Dine: The Man Who Created Detective Philo Vance* (New York: Scribner, 1992).

Mallowan, Max, *Mallowan's Memoirs* (London: Collins 1977).

Marsh, Ngaio, *Black Beech and Honeydew* (London: Collins, 1976, rev. ed. 1981).

Mayo, Oliver, *R. Austin Freeman: The Anthropologist at Large* (Hawthorndene, South Australia: Investigator, 1980).

Meredith, Anne, *Three-a-Penny* (London: Faber, 1940).

Morgan, Janet, *Agatha Christie: A Biography* (London: Collins, 1984).

Newnes, Stan, *Arthur Morrison* (Loughton: Alderton, 2008).

Osborne, Charles, *The Life and Crimes of Agatha Christie* (London: Collins, 1982).

Pike, B. A., *The Short Stories of Margery Allingham: A Definitive Listing* (*CADS* magazine supplement 15; Benfleet: *CADS*, 2013).

Powell, Violet, *The Life of a Provincial Lady: A Study of E. M. Delafield and Her Works* (London: Heinemann, 1988).

Prichard, Mathew, ed., *Agatha Christie: The Grand Tour* (London: HarperCollins, 2012).

Rahn, B. J., ed. *Ngaio Marsh: The Woman and Her Work* (Lanham, Maryland: Scarecrow, 1995).

Reynolds, Barbara, *Dorothy L. Sayers: Her Life and Soul* (London: Hodder, 1993).

Reynolds, Barbara, ed., *The Letters of Dorothy L. Sayers* (vol. i, London: Hodder, 1995; vols. ii to v, Swavesey: Dorothy L.Sayers Society, 1997–2000).

Robyns, Gwen, *The Mystery of Agatha Christie: An Intimate Biography of the First Lady of Crime* (New York: Doubleday, 1978).

Rooney, David, *The Wine of Certitude: A Literary Biography of Ronald Knox* (San Francisco: Ignatius, 2009).

Sarjeant, William A. S., *Punshon's Policemen: The Two Detective Series of E. R. Punshon* (*CADS* magazine supplement 6; Benfleet: *CADS*, 1995)

Stanford, Peter, *C. Day-Lewis: A Life* (London: Continuum, 2007).

Stewart, A. W., *Alias J. J. Connington* (London: Hollis & Carter, 1947).

Stone, Alzina, ed., *Dorothy L. Sayers: The Centenary Celebration* (New York: Walker, 1993).

Thompson, Laura, *Agatha Christie: An English Mystery* (London: Headline Review, 2007).

Thwaite, Ann, *A. A. Milne: His Life* (London: Faber, 1990)

Turnbull, Malcolm J., *Elusion Aforethought: The Life and Writing of Anthony Berkeley Cox* (Bowling Green, Ohio: Popular Press, 1996).

Van Hoeven, Marianne, ed., *Margery Allingham: 100 Years of a Great Mystery Writer* (London: Lucas, 2003).

Vernon, Betty D., *Margaret Cole, 1893–1980: A Political Biography* (London: Croom Helm, 1986).

Ward, Maisie, *Gilbert Keith Chesterton* (London: Sheed & Ward, 1944).

Real-Life Crime

Alan, A. J., et al., *Great Unsolved Crimes* (London: Hutchinson, 1935).

Beales, Martin, *Dead, Not Buried* (London: Hale, 1995).

Borowitz, Albert, *Blood & Ink: An International Guide to Fact-Based Crime Literature* (Kent, Ohio: Kent State University Press, 2002).

Browne, Douglas G., and E.V. Tullett, *Bernard Spilsbury: His Life and Cases* (London: Harrap, 1951).

Clarke, Kate, *Lethal Alliance* (Hay-on-Wye: Carrington Press, 2013).

Connell, Nicholas, *Walter Dew: the Man Who Caught Crippen* (Stroud: Amberley, 2005).

Cyriax, Oliver, *The Penguin Encyclopedia of Crime* (London: Penguin, rev. ed. 1996).

Flanders, Judith, *The Invention of Murder: How the Victorians Revelled in Death and Detection and Created Modern Crime* (London: HarperCollins, 2011).

Gaute, J. H. H., and Robin Odell, *The New Murderers' Who's Who* (London: Harrap, 1989).

Goodman, Jonathan, *The Slaying of Joseph Bowne Elwell* (London: Harrap, 1987).

Haste, Steve, *Criminal Sentences: True Crime in Fiction and Drama* (London: Cygnus Arts, 1997).

Jesse, F. Tennyson, *Murder and its Motives* (London: Harrap, rev. ed. 1952)

Jones, Christopher, *The Maybrick A to Z* (Birkenhead: Countyvise, 2008).

Normanton, Helena, *Notable British Trials: Alfred Arthur Rouse* (London: Hodge, 1931).

Rhode, John, *The Case of Constance Kent* (London: Bles, 1928).

Rose, Andrew, *Lethal Witness: Sir Bernard Spilsbury, Honorary Pathologist* (Stroud: Sutton, 2007).

Rose, Andrew, *The Prince, the Princess, and the Perfect Murder* (London: Coronet, 2013).

Stashower, Daniel, *The Beautiful Cigar Girl* (New York: Dutton, 2006).

Summerscale, Kate, *The Suspicions of Mr Whicher* (London: Bloomsbury, 2008).

Weis, René, *Criminal Justice: The True Story of Edith Thompson* (London: Hamish Hamilton, 1988).

Whittington-Egan, *The Ordeal of Philip Yale Drew* (London: Harrap, 1972).

Whittington-Egan, Richard, *The Riddle of Birdshurst Rise* (London: Harrap, 1975).

Wilkes, Roger, *Wallace: The Final Verdict* (London: Bodley Head, 1984).

Young, Filson, *Trial of Frederick Bywaters and Edith Thompson* (London: Hodge, 1923).

Historical Context

Gardiner, Juliet, *The Thirties: An Intimate History* (London: Harper, 2010).

Graves, Robert, and Hodge, Alan, *The Long Week-End: A Social History of Great Britain, 1918–1939* (London: Faber, 1940).

Marr, Andrew, *The Making of Modern Britain: From Queen Victoria to VE Day* (London: Macmillan, 2009).

Symons, Julian, *The Thirties: A Dream Revolved* (London: Cresset, 1960).

Magazines, etc.

The principal fanzines, magazines and journals to which I have referred are *CADS* (*An Irregular Magazine of Comment and Criticism about Crime and Detective Stories*), edited by Geoff Bradley; *Clues: A Journal of Detection*, currently edited by Janice M. Allan; and *Give Me that Old-Time Detection*, edited by Arthur Vidro. The newsletters of the Dorothy L. Sayers Society, together with other publications such as the 'Sidelights on Sayers' and the proceedings of its conferences, and the Margery Allingham Society's newsletters, contain a wealth of material. Back issues of *The Armchair Detective*, founded by Allen J. Hubin but no longer published, remain a mine of information. Countless newspapers in the UK and overseas contain useful details, while many Wikipedia entries provided at least a starting point for further inquiry, often proving at least as reliable as conventional sources. The reviews contributed by Dorothy L. Sayers to the *Sunday Times*, and those written by Anthony Berkeley (usually under the name Francis Iles) for various newspapers and magazines, were of especial value. Some of the inscriptions in books discussed in the text are to be found in my personal library, as is Sayers' annotated copy of *The Trial of Constance Kent*, while others have been shown to me by their owners. A happy development of the internet age is the proliferation of websites, discussion groups, and blogs which cover Golden Age books and writers. There are far too many to list, but the Golden Age Detection site is a very useful resource, while Allen J. Hubin's monumental bibliography has been updated online. Links to many relevant blogs may be found at:

www.doyouwriteunderyourownname.blogspot/

Index

Index of Titles

MARTIN EDWARDS is an award-winning crime writer and an internationally renowned commentator on detective fiction. His Lake District Mysteries include *The Coffin Trail*, which was short-listed for the Theakston's prize for best British crime novel. He has also published eight non-fiction books, eight novels about Liverpool lawyer Harry Devlin, two stand-alone novels, over 50 short stories, and has edited 22 anthologies. His awards include the CWA Short Story Dagger and the inaugural CWA Margery Allingham Prize. Alongside his writing, he is Archivist of the Detection Club and the Crime Writers' Association, series consultant to the British Library's Crime Classics books, and consultant to a national law firm. *The Golden Age of Murder* is the result of years of research and a lifetime of reading.